RESURRECTION

A ZOMBIE NOVEL

Michael J. Totten

Michael J. Totten is a novelist and a foreign correspondent who has reported from the Middle East, Eastern Europe, Latin America, and the former Soviet Union.

His first book, *The Road to Fatima Gate*, won the Washington Institute Book Prize in 2011.

He lives with his wife in Oregon and is a former resident of Beirut.

ALSO BY MICHAEL J. TOTTEN

The Road to Fatima Gate
In the Wake of the Surge
Where the West Ends
Taken: A Novel

RESURRECTION

A ZOMBIE NOVEL

MICHAEL J. TOTTEN

First American edition published in 2014 by Belmont Estate Books

Cover design by Kathleen Lynch
Edited by Elissa Englund

Manufactured in the United States on acid-free paper

FIRST AMERICAN EDITION

Totten, Michael J.
Resurrection: A Zombie Novel
ISBN-13: 978-0615964331
ISBN-10: 0615964338

For Dean and Kris

Contents

PART ONE

ALL IN ASHES

CHAPTER ONE

Hughes shot at Annie Starling the moment he saw her. Just pointed his Mossberg pump-action shotgun at her and fired.

Frank drove and had to weave all over the place to get around wrecked and abandoned cars on the road. Hughes didn't look ahead. He watched the tree line, guarding against a flank attack. The Chevy could be assaulted from the side with just a few seconds' warning. The trees were less than thirty feet from the road. Hughes could not screw around, and he had to shoot fast.

So when he saw the woman charging out of the trees fifty yards ahead, he just reacted. She was shrieking and flailing her arms, and the whole front of her shirt was soaked in blood. Her face was smeared with it. Hughes didn't blame himself, not even in hindsight. She looked like a threat, so he fired.

But he didn't see the mangled Toyota in the Chevy's path. Frank swerved around it at the precise moment Hughes saw her, and by the time he squeezed the trigger, Frank had already turned the Chevy a good thirty degrees. Hughes' shot went wide. Real wide.

The woman screamed.

Frank slammed on the brakes as she dove behind an abandoned Mercedes.

"Don't shoot, don't shoot!" she said.

"Shit," Frank said.

"Well, I'll be goddamned," Hughes said and stepped out of the vehicle. He heard no sound but the Chevy's idling engine and his boots crunching on road grit.

Frank killed the engine—a wise decision, as they'd made far too much noise already—and absolute silence fell over the road. Hughes heard no people, no cars, no distant trains, no airplanes, no hum of electricity in the power lines. Nothing. The air was still. No wind, no radio waves pulsing through the atmosphere, no vibration from living things in any direction.

They were safe then, at least for the moment, but he took the shotgun with him. He wasn't going to shoot at the woman again, but he sure as hell wasn't about to go out there unarmed. She had come running out of the trees, and for all he knew she had been *chased* out of the trees. He wouldn't have stepped out of the vehicle unarmed either way. It was a new rule that would last the rest of his life.

"It's okay, lady," Hughes said and raised both hands in the air. He removed his finger from the trigger guard and pointed the Mossberg at the sky. She stayed hidden behind the Mercedes. "I'm not going to shoot you. And I'm real sorry I tried. I made a mistake."

The woman made no sound. If Hughes hadn't seen her duck behind the car, he'd have no idea she was there.

"I promise you," he said. "I'm really not going to hurt you. Come with us. We'll take you to a safe place. You won't last long out here by yourself."

She peeked her head over the Mercedes' roof and saw his hands in the air and the gun over his head. Then she stood all the way up. She looked terrible, worse than anyone Hughes had ever seen. Her shirt wasn't just soaked in blood. It was also caked with gore. Her long hair was so filthy and matted with God-only-knew-what that he wasn't even sure what color it was supposed to be.

She, too, raised her hands in the air as if she thought Hughes wanted to take her prisoner. They just stood there and looked at each other, both with their hands in the air proving to the other that they meant no harm.

Hughes lowered his first and pointed the Mossberg at the ground. She lowered her hands more slowly and carefully.

She hadn't bathed or even washed her face. She did not have a supply bag or a backpack or even a weapon. She must have been dehydrated and was possibly starving. Obviously she was traumatized and probably couldn't think clearly. Hughes had been lucky so far by comparison. Damn lucky.

Hughes could only imagine what kind of horror she'd experienced recently. Was somebody killed right in front of her? Maybe someone was killed right on top of her. Perhaps she killed one of those *things* right on top of her. She didn't have a gun, but maybe she lost it. Maybe she used a knife or a crowbar or even an ax. Hughes shuddered. Whatever had happened, she had been in extremely close contact.

She tilted her head ever so slightly. The tilt was barely perceptible, but Hughes was a perceptive guy. She flicked her eyes around, studying Hughes' face, his shotgun, the red Chevy, Frank leaning forward at the wheel, and the line of ruined cars on the road stretching on to infinity.

"I didn't mean to shoot at you, lady," Hughes said. "I thought you were one of those things."

"One of what things?" she said.

H ughes would have let her sit by the window, but he was a big guy and he couldn't sit in the middle without crowding into the gear shifter. She had to sit crammed between him and Frank, but they weren't going far.

Besides, he was the truck's security detail. He needed to be able to shoot out of the window. The U.S. military certified his Mossberg 500 Persuader pump-action shotgun as combat-reliable. With the pistol grip kit, it worked well for law enforcement, as well, but it's designed for home defense mostly and for close-quarters fighting. It's not always great in the field, but it was fine indeed for fighting on two-lane roads through the forest.

"What's your name?" Hughes said.

"Annie," she said. "Annie Starling." She put her face in her hands and leaned forward so her shoulders wouldn't touch his or Frank's. Hughes was grateful for that. She was covered in blood and might be infected. Dried blood, but still. Hughes' white T-shirt and faded khakis were covered in all manner of grime, but he looked and probably even smelled brand-new next to Annie.

"I'm Levan," Hughes said. "Levan Hughes. Most people just call me Hughes. This here's Frank."

"Hi, Annie," Frank said and tipped his baseball cap. "Sorry about the scare back there."

"Where are you taking me?" Annie said.

She was shaken up and afraid. Hughes could see that. He was used to making people a little bit nervous. He was a 240-pound black man— all muscle, no fat, and no bullshit. He didn't smile much. Not everyone was cool with that when they first met him. Few people were, actually, especially small and vulnerable women like Annie Starling. He knew they weren't afraid of his skin color, or at least not his skin color alone. Hardly anyone would even notice him if he weighed 160, wore a jacket and tie, and carried a folded-up *New York Times* under his arm. They were afraid of his size and his bearing. He knew how to kick the shit out of people, and that came across.

So he wasn't the least bit surprised that Annie Starling cringed a bit in his presence, especially since he'd just shot at her.

"We have a safe place," Hughes said. "We'll take you there. But first we have to go shopping. We'll get some things for you too. Some clean clothes and a weapon."

Annie said nothing. She just leaned forward and twisted the ring on her right hand. It was on her fourth finger, but the wrong hand for a wedding band.

Hughes shifted his weight and leaned hard into the passenger door to give her a little more space. He felt bad for shooting at her. And she smelled bad. Everyone smelled bad now, but Annie Starling smelled worse than anybody.

"Do you know what happened to you?" Hughes asked her. He doubted she did.

I thought you were one of those things.

One of what things?

Annie said nothing.

"Do you have any idea what's going on?" Hughes said.

Annie said nothing.

"She must have amnesia," Frank said. "Something real bad must have happened."

"She's sitting right here," Hughes said. "She can hear you."

He figured it was best to fill her in later. She seemed to be in no condition to take it all in at the moment. Kyle could explain everything when they returned to base. Hughes was not a great talker and never had been. Hughes was all about doing things and doing them quietly.

He'd been a bail bondsman up in Seattle. Before. He headed south toward Portland after he lost his family, but he doubted he'd ever get as far as Oregon now. Not in these conditions. Not without a helicopter. And he doubted anyone would be flying him anywhere in a helicopter anytime soon.

As they got farther from the I-5 interchange, the number of cars sitting on the road thinned out. I-5 was impassable in both directions. Because of the evacuations. People in Portland wanted to get to Seattle. People in Seattle tried to get down to Portland. Hughes shook his head when he thought of it. Just a panic response. When things got real bad, *anywhere but here* seemed like a plan. But small towns were better than big cities, the countryside better than small towns, and the wilderness better than anywhere.

Hughes had no particular reason to head south. Perhaps he should have bugged out for the mountains. He didn't know how to survive in the mountains, but they were sure as hell less dangerous than what Seattle had turned into. Things were probably no better down in Portland or up in Canada. The entire world was infected. No place was more jacked up than India. Maybe a few island nations were doing okay, but that was it. Micronesia probably wasn't affected, but how long could a string of minuscule islands in the South Pacific get by in a world by themselves? They could just go back to a fishing and coconut economy, he guessed. Micronesia actually wouldn't be a bad place to be, now that he thought about it.

"When was the last time you had a meal?" Hughes said to Annie.

"I don't know," Annie said. "I don't feel hungry. But I should probably eat. And I do feel pretty thirsty."

Hughes reached under the seat and pulled out an unopened bottle of water.

"Here," he said as he twisted off the cap and handed it to her.

She nodded and took it. And she relaxed a few increments. She seemed just slightly less afraid of him now.

Hughes wanted to ask whose blood was on her face, but he guessed she wouldn't know. He thought about warning her that wetting her lips might remoisten the blood, that she might get some in her mouth, but it wouldn't make any difference. She was either infected by now or she wasn't, and Hughes was pretty sure at this point that she wasn't. A person could only last a few hours at most after exposure to the virus, and if she'd been exposed in the past two or three hours, she wouldn't have asked what *things* he was talking about.

"What on earth happened here?" Annie said. Frank swerved the Chevy around abandoned cars. Some had busted-out windshields. Some still had their doors open. The road was so jammed up that Frank had to spend most of his time driving clear off the shoulder and onto the grass.

Hughes sat silent for a moment. "Things have been like—this—for more than a month now," he finally said. "You can't remember anything?"

"I know who I am," she said. "I remember my whole life. But I don't remember any of this. Whatever this is. These cars have been here for a *month*?"

Hughes tried to see the world around him through Annie's eyes. Tried and failed. There were too many incomprehensible things to take in. Wrecked cars. Abandoned cars. No moving traffic. No pedestrians. A boarded-up café on the side of the road. Downed power lines that normally would spark with electricity. The road covered in branches and leaves and everything else that had blown onto it since early September, none of which would ever be cleared. It would just keep piling up. He wondered how much longer any road in the world would still be passable. Roads in the Pacific Northwest would likely be finished in less than a year without cleanup and maintenance.

He saw a dead body in the grass on the right side of the road just up ahead. Actually, *body* didn't quite say it. It was mostly just bones. Almost all the meat had been picked clean.

"Oh my God," Annie said and covered her mouth with her hands. There could be no doubt in her mind that the skeleton once belonged to a human.

She didn't say anything else. Just turned her head so she could keep staring at it in horror as they drove past.

"Brace yourself," Hughes said. "There are probably more up ahead."

They were coming up on the little town now, the kind of place people hardly notice and don't even remember driving through after they've passed it. The town where Parker had told them he saw an outdoor-sporting-goods store that looked like it hadn't been looted yet. Parker had no time to hit it before, so Hughes and Frank were going back to it now. As soon as they reached the outskirts of town, Annie would see a whole lot more bodies and probably worse.

"What *happened*?" Annie said.

Hughes had to tell her something. He could hardly believe it was necessary. Annie must be the only human being in the world who didn't know.

"Plague," Hughes said. "Worst plague you ever saw. Amazing that you don't remember."

"Where's a safe place we can go?" Annie said.

"We have a place," Frank said. "Back behind us a couple of miles. We'll take you."

"I mean, how can we get away from all this? It can't be like this everywhere."

Hughes said nothing. Frank said nothing.

They drove on in silence for another minute or so. Hughes saw buildings ahead set back a ways from the road. Stores with parking lots out front. Buildings meant bodies. He put his thick arm out the window and leaned hard into the door. He might need to shoot again soon.

"More bodies ahead," he said, to warn Annie.

She saw them. Five bodies, mostly just skeletons, lying in the road next to a Jeep with its doors flung open. This time she didn't say anything. Didn't place her hands over her mouth. Didn't react. Just stared as they drove past.

Dozens of bodies were strewn across a parking lot in front of a feed store. They, too, were mostly just bones. Torn but now dried bloody clothing was scattered all over the place.

"This is what the plague does?" Annie said as much in amazement as horror. "Destroys the whole body? Like flesh-eating bacteria?"

They drove past the feed store and past two more skeletons in the road. Frank swerved around them.

"No," Hughes said. "That's not what the plague does at all."

Hughes would wait and tell her the rest later. It was too much to take in all at once.

"There," Frank said and pointed at a one-story building with a sign on the roof that said "Adventure Outfitters." "That must be the place."

They turned into the parking lot. It was empty of cars and of bodies. The front door was not boarded up. Hughes saw tents and backpacks and lanterns and boots displayed behind unbroken windows, just as Parker had said.

Frank stopped the truck in front of the door and put it in park.

"Okay," Hughes said to Annie. "Here's the deal. We're going to be attacked, so we have to move fast. We run in there, grab a couple of each item, throw them into the truck, then we *move*. Stay close to me. Don't venture off more than a couple of feet."

He and Frank opened the Chevy doors and got out. Annie stayed put for a moment until Hughes beckoned her with a wave of his hand.

"Who do you think is going to attack us?" Annie said. She stepped onto the pavement and looked around with unease. "It doesn't look like anyone has been here for months."

"Sick people," Hughes said. "The plague makes them aggressive."

"*Really* aggressive," Frank said.

Hughes broke through the glass door with the butt of his shotgun. He instinctively expected the screech of an alarm, but of course the power had been out for weeks, and the shattering glass was the only sound in any direction. The silence before and after was total.

He still hadn't gotten used to such quiet in an environment built by humans. Even the forests were louder than this. At least in the forest you could hear birds, insects, streams, and falling pinecones. Here there was no sound at all, the unreality almost dreamlike.

He reached in through the glass, careful not to cut his wrist on the jagged edges, and unlocked the door.

Frank flipped on a Maglite and swept the beam across the checkout counters and into the gloom. "Looks undisturbed," he said. "No one has been in here."

"Those bones we saw back there …" Annie said.

"Yeah," Hughes said.

"How long have they *been* there?"

Hughes stepped inside. "A month," he said in a voice just over a whisper. "Maybe two months." He scanned the store and swept the Mossberg back and forth, his finger inside the trigger guard. On the right was the clothing section. All-weather jackets, fleece pullovers, high-tech wilderness pants, gloves, hats, and wool socks.

"Then how could the bodies have decomposed so quickly?" Annie whispered. "The animals got to them already?"

"Those bones weren't picked over by animals," Hughes whispered.

She squinted.

"Later," Hughes said. "We'll explain it all back at home base. Grab some warm clothes that look like they'll fit you. Get at least two of everything."

Hughes led Annie to the clothing section as Frank picked up a handbasket to stuff items in. They didn't have enough time to fill a shopping cart.

"I'm getting food," Frank whispered. "It's right here next to the clothing." He grabbed packages of freeze-dried turkey tetrazzini and chili mac that could be "cooked" in the wilderness just by adding hot water. The expiration dates were years into the future.

Hughes watched over Annie as she grabbed two fleece pullovers and two pairs of pants off the rack. "Get five pairs of socks," he whispered, "or your feet are going to rot. And grab some strong boots."

He heard nothing in the store but himself, Annie, and Frank. If one of those things was in there, they'd know by now. The only quiet way in was through the front door. He lowered the shotgun, took his finger out of the trigger guard, and beckoned Annie to follow him toward a large glass counter displaying the expensive items the store owners didn't want to be shoplifted.

"Frank," he whispered. "Over here."

Frank sidled up behind Hughes and shined his Maglite through the glass. Hughes saw exactly what he was hoping to find. Hunting knives, GPS systems, and one-eyed night-vision devices.

"Sweet," Frank said.

"Grab those night-vision monocles," Hughes said. "Grab several. We won't be able to recharge the batteries."

"Sure, we will," Annie said. She held something in her hand. "It's a portable solar panel. Says it's for charging cell phones and iPads while camping."

Hughes lit up. "Get as many of those as you can carry."

"There must be some first-aid packs in here somewhere," Frank said. Hughes saw that Frank had placed five night-vision monocles in his basket.

"Go find some," Hughes said. "Get the biggest packs you can find. One minute."

Hughes grabbed a water filter, a small camp stove, a compass, and navigation maps of Oregon, Washington, and British Columbia. He collected six small emergency blankets made of reflective Mylar, two hunting knives, two more portable solar panels from where Annie had found hers, a handheld GPS that looked like it might plug into the panels, two winter jackets, two sleeping bags, seven candles, packs of waterproof matches, fistfuls of fleece hats. He stuffed everything into the biggest backpack he could find. He slung the weighted-down backpack over one of his shoulders and grabbed a second empty one for good measure, then hustled toward the front door.

"Time to move," he said. "Frank. Annie. Let's go. We can't push our luck."

Hughes tossed his items into the Chevy's truck bed. Frank and Annie followed him out and set their items next to his.

"Shh," he said and held up his hand. Everyone cocked their heads and stopped breathing for a moment.

"I don't hear anything," Annie whispered. She shuddered at the implications. The poor girl still didn't know what was happening.

"I don't either," Frank said, though unlike Annie, he looked relieved. Hughes thought for a moment.

"If anything heard us pull in here," he said, "they'd be here by now." Frank nodded.

Annie said nothing.

"Nothing is coming," Hughes said.

"How do you know?" Annie said.

"If something was coming," Hughes said, "believe me, we'd know."

"But how?" Annie said. "How would you know if someone is coming?"

"You'll find out when it happens," Hughes said.

The last thing Annie remembered was visiting her older sister Jenny in Olympia. She had no idea how much time had passed since then and when all—this—happened.

She had driven down for the day from Seattle. Both she and Jenny moved to Washington State from South Carolina—Jenny because she got a job working for a congressman and Annie because she had broken up with her live-in boyfriend of two years and felt the need to start over. Jenny told Annie the Northwest was a fabulous place to live, and Annie figured that made it as good a place as any to reboot her life. Seattle was as far from South Carolina as a person could get in the United States without moving to Alaska or Hawaii, and since her sister was out there, she would not be alone.

She lived near the University of Washington campus just north of downtown Seattle. She clearly remembered hopping in her Saturn and driving down I-5 to Olympia. She and Jenny picked up some lattes at the Starbucks downtown near the state capitol building and drank them across the street on a park bench. It was a warm late-summer day. She remembered thinking the moderate dry heat of summer would soon be replaced with the cool musty air of October. There was no plague, nor talk of any plague.

The next thing she knew, she was waking up on the forest floor aching and dehydrated and covered in blood and gore. She reeked something awful and her mouth tasted like a rat had died in it. She got up, stumbled around for a few moments, and heard Hughes and Frank's truck on the road just a few dozen yards away. And now she was in the truck heading to what Hughes said was their home base inside a grocery store.

A grocery store? They lived in a grocery store?

Where the hell had she been living these last couple of months?

"What's the date today?" she said.

"Dunno," Hughes said. "Must be early November by now, I guess."

"It feels like a whole year has passed since this happened," Frank said. "But I guess it has only been a couple of months."

Early November. It was, what, early September when she was at her sister's? So she was missing a solid two months of memory.

"How far are we from Olympia?" she said.

"You don't know where we are?" Hughes said.

"It looks like the same general area," she said, "but no, I don't know where we are."

"Olympia is fifteen miles north of here," Hughes said. "Portland is an hour and a half to the south. At least it would be if the roads weren't so bad. It would take a week to get there in these conditions. The freeway is impassable. We'd have to walk."

She looked through the windshield in amazement. Both sides of the road were jammed with stopped cars. They spilled out of their lanes and onto the shoulder. Some of the doors were left open. What on earth had happened to everybody? Were all of them struck down by the virus? Even while out in their cars? Where did they go? Was there a refugee center somewhere? She swallowed hard, not sure she wanted to know the answer just yet.

"How does the virus spread?" she said.

"Bodily fluids," Hughes said. "It's not airborne, thank God. We wouldn't be alive if it were. Don't touch anything that's dead. Don't touch anything if it looked like something dead touched it. If you get blood or fluid of any kind on your hand, you scrub that bitch down. I can't believe you're not sick with all that blood on your shirt and on your face. I'd tell you to keep your fingers the hell out of your mouth, but if that virus was on you somewhere, you'd be infected by now. That's for damn sure."

"What are the first symptoms?" she said. She saw the five skeletons next to the Jeep they'd passed earlier.

"Sore throat," Hughes said.

Annie had a sore throat.

"Coughing."

But that was probably because she was dehydrated.

"A fever like you wouldn't believe. Then coma. It only takes a couple of hours. Some people go down within minutes."

She caught herself rubbing her throat and stopped. She didn't want them to think she was getting sick.

"Water?" Hughes said. He'd noticed her rubbing her throat. She wasn't surprised. Hughes didn't look like the type of guy who let much get past him.

"Thanks," she said as he reached under the seat and handed the bottle to her again.

There was something else Hughes wasn't telling her. Frank had said the virus makes people aggressive. Like rabies? Does that happen before or after the coma? How could it happen after?

Pine needles and leaves covered the road ahead. The cars were covered too. Off to the right she saw the burned-out husk of what was once a Volkswagen Bug. They passed a boarded-up mom-and-pop gas station on the left side. She wondered what happened to mom and pop.

"How many people do you suppose have been killed?" she said.

Hughes and Frank looked at each other.

"Pretty much everybody," Frank said and rubbed his mustache.

She sank in her seat. Pretty much everybody? How was that possible? Not even the Black Death killed pretty much everybody.

But somehow that felt right. It didn't sound right, but it felt right.

She didn't remember any of this, but the weird thing was that she almost remembered. She felt as if she were watching a movie that she had seen a long time ago as a kid. She had no idea what was going to happen next, but she sort of remembered things as they happened. She didn't know what Hughes and Frank were going to say when she asked them a question, but everything they did say seemed right, like some part of her knew. Her mind was throwing up walls, leaving her stranded somewhere between amnesia and denial.

Frank swerved around a tight knot of cars in the road and had to drive most of the way to the tree line to get past them. Annie felt Hughes tense up as they neared the edge of the forest. He had that gun of his pointed out the window and was ready to pull the trigger. He looked like he *wanted* to pull the trigger.

Frank swerved back toward the asphalt after clearing the pileup. "Bogie at eleven o'clock. Hold onto something."

Annie glanced left. A man came charging out of the trees on the other side of the road. He was covered in blood and screaming like he was terrified or enraged.

"Watch out!" Annie said. "There's a—"

But Frank swerved into the man's path and swiped him with the side of the Chevy. The impact sounded like someone threw a sack of potatoes at the driver's-side door. The man bounced off the vehicle and flopped onto the shoulder. Frank kept going and checked the mirror.

"It's down," he said.

"You just hit that man!" Annie said. "You probably killed him. Did you do that on *purpose*?"

Silence in the truck.

"Annie," Hughes said and shook his head. "He was one of the infected ones."

"You thought I was infected."

"He was covered in blood."

"I'm covered in blood."

"He was screaming. You heard him."

"So you killed him?"

Frank and Hughes said nothing.

Something was wrong with her brain. What Frank did seemed wrong but felt right. Why? Her gut knew something her mind couldn't access. Her short-term amnesia, her denial, her mind blockage—whatever it was—was tenuous. It wouldn't last. Her memories were just barely below the threshold of consciousness.

She looked at the body in the rearview mirror. It did not appear to be moving or even twitching. The man was already covered in blood and gore before Frank hit him. Aside from the fact that he no longer moved, he looked no worse now than he did when he ran out of the trees.

"Can we stop for a second?" Annie said.

"What for?" Frank said.

"No," Hughes said.

"I want to go back and get a closer look at that man," she said.

"He wasn't a man," Hughes said. "Not anymore. He was one of those things."

He wasn't a *thing*.

"Infected or not," Annie said, "he was a man."

Hughes said nothing.

"We can't stop here, Annie," Frank said. "The truck's noise attracts them. We're damn lucky none of them followed us to the sporting-goods store. And anyway you don't want to get too close to even the dead ones.

Bodily fluids and all that."

She needed to study that body, but she didn't know why. Probably just her brain-lock trying to resolve itself. Her memory, her knowledge and understanding of the insanity all around her, was trying to punch its way out through whatever barrier had been put in place. Stopping to think and scrutinizing things might help, but Frank wouldn't stop, and Hughes wouldn't let him stop if he wanted to.

They rounded a few more corners and arrived at the outskirts of another town, the kind of outskirts that look exactly like outskirts everywhere in the country. Gas stations, fast-food joints, used-car lots, Jiffy Lubes. The place had been torn to pieces just like the last town they passed through, but here the streets were entirely empty of cars. Everyone had evacuated.

Trash, branches, leaves, debris and broken glass covered the streets, the sidewalks, and the parking lots. A pickup truck had smashed into an electrical pole. What looked like a used-car lot had exploded and burned to the ground. Dead bodies—bones, mostly—were strewn all over the place. The windows of a Burger King were covered with nailed-up boards blackened by fire.

Was the Burger King boarded up to keep people out or to keep people in? Why had the car lot burned down?

Though the details weren't familiar, the brushstrokes were. She was certain she'd never been there before, but she felt a sense of déjà vu coming over her. Something was banging inside her head and trying to get out. Something of earthshaking significance. She could feel it, like a just-forgotten dream on the other side of the mist.

Why couldn't she remember? There was a reason she went into brain-lock. Something had happened to her. Something that didn't happen to Hughes or to Frank.

CHAPTER TWO

Kyle Trager stared while Parker cleaned his guns. Parker had parts from three handguns greased up and spread out before him on the counter of the checkout aisle, the one nearest the grocery store's door where there was more light.

"We should shove off tomorrow," Kyle said. "Get a boat and head up to one of the islands."

Parker set down a pistol and his oil rag. "None of us has seen a better place than where we are right now. It's secure and our food will last months."

They were holed up in a well-stocked grocery store in a medium-size suburban-looking town just off the interstate. A nearby lumberyard provided all the wood and nails they needed to board up the windows and fortify the front and back doors. They had no electricity, but plenty to eat.

"We're only safe here," Kyle said, "until we get attacked by 200 of those things at the same time. We'll never be safe on the mainland. We need an island."

"Those things aren't going to last," Parker said. "Winter is coming and they're running out of food. We stay here, wait for them to start dying off, and then we can go to your little island."

Kyle's group of five had only cohered a week or so earlier. He and Frank were traveling together when they ran into Hughes and Carol. Then the four of them found Parker rummaging around in somebody's van. They all understood there was safety in numbers. They didn't even discuss whether or not they should stick together. They did it instinctively.

And they were all thrilled when they found an unlooted grocery store. It must have been the only one in all of Washington State. It was a great place to hole up for a while, but it wasn't home. Surely it wasn't secure enough to stay there all winter, but Kyle couldn't get Parker to see that. They'd been butting heads ever since Kyle first suggested sailing north to the islands.

Somebody was bound to emerge as a leader eventually. That's how these things usually worked, but it hadn't happened yet. Even if the leader wasn't a boss issuing orders, somebody would have the most influence. That person was bound to be Kyle or Parker. Theoretically it could be Hughes, but Hughes didn't seem interested. He didn't talk much. And silent types can't be leaders.

Frank wasn't incompetent, exactly, but he was definitely sidekick material. No one with any sense would want Frank making decisions, including Frank.

Carol was out of the question. She was a nervous wreck, a total disaster. She wanted someone to tell her exactly what she should do and when she should do it.

That left Parker and Kyle, but Parker was bullheaded, difficult, and just … off. It wasn't only the guns. The man looked like a slob with his cargo pants, army jacket, and big scruffy beard. Hadn't he heard of razors? There must have been hundreds of disposables in the toiletries aisle. The world was fast running out of just about everything, but Kyle figured he could easily loot a lifetime supply of disposable razors. And Kyle thought it was important to look like a civilized person, now more than ever.

"You want some more light?" Kyle said to Parker as he ran the oil rag through the barrel of one of his pistols. "I could bring some candles over."

"I'm fine," Parker said and didn't look up from his work. He faced the line of windows so he wouldn't get in the way of the light, though there wasn't much to get in the way of. Every window in the grocery store was boarded up. Only twelve or so inches were left exposed at the top to let in some sun. They had to be conservative with the candles.

At least the water still worked—for now, anyway. And it came out of the sink with incredible force. Apparently the pressure just kept building up since hardly anyone was left alive to release it, but it too would eventually break like the electricity had.

Kyle didn't like it when Parker cleaned his guns. Didn't like it at all. Parker cleaned his guns all the time, every single day, even when he hadn't fired them since the last cleaning.

He did it to intimidate everyone else. Kyle was sure of it. No one was really in charge, nor had Parker tried to appoint himself boss, but he wanted to make damn certain everyone took his feelings into account. Theatrically cleaning his guns was a big part of it.

Parker also wanted to make Kyle feel inadequate and incompetent. How can you expect to lead this group if you can't even clean a damn gun?

Kyle was no kind of idiot. He knew how to shoot. His father showed him how when he was a kid. And he had gone shooting dozens of times with his friends on the range and in the forest. He just didn't own a gun. His home state of Oregon was awash in guns. It had more guns than people. There just weren't as many guns or gun owners in the city, and Kyle was a city person.

He had worked as a computer programmer in the suburbs of Portland. That's where he was when the plague struck. He headed north into Washington, but not to Seattle. That would not have been smart. Seattle wasn't safer than Portland. Seattle was the first American city to be hit with the virus. Kyle aimed straight for Olympia at the southernmost point on Puget Sound, an island-studded inlet extending hundreds of miles inland from the Pacific Ocean. From there he planned to take a boat to the San Juan Islands just shy of the Canadian border. That was a plan that made sense. Those things couldn't get to him on an island.

Carol stepped out of the walk-in cooler with a broom in her hand. She'd been in there sweeping the floor again. A now-dry meltwater stain spread out from under the door. The walk-in cooler wasn't cold anymore and would never be cold again, or at least not any colder than the rest of the store once winter set in. They decided they'd use it as their fallback position if those things ever got past their defenses at the windows and doors. There was only one way in and out. As long as they had enough bullets—or cartridges, as Hughes and Parker liked to call them—they could shoot those things one at a time as they came in.

"How you doin', kiddo?" Kyle said to Carol.

"I'll feel better when Hughes and Frank get back."

"They should be back pretty soon. They must have found some good stuff."

Parker ignored them. He was all-consumed by his guns.

Kyle wasn't sure what kind of guns they were and he wasn't going to ask. He knew his own weapon was a Glock 17. That's what Hughes had called it when he gave it to him. And Kyle knew how to use it. Using a handgun isn't hard. He always thought it was strange when a character in a movie asks another character if they know how to use one. What's to know? Flick off the safety, point it at whatever you want to splatter, and squeeze the trigger.

Kyle heard something outside. Carol and Parker heard it too. Parker turned his ears toward the noise and Carol took a step back. Kyle heard it again. It sounded like soft padding footsteps. It wasn't one of those things, then. A dog, most likely, though it could have been just about anything. Kyle had seen deer and even a bear in urban environments in the past couple of weeks. He figured it was only a matter of time before he saw mountain lions.

"I'm with Kyle," Carol said, her voice shaking. "It's not safe here. We should head to the islands. I don't think I can stay here for three months. Look at us. Even you two get jumpy when it's only a dog outside the door."

Kyle felt sorry for Carol. The poor thing would be scared out of her mind whether or not they stayed hunkered down in their fortified grocery store. Carol would be jumpy in an underground government bunker. She dealt with it by keeping herself busy with obsessive-compulsive cleaning. She cleaned everything in the store over and over again. She kept scrubbing down the meat and produce trays even though the meat and produce were long gone, spoiled and reeking and thrown out the back where the stench could waft away. It didn't entirely waft away, of course. The store still smelled like a garbage can. Everything but the air, though, was as clean as it could possibly be, thanks to Carol's nervous habit. She even made several rounds down the aisles straightening every cereal box, every bottle of olive oil, and every box of macaroni and cheese, but it was all rather pointless. Once things were straightened, they stayed straightened. You could mop a clean floor, but you couldn't make straight boxes of macaroni and cheese any straighter.

"How exactly do you two expect to get to a boat from here?" Parker said. "We're at least fifteen miles away from the water. We'd have to walk. You've seen the roads. We sure as hell aren't getting there in a car."

"We can take bicycles," Kyle said. "We can weave around the abandoned cars, and we can ride faster than those things can run."

"But we can't carry supplies," Parker said. "All this food will be wasted."

"That will be true whether we go now or wait," Kyle said.

"But if we wait," Parker said, "we won't have wasted the food. And there will be fewer of those things running around."

"Maybe," Kyle said. "But there will be none of those things on an island."

"You don't know that. What if we get all the way up there and the islands are all infested?"

"We'll be on a boat. Those things can't get to us if we're on a boat."

"You don't know that either."

Kyle said nothing. He couldn't be certain, but he was pretty sure those things couldn't swim. Or, if they could, they wouldn't be able to climb onto a boat from down in the water before getting whacked in the head with a crowbar.

The grocery store was a fine place to dig in for a while, but it couldn't last. And Kyle did not enjoy being there. He couldn't relax, and neither could anyone else.

They needed more than just food. Hughes and Frank were on a supply run at a sporting-goods store, but they also needed medicine and clean clothes. And they needed warm clothes. The cold rains of November were coming. They'd eventually all get trench foot if they could not keep their socks clean. Kyle also needed a new shirt. His red flannel was comfortable, as were his blue jeans, but they had been ripe for weeks.

It was impressive, though, what they'd done with the place.

An entire grocery store in this little suburban-style town off the interstate hadn't been looted. There was another store, a bigger, fancier one with vast health-food aisles a half-mile or so away. That one had been stripped practically bare. This store had survived the initial panic and the mass exodus.

It looked like the kind of place customers with money would have avoided back when things were still normal and places like this were still open for business. The floor was made of chipped 1970s tiles. The subflooring was even exposed in some places. The off-white walls couldn't have been painted once in the past decade. Kyle marveled at the long black smudges at head level. How did those get there? The fluorescent tube lights above had long gone dark, but they must have made the place look like the inside of a meat locker when the power still worked. No matter how many times Carol doused the place with Lysol, the air was infused with the sweet tang of rot. And to top all that off, there was nowhere soft or comfortable to sit or lie down. The place sucked, aside from the fortifications and food.

But they had most of what they needed inside. Cans of soup. Cans of spaghetti and ravioli. Cans of clam chowder that dubiously claimed to be restaurant quality. Cans of baby food. No one had a baby, nor had anyone tried to eat any baby food yet, but it had to be fine in a pinch. Nobody was interested in the canned vegetables, but Kyle figured that would change soon enough and they'd all be happy to have them.

The breakfast aisle was popular. The Pop-Tarts and granola bars were okay, but a few aisles down were bags of powdered milk that could be reconstituted with water. And since the store's picnic section had thin cardboard bowls and plastic spoons, they could eat an actual breakfast that was exactly like some of the actual breakfasts they used to eat before the world went over the cliff. Rice Krispies and Froot Loops were bound to get old eventually, but they sure beat cold soup.

They had beef jerky and dried meat sticks, which were fantastic, though hardly substitutes for cheeseburgers and steaks. The fruit roll-ups and jam tasted all right, but eating those just wasn't the same as crunching into a tart apple or sucking juice and pulp from an orange.

No one felt guilty or childish when eating peanut butter out of the jar. It tasted good, and it was heavier and felt more nourishing than most of the other foods they could still eat. Peanut butter stuck to their ribs. It was the new steak and potatoes.

The other best thing was the tuna-fish section. They had so many cans of tuna that everyone was already sick of eating the stuff. But also right next to the tuna in the very same section were cans of chopped turkey and chicken. It came in cans that looked identical to the tuna-fish cans. Kyle didn't know such items even existed until now, and he dug into one before even bothering to open a fish can.

They weren't short on beverages. They had an entire row of warm Coke and Pepsi and Root Beer and Sprite. Warm soda tasted more syrupy than usual, but that was okay. They also had a substantial selection of flavored iced tea and sports drinks. And, of course, beer and wine. Parker was working his way through various craft beers, but Kyle preferred red wine now that the power was out and the refrigerators were off. He liked a good craft beer as much as any Northwesterner, but the stuff was warm now and it wasn't the same. At least wine was supposed to be kept at room temperature.

The fresh meat, fresh fruit, fresh vegetables, milk, butter, and frozen food were finished. All that stuff was just chucked out back. It reeked back there something awful, like 10,000 trash cans. The whole mess of rotting food was coalescing into a putrid sludge oozing with bacteria and swarming with insects. Kyle was certain by now that it was a biohazard. The whole store smelled like that when they first got there. Getting rid of the spoiled food was a spectacularly unpleasant task that Kyle would never forget.

He also wouldn't forget how they'd fortified the place. That, Kyle thought, was something for the history books—assuming history books would ever be written again. Kyle didn't know how many people were left in the world, but he was certain it was one percent at the most.

They were safe for now—sort of—but they couldn't stay there forever. The food would run out eventually, and they'd have to leave. They'd have no way of finding or producing more food, not here, not in this place, and probably not any other place that was suburban or urban. They'd need to grow food and hunt food, and that required a rural location.

And they needed long-term security. What better place for that than one of the San Juan Islands? Those things couldn't get to them there. They could live in houses and plant crops and hunt deer and fish. They could stock up on medicines and install solar panels and turn on the lights and even watch movies. Their lives could be relatively stress-free and idyllic in a mild climate with plenty of rainwater.

But if they stayed too long in that store on the mainland, they'd die.

"If you want to stay here," Kyle told Parker, "then stay. I can't stop you. I'm not even going to try. But I'm taking everyone who wants to come with me up to those islands."

Parker, his guns freshly oiled, sat on the floor near the front door and watched his companions through slitted eyes. Carol was on another one of her cleaning jags. Kyle paced and thought and talked too much as usual. Hughes and Frank hadn't returned yet.

He wasn't sure they'd ever return.

The fortified grocery hadn't been attacked yet, but their luck had to run out eventually. They were on the outskirts of a town, for God's sake. The place should be crawling with the infected. Parker figured it would take at least another month before most of those things starved, if not longer. It depended on how much food they could find in the meantime and how well they could adapt while suffering their ... affliction.

He doubted those things could adapt. The virus spread with unspeakable speed and ferocity, but Parker didn't think it had a long life span. It did far too much damage to the host's mind. The basic and primitive lizard part of the brain seemed to be all that was left, and even that was distorted beyond recognition.

Kyle's pacing and Carol's incessant cleaning annoyed him, but on some level he was actually grateful. They made just enough noise to drown out the quiet. Not enough noise to attract a horde, but enough that Parker could forget that he was a witness to the end of all things.

The end of all things. He still hadn't wrapped his mind around that. The implications of more than six billion dead were too overwhelming, like contemplating the number of molecules in the ocean or the number of stars in the galaxies.

And it wasn't just the number of dead. Everything was falling apart. Flip a light switch and nothing happens. Want gas for your car? Get a hose and siphon it out of somebody else's. Want fresh milk for your cereal? Find a cow that hasn't yet starved or been eaten. Water exploded out of the faucet when he twisted the tap, but that wouldn't last. Nor would the boxes of dry goods that hadn't expired. What would they do when they ran out? Farm? Where? How? None of his companions knew the first thing about farming.

He didn't even like his companions. Hughes was okay, but Frank was useless if nobody gave him an order. Carol was dead weight. She had no asset aside from her gender. If enough humans could figure out a way to survive and rebuild in this broken new world, some of them would have to be women for obvious reasons, but that was the beginning and end of Carol's usefulness. She couldn't fight, couldn't think straight, couldn't drive on the roads, couldn't carry anything heavy, and failed to offer a useful opinion on anything.

Kyle, on the other hand, talked and thought too much about everything. And he was practically still a kid. Parker was pushing forty, but Kyle couldn't be a day over twenty-five. Parker remembered how stupid he was in his twenties. He thought he had it all figured out, but all he'd really done was survive adolescence.

And that button-up flannel shirt Kyle wore. Good grief. The grunge look went out of style long ago, even in Seattle. Kyle needed practical clothes like what Parker was wearing: water-resistant cargo plants, a black fleece sweatshirt that kept him warm even when wet, and his favorite olive drab army jacket.

And the dumb kid shaved every day, a spectacular waste of effort and time. Kyle kept his face baby's-ass smooth as if he might get a date. A date with who? Carol?

Worst of all, though, Kyle was a goddamn lunatic for thinking they ought to leave their food and fortifications behind for some mythical island where unicorns romped in the fields and fairies lived in the trees.

An island would be nice, sure, if they could beam there like in *Star Trek*, but their grocery store was a castle. They had food, water, bathrooms, basic medicine, clothes, blankets, and a whole row of gas cans by the back door.

Every single window was boarded up with plywood except for slits at the top to let in some light. Two-by-fours braced the front and the back doors. No one, and no thing, could force its way in unless it was driving a truck or wielding an ax.

Hughes and Frank had hauled the lumber, nails, and hammers in the Chevy from a hardware store down the street. They did it at night. The darkness at night now that the power was out gave him the creeps. Billions of new stars seemed to leap toward the planet from the farthest reaches of space, but Parker couldn't see a damn thing if the moon wasn't up.

Only once since he was seven and afraid of his closet did he feel real fear of the dark. He'd gone on a camping trip with a buddy who marched him and his sorry ass seven miles up a trail in the Olympic mountains. That was maybe ten years ago. The scenery was spectacular. Parker had never seen anything like it because there is nothing else like it. The Olympic Peninsula produced the only true temperate rain forest on earth. Not even the other lush forests of Washington and Oregon are like the forests in the Olympics. Everything's wet all the time. Baby trees grow from the sides of fallen dead trees, sucking nutrients from their predecessors like cannibals. Curtains of moss the size of houses hang from the canopy.

Unlike in the volcanic Cascades, where they're few and far between, black bears are thick on the ground in the Olympics.

And that was the problem.

Sometime after midnight he crawled out of his tent to urinate and a near paralyzing fear of the darkness struck him at once. He couldn't see shit, not even stars. There was no ambient artificial light from a city in any direction. The nearest house was more than fifty miles away, and he was pretty sure the nearest town was in Canada. He turned on his flashlight, but it only cast a dirty yellow splotch on the underbrush. The rest of the world remained shrouded in pitch.

He might have felt okay had the forest been silent. At least he'd know a bear wasn't stomping around somewhere nearby. But the forest was not silent. Water dripped from the trees in every direction. His ears seemed to work overtime since he couldn't see. The part of his brainpower that normally processed sight was freed up to listen for sound. The dripping water sounded like an afternoon rainstorm. If a hungry 350-pound omnivore stepped on a branch somewhere nearby, maybe he'd hear it. But if a 350-pound omnivore sat on the path right in front him just waiting for Parker to get a little bit closer, he'd be torn to pieces by claws and by teeth the instant he bumbled into it.

He hurriedly pissed in the bushes and scrambled back to his tent.

The dark of the Olympic National Forest put a fright into him that was primal in its intensity. He didn't think it was possible to be any more afraid of the dark than he was on that night in the forest, but he was wrong. He was so very wrong.

How many bears live in that forest? A couple of hundred at most? In the now-darkened cities of the Pacific Northwest, thousands of those *things* were loose on the streets.

Possibly hundreds of thousands.

And the nearest artificial light was on the international space station.

Parker was not going to leave the confines of his fortress unless he fucking well had to.

Hughes had figured out how to board it up without generating as much noise as a construction site. He blew up the used-car lot down the street. Hughes and Frank first doused the building with gasoline, but they dumped the lion's share on the hoods of all the vehicles lined up out front. And they dropped a match.

The noise was unfuckingbelievable once the cars started exploding. It attracted hundreds of those things. They threw themselves into the flames like moths into a campfire. Most burned to death. Others were blown to pieces when the gas tanks ignited. None heard or otherwise noticed Parker and Kyle as they drove sixpenny nails into plywood and transformed their grocery store into a castle.

Parker was impressed with Hughes for coming up with that plan. It was a good idea, a big idea, and if Carol hadn't been so freaked out by the explosions, it would have been fun.

He heard something outside, tiny and faint through the boarded-up windows, most likely Hughes' truck. All sounds were magnified now. The silence of the earth itself seemed to make noise. Parker thought the "sound" of silence might be the onset of tinnitus in his ears, an incessant ringing that he never noticed before beneath the hum of civilization.

Or maybe what sounded like faint tinnitus was really just the sound of the earth, of insects crawling on pavement and grass, of drifting and subducting tectonic plates, of oozing magma miles below, and the hum of the planet's magnetic field. Maybe he was just imagining things. Maybe silence itself had a sound that he never noticed before because silence had never existed.

Even the quietest night in his Seattle neighborhood had plenty of sounds: cars on the interstate, even though it was miles away; planes coming into the Sea-Tac airport from the East Coast and from Asia; trains on their way up to Vancouver in Canada; ships coming into Puget Sound from the ocean. All those things made noise. Even the wires in his house buzzed with electricity. Now there was nothing.

It was worse at night when absolute silence met absolute darkness in a world full of absolute danger. Those things were somewhere out in that void. Hundreds of thousands of them just waiting for stimulus.

But now he thought he heard Hughes' truck somewhere in the distance.

"Is that them?" Carol said.

"Don't know," Parker said.

"It has to be them," Kyle said. "They're actually a little bit late, and we haven't seen another person in days."

Parker stood. Maybe that was Hughes and Frank's truck and maybe it wasn't. He picked up his freshly oiled Beretta M9.

Kyle picked up a hammer.

The vehicle pulled into the lot and stopped. Parker couldn't see through the door since it was boarded up like the windows. He'd cut a tiny piece out of the plywood so he could reach the door's locking mechanism, but that missing piece was only the size of the lock. He stood by the door and waited until he was sure it was Hughes and Frank outside before unlocking it.

Parker heard Hughes' voice. "We need to get inside. Those things are attracted to noise. We got lucky before."

Then he heard a woman's voice. Who was that? He couldn't quite make out what she said, but that definitely wasn't Frank he was hearing.

Parker opened the door.

"Hey," Hughes said.

"Parker," Frank said and nodded.

Parker squinted at the light and saw the woman. She was covered head to toe in blood and matted gore. "Jesus Christ. What the hell happened to you?"

"I'm okay," she said. "My name's Annie." She wiped her hands on her pants. They came off no cleaner than before. He could tell she was thinking of shaking his hand, but she saw the look of disgust on his face and put her gross hands in her pockets instead.

"Just get inside," Parker said as he scanned the parking lot and the street outside. "And don't touch anything until you get cleaned up and changed."

"We got some good stuff," Frank said as he stepped through the door.

"Shh!" Parker said. "Just get inside in case anything followed you."

That should be the last supply run for a while, Parker thought. If they kept going out there in the truck, eventually they'd bring dozens if not hundreds of those things back to the store on their tail.

Hughes gestured for the woman named Annie to walk ahead of him. Parker stepped out of her way and locked the door behind Hughes. The amount of light in the store fell by half when he shut the door.

"I'm Annie," the woman said to Kyle and Carol.

"Whoa," Kyle said when he got a good look at her.

"Oh, honey," Carol said.

"Sorry," Kyle said. "I'm Kyle." He tentatively reached out his hand and shook hers. "This is Parker and Carol. Come on, let's get you cleaned up. There's a sink in the back that still works."

This Annie person was a biohazard on legs.

"She clean?" Parker said to Hughes.

"I think so," Hughes said.

"You think so? Annie, your clothes will need to be burned."

"Oh," she said. "My clean clothes are still in the truck."

"Just wait," he whispered, annoyed. "We can unload the truck later. Right now we need to be quiet in case those things heard you pull in here."

Kyle took her into the back where the sink was.

"Where'd you find her?" Parker asked Hughes.

Hughes and Frank looked at each other.

"She came running out of the trees," Frank said, "looking like one of those things. You saw her. All that blood on her face and all over her shirt. She was waving her arms around and looking all crazy so Hughes shot at her."

"I take it you missed?" Parker said.

"I fired the Mossberg as Frank swerved around a car," Hughes said. "So, yeah, I missed. She's really damn lucky."

Parker said nothing. He wasn't thrilled to have another person around. With himself, Kyle, Hughes, Frank, Carol, and now this Annie person, there were six of them. An even number. Parker didn't like even numbers. An even-numbered group could be deadlocked on decisions.

And Parker didn't like the looks of this Annie. She was what, twenty-five years old at the most? Kyle's age and Carol's gender. A crap combination. Could she pull her weight? Well, maybe. She had blood all over herself, which meant one of two things. Annie was about to turn into one of those things or she'd killed a bunch of those things. Parker couldn't imagine Carol squishing a bug.

"Something's up with her," Hughes said.

Parker raised his eyebrows. "What?"

"She doesn't remember anything."

"Well, that's just great."

"She knows who she is. She remembers everything except the last couple of months. She didn't even know about the plague until Frank and I told her."

"Can you believe that shit?" Frank said.

"She must be traumatized," Carol said.

"You think?" Parker said.

Hughes grabbed Parker's arm. Parker knew what that meant. Don't be an asshole. Hughes was the only person Parker would let get away with that. Not that he could really stop him.

Kyle returned from the back of the store.

"Annie's washing up," he said. "She really wants to change out of those bloody clothes as soon as it's safe to unload the truck."

Everyone got quiet. Parker stepped up to the door and pressed his ear against the plywood, the Beretta M9 in both hands. He heard nothing but the sound of the sink running in back as Annie washed up. "Quiet out there. We might be okay."

Ten more minutes, he thought, and if nothing comes and bangs on the windows and doors, they can slip out and unload the truck.

Annie shut off the sink and Parker could hear his tinnitus again. Or the hum of the earth. Or whatever it was. He heard nothing else but his own heartbeat and his breathing.

Kyle approached the door. He, too, placed his ear next to the boards. He didn't seem to hear anything either.

Parker thought that was too good to be true. Something had to be out there. They were in a town, for Christ's sake.

They both pressed their ears to the boards again.

Then Parker heard something that sounded like footsteps on asphalt. Not the footsteps of a dog or a cat and certainly not a rat. Not a deer or a coyote or any other animal that might have wandered into town now that people were gone. No, Parker heard the footsteps of humans.

Or things that used to be human.

He and Kyle stepped away from the door.

Parker twitched when Annie whispered from just behind him, "Is it clear?" He didn't know she was there. He didn't hear her sneak up on him. So that was a point in her favor. She knew how to move really damn quietly when she had to.

"Shh," Parker said.

The footsteps outside grew louder.

"They're regular people," Kyle said. "Not infected. Those footsteps sound normal."

The footsteps stopped outside the door. After a moment of silence, somebody knocked.

Parker flicked his Beretta's safety off.

Kyle felt a surge of elation when he heard the knock on the door. More survivors!

But Parker looked spooked. The man stepped back and pointed his pistol right at the door.

"Who's there?" Parker said.

"Please," said a man's hushed voice outside. Kyle could barely hear him through the boards. "We've got wounded out here. We need help."

"How many are you?" Parker said.

"There are three of us. Please."

"Are any of you infected?" Kyle said.

"No. But we were attacked. Not by the infected, but by other people. Then we saw your truck. You've got to let us inside before they see us. They're armed."

Kyle looked first at Parker and then at Hughes. Hughes nodded. So did Parker. Kyle unlocked the door and opened it.

Outside stood three men wearing black and pointing pistols at Kyle's face.

"Shit," Parker said.

The man in the center, the tallest of the three, saw Parker's gun and aimed his pistol squarely at Parker's head.

Kyle heard Carol skitter away, but he had no idea how the others were reacting. He could not take his eyes off the intruders and their guns. Kyle still held a hammer in his hand and wouldn't let go of it.

"You'd better let us in," said the tall man, "before some of those things see us." He was the one who had spoken through the door. The leader.

"I thought you said you were attacked by people," Parker said.

"I did," said the tall man.

"Which of you is injured?" Kyle said.

The tall man sighed. "None of us. But you will be if you don't back up and get out of our way. We're coming in."

Kyle stepped aside but kept hold of his hammer. The men stepped inside, but Parker stayed right where he was, barely a dozen feet away, and kept his handgun pointed at the intruders.

"Bobby," the tall man said. "Lock the door."

The one who answered to Bobby reached behind himself and closed the door. Half the light in the room vanished. Bobby fiddled with the lock.

"Were you followed?" Kyle said.

"We're all clear. There's nothing else out there. We've been searching the area for more than an hour. We could all pull our triggers right now and nothing would hear us."

"We pull, you die," Parker said. He held his gun level.

"You die too," said the man. "And you die first. You can shoot one of us, but we will shoot all of you. So I strongly suggest you lower your weapons and that you do it now."

Kyle set down his hammer. Hughes held a crowbar, but he set it down a little more slowly and a lot more reluctantly. Parker wouldn't budge. Kyle wasn't sure he even blinked.

"I am not setting my gun down," Parker said.

Kyle wasn't sure if he should be glad Parker kept his weapon trained on the man or if Parker was being reckless. He was probably being reckless.

"You'll all die," the man said.

Definitely reckless.

"The hell do you care?" Parker said. "You'll be dead. It won't make a rat's-ass bit of difference to you if the rest of us die. So I know as a fact you aren't pulling that trigger. You may as well stick that gun in your mouth and shoot your own brains out the back of your head."

The two men stared at each other. Nobody moved. Nobody breathed.

"Guys—" Annie said, but Parker shushed her.

"So we're at an impasse," the man said.

"You're goddamned right we are," Parker said and took a step forward. All three straightened their arms and inched their guns closer. "And we're at an impasse in my house. Step outside, and you're free to go wherever you like. We won't chase you. But if you don't go, at least one of you dies. Maybe all three of you."

"Everybody relax," Kyle said. "No one's going to shoot anybody. We have plenty of food here and lots of space to spread out in."

"Kyle," Parker said. "Pick up your hammer."

Kyle didn't move. Was Parker nuts? This was no time to escalate.

"Everybody just chill," Kyle said. "We have plenty of food, plenty of water, plenty of space, and we obviously have plenty of weapons. We're better off sticking together. We have no reason to fight, and if we work together we'll be safer next time we're attacked."

"He's right," said the tall man to Parker. "So why don't you just drop the gun."

"Our house," Parker said. "You drop 'em."

Kyle glanced at the faces of his companions. Hughes looked ready to rip heads from torsos and could probably do it if he wouldn't get himself shot first. Frank looked too nervous to do anything. Annie seemed to be afraid of everyone in the room. Carol was nowhere to be seen, hiding in the walk-in cooler most likely.

Somebody had to drop their gun first. And it was far more likely to be Parker since it was three against one. But he wasn't going to drop it. He was going to get himself and possibly everybody else killed. So Kyle walked up to Parker and snatched the pistol out of his hands.

Parker gasped. Bobby just chuckled.

Kyle was surprised at how easy it was. And he was just as surprised that he did it. He didn't plan on grabbing the gun. Didn't think about it at all. He just reacted and suddenly found himself with Parker's Beretta. He took a few steps back so Parker couldn't grab it again, then set it down on the floor.

"You're a real stupid sonofabitch, you know that?" Parker said and raised his hands in surrender.

"Okay," said the tall man. "Everybody just take it easy. Bobby, Roland, put your guns away." The two men holstered their weapons. "Now I'm putting mine away too." He then tucked the pistol into the front of his pants.

"Kyle," Parker said and shook his head. He looked like he was about to say something else, but then he paused. He seemed to remember something, and Kyle thought he knew what it was. Parker had two more cleaned and oiled pistols next to the cash register in the checkout aisle. They weren't visible from the door. Parker wanted to go for them. Kyle could sense it. And Kyle wouldn't let him. He wasn't about to tell the three strangers that there were guns over there, but he also didn't want Parker picking one up and starting a shootout. So Kyle slowly moved to the checkout aisle himself and blocked the path to the register.

Parker sighed. He knew what Kyle was up to.

But Kyle was right to do it. The tension in the room had just been defused. He could understand why the three strangers came in with guns drawn. They had no idea who or what they might find in the store. The law had gone silent. There were no patrol cars out there, no sheriff's deputies, no detectives, no jails, no judges, no justice. Everything and everybody was dangerous, including other survivors.

Thanks to Kyle now, though, everybody's gun was tucked away or at least on the floor. They could talk.

"I'm Kyle," he said, and stuck out his hand for the tall man. The tall man shook his hand and relaxed slightly.

"Lane," he said. "This here's Bobby and Roland."

Bobby nodded curtly. Roland just stood there.

"I'm Frank," Frank said. "The big guy with the shotgun is Hughes."

Hughes eyed Frank sideways and nodded—suspiciously, Kyle thought—at Lane and his boys.

"I'm Annie," Annie said. "I'd say it's nice to meet you, but—"

"You're covered in blood," Lane said.

"I'm not infected."

"You sure about that?"

"She's not," Kyle said. He sure hoped he was right.

Lane nodded, though a bit warily. He had no idea that the rest of them didn't know Annie, that she was a stranger to all of them and had arrived for the first time just moments before.

"Sorry for coming in here like this," Lane said. "But it's dangerous out there. I'm a police officer. You wouldn't believe the things I had to deal with when everything was coming apart." Then he checked himself. "Well, maybe you would."

"You were a cop?" Hughes said and tipped his head back.

"Up in Seattle."

"Which precinct?" Hughes said he'd been a bail bondsman up there, so it stood to reason that he'd know some cops.

"Fifty-seventh," Lane said.

"What do you think of Chief Berenson?" Hughes said.

"The police chief?"

Hughes said nothing.

Lane shrugged. "He's okay. Or he was anyway."

Everybody got quiet. Bobby and Roland's body posture shifted an iota or two. They looked at each other. They looked at Parker. They looked back at Lane.

Shit, Kyle thought.

Lane nodded to Bobby.

Bobby unholstered his weapon and pistol-whipped Parker. The gunmetal hit the side of Parker's head with a hard and wet smack.

Roland drew down on Hughes.

Kyle took several steps back. Away from the hammer at his feet. Away from the Beretta he'd taken from Parker.

Annie backed up too and covered her mouth with her hands.

Frank said, "Sonofabitch."

CHAPTER THREE

Parker woke and found himself crammed in a corner just past the cereal aisle with his wrists and ankles bound together with duct tape. Above him loomed a refrigerator stocked with warm cans of Red Bull. His head hurt like a bastard where—what was his name? Bobby?—cracked him upside the skull with the butt of his pistol.

And his beard itched. He hadn't shaved once since he escaped Seattle. He couldn't be bothered. The hell did it matter what he looked like? Everyone looked like shit now. But the beard itched and his hands were tied so he couldn't scratch it.

That Lane character crouched next to him while lazily pointing his gun at the floor. "Morning."

Parker tried not to wince from the pain in his head.

"We've been waiting for you to wake up," Lane said. "I have an announcement to make. But I should first tell you we swept through the place and confiscated all of your weapons."

"We would have shared," Parker said.

"I didn't exactly get that impression." Lane stood. "Not from you, anyway." He turned around and raised his voice. "Listen up, people." He then left Parker behind in the back and joined everyone else at the front. "Your friend back there is with us again, so I'm going to tell you what's what and I'm going to make it real simple."

Parker could hear Lane just fine from the back of the store. It's not like there was any other noise in the world to drown out his voice.

"This store is ours now," Lane said.

Parker heard a panicky *no* out of Carol.

"We've taken your guns. We've taken the keys to the Chevy. And you're all evicted."

"Can't let you do that," Hughes said. Parker couldn't see Hughes from his place on the floor, but he could imagine the look on Hughes' face.

I'm only going to say this once," Lane said. A hush fell over the store. Parker wanted to rip the man's guts out. "If you decide you aren't going quietly, we'll shoot you. Bobby and Roland both think we should shoot you right now either way, but I told them no. It's unnecessary if you cooperate. And I don't want to waste ammunition. You can fend for yourselves out there. You've survived this long. Find somewhere else and we will not bother you. But if you resist, we'll dump your corpses out in the intersection."

No way was Lane a cop like he'd said. Parker didn't believe it. He wasn't the world's biggest fan of cops, but even the dirty ones were better than this guy.

"I have a suggestion," Kyle said.

Parker groaned.

"Did you not hear what I just said?" Lane said.

"I actually think you're going to like my suggestion," Kyle said.

Parker was going to have a long talk with Kyle if they ever got out of this. A long talk.

"*What?*" Lane said.

"We have a plan," Kyle said. "We weren't going to stay here much longer anyway."

"*What's* your plan?"

"We're on our way up to Olympia. To the marina. We're going to pick out a boat and sail to the San Juan Islands."

You motherfucker, Parker thought.

Lane said nothing.

"You could come with us," Kyle said.

Parker promised himself he'd kick Kyle's ass. *Promised.*

Lane said nothing again for a moment, then replied, "It's an intriguing idea. But why would we go with you?"

"Because I know how to sail. I'm not an expert or anything, and I don't own a boat, but I used to go up there with a buddy of mine. I helped him out with his sails. I know how they work, and I can get us there as long as the wind isn't coming down from the north."

Lane said nothing.

"Do you know how to sail?" Kyle said. "Any of you?"

Nobody said anything.

"That's a fine idea," Lane said. "And no, I don't know how to sail. But there are plenty of islands and plenty of powerboats up in Olympia."

"You have keys to one of those boats? Or know how to hotwire one? I don't imagine they taught you how to hotwire a pleasure boat at the police academy."

Lane said nothing.

"The entire world is overrun with those *things*," Kyle said, "and you want to make enemies out of us over a grocery store? Seriously? Almost everyone's dead. Your biggest concern in a grocery store shouldn't be six other people. It should be the expiration dates on those soup cans. What you need is a secure perimeter and people to help you figure out how to farm."

Lane said nothing.

"Am I making sense here, Lane, or are you bound and determined to stay here while we go rebuild somewhere safe?"

Parker had to admit Kyle made sense, but Lane and his boys would still have to be dealt with. Kyle, too, would have to be dealt with one way or another. Surrendering to Lane was an act of towering asininity. It damn near got all of them killed. It still might get all of them killed.

Parker had no intention of going anywhere with Lane unless it was outside to the parking lot to beat him to death, but if the asshole would agree to Kyle's plan for the time being, it would buy them some time. He didn't know what was going to happen, exactly, but whatever it was, sailing to the San Juans with that crew was not it.

"Look," Kyle said. "You guys aren't exactly shaping up as our dream companions, but I'll take you up to the islands if you chill out and give us our guns back. Because if you throw us out without weapons, we'll die. And you'll die, too, because you will never get to a truly safe place without me."

The whole store was silent for a few moments.

"It's not a half-bad idea, boss," said one of the others. What was his name? Ronald? Roland?

Lane said nothing. Parker couldn't see Lane's face from the back of the store and had no idea what he was thinking.

"Hey!" Parker shouted. "Either throw us out or come with us to Kyle's island, but untie me. This is bullshit. I'm unarmed."

"We'll get to you in a minute," Lane snapped.

Parker heard nothing for another few moments. Were they whispering? Consulting with each other through facial expressions? What?

Lane finally spoke. "All right. We'll take you up on that offer. We'll go to the islands together. But I am in charge. You will do what I tell you. We keep all the weapons. Roland, go outside and push one of those Dumpsters against the back door. And take the wheels off so it won't move again. Bobby, go untie our friend Pablo back there."

"Parker!" Parker said. "My name is Parker. Not Pablo."

Nobody answered him.

Bobby ambled toward Parker down the cereal aisle with a hunting knife in his hand. He took his time about it. Parker could tell that Bobby would rather cut Parker's throat than the duct tape around his wrists, but Bobby also looked like the type who does what he's told. Whatever. All three of them—Lane, Roland, and Bobby—would be out of the way soon enough.

Bobby crouched and cut the tape around Parker's wrists. Parker felt no pressure at all to say thank you, nor did Bobby seem to expect it.

Parker stood up, brushed off his pants, and joined the rest of his group. His head throbbed and he felt a bit dizzy. Nobody but Hughes wanted to look at him. Annie even seemed a little repulsed. Did none of them appreciate what he'd tried to do? They saw him as a troublemaker, but come on. The old world was finished and so were its rules. Predators like Lane and his boys could not be put into jail anymore. They had to be resisted and killed or they'd be the ones ruling the rubble and ashes.

Perhaps Parker made the adjustment more quickly because he was never any good at the old rules in the first place. No one taught him how.

His mother married his father, but her true love was the bottle. She poisoned body and mind with bourbon and wine. Parker still couldn't stand the stench of hard alcohol.

She abused him mercilessly when she drank. "Your father hates you," she'd tell him, and he'd run off and cry in his room. Only when he got older did he realize his father didn't hate him, that the monster he was supposed to call Mom spoke for herself.

"You're going to spend your life in jail if you don't straighten up," she'd say. "Jail!"

Then one day she hit him. He was just six years old, but even at that age he knew that he'd never forget it. She slapped him so hard and so violently across the side of his face that his teeth cut into his cheek and he spit blood.

Later he saw her on the couch curled into a ball, crying, with her hands on her face, her back seized with convulsions.

She killed herself and a family of three when he was nine. Behind the wheel with her blood alcohol at four times the legal limit. Head-on collision.

His father didn't handle it well. He never handled anything well.

He tolerated his wife's abuse throughout their marriage. Never challenged her. Never stood up for Parker when he was abused either, not even when she drew blood. His father just kept saying that Mom was sick and that we should try to understand and do what we can to make her feel better.

After she killed herself in the car, his father retreated into a shell of his former self, which wasn't much to begin with. Parker never saw him cry, never even heard him say much about it. His father hardly even spoke for a year.

Parker detested him. Detested him for not protecting him from his mother. Detested him for not forcing his mother to stop. Detested him for not saying "I love you" when he knew good and goddamned well that his mother was telling little Parker that his father hated him.

His father became the ultimate anti–role model.

I will never be like him, Parker swore. Never.

And no one will ever beat me again.

Annie thought about running. She wasn't going to do it, but she couldn't help being tempted to run for the door and just get the hell out of there. All these people she found herself with were bad news.

Hughes had shot at her.

Parker damn near started a firefight.

Bobby hit Parker in the head with his pistol.

Lane threatened to dump everyone's corpses out in the intersection.

How much worse could the plague be?

But she knew that was wrong. She didn't remember the outbreak, the evacuations, or what had happened to her personally, but everything was starting to feel more familiar. She knew those infected people—those *things*, as the others called them—were far more dangerous than anyone inside the store.

The only person she actually liked so far was Kyle. She wasn't convinced it was a great idea to take Parker's pistol away, but Kyle seemed like a decent enough person, and he was right that they had to get off the mainland. Some of the islands were connected to Seattle and Tacoma with bridges, but you had to take a boat to the rest. Some of the islands had little towns on them and some of them didn't. Some didn't even have people.

She had never been to the San Juans, but everyone said they were the prettiest. And they were the farthest away. They were all the way up next to Canada. She wondered at this point if international boundaries still made any difference. For all she knew, the governments of each country were hiding out East in bunkers and had no idea what was happening in the West.

She didn't like being so far from home. She grew up in Georgetown, South Carolina, midway between Myrtle Beach and Charleston. Her hometown felt cramped and cloying and small during her teenage years, but she later had to admit that it was delightful. Its cute-as-a-button downtown wouldn't have looked out of place in some parts of Europe were it not for the subtropical vegetation and climate. It became too small for her, though, and even while she lived there for eighteen years and a month, she felt like Charleston, a bigger city that was much more her style, was where her home compass pointed these days.

She only lived in Charleston a few years, but the city had been part of her life for as long as she could remember. It was only an hour from where she grew up. Her mother's sister Aunt Susie lived there, and Annie's parents took her to visit several times a year when she was growing up. And when she was fifteen years old she sneaked to the city a couple of times on the sly with her sixteen-year-old boyfriend—whom her parents didn't approve of, of course—who had a driver's license and libertarian parents.

Annie always felt a rush of excitement when she showed up in Charleston. It's bigger and more important than her hometown, and it's heartbreakingly lovely. No one builds cities like that anymore. Charleston celebrated its 400th birthday before she was born. It was founded 200 years before America declared independence from Britain.

The city haunted her when she was awake, and it appeared in her dreams when she slept. Even though leaving was an impulsive mistake, she never would have appreciated the beauty and charm and homeyness of Charleston had she never left South Carolina. Her only real regret was that she never made it back before it was destroyed like everywhere else.

Better to die at home with her family near the old waterfront amid her favorite palm trees.

The city's age comforted her with a sense of continuity with the past that was thinner out West. Charleston had weathered revolution and war and yet it still stood. Until the plague struck, Seattle and Portland had never weathered anything other than rain. And now they were ruins. She knew she was kidding herself, but she liked to imagine that Charleston somehow still stood, that it was less damaged by the terrible events sweeping over the world. But she could never go back. And she knew like she knew her own name that the city would not be the same if she did.

A ll right, listen up," Lane said. He stood up front near the windows where a little more light came into the store so everybody could see him. Annie watched from a distance. Everyone watched from a distance. Everyone but Bobby and Roland, who did not leave his side and always had their weapons in sight.

Annie couldn't figure out why they had to be so aggressive. Survivors should stick together and not fight each other.

"Kyle," Lane said. "I need you up here so we can figure out this boat thing. Parker, you too. I want to keep an eye on you. And Annie, you go outside and unload that truck. Hughes tells me you've got a bag of fresh clothes out there."

"I do," she said. "Thank you."

Finally, she could clean up properly. She had half washed the blood and mud and muck off her hands and her face, but she still looked and felt like she'd crawled through a charnel house. She twisted the ring on her finger and pulled on it a bit, revealing a clean white band of skin underneath, the only place on her body that wasn't disgusting.

"What *happened* to you, anyway?" Lane said. "I—" He paused. "Wait." Squinted at her just slightly. "Don't I know you?"

She didn't recognize him at all.

"I don't think we've met," she said.

He folded his arms over his chest and looked at her harder. "I'm certain we have. You look more than familiar."

"I don't know many cops in Seattle. But maybe you pulled me over one time." She doubted he was really a cop like he'd said, but she had to say something.

"No. I've seen you recently. I know you from after all—this— happened. Not from before."

He could be right. She didn't remember anything between coffee with her sister in Olympia and Hughes shooting at her on the road. Maybe she *had* met Lane before. During the interval.

"You don't look familiar," she said.

Lane didn't know she'd lost part of her memory. Nobody told him.

He was silent for a couple more moments. He kept staring. Then he said, "This is driving me crazy. How could I not know where I've seen you? I've hardly seen anyone recently."

She was getting a little spooked now. Was something blocking *both* their memories, only whatever it was blocked hers more strongly than his?

"I'd better go get the stuff out of the truck now," she said.

Lane stared at her for another couple of seconds, then nodded. "Yeah," he said. "Go get the stuff. Bobby, go with her. Make sure none of those things are outside."

Bobby gingerly went out ahead of her, scanning the lot, then looking left and right before squinting in the distance across the street. She followed him out, hefted the large backpack Hughes had stuffed with supplies over her shoulders, grabbed her bag of clothes, and took everything inside. Bobby followed her in without carrying anything. She made two more trips with Bobby ostensibly covering her in case she was attacked, but she knew his real job was to mind her.

She laid everything against the wall near the front door.

"Parker," Lane said. "Unload this stuff."

Parker huffed and took his sweet time.

"I'm going to change my clothes if you don't mind," Annie said.

Lane nodded. "Please do."

She grabbed a flashlight and took her clothes into the women's restroom in back and shut the door. There were no windows in there, and therefore no light with the door closed. Nor was there a bathtub or shower, of course. Just a toilet, a sink, a mirror, a roll of paper towels, and vulgar scribblings on the wall next to the toilet. She flicked on the flashlight, set it on the back of the sink, and took her nasty clothes off.

She smelled bad. That was especially noticeable now.

She was certain there'd be no hot water, but she twisted the knob anyway and water damn near exploded out of the tap. It roared out with incredible force.

That couldn't be normal, though she had no idea what would cause it to happen.

The water was cold, of course, but there was liquid soap in a dispenser on the wall. She shivered as she cleaned herself as well as she could, starting with her armpits and working down toward her feet. She felt a wound on the back of her shoulder that had scabbed over. It didn't hurt. She hadn't even noticed it until now and had no idea how it got there. But if it was long past hurting, it was most likely long past getting infected, so she didn't worry. She dried herself off with towels from the roll and spent ten minutes scrubbing the gross mat of God-only-knew-what out of her hair under the faucet with hand soap.

When she put on fresh clothes, she felt like a new human being. She must have been waiting ages for this, but she could only remember waiting the past couple of hours. How much time had passed since she woke up on the forest floor just before Hughes shot at her? Four hours at the most? It felt like four weeks.

She shone the flashlight in her face and studied herself in the mirror. She looked presentable now. Pretty even, not like a ghoul. Her hair was longer. It was down past her shoulders now. She supposed that's what happens when you lose eight weeks of memory since your last haircut.

Her amnesia was damn peculiar and not what she would have expected. Even though she couldn't remember anything about the last two months, her sense of confusion was going away. Everything made sense now. She could only explain it one way. Her conscious mind couldn't access all of her memory, but her subconscious mind did not have that problem.

The plague and its attendant destruction was such a tremendous event that it rewired her brain. So while she couldn't remember the events, she sure as hell noticed the rewiring. She thought of an axiom from her psych class in college up in Seattle: *neurons that fire together, wire together.* Her professor used smoking as an example. Smokers make all kinds of associations with cigarettes. Drinking coffee, having a beer, getting in the car, stepping outside. That's why it's so hard to quit. Coffee, beer, driving, even stepping outside make smokers who are trying to quit think of cigarettes. A person suffering from amnesia who had no idea they were a smoker would *still* think of cigarettes if someone gave them a beer. That's how powerful brain wiring is.

If epic devastation wasn't powerful enough to reroute her circuits, nothing was.

She was no longer the same person she used to be. And while she couldn't remember her transformation, she sure as hell noticed that she was transformed.

Her sense of danger was more pronounced. She understood on a cellular level that required no explanation from Kyle or Hughes or anyone else that the entire planet was hostile, that resources had to be scavenged, that law and order were finished, that she had to fend for herself, that every single thing that humans had ever built anywhere—except perhaps Egypt's great pyramids—would be ground down. She had internalized these truths and imprinted them into her being. Amnesia couldn't change that even if she couldn't remember it happening.

But something *else* had also imprinted itself into her being. Something else had happened to her. Something aside from the plague. Something aside from the probable deaths of everyone she had ever known. Something aside from the fact that she'd never see her Seattle apartment again, never see South Carolina again, never see anybody she recognized ever again, and might not even survive the next twenty minutes. Something in *addition* to the fact that the world was in ashes.

She sensed a secret knowledge buried somewhere inside that was banging on the lid of her subconscious and trying desperately to get out. She knew it as well as she knew her name was Annie Starling. But what *was* it? What was she forgetting? What on earth could it possibly be?

She stared hard at herself in the mirror.

Look, she thought. Look hard. The answer is there.
But she couldn't remember.

CHAPTER FOUR

Kyle liked and trusted cops, but he wasn't at all convinced that Lane was a cop. What kind of cop would take people hostage and threaten to kill them for food? At least Lane's goons weren't waving their guns around anymore, and Lane contented himself for the time being with just barking orders.

He told Kyle and Parker to unload the supplies Hughes and Frank had picked up at the sporting-goods store.

"I'm sorry," Kyle whispered to Parker while they unpacked the large backpack, "for taking your gun."

Kyle didn't actually think he'd made a mistake when he disarmed Parker. He very well may have saved Parker's life, along with everyone else's. Parker didn't see it that way and was still upset about it, and Kyle was ultimately on his side.

Lane stood near the front door like he was guarding it, with Bobby and Roland armed at his side. Annie was washing up in the bathroom. Carol was hanging back in the walk-in cooler as usual. She seemed to like having a second door between herself and the outside. Hughes and Frank sat on the floor next to the beverage aisle in back.

Parker didn't respond to Kyle's apology. He just removed what appeared to be night-vision goggles from the pack and set them down on the floor.

"Well, what do we have here?" Lane said when he saw the night vision. "That is some fine-looking equipment." He seemed to know what he was looking at.

Kyle pulled the extra socks, gloves, fleece pullovers, and hats out of the bag and held them up. "Where do you want all this stuff?"

"Leave it up here by the door," Lane said. "All the equipment and guns will be kept here from now on. This area is off-limits to everybody but me, Bobby, and Roland. Got it?"

"Oh, believe me, we got it," Parker said.

When they finished unloading the gear, Lane said, "Good work, boys."

Parker grunted and headed back toward the bathrooms. Kyle followed him into the gloom.

"We need to get our guns back," Parker said. They didn't have to whisper now. They just had to talk quietly.

"We can't shoot them," Kyle said. "It will be noisy. We'll draw a hundred of those things down on our heads."

"Lane is our number-one problem right now."

"We can wait until—"

"No. We're not going with them on your boat."

Parker shuffled off farther into the back of the store. Kyle went with him.

They could have just fled out the back, but Roland and Bobby had blockaded that door from the outside with a Dumpster. Supposedly they removed the wheels so it couldn't be moved again, at least not from inside the store.

"The old rules are off," Parker said. "These people aren't civilized. And frankly neither are we. Not anymore. If we don't kill them—and I mean as soon as fucking possible—they're going to kill us eventually."

"Lane says he was a cop."

"You actually believe that?"

"Not really, no. But disasters change people. Were you like this before?"

Parker said nothing.

Kyle figured Lane would settle down once he realized the others weren't a threat—as long as he could convince Parker to settle down and stop looking like a threat waiting to happen all over again. And it was *possible* that Lane was a cop. Everyone left alive in this world was wandering around in some kind of trauma. Parker was right that the old rules were off, so why should he expect Lane to abide by them any more than anyone else? So yeah, it was entirely possible that Lane once was a cop. Kyle sure hoped so. If Lane had been a cop, everything would be fine.

H ughes didn't like or trust cops at all. But Lane was no kind of a cop. Hughes had asked what Lane thought of Chief Berenson, but there was no Chief Berenson. The police chief's name was Anderson. As a bail bondsman, Hughes knew that.

Lane was a liar. A thief. He took hostages. He'd probably killed people. And he was no kind of cop.

That was for damn sure.

L ane wasn't a cop, nor was he sure anyone believed he was ever a cop, but he didn't care because he was charge.

Bobby and Roland did what he told them to do when he told them to do it, but the truth was that Lane would be lost without them. He had a crew of six until a couple of days earlier. They were robbed at gunpoint of everything they had—their food, their water, their gear, their guns, everything. Then they were torn to pieces by a pack of hunters. They were unarmed and defenseless and scavenging for food in an abandoned house when a pack of them swarmed inside the front door and ripped apart four of his companions. The pack would have been no big deal if they still had their guns, but everything but their clothes had been stolen. The only reason Lane, Bobby, and Roland were still alive was because they managed to slip out the back while the shrieking screams of his friends and the hate-filled screams of those hunters faded away in the background.

Not two hours later they came upon a massacre site. A small group of men had been overwhelmed by another pack—no, a *horde*—so large their guns couldn't save them.

But those guns saved Lane, Bobby, and Roland. They felt no compunction whatever in stealing guns or anything else from the dead.

Nor did they feel much compunction about taking guns or anything else from the living. Not anymore. Better to steal than have your stuff stolen.

Never again, Lane swore to himself, would he let anyone take his weapons away. There were new rules afoot. Rob or be robbed. Kill or be killed. Rule or be ruled. And don't be a sucker.

Lane wasn't a cop and he wasn't a sucker.

He summoned Kyle to his place near the front door with a wave of his hand. Annie followed even though he hadn't summoned her.

"So how are we getting to this fabled boat of yours?" Lane said to Kyle. "We can't go in a vehicle. The roads heading north are too jammed."

Kyle opened his mouth to say something, but Annie interjected.

"Can I make a suggestion?" she said.

"I didn't ask you," Lane said. "But what? But what's your suggestion?"

That girl gave Lane the creeps. He still couldn't remember how he recognized her, but a feeling rose in his gut that told him she was dangerous. The threat-detection radar in the lizard part of his brain wouldn't shut up about it. She didn't look dangerous. Not at all. She seemed smart and capable. Maybe that was part of the problem.

"I think we should take bicycles," she said.

"Bicycles," Lane said.

"Yes," she said. "Bicycles. We can weave around abandoned cars and ride faster than anything that tries to chase us."

"That's exactly what I was thinking," Kyle said, smiling. "It's a good idea."

"I didn't ask you," Lane said.

"Actually, you did just ask me," Kyle said.

It made sense, and Lane had considered the same thing himself, but there was a problem. "We won't be able to carry as many supplies."

"We can carry enough," Kyle said. "We make another run at the outdoor store up the road, get a few more huge backpacks, load 'em all up, and ride off to Olympia. Shouldn't take more than a couple of hours. But I think we should wait until dark and ride up there by moonlight. We can get more night-vision devices when we pick up the backpacks."

Lane nodded. "I'll send some of you up there on a supply run. And I'll send Roland with you so you'll have protection in case you're attacked."

Lane still wasn't sure what to do with all these people once they got to an island. That Parker character would have to be dealt with, of course, and maybe the big black guy too. The others were on probation. Kyle might turn out okay. He wasn't stupid and he seemed okay with following orders. Frank wasn't outstanding material, but he probably wouldn't cause trouble. Probably.

But something was up with Annie, and Lane wouldn't know what to do with her until he knew exactly what it was. Why did he know her face? And why did she give him the creeps? He didn't get the feeling he knew her from the distant past. He felt like he'd seen her somewhere in the past couple of days. But he'd hardly seen anyone the past couple of days. How was that possible?

"Annie," he said. "You and Kyle are on bicycle duty. Go out and find one for everyone. Bobby will go with you for protection."

"You want us to go now?" she said.

"Yes, now."

"Isn't someone taking the truck to the outdoor store?"

"You don't need the truck. Go on foot, find three bicycles, ride them back, then go out and find more. You'll be fine. Bobby will be with you. You're less likely to get attacked if you don't take the truck anyway because you won't make as much noise. There are rows of houses behind the store. You probably don't need to go more than two or three blocks to find bikes."

"But—"

"Girl. You do what I tell you."

She clamped her mouth shut and swallowed.

She didn't look dangerous. She looked like a scared college student. But some knowing part of his mind could not stop flashing a *red alert* whenever he saw her face. He studied her hard but could not figure out why he couldn't remember.

Annie knew the real reason Lane sent Bobby with her and Kyle to scavenge for bicycles. Bobby wasn't their bodyguard. He was Lane's bodyguard. Lane didn't want Kyle and Annie scavenging for weapons instead of for bicycles.

Bobby unholstered his pistol with one hand and picked up two crowbars with the other.

"Let me see one of those," Kyle said and reached out his hand.

Bobby jerked away. "You can have one of these when I tell you."

This wasn't going to work, Annie thought. They didn't need to like each other, but they did need to work together out there, especially if they were attacked. She approached Bobby slowly and placed her hand on his shoulder.

"Hey!" Bobby said and shrugged her away. "Keep back."

This was going to be worse than she thought.

"Let's try to be civilized," Kyle said. "We aren't your enemy. Our enemies are outside. We all need weapons if we're going out there."

"You can have one when I say you can have one," Bobby said.

"You keep your pistol," Kyle said.

"You're goddamn right I'm keeping my pistol," Bobby said, his upper lip curling.

Annie wanted to argue but decided against it. Bobby would eventually settle down, especially if she and Kyle didn't spook him by invading his space. She decided to be as nice as she could, to pretend she and Bobby were friends. If she acted like his friend long enough, it might become less of a lie after a while.

"After you," Bobby said and gestured for Kyle to go out ahead. Bobby was not going to turn his back on anybody.

Kyle unlocked the front door and peered out. "Looks clear," he said and stepped out. Annie looked over at Bobby. He motioned her out with his eyes.

She stepped outside and was overwhelmed with the putrid stench of rotting trash. The odor was faintly detectable inside the store, but outside she could taste it.

She looked out at a generic suburban street that could have been just about anywhere in the country—with strip malls, big-box stores, and fast-food joints—but absolutely everything was ruined. Windows were either broken or all boarded up. Pieces of glass crunched underfoot. No cars on the street. Trash blew in the wind. What looked like a used-car lot had exploded, its charred remains looking like the architectural equivalent of bones littering the parking lot.

Everything was quiet and still. The setting just didn't seem real, as if this whole thing were some kind of elaborate put-on. And where on earth were these *things* everyone kept talking about? The only one she'd seen—and an alleged one at that—was the man Frank hit with his truck not twenty minutes after Hughes had fired his shotgun at her.

"I think I remember seeing a bike shop not far from here," Kyle said. "Down that way, I think."

He pointed toward the east, or the direction Annie assumed was east. She had a decent sense of direction, but she still wasn't entirely sure which town she was in or where it was in relation to everywhere else.

"So let's head that way then," she said. "Better to get bikes from a store than from people's garages. It's quieter and won't take as long."

"Bobby?" Kyle said.

"Fine. Let's go."

"We should walk down the middle of the street," Kyle said. "We'll be a little more visible, but we'll be farther away from the buildings. In case some of those things come out running at us."

"Those ... things, as you call them ... could be in these buildings?" Annie said. Most of the windows and doors were boarded up.

"They could be anywhere," Kyle said.

"Enough talking," Bobby said.

So they walked "east" and said nothing. Just down the street a ways on their left was the blown-up car lot. On their right was an ex–Burger King. Up ahead were more strip malls and big-box stores, including a

Target. There might still be items worth scrounging in there, she thought, except the windows were smashed in.

They walked for a good twenty minutes saying nothing and hearing nothing, and part of Annie found the whole business exhilarating. Who would ever expect to *see* something like this? American cities and suburbs had always looked and felt permanent. On some level she knew they weren't, of course—everything falls apart eventually—but it never occurred to her that they could slide into decay so rapidly. She certainly never expected to see everything disintegrate at once.

She felt a few drops of rain on her face, but only a few. The Northwest's weather was bizarre. Some days it rained so lightly she could be outside for hours and not really get wet, while rainstorms in South Carolina could drench her to the skin faster than if she stood with her clothes on in the shower.

Harder rains were coming, however, if it really was early November like the others were saying. The dry summer season was over and November's rains were the worst. Soon the rain would fall without stopping for days.

Life was about to become a lot more complicated. She loved the smell of fall, the earthy fragrance of mulch and dead leaves and coldness and rain, but that was absent now and replaced by the retch-inducing slum reek she'd once encountered on a trip abroad to India. Maybe the late-autumn rains would wash the stink off this town. She doubted the stench of rotting trash and—what else, dead bodies?—could last through the season.

Nature was coming back fast and hard. How long before she saw bears in the streets? And how long before moss, grass, and even trees start growing on top of the pavement?

"So what did you do?" Annie said to Kyle as they walked. "Before all this."

"Huh?" Kyle said. He heard her, but he hadn't actually heard her. His mind was somewhere else.

"I asked what your job was," she said. "Before all this."

Kyle shook himself back to his immediate surroundings.

"I worked in high tech. Programming computers. The job paid well, but it never really defined me. At least I didn't define myself by my job."

"So what defined you?" she said.

Kyle ignored her and stopped in the middle of a four-way intersection. The wind kicked up and Annie heard the darkened traffic signals creaking as they swung on their cable under the dishrag sky.

"What?" Bobby said.

Kyle said nothing for a moment. He just stood there with his hands on his hips and looked to the left and the right. "I think," he said, "that I saw the bike store down there." He pointed toward the right. Toward the south? The suburban business district continued in that direction just as it did straight ahead, but there was less debris on the streets to the right.

"So let's go then," Bobby said.

"Right," Kyle said.

So they headed right, toward what Annie thought was south. They walked in silence for a few minutes, passing a boarded-up bank, a gas station with the windows smashed in, a car that had accordioned into an electrical pole, an ambulance turned onto its side, and an apparent massacre site next to an Arby's fast-food joint with bones and torn clothing and bloodstains smeared on the pavement.

Then the street exploded 100 feet in front of them. The pavement ruptured and a geyser of water erupted into the air as loud as a car bomb.

Annie turned away and covered her face with her arms.

"Shit!" Bobby said.

"Off the street," Kyle said. "Now." Annie felt him gently push her toward the overturned ambulance across the street from the Arby's. "Before it happens again."

"The fuck *is* that?" Bobby said. He bolted toward the ambulance ahead of Annie and Kyle as though he had completely forgotten he was supposed to be in charge and keeping an eye on them from behind.

"It was bound to happen eventually," Kyle said.

Annie, panting and her heart racing, ducked behind the ambulance.

She had no idea what on earth was going on, but it sounded like Godzilla was breaking through the street from underground.

"*What* was bound to happen eventually?" Bobby said. He really did seem to forget they were supposed to be enemies.

"Water pressure," Kyle said. "It's been building up in the pipes for months because hardly anyone is releasing it from the tap."

Of course, Annie thought. That explained why the water had burst so forcefully out of the sink.

"The pipes couldn't keep taking the pressure forever," Kyle said, "so now they're exploding. It's probably happening all over the world. We're going lose the water back at the store."

Annie felt the pavement thrumming under her feet.

"Oh shit," Bobby said. "This is not good."

"Yeah," Kyle said.

Annie knew exactly what they were thinking. They were not just worried about losing tap water.

"Bobby," Kyle said. "Give me one of those crowbars."

Bobby stepped back, remembering now that they were adversaries. Then he stopped. "Fuck."

"They're coming," Kyle said. "We can't stay here. And you need to give us those crowbars."

Annie heard something new. It was hard to hear over the roar of the water, but it was coming from behind the Arby's building. It sounded like pounding on pavement.

"It's them," Kyle said.

"Fuck," Bobby said and pointed his pistol toward the Arby's.

The sound grew louder. Annie stepped behind Bobby since he was the one with the gun.

"Bobby," Kyle said. "Give me one of those crowbars."

"Me too," Annie said. She could hear the sound clearly now. It was definitely feet running on pavement. Running hard. She was nearing panic and felt like her heart might explode.

"I got this," Bobby said between breaths. He was damn near

hyperventilating and he couldn't hold his gun steady.

"No you don't," Kyle said and reached toward him.

"Stay back!" Bobby said and pointed his gun at Kyle for a moment before pointing it back toward the Arby's.

The sounds of running grew louder.

And then Annie saw them.

A dozen ragged people sprinting right toward her. Their clothes and faces and hair were drenched in blood and mud and gore, their faces snarling in vicious expressions of hatred and rage. They ran straight at Annie and Kyle and Bobby, and they ran as though they would never get tired.

And when they laid eyes on Annie and Kyle and Bobby, they screamed. Every one of them belted out war cries loud enough to burst their own vocal cords.

Bobby gasped and fired his handgun—*pop pop pop*—into the oncoming pack. He gripped the two crowbars in his left hand while firing again with his right.

Now Annie understood why everyone else called them *those things*. They looked like people, but they sure as hell weren't acting like people.

One of them fell, but Bobby fired wildly and missed most of his shots.

Annie couldn't believe how *fast* they were. She expected them to be slow. Weren't they supposed to be sick? How could sick people run like that?

"Bobby!" Kyle yelled. He came up behind Bobby and wrested the crowbars from his left hand. Bobby released them, but too late. Those things were nearly upon them.

Annie took one of the crowbars from Kyle. Bobby dropped three more of those screaming things before his gun dry-clicked.

"Shit!" Bobby said. And the pack was upon him.

Kyle smashed one in the side of the head while another threw itself at Bobby and bit hard into his forearm. Bobby screamed and fell on his back, the thing still latched by its teeth onto his arm. Kyle smashed it in the head. Then smashed another. The now-dead one that bit Bobby slumped to the ground while Bobby rolled away from it.

One of them, a man, ran right at Annie. She swung her crowbar as hard as she could and shattered its arm. It fell to the ground, made a sound between a grunt and a roar, and looked at her with hatred. Its eyes seemed intelligent. Full of hate, but intelligent. No, it wasn't intelligence she was seeing. It was *focus*. Then it stood up and lunged for her. She swung again and clipped it in the shoulder. It staggered.

"Help!" she said.

Bobby was on the ground, useless, bleeding, and moaning in pain.

Kyle faced two by himself.

No one could help her.

She backed up. The thing in front of her just stood there, wounded and stunned with its arms broken. But it still had its teeth like the one that had just bitten Bobby.

She wanted to say something. This thing wasn't a thing. It was a human being. A man. It was a *he*. She instinctively wanted to reason with him, but she could tell by the look on his face and in his eyes that he was beyond understanding or caring, like a cornered, aggressive animal.

He stared at her, hating her, yet looking strangely detached at the same time. He—it—looked at her as if she were food.

It was going to lunge again. She could tell. It bared its teeth.

She went straight for the head and heard a sickening wet *thwack* as she burst its skull like a melon.

It went down like a marionette with its strings cut.

Annie heard three things. Her own rapid breathing, her heartbeat in her ears, and Bobby moaning in agony on the ground.

She looked around. Dead bodies everywhere. Dead people stricken with some awful disease that make them violent. None remained standing, but two were still twitching and one was trying to crawl.

She hugged Kyle. She hugged him hard and couldn't stop shaking.

"God," she said and gasped. "Are you okay?"

"I'm okay. You?"

"I think so." She could feel her heart slamming inside her chest and against his.

Kyle let her go and turned to Bobby. "He's bitten."

Bobby lay on his side now, clutching his wounded arm and whimpering.

"He'll be okay," Annie said.

"No, Annie," Kyle said. "No, he won't."

CHAPTER FIVE

Kyle helped Bobby up while Annie stood aside nervously. He no longer felt any hostility whatsoever toward Bobby, nor did Bobby seem to feel any toward him. But he wondered if Bobby would feel the same way if he hadn't been bitten.

Bobby closed his eyes hard and blinked as if he couldn't quite focus. Kyle realized the poor man was in shock. Bobby's face had gone white, his hands clammy and cold. He covered the bite wound with his good hand. Sticky blood seeped between his fingers. The wounded arm was drenched in the stuff, as were his shirt and his pants.

Kyle needed to be damn sure not to get any of Bobby's infected blood on himself or on Annie.

"Don't tell Lane," Bobby said and winced.

"He'll know, Bobby. Look at yourself."

Bobby didn't look at himself. Instead he raised his gun and pointed it in Kyle's general direction. Kyle knew Bobby's magazine was empty. He'd heard the dry click of the firing pin just before that thing sank its teeth into Bobby's arm. Bobby must have remembered because he holstered it and staggered off to the side.

"Why don't you give me that," Kyle said.

"No."

"We might get attacked again. That geyser down the street isn't getting any quieter. It's going to attract every one of those things for a mile in every direction."

"The fuck do I care?"

"Bobby!"

"I mean, here, take it." Bobby unholstered the weapon and handed it over. He reached into his pants pocket and pulled out a full magazine and handed that over too. Kyle loaded the weapon and checked the safety.

"I can't go back there," Bobby said. His lips trembled. He was more afraid of returning to the grocery store than staying out on the street.

"Why not?"

"Lane."

"He doesn't seem like the easiest person," Annie said.

"He's fine," Bobby said. "He's great. He saved my life. I'd be dead if it weren't for Lane. But I've been bit. I know what he's going to do."

"We don't kill people who have been bitten," Kyle said.

"Then you're an idiot," Bobby said. "You should shoot me right now."

Kyle motioned them along. They needed to get away from that geyser, which was filling the street with an ever-expanding lake. Soon enough the bodies of those things they'd just killed would be in the water.

"The virus is transmitted through bites!" Annie said as though she had only just now figured it out.

"Well, yeah," Bobby said. "Where the hell have *you* been, girl?" He grimaced in pain and stopped for a moment. Then he looked at her squarely. "I'm sorry for … you know. For everything."

"It's okay," Annie said. "Let's go back and get your arm bandaged up."

"You *really* shouldn't touch me," Bobby said and stepped away from her and from Kyle. "Don't get any of this blood on you or you might turn too. I couldn't go back in the store like this even if Lane would let me. It wouldn't be fair to you guys or the others."

But he kept walking toward the store with them. He wasn't ready to sit down and die yet. Kyle didn't know what he should do, because Bobby was right that he shouldn't go back to the store. He was infected. His blood was contagious. And he'd turn soon. Into one of them.

The sound of the geyser behind them was quieter now, partly because they weren't as close to it anymore, and also because the pressure seemed to be easing.

Kyle shuddered when he imagined what Bobby would look like after turning. He would be both Bobby and not-Bobby. Mostly not-Bobby.

There was something deeply and terribly wrong with those things, something aside from the obvious, something Kyle couldn't quite put his finger on, something that made them *things* instead of people with a disease that made them violent. They looked different in ways too subtle to identify consciously but that were somehow obvious all the same.

A friend of Kyle's from the high-tech industry in Portland worked on computer animation at home on the side. He hoped to eventually land a job making video games. And he once told Kyle about something all advanced computer-animation artists had to beware of, something they called the uncanny valley.

The uncanny valley refers to the instinctive revulsion people feel when they see something that looks almost human but isn't quite. A robot that looks ninety-nine-percent human will make people far more uneasy than one that only looks seventy-five-percent human. The same applies to animated characters. They need to look 100 percent human or they need to be obvious fakes. Otherwise they'll be creepy.

The part of the human psyche that feels wary of the almost-but-not-quite human was what recognized the infected as the infected. Their aggression made them obvious too, of course, but Kyle was certain he'd be able to spot an infected even if it was just standing there and not doing anything. He'd seen a few of them briefly standing around before the aggression kicked in, and they stood at weird angles in odd postures that didn't look comfortable, as if comfort and properly ergonomic body mechanics no longer had any meaning.

Since they were so wrong on the inside, it made sense that they looked wrong on the outside, but they hadn't been transformed physically in any obvious way. It's not like their skin turned green or their eyes went red. But they exuded an alien vibe. They seemed to lack language. They didn't use it at least, nor did they seem to understand it anymore. They obviously didn't have empathy. They were impervious to reason, and they seemed to be impervious to emotions aside from hunger and rage. Kyle's cat had been more in tune with Kyle's emotional state than these things were. The instinctive human revulsion to cannibalism was replaced by an instinctive drive to cannibalism.

Maybe that's what it was more than anything else. Those things didn't see themselves as cannibals. They didn't kill or eat each other. They only killed and ate people who had not been infected. Which meant they recognized each other just as clearly as Kyle recognized them. So perhaps their aversion to cannibalism had *not* been abolished. They just no longer saw uninfected people as people.

The feeling was mutual. Those things were no longer people. Not really, not anymore. Kyle and Hughes and Parker were people. Even Lane and Bobby and Roland were people. But those things had exiled themselves from the species. Kyle had more in common with primitive hunter-gatherers and probably even Neanderthals than he had with them.

He, Annie, and Bobby reached the intersection where they needed to turn. The grocery store was only twenty or so minutes away now. And Kyle had Bobby's pistol loaded with a full magazine. It occurred to him that he could sneak into the store and shoot Lane and Roland before either of them had a clue what was happening. It's what Parker would do, for sure, and it's what Parker would advise Kyle to do if he could. Parker could be a bit unhinged, but he was right about one thing. They really did live in a world with new rules. A world with no rules, in fact.

Bobby was going to die. He couldn't be saved.

Lane and Roland also needed to die. Kyle could see that now. He'd be content if Lane and Roland just left and went their own way, but that wasn't going to happen, and if they did go away, they'd no doubt make trouble for whatever other poor survivors they ran across. No, Lane and Roland needed to die. But Kyle didn't want to pull the trigger. He could be honest with himself about that. He'd rather have Parker or Hughes do it. Or, if he had to do it himself, he'd rather have a plan that involved something a little better thought out than *run into the grocery store blind and shoot them on sight.*

Annie had blood on her shirt all over again. She hadn't even been clean for two hours. Kyle was drenched in the stuff. Their clothes would have to be burned. She knew that, right? Despite the fact that parts of her memory seemed to be wiped.

But he pointed at a blood-soaked spot on her shirt and said, "Don't get any of that in your mouth," just to be sure.

A nnie felt surprisingly at ease considering what had just happened. The adrenaline had washed out of her system, and her heart and breathing rates were normal again. Her body seemed to have adjusted to violence and terror during the time she couldn't remember.

She supposed her partial amnesia was her mind's way of protecting itself from trauma so she could still function. It seemed to work, because she functioned just fine.

Bobby stopped on the sidewalk. "Sorry. I need to sit down."

He looked dizzy and about to fall over. Annie didn't like Bobby one bit, but she instinctively wanted to reach out and help him. He was mortally wounded, after all, and it's hard to hate a man when he's dying. Then she remembered she wasn't supposed to touch him. If he'd contracted the disease, he'd be shedding the virus from the wound in his arm. But she hardly saw the point of such caution since she and Kyle were already drenched with infected blood.

Annie got close enough to Bobby that she noticed something she hadn't seen before. He had a small knife clipped to his belt in a little sheath, the kind that might be marginally useful while fishing or camping but practically useless for someone being swarmed by the infected. But a three-inch knife was better than no knife. She wanted it.

"We're almost back to the store," Kyle said. "We're not safe out here and the store is only five blocks away. We need to get inside. But you're right that you can't come inside with us."

Bobby eased himself down onto the sidewalk. "Just leave me here. And give me my gun."

Bobby's gun. She and Kyle might be able to do something about Lane.

"Either give me my gun back or shoot me," Bobby said.

Kyle said nothing. He said nothing for a long time.

Bobby pitched forward and had to support his head with his hands. "Whoa," he said and blinked like he had something in his eyes. "The virus is really coming on fast with me."

"How long does it usually take?" Annie said.

"Couple of hours usually," Kyle said. "But sometimes it's faster."

"It's real fast with me, bro," Bobby said. He blew out his breath and closed his eyes. "Look, I know what you're thinking. I'm dying, but I know what's going on. You want to shoot Lane. I get it. But you don't want to shoot me. I get that too."

Kyle said nothing.

"I'm going to die anyway. I'll be a dead man walking if you let me turn. So if you don't want to shoot me, hand me the gun and I'll do it myself. Then you can have the gun back."

"Lane will hear the shot," Annie said. So will other infected, she thought.

"Those things will hear the shot too," Kyle said. He paused and looked hard at Bobby. "You asked me not to tell Lane."

"What?" Bobby said.

"Earlier," Kyle said. "Right after you were bitten. You told me not to tell Lane because you knew what he'd do if he found out. But if you want me to shoot you, what are you afraid Lane is going to do?"

S ound travels clear and far in a world gone quiet. The patter of a man's footsteps travels four blocks, the slam of a car door more than a mile. Tipped-over trash cans are even louder. The sound of gunfire seems to encircle the world.

It took Lane but moments to figure out that explosion. The roar of rushing water gave it away. The mains under the streets were bursting from the pressure, and the weakest point blew.

The following sounds were even clearer. A shrieking pack of hunters followed by the report from Bobby's pistol followed by silence.

All this took place at least a mile away, but sound travels clear and far in a world gone quiet.

What he could not know is whether Bobby, Kyle, and Annie were still alive.

Everyone in the store heard the same things, of course. That hysterical Carol lady had no idea what was happening, but Parker and Hughes eventually figured it out and explained it to her. Hughes gave her a bottle of water to drink so she'd keep quiet.

Lane was beginning to change his mind about Hughes. Hughes might be okay. He was smart and competent. Naturally Lane didn't trust him, and he felt with dead certainty that the lack of trust was mutual, but he might try giving Hughes an iota of latitude to see how he handled it.

But he'd need Bobby to return in one piece for that. Controlling the group wouldn't be easy with only Roland on his side. He needed two wingmen. The extra guns were locked in the truck outside and Lane was the only one with a key (as far as he knew), but three armed men were much more intimidating than two. Holding off a potential insurrection with just two would be very difficult indeed when it came time for those two men to sleep.

No matter what else happened, though, he had to get rid of Parker. He was not going to change his mind about that. The only question at this point was when.

Lane summoned Roland.

"They should be back by now if they survived," he said. "Unless they're injured."

"Or bit," Roland said.

"Or bit. Go out and check. See if they're on the road. And go out there very carefully. It's been noisy. That pack of hunters might still be out there and they can hear just as well as we can."

Roland nodded.

"Take two guns," Lane whispered. "You can give one to Kyle if he's still alive and you don't have any choice, but don't give one to Annie. I don't trust her."

Roland frowned. Lane hadn't shared his feelings about Annie with anyone. "What's wrong with Annie?"

"I'm not sure. There's something wrong about her. I haven't figured out what it is yet, but I will. We'll talk more later."

Roland nodded again and slipped outside.

Lane turned to face his prisoners alone.

K yle made another quick scan of the area to make sure nothing was coming at them, then sat on the curb next to Bobby and Annie. They could not stay outside, but something had to be done with Bobby. Kyle couldn't just leave him there.

"He won't shoot me," Bobby said. "Lane won't risk attracting those things with a gunshot unless he doesn't have any choice."

Kyle nodded. "Of course."

"Which means he'll beat me to death." Bobby lowered his head and covered his eyes with his right index finger and thumb. "I should never have walked this far. You should have shot me back there."

"What do you want to do?" Annie said. She sounded like she actually cared. Kyle was surprised at how nice she was being, considering how Bobby had treated her less than an hour ago.

"Just give me my gun," Bobby said. "I'll walk a few miles and do it myself."

"Somebody's coming," Annie said.

Kyle drew his pistol, bolted upright, and saw a figure walking toward them halfway between themselves and the grocery store. It looked like Roland. He was walking straight at them with a gun in his hand. Kyle turned slightly to conceal the gun in his own hand.

"Fuck," Bobby said. "This isn't good, man."

"It's okay," Kyle said. "I'll talk to him."

Roland walked ramrod straight and with purpose.

Kyle waved as if Roland was friendly, hoping to defuse the situation ever so slightly, but Roland kept advancing

Annie stood up and leaned into Kyle. He felt a warm rush in his chest cavity despite the approaching danger.

Roland finally reached them and stopped and stared at Bobby. Kyle kept his gun out of sight. Bobby looked at his feet.

"He hurt?" Roland said.

"Yeah," Kyle said.

Bobby said nothing. He rested his good arm on his knees and buried his face in the crook of his elbow.

"He bit?" Roland said and tensed up.

Nobody said anything.

"So he's bit," Roland said. "Shit."

Nobody moved or said anything for a few moments.

"Wait here," Roland said. He turned to walk away, then he stopped and turned back around. "Where's Bobby's gun?"

"I gave it to Kyle," Bobby said.

"Give it to me," Roland said and pointed his own weapon at Kyle.

"It's okay, man, he's cool," Bobby said.

"Give it to me," Roland said again and jabbed the nose of his weapon in Kyle's direction.

Kyle instinctively raised his hands in the air in surrender, but he couldn't bring himself to hand over the weapon. He thought about pointing it in Roland's direction, but he couldn't bring himself to do that either. Roland would shoot him.

"Just fucking hand it, Kyle. You want to get in a duel out here? You think that's going to make this fucked-up day any better?"

Roland had him. There was nothing else he could do but slowly set the gun down and step away.

"Good boy," Roland said as he picked it up off the pavement, never taking his eyes off Kyle's. "Now wait here and keep an eye on him. I'll be back in a couple of minutes."

Lane cracked open the front door and peered out, but only for the briefest of moments. He couldn't take his eyes off the interior of the store for more than a second or two in case Parker or Hughes decided to creep up behind him.

Roland was on his way back. By himself.

Christ. Keeping all these people in line was going to be a bitch and a half if something happened to Bobby.

Lane could tell by Roland's walk that he wasn't happy. The man didn't exactly have a spring in his step.

He closed the door and turned back to his prisoners. Carol was hiding in the cooler as usual. Frank was in the bathroom. Parker and Hughes sat on the floor in the back near the Red Bull.

Roland stepped inside and shut the door behind him. "Bobby's been bit," he said.

Lane exhaled. He knew it. "And the others?"

"The others are fine."

Well, that's just great.

"You know what to do then," Lane said.

"That's why I came back," Roland said. He picked up a hammer and rummaged through the pile of extra clothes until he found the scarf for his face.

"Do it carefully," Lane said. "And don't touch him. Do not. Touch him."

"I've done this before, boss," Roland said and slipped back outside.

Kyle kept a close watch in every direction. He might be able to handle a handful of those things, but any more than that and he'd have to take Annie back to the store at top speed and leave Bobby alone to his fate.

"He's going back to tell Lane," Bobby said.

"Seems so," Kyle said.

"He's going to beat me to death with one of those crowbars."

"I'll talk to him," Kyle said.

"And he's going to listen to you? He won't even listen to me. He only listens to Lane."

"Can't we at least wait until—you know," Annie said.

"Lane won't chance it," Bobby said. "I'm contagious. So you know what? Lane's right. And you should step back. You should have just shot me as soon as it happened."

"I told you," Kyle said. "We don't do that."

"You seem like nice people," Bobby said. "You're too nice. It's going to get you killed."

Kyle swallowed.

"I'm so sorry," Annie said. And Kyle could tell she really was. He was sorry too. But if Bobby hadn't been bitten, he'd still be hostile.

"Look," Bobby said. "I know Lane. He's not complicated. And he's not a bad guy. I know how it looks, but he's not. Just do what he tells you to do and you'll be okay. He'll lighten up if he trusts you. And he'll keep you alive."

"Roland's coming back," Annie said. "And he has a hammer."

"Oh Jesus," Bobby said and covered his face with his hands.

"I'll talk to him," Kyle said.

Bobby just moaned.

"I'll talk to him," Kyle said again.

Roland was coming at them fast and angry. He had a pistol in one hand, a hammer in the other, and a scarf wrapped around his neck.

Annie leaned into Kyle. This time he did not feel a warm rush. He felt revulsion, not at her but at what he knew was going to happen.

"What's the scarf for?" Annie said.

Kyle was pretty sure he knew what the scarf was for.

Roland stopped when he reached Bobby. "Step back."

"Make it painless," Kyle said.

"I've done this before. Step back."

"I didn't ask if you'd done this before. I said make it painless."

"Motherfucker," Roland said and pulled back the hammer as if he'd hit Kyle if he didn't shut up and step back.

Kyle and Annie stepped back.

Roland pulled the scarf up and covered his mouth. "He won't feel a thing," he said, this time in a more civilized tone. "He's my friend, and I'm not a sadist."

Bobby turned away from Roland and showed him the back of his head. He covered his ears with his hands and said, "Do it."

Annie hugged Kyle and buried her face in his chest so she would not have to look. But Kyle was certain she heard it.

And when Roland was finished, the scarf over his mouth was flecked with blood.

Annie took the small knife from Bobby's belt when Kyle and Roland weren't looking. It took less than a second. It came right off because it was held in place by nothing more than a strap and a snap.

CHAPTER SIX

Lane ordered all the men but Roland into the cooler for the night. Carol and Annie were allowed to sleep on the floor near the bathrooms, but Hughes, Frank, Kyle, and Parker couldn't be trusted, especially not in the dark, not when Roland and Lane were down a man and needed to sleep.

Hughes took it in stride. He wasn't planning to move against Lane or Roland in the night anyway. They'd be on guard. Sure, it was dark. One would be asleep and the other one tired, but they'd be on guard. They'd expect an attack and be ready to shoot.

The best time to strike would be when Roland and Lane are distracted, preferably by a pack of those things. They couldn't possibly make it all the way to Olympia and then up to an island without running into a pack or even a horde. That's when Roland and Lane would go down.

So what did Hughes care if he spent the night locked in the cooler? All he wanted was sleep. Roland and Lane wouldn't sleep well—that was for sure—but Hughes would. In the morning he'd be fresh and rested and ready to kick the shit out of sleep-deprived Roland and Lane.

Frank grumbled under his breath about being locked up. Hughes understood. Kyle cringed when Lane padlocked the door. Hughes understood that, as well. But Parker banged on the door and shouted that Lane was an asshole. That, Hughes did not understand. That was just stupid. Parker might make an outstanding foxhole companion, but he was no good at all under purely psychological pressure.

The cooler was big enough for everyone to spread out. It was a long rectangular metal box about the size and shape of a shipping container. Hughes and Frank took spots on the floor near the back. Parker sat by the door, no doubt so he could bang on it some more when he got mad. Kyle stayed up there with him. Those two were always fighting. Kyle was perfectly welcome in the back away from Parker and his combustible attitude, but those two had some issues to resolve. Hughes could hear them arguing in low voices. Maybe they'd come to terms. They'd better, or Hughes would crack their heads together once Lane was out of the way.

Hughes lay on his back on the steel floor and laced his fingers behind his head. Frank stuck a Maglite between his teeth so he could use two hands to move some boxes out of his way.

"Ain't this a bitch," Frank said.

"S'all right," Hughes said. "Just try to get some sleep. Rest up for tomorrow."

Frank took the Maglite out of his mouth and kicked the last box out of the way. Then he shut the light off and fidgeted while trying to get comfortable on the floor. The cooler was pitch black now, so Hughes closed his eyes. He saw spectral purple afterimages on the back of his eyelids.

The electricity had been off for a long time. The walls and the air inside had long ago adjusted to the ambient temperature in the store, which wasn't much different now from the ambient temperature outside, which was getting colder by the day. Still, Hughes felt just a tiny bit colder inside the cooler. It was probably just his imagination.

Frank finally stopped fussing around and got still. "I wonder if the president got bit," he said in the darkness.

"The president of what?" Hughes said.

"Of the country," Frank said.

"The hell you talking about, the president getting bit?"

"Can you imagine him chasing his staff around the White House?"

Hughes chuckled and shook his head in the dark. "Frank, my man."

"Go ahead and laugh, but it's not funny. Just about every famous person you've ever heard of has either been bitten or eaten. Think about it. Stephen King. Justin Bieber. John McCain. Bit. Imagine getting chased in Hollywood by Arnold Schwarzenegger after *he's* been bit."

"Jesus Christ, Frank. The president hasn't been bit. He's in a bunker somewhere."

"Okay, but Arnold Schwarzenegger isn't in a bunker somewhere unless he dug it himself in his yard."

"Go to sleep, Frank."

"I can't stop thinking about this stuff."

"Then think about it quietly, okay?"

Hughes' back hurt. Sleeping on the floor wasn't doing him any favors. He rolled onto his side to relieve the pressure, but the pain just moved into his shoulder.

"A buddy of mine used to work summers as a mechanic down in Antarctica," Frank said. Hughes sighed. Frank was not going to be quiet anytime soon. "They even sent him to the station at the South Pole once. How awesome would that be?"

Hughes just wanted to sleep, but he didn't want to be rude and couldn't get comfortable anyway. Frank wasn't the smartest person around, but he was an okay guy, and anyway he was Hughes' friend.

"You want to go to the South Pole?" Hughes said. He had no idea they had a station down there.

"Well, kind of," Frank said. "I mean, it would be cool, wouldn't it? That's not something you see every day. The guys at the South Pole station are probably fine."

Yes, Hughes supposed the scientists at the pole probably were fine for the time being. "Until they run out of food and fuel. Nobody's going down there to get them."

Hughes imagined himself stuck in Antarctica. What would he do? Would he even try to get back to the warm parts of the world, or would he hold out on the ice as long as he could until he died peacefully? Freezing to death had to be better than getting chewed up by teeth. He imagined a team of scientists braving the most hostile conditions on earth and actually making it back, only to return home to—this.

"You know it's winter down there in August?" Frank said.

Yes, Hughes knew it was winter in August on the bottom half of the world. "So I guess it's spring for them now that we're going into November. How many people are down there?"

"I don't know. Not a lot. They have a pretty small crew during the winter. My buddy left at the end of the summer. Most people leave then. The ones who stay are hard-core. Everybody goes a little bit crazy. My buddy says they have a name for it. They call it going toast."

Going toast. Hughes liked that. Going crazy was going *toast.* He wasn't sure what it meant, exactly, but he liked the sound of it.

Everyone left in the world was probably going a little bit toast.

Carol? Jumping at her own shadow and cleaning everything over and over? Toast.

Annie? Toasted, for sure. The biggest catastrophe in the history of the species had just laid waste to the planet, and the poor girl couldn't remember a bit of it.

Parker? That guy was still in the toaster.

And Lane? Lane was *burnt* toast. Burnt and black and stinking up the whole kitchen.

Hughes was sure he'd go toast himself soon enough. Somehow he hadn't already. Mostly because he didn't feel anything anymore. Then again, he could be kidding himself. Maybe feeling nothing was his own way of going toast.

He couldn't help but wonder if his family might still be alive if they lived in New York or Chicago or Houston instead of Seattle. Because the only places in the world hit harder than Seattle were Calcutta and Moscow.

That's where it started. In Russia. Some dinky Arctic research town in Siberia was the first to get hit. A scientist up there was bitten by what everyone thought was a rabid fox. The guy *turned* and then bit his doctor. Since he was the only doctor around, they flew him to Moscow for treatment. The doctor bit a dozen passengers on the plane. He ripped a woman's throat out with his teeth before a mob jumped him and bashed his head in with a fire extinguisher. After they emptied the plane, it was absolute mayhem at Moscow's international airport.

No one had a clue what was happening, and it took the Russian authorities much longer than it should have to shut everything down.

They might have managed to contain it had they understood, but they did not understand.

Most of the Russian infected stayed home, but someone in Moscow who got bitten but was otherwise initially fine flew to Paris. Another boarded a plane to Seattle. A third flew to Cape Town, and a fourth to Mumbai. And it spread like a motherfucker from there. Quarantines were impossible. Governments everywhere were two or even three steps behind.

Since the plague's insertion point in America was Seattle, the East Coast had more warning. Things might be a little bit better over there. Local governments could be two or three steps ahead. By the time the virus spread through Oregon and reached California and Idaho, the U.S. government knew what was happening. Containment was no longer possible, but at least they knew what was coming. New York, Miami, and Boston might not have had a single case before they knew what was coming. Maybe the Army was out in the streets. Northeastern Canada could have cut itself off completely for all Hughes knew. The Caribbean islands almost certainly did. Puerto Rico and Cuba might still be intact.

But Seattle was the worst place to be. Hughes' family stood no chance, not only because they lived at ground zero but because of his wife's … situation.

Sheila had been depressed for years. She went weeks in a row without leaving the house or even getting out of bed except to use the bathroom. Hughes earned just enough from his job that she didn't need to work, so when Tyler was born, they agreed she should spend at least a few years taking care of their son. But it wasn't long after she became a stay-at-home mom that she sank into a personal hell from which she never emerged.

Hughes never did figure out why. It wasn't because she stayed home. He hadn't forced her. He wasn't that type of guy, and it was her idea anyway. She seemed to love it at first. She took more pleasure in taking care of that boy than anything else. But something switched on or off in her head and sent her spiraling into a void.

Sheila's morbid depression frightened their son Tyler. He was too young to understand it. Hell, Hughes didn't understand it either. At least he was an adult and knew these things sometimes happened to people, but he had no idea how to explain it to a six-year-old. Tyler did his best, though, to handle it stoically. He didn't cry, didn't complain, didn't needle his mother about it. He was going to be just like his father. At least he would have been had he survived.

Hughes guessed she had some kind of chemical imbalance that altered her personality, but she never had a brain scan, never saw a doctor who did anything more than prescribe pills. And one day she just pulled the sheets over her head and never got up again, at least not for long.

The one day in her life when Sheila should have stayed in bed was the first time in over a month that she went into the living room and opened the curtains to let in some light.

Five of those things burst through the window.

She knew what was happening out there. Hughes had told her, but she paid little attention. News of the plague didn't seem real to her clouded mind, as if it were just some story on the radio. It had to be seen to be believed, and Sheila hadn't seen anything. It didn't fully register for Hughes either until he went to the hardware store for supplies and found the door ripped off its hinges, the shelves stripped down to leftovers, and one of those things hunched over the body of the store clerk.

Or maybe Sheila just didn't care. Perhaps she surrendered. Surely it must be easier for a morbidly depressed person to face the fact that the world was circling the drain. Sheila's world had already circled the drain. Maybe she was suicidal there at the end. Opening the curtains was just her way of taking a bottle of pills. Hughes had to admit that was possible.

But he never wanted to know for sure because he'd never forgive her. One of those things damn near took Tyler's head off before Hughes put a bullet through its spine.

His poor boy. Tyler fell to the kitchen floor, convulsed like he was being electrocuted, and bled out in less than a minute. At least he didn't

suffer for long, and he died before he could turn. Hughes didn't have
to put his boy out of his misery, nor did he have to shoot his boy to
defend himself. Hughes doubted he could have done it. Unlike Sheila,
his survival instinct was still intact, but if he'd had to kill his own son,
even in self-defense, it would have been the second-to-last thing he ever
did.

Sheila wasn't as lucky as Tyler. She, too, was bitten, but she was
bitten in the back while running into the bedroom. Hughes popped the
one that bit her and finished the other three off in the hallway, then he
barricaded himself next to his wife in the bedroom and did everything
he could to make her last hours comfortable. He waited until she slipped
out of consciousness before suffocating her with a pillow.

He buried them out in the yard before he left town.

Hughes hadn't grieved yet. He had not even started. That particular
circuit in his head had switched off. A whole series of pathways in his
brain just went dark. He noticed it happening. The emotional part of his
personality went into sleep mode and stayed there.

Maybe something like that was what happened to Annie, only she
lost her memory instead of her feelings.

Hughes knew his emotions hadn't died, though. They were just
resting. They would be back.

Lane will be one lucky bastard if he dies one way or another before
it happens.

Annie's first night since she woke in the forest didn't go well. Lane
had designated a place for everybody to sleep, and she and Carol
were sent to the floor near the restrooms. He promised everyone that
he'd ease up when they got to the island and could spread out, but Annie
didn't believe him.

She lay on the cold floor next to Carol. They covered themselves in
warm jackets and used fleece sweatshirts for pillows.

It's too bad, she thought, they couldn't spend the night in a motel.

There had to be one nearby. But of course it wouldn't be safe.

She felt comforted by the fact that she could see. Lane had placed a candle in one of the checkout aisles, no doubt so he'd know if anyone tried to sneak around. She didn't like his reasons, but she approved of the results. The stuttering shadows on the ceiling and walls reminded her of more peaceful times.

But she thought the light, faint as it was, might put them in danger since the boards didn't reach all the way to the tops of the windows. If sunlight could get in during the day, candlelight could get out at night.

She was more afraid of the dark, though. She hadn't yet seen the total darkness of night in a world with no power. She couldn't remember seeing it anyway. She'd have to experience it for the first time all over again, and she wasn't ready for that. Even the tiniest sounds would freak her out. She thought about taking the ring off her finger and letting her hand breathe, but she didn't want to lose it on the floor so she just twisted it.

Carol was lying next to her. The poor thing was even more of a wreck, but her presence still gave Annie comfort.

"How you holding up, Carol?" Annie whispered.

"Okay, I think," Carol said. "Thanks." Carol did sound okay, especially under the circumstances. Maybe Annie's presence was helping her too. "How are *you* holding up?"

"Okay. I'm a little bit numb."

They were silent for a few moments. They both seemed to want to talk, but didn't know what to say. Annie figured she should start with the basics. "How did you meet these guys?"

"Hughes found me on the road. He was on his way down to Portland. I was on my way up to Seattle. The roads were so jammed with cars that everyone had to walk. And then—"

Annie heard Carol swallow hard.

"It's okay," Annie said. "You don't have to talk about it."

"I probably should talk about it." She sounded a little more sure of herself now. "I'm not usually like this."

"What did you do before?"

"I owned a restaurant in the Pearl District in Portland."

"Wow."

"You know that part of town?"

"No, but it sounds fancy."

"It is. It's an old warehouse district that was gentrified by artists back in the '90s, then upgraded again by people with money. It's like SoHo in New York. Very prestigious, very expensive. Well, at least it was like SoHo in New York. Now I guess it must look like this place."

Annie listened to her own breath. She could hear her heartbeat in her ears and the blood rushing into her head. She wondered if the Pearl District was as quiet as this place, or if it was loud because it was overrun with infected people.

"We were attacked," Carol said.

"In Portland?" Annie said.

"No. On the road. Me and Hughes. Everyone, actually. There were thousands of us. We all had to get out of our cars and walk. I stayed on the right side of the road. Everyone did. Those going north walked on one side and everyone going south walked on the other side. Like we were driving, you know? You drive on the right side while oncoming traffic is on the left."

"That's when you were attacked?"

"We heard screams up ahead. The screams must have been a half-mile away at first, but they were loud. Incredibly loud and coming from the north. Everyone on my side of the street stopped. It was a pedestrian traffic jam. Then I started to get pushed the other direction. People who had been walking north were running south. People on the other side of the road were running now too. We weren't going in two directions anymore. We were all running in a single direction. South. Away from the screams." Carol paused, then continued. "It was those things. Hundreds of them. Maybe thousands. A whole army of them pouring out of Olympia."

Annie could only imagine how terrifying that must have been. No wonder Carol was such a disaster.

An army of those things. Pouring out of Olympia.

Where her sister Jenny lived.

"I ran down the middle of the road," Carol said, "where it was a little less crowded. There were cars, but less people. That's when I saw Hughes. He was on the other side. I ran over to him because he looked like the kind of man who might protect me. You know? And he did. I might have thought he was scary if I saw him at night out by myself, but a big guy like him was exactly what I needed right then. So I ran up to him and grabbed his arm like it was a saving banister. He let me. As if what I'd just done was the most natural thing in the world. 'Come on,' he said. 'We should get in one of these trucks and get down.' So we did. We found an unlocked SUV with tinted windows and we got inside and locked the doors. He got on the floor in the back and I crouched down in the front."

"Sounds like a good idea," Annie said. "Lucky about those tinted windows, I guess."

"It was a good idea. It's the only reason I'm still alive. But that's when it got really bad."

Carol stopped talking. Annie wasn't sure if she had paused or if she didn't want to continue. Annie wasn't going to ask. She didn't want to push it. If Carol owned a restaurant in a prestigious part of Portland, she must normally be a competent and capable person, but now she was shattered. Like everyone else.

"I couldn't see anything," Carol said. "I didn't dare sit up to look out the windows. It didn't matter that they were tinted. Tinted windows aren't like one-way glass, you know. You can sort of see through them. I didn't want anyone or anything to see any movement inside. But mostly *I* didn't want to see anything outside. And it's probably a good thing I didn't because if I could have seen what I was hearing, I wouldn't have made it."

Carol stopped talking again and Annie said nothing. Carol would either tell her the rest or she wouldn't.

The silence felt a little bit awkward. Annie wanted to press Carol for more, but she didn't. Finally, Carol finished her story unprompted.

"The screaming kept getting louder. Those things were screaming and so were the people. First people were screaming in terror and then were screaming in pain. They were being eaten alive, Annie. It was happening right outside the truck. They were being slammed against the side of it. There was this constant *banging*. The side window above my head cracked. I thought those things knew we were in there and were trying to bust their way in."

Annie shuddered. She was not going to ask what she saw when she and Hughes finally climbed out of the truck. Surely Carol would never forget it, but also she might never want to discuss it. She reached toward Carol, found her hand, and clasped it.

They lay like that for a while, two new friends holding hands in the darkness. It felt good. Annie felt better than she had all day. She even forgot, for a moment, that she was being held hostage by Roland and Lane.

But Roland and Lane seemed like the least of her problems after hearing Carol's terrible road story. She couldn't get those images out of her mind.

Carol eventually let her hand go. Annie could hear her trying to get comfortable on the floor. It was impossible, but they both had to try.

Annie missed home so much that she ached. She wanted nothing more than to return to South Carolina even if it was a smoldering ruin. People breathe differently, more deeply, when they're in the place where they come from. Annie breathed differently in South Carolina. She breathed differently in the whole American South, not just in South Carolina. The South was home. She didn't like everything about it, but it was the place that raised her. It fit like a dress made just for her. The Northwest felt a little bit off, and a little bit foreign, even before all this happened. Not because there was anything objectively wrong with the Northwest, but because it wasn't home.

Maybe things weren't as bad in South Carolina. The virus came from

Russia—that's what Kyle told her, anyway—and it entered the United States in Seattle. So maybe the eastern part of America had more time to prepare. Maybe there were more survivors out there. The government might still even function. It was possible, right? She couldn't really see how, but she had to believe it was possible.

Annie finally drifted off into a frightening dream world.

She ran down Fifth Avenue in downtown Seattle alongside hundreds of other people with the sound of screams, gunshots, explosions, and sirens behind her. Cars crashed into each other ahead of her. People jumped out of windows and onto the street. Some of them jumped from so high, they were instantly killed when they landed.

She woke up gasping and sweating and felt Carol's reassuring hand on her shoulder.

"It's okay," Carol said. "You were just having a dream."

When Annie finally fell back asleep, she fled a pack of the infected through a forest.

CHAPTER SEVEN

Parker was pissed. He felt a deep, abiding hatred for just about everybody. He could not fucking believe Kyle had Bobby's gun in his hand out on the street and didn't take Roland out. This whole thing would be over by now if he had.

But, no. Kyle couldn't man up. Nor could Annie, who obviously had a silly girl's crush on the dolt, inspire him in any way whatsoever to do what any fool should have known had to be done. And now Lane had him and the others locked in the cooler. Kyle couldn't even do the decent thing and give Parker some space.

"At least they're down one," Kyle said.

"No thanks to you," Parker said.

Kyle said nothing.

Parker couldn't see a damn thing. He idly wondered what Hughes and Frank were whispering about, but he didn't actually care. He pulled his army jacket tight against him so he wouldn't freeze to death on the floor.

"We only need to take one more of them out," Parker said. "Preferably Lane, but taking that other asshole out would have worked too. You could have done that today."

"Yes," Kyle said. "I could have shot Roland. And told every one of those things for miles in every direction right where we are. The water main brought a pack down on our heads when it exploded. There's no telling how many more surged into the area. And besides, you don't know what Lane would do if he found himself the last one standing. He might just start shooting."

"Then shoot back." Parker wanted to smack Kyle upside his head, but it was dark and he had only a vague idea where Kyle's head even was.

"Listen," Kyle said. "We'd be out on the streets with nothing if it wasn't for me. I was the one who talked Lane into letting us stay here by offering to take everybody up to the islands."

So what?

"Sure," Parker said. "We'd be out there and disarmed. Instead we're *in here* and disarmed and being held hostage. This is better *how*, exactly?"

"At least we're safe from those things. None of them can get us in here."

"You hope."

"I do. You should try it sometime."

He'd need to do something about Kyle. What, he had no idea. But he had to do something.

He should also try being less of an asshole. Things could only end badly between him and Kyle if they couldn't learn to get along, but things weren't going to end any better if Kyle couldn't get all of his shit in one sock.

Parker was supremely annoyed with just about everyone, but he needed them to survive. He knew that, and he knew it consciously, but he still yearned for freedom from his dumb companions. He especially yearned to be free of Kyle. At the same time he feared dying violently and alone. Out there on his own? He'd be torn to pieces in the howling darkness for sure. He had to figure out a way to connect with these people. He had to.

Sometimes he felt twinges of envy for Kyle's naiveté. How nice it must be to feel hope in this world, to believe all they had to do to build a new life is sail north. Did Kyle not understand that a person could die now from a toothache? A person could fucking well die from it. The infection could spread to the brain. Sure, they could raid pharmacies for antibiotics, but all the medicine in the world would expire eventually and most of the pharmacies had been looted already. Primitive man's life expectancy was about thirty. Parker was pushing forty.

He huffed, lay on his back, willed himself to get tired, and failed. He could not switch his brain off. As usual when he could not switch his brain off, he thought about Holly.

He'd been married once. Met his future wife at a trendy café named Spinoza's in Seattle's Ballard neighborhood. It was the kind of place Parker always hated, not only because he didn't fit in there but because it attracted the kinds of people he wished never colonized his neighborhood to begin with—the young, the hip, the beautiful, and the moneyed. Ballard used to be an honest and slightly gritty place for men who worked the docks, the ship locks, and who made things with their hands. It was never intended for soft people who lived in undeserved luxury and made boatloads of cash clicking away on their laptops.

The only reason he went into Spinoza's that day at all was because he needed the bathroom. But when he saw a young woman sitting there by herself with her newspaper and a latte, he couldn't help himself. He decided to order one too and see if he could gin up the nerve to take the empty table next to her.

There was something about her, though he couldn't quite figure out what it was. Not even after they married could he figure out what it was. She was attractive, sure, but not the most attractive he'd ever seen. She seemed friendly and approachable enough, though he had no idea why he would think that since she was just sitting there reading the paper. There was just something … gravitational about her, like she'd been engineered just for him.

He ordered awkwardly at the counter. He'd never had a latte, a cappuccino, or an Americano. He didn't even know what they were. But he couldn't just say "I'll have a coffee." They didn't have regular coffee in those kinds of places.

The pretty woman with the newspaper sat far enough from the counter that she couldn't hear him fumble his order, and thank heaven for that or he wouldn't have sat next to her. She looked so peaceful and content, so at ease in the world as she flipped strands of her brown hair over her ear.

He didn't intend to hit on her or ask her out for a date. He just wanted to enjoy the pleasure of her attention even if it only lasted a couple of seconds.

She sat by herself at a table for two. He sat next to her at another table for two and placed his drink in front of him. It looked like a dessert. He expected it to taste like one too, like a coffee meringue pie or something. Normally he drank plain old coffee, black, but the creamy and bitter whipped goodness in his mug, despite being foofy and gay, was outstanding. Wow, he thought. This *exists*?

"This coffee is extraordinary," he said.

"Isn't it?" the woman next to him said. The corners of her eyes crinkled up when she smiled over her mug.

God, Parker thought. I love this woman. He didn't know why. He just did.

Her name was Holly and she was a regular at Spinoza's. She had gone to school with the café owners. He told her he was new to fancy coffee and she seemed delighted to explain all the options.

They were so very different, but they were married in less than a year.

He built cabinets for a living. She worked in an office downtown as a paralegal. His friends were working class. Hers were professional. He loved the outdoors. She enjoyed fancy meals out. He drank beer. She liked red wine. Once in a while he embarrassed her when they went out with her friends, and he knew he seemed a little rough around the edges in mixed company, but she loved him and he couldn't imagine living without her. She had a soft and gentle soul and seemed to appreciate his brusque masculine qualities—she was genetically hard-wired to do so, after all—until one day he hit her.

He didn't mean to. Really, he didn't. It just happened. They were arguing about money, which was a stupid because they both made plenty. He wanted a motorcycle and could afford it. She wanted to spend the money on granite kitchen counters instead.

She might have talked him into it, too, but instead she said she was tired of being a slave to his lower-class lifestyle.

He'd never hit anybody before. He looked like the type of guy who had been in a couple of fights, but he hadn't.

He didn't hit her too hard. It was really more like a slap. He didn't strike her with a closed fist, didn't break any bones, didn't make her bleed, didn't even leave a mark that lasted more than five minutes. But he did strike her cheek, and he'd never forget the sound or the look on her face when he did it.

Her entire life shattered in one instant.

She'd never forgive him, not in her heart, and he knew it.

He could not have been sorrier. That slap hurt him more than it hurt her. It sounded ludicrous when he said so, and she screamed that it was the most outrageous thing she ever heard, but it was true. It changed him as a person. It sentenced him to be a different kind of man for the rest of his life, the kind of man who hit women. A domestic abuser. A *wife-beater*. He never did it again, nor would he ever—no, really, he wouldn't—but he would spend the rest of his days as a man who had once smacked a woman.

Eventually she could look at him again, and a little while later she could talk to him again, and eventually she even had sex with him one last time, but it ended in tears, and at that moment he knew it was over. She never slept with him again. Never even hugged him again. She left a few months later and said she was sorry but she wouldn't be back. She cried when she left and she even said that she'd miss him, but she was true to her word. She never came back.

That was two years ago. Parker thought about her every day since. After the plague swept the world, he worried about her so hard he vomited.

What happened to her? Was she alive? Did she get bitten? Was a distorted version of her out there somewhere, diseased and warped beyond recognition? What would he do if she came at him on the street baring her teeth? Would he shoot her? Would he smash in her skull with a crowbar?

Would he smash in her face if he had to?

Kyle was stuck. He didn't regret anything, didn't feel like he'd done anything wrong, but at the same time Parker did have a point. Kyle had to admit it. If he'd taken out Roland when he had the chance, they would not be locked up. There was no way Lane could subdue everyone if both his cohorts were dead and Kyle had Bobby's gun.

Some of those things would likely have heard the gunshot. Kyle and his crew might have to barricade themselves in the store or flee in the truck. But at least they'd be free of Lane.

But then Parker or Hughes or Annie—Annie!—would blame him for bringing those things down on their heads when he knew perfectly well that there were more in the area now due to the explosion down the street. Sure, they could flee in the truck, but they couldn't take the truck all the way to Olympia. The roads were all snarled. So where would they go? Just drive a few miles, get out and walk, and hope for the best?

So yeah, Parker was right in a way, but at the same time, he wasn't. Kyle didn't actually know what he should have done or what he should do next.

He wasn't one for confrontation and never had been, not even when he was picked on in school. It's not like he ever *had* to fight back. Only two other kids ever bothered him much. Kyle wasn't an outcast, but almost everybody got picked on by somebody in school.

A kid named Tim was the first. Tim wasn't a bully. He wasn't even all that big or intimidating. Kyle never did figure out why, but Tim just wanted to fight somebody, and he apparently picked Kyle because Kyle didn't look threatening. Kyle had no fight in him at all and that came across.

So Tim just walked up to him one day between classes out in the hall and punched him in the shoulder. Not hard enough to get himself suspended for assault or for fighting, but hard enough to piss off Kyle and get his attention.

"Meet me behind the gym," Tim said and narrowed his eyes, "after school's out today."

Kyle rubbed his shoulder. It didn't hurt all that bad. The rubbing was an instinctive response. Kyle realized it made him look weak, so he stopped.

"What for?" Kyle said.

"So I can kick your ass."

Tim was serious. Kyle could tell. Kyle was baffled. And of course he didn't show behind the gym.

The next day Tim approached Kyle again in the hallway between classes, but this time he didn't start swinging. "So, you're afraid to fight me, eh?"

Kyle sized Tim up. He wasn't afraid. He just didn't see the point in fighting for no reason.

"I'm not *afraid*." He sounded anything but convincing to even himself, but the truth was that he really wasn't afraid. "It's just stupid."

"You're afraid," Tim said in a mock little-kid voice. "Kyle's *afwaid*." Tim laughed and sauntered off, no doubt feeling terrific about himself. And he never bothered Kyle again.

That, Kyle decided, was how you handled a bully. Don't let him rile you up. Don't fight if it's not strictly necessary. The thirteen-year-old version of Parker, Kyle was certain, would have fought Tim. Both would have been hurt and suspended. What, exactly, would have been accomplished?

Kyle wondered what had happened to Tim. Did he grow up to become a well-adjusted adult? Or did he beat his wife and kids? What if he went to jail? What if Tim was in jail right now, protected from those things by steel bars but starving to death because he couldn't escape to find food?

Two years later another kid picked a fight with Kyle for no reason, only this time the result was quite different.

It was Kyle's sophomore year in high school. The kid's name was Brady. He wasn't anything special, not at all the kind of kid you'd think was a bully if you only got a quick look at him. But for whatever reason, he wanted to get scrappy with Kyle.

It all came to a head when the two boys found themselves in shop class together. Brady made one taunt too many, and though Kyle could no longer remember what Brady said, he wouldn't forget what happened next. Brady was hectoring Kyle from the next work table, and Kyle stood up from his bench with a wrench in his hand and took two steps forward.

Brady looked terrified, as if Kyle were gearing up to break open his skull.

The shop teacher, Mr. Horton, heard the commotion and saw what was happening. "Break it up right now or you're both suspended!"

The only reason Kyle stood up with a wrench in his hand is because the wrench was already in his hand when he stood up. He wasn't going to *do* anything with it.

Brady never bothered Kyle again. The following year, junior year in high school for both of them, the two even became sort of friends. Brady had mellowed, and they found themselves in the hallway talking about computer stuff once in a while. Brady, Kyle figured, might have turned out okay, at least until the world ended.

So maybe, Kyle thought, if he stood up for himself a little, he and Lane could become friends after Kyle whisked him safely away.

L ane sat on the floor and leaned against the boarded-up door while Roland slept at his feet. He held his pistol in his right hand and a flashlight in the other. Anyone who approached in the dark would be shot.

Things were no good now that Bobby was gone. No, they were not good at all. Something different had to happen and fast. He'd have a man-to-man talk with Hughes. He'd offer Hughes a job as one of his wingmen, possibly even outranking Roland.

And he'd need to get rid of Parker. Tomorrow.

He heard two sounds. Roland's deep breathing. And Annie as she thrashed about in her sleep.

Annie dreamed that she had been bitten. She dreamed that she went into some kind of coma. And she dreamed that she came out of that coma in some kind of rage.

She chased people and screamed her throat out while chasing them. She chased them out of a camp and into a forest.

She caught someone who looked like a teenager and sank her teeth into his back. Her prey screamed, but it was too late for her prey. She'd gotten it and now it was hers. She straddled it and placed her hands on its shoulders and shoved its head into the ground and onto some rocks. The pathetic thing whimpered. Then she leaned forward and bit into its neck while it writhed and wriggled and screamed.

Others joined in. Predators like her. Hungry hungry predators. Predators who hated the weak who were responsible for their hunger. Predators that ripped the flesh from the prey she'd caught with their teeth.

She woke screaming.

Lane leaned forward when he heard Annie screaming and placed his finger inside the trigger guard.

Kyle snapped out of his half-asleep state when he heard somebody screaming. It sounded like Annie.

Hughes twitched awake and jumped to his feet when he heard a girl screaming. Were they under attack? Shit, where was his shotgun?

Parker woke to the sound of somebody screaming. The hell's going on *now*?

He couldn't see anything. That bastard Lane had locked him up in the cooler.

Parker heard scrambling next to him. Kyle shouted and banged on the metal door with the flat of his hand. "Annie!"

Annie seemed like a sweet kid, but good grief. What a head case. And Kyle was falling for her like the putz he was. Why couldn't he see that she was trouble?

Annie stopped screaming as abruptly as she had started. Parker heard Carol's faint voice from the other side of the door, though he couldn't quite make out what she said.

"Girl just had a bad dream," Hughes said. "Shit. And I was deep asleep too. Won't be again for at least another hour after all that."

"Annie, are you okay?" Kyle said through the door.

"I'm fine," she said. "I just had a—really bad dream. Sorry everybody."

Parker tried to get back to sleep, but instead he thought about jabbing his thumbs in Lane's eye sockets.

Annie had the dream again, only this time she was in a city. A hungry hungry predator in a city. A city empty of food. Empty of prey. Her prey that was her food. Her cattle run wild.

She found a house. Sound inside. Light inside. Sound and light meant prey and food and more food. One of her prey opened the door. Her prey stepped outside. Her food stepped outside. She screamed, alerting the others, and ran and pounced and bit it and chewed.

Warm blood in her mouth, on her chin, on her chest.

Yelling inside the house. Those things, her food, were yelling at her from inside the house. She looked up, snarled, and saw the face of one of those things.

She knew that face.

Lane.

This time when Annie woke she could not be consoled.

Roland stood watch at the gate, but Lane still couldn't sleep when it was his turn. Not after that girl woke up screaming again. The other woman, Carol, eventually calmed her down, but Annie's screams must have been heard from ten blocks away in every direction.

The boarded-up door wasn't really a gate, but Lane thought of it as one anyway. It functioned as a gate—a gate to his castle and everyone else's prison.

A breach from either direction would mean death and destruction.

When he saw the faint light of dawn breaking, when just the tiniest hint of blue washed over the store and onto the beverage rack in the back, he knew he was in trouble. He could not be effective without any sleep. One more night like this and he would be finished. He needed Bobby, but Bobby was gone.

Something different needed to happen, and it needed to happen today. He had to flip Hughes and kill Parker. And if that didn't work, he would have to kill everybody but Roland and Kyle.

Roland was loyal. Kyle knew how to sail. And Kyle will do what he's told.

Nobody said a word about Annie's nightmares in the morning. Thank goodness for small mercies, she thought, because she did not want to talk about it, not even with Kyle.

She was eating a breakfast of blueberry granola bars and Rice Krispies sans milk when she saw Lane stride over to the walk-in cooler where he had locked up the men. He pounded on the door and then opened it.

Parker was the first to emerge. "Everybody sleep all right?" he said sarcastically when he came out.

Nobody replied.

She cleaned up her breakfast area and slipped past the men and into the women's room. A shower would be nice. She'd crawl over a pile of corpses for fresh clothes from a warm dryer, but a cold scrub-down in front of the sink would have to do.

She opened the tap. Hardly any water came out. The system had finally broken.

Everything was broken. Apparently including her mind.

Her hands shook as she looked around for something to stop up the sink with, but there was nothing. Only a thin trickle of water came out of the faucet.

She took off her shirt and rubbed meager amounts of cold water under her arms. This was it, she thought. The last time she'd get to bathe with water out of a pipe. Bottled water had to be conserved for drinking. At least there were plenty of deodorant sticks in the hygiene aisle.

More cold water went onto her stomach, her breasts, her forearms, her neck, and her shoulders. With her fingertips she felt that scab again on her back. She'd noticed it yesterday but hadn't paid it much mind. She'd been far more interested in scrubbing the blood and gore out of her hair. But now that she was more or less clean and intact, the scab was more noticeable. And more irritating.

She turned halfway around and craned her neck as far as it would go so she could see her back in the mirror.

She screamed in shock and alarm when she saw that the wound was a perfectly shaped human-sized bite mark.

Those dreams she had weren't nightmares.

They were memories.

CHAPTER EIGHT

Kyle slapped the bathroom door. "Annie!" he said, his heart racing. "What's going on in there?"

She was crying hysterically from down near the floor.

"Hell's her problem?" Roland said from his post in the front.

"She's had a rough couple of weeks," Kyle said and slapped the door again. He tried the knob, but it wouldn't turn.

"The rest of us have been on vacation?" Roland said.

Kyle ignored him. "Annie!" Parker and Hughes joined him at the door.

"We need to calm her down," Parker said. "Dangerous making this kind of racket in here."

"Would you please," Kyle said, "worry about someone other than yourself for a change? Annie!"

"I'm worried about everyone here, Kyle. If enough of those things outside hear us, everybody could die, including your girlfriend."

Annie quieted down.

"Annie," Kyle said. "Can you open the door? Let me help you."

After a moment's pause she said, "I'm okay." She did not sound okay. "I'm sorry, just give me a minute."

"I'll be right out here," Kyle said.

Jesus, what was wrong with that girl? He had feelings for her, he could not deny that, but if he'd met her a few months earlier, before it all went sideways, he'd be spooked off her. He'd dismiss her as damaged and high-maintenance. But he couldn't dismiss her like that. Not now.

Everybody was cracking. Lane and Roland were damn near psychotic, though they might have been fine even recently. Parker was borderline. Carol was a human-shaped basket case. Frank wasn't bright enough to freak out in any way that was interesting. Hughes seemed to keep it together okay, but Kyle was sure that was just a facade.

And what about Kyle himself? How was he doing, *really*?

The bathroom door opened. Annie emerged with her cheeks puffy and her eyes bloodshot and wild. Kyle wanted to hug her.

"My memories came back," she said.

She remembered it all, including what happened right after she had coffee with her sister in downtown Olympia. She had gotten back in her car, turned on the radio, and driven toward Seattle. NPR said a bizarre outbreak of some rabies-like virus at Moscow's Sheremetyevo International Airport was wrecking havoc in Russia and spreading at an alarming rate in Europe and Asia. There was even a possible outbreak in Seattle, but that could not yet be confirmed.

That was why her memory had ended with meeting her sister. It was the last normal thing she did before the world changed.

She remembered hunkering down in her apartment until fear and dread and chaos and death swept her neighborhood. She remembered running in terror down the streets and all but crashing into her friend Blake from college. Blake who she suspected had a thing for her. Blake who owned a motorcycle. Blake who gave her a ride.

They rode the interstate toward Olympia. They both wanted out of Seattle, and Annie had to get to her sister. She and Blake could stay with Jenny if it was safer. But Olympia wasn't safer. It swarmed with the infected, so they rode onward toward Oregon. Portland would almost certainly be just as dangerous, but they planned to turn first and head inland, east, toward Mount Rainier National Park, where nobody but park rangers lived.

She and Blake didn't make it. The interstate was so jam-packed with cars from the mass exodus that they couldn't even ride on the shoulder. They had to ride on the grass next to the interstate, and even that was crowded with cars in some places. People were milling about everywhere on the sides of the freeway, some walking north, some walking south, and some heading down side roads and even into the trees.

They took a side road to a back road to a dirt road to a track to an empty cabin in a dark forest that looked and felt prehistoric. She and Blake went inside and found a pantry full of food. Out back they found gas cans for a generator and some prechopped wood for the fireplace.

They went inside, drew the curtains, locked the doors, made no sound.

A hushed stillness settled over the world.

Annie and Blake lived there for weeks, subsisting on dry goods in the pantry but not daring to start a fire or use the generator.

Nobody ever came up the road.

The food ran out, as they knew it would, but they waited before looking for more. Waited four days until hunger compelled them to get back on Blake's motorcycle and ride to the nearest town—some exurb outside Olympia that might have unlooted food in a store if they were lucky.

The motorcycle made a terrible racket that seemed like the only sound on earth. Every infected person within a five-mile radius must have heard it, but there was nothing else they could do. They might die looking for food, but they would surely die if they stayed in the cabin. Leaving at least gave them a chance.

They rode fast and hard on the back road, but the main road was snarled with cars. Blake steered carefully around them and had to take the bike onto the shoulder a couple of times. After clearing a Greyhound bus on the road, they were mobbed by a swarm of the infected and thrown over the handlebars. Four or five of them poured on Blake at the same time. She was unarmed. She couldn't save him. So she ran away screaming and one of them, also screaming, launched itself at her from the side and they went down together.

It bit her on the back beneath her shoulder. She remembered it clearly now. The pain was exquisite, like someone was digging out her flesh with a jagged-edged scoop. That thing actually tried to take a bite *out* of her. It wanted to eat her alive. But she turned over and flailed, kicked, and punched it as hard as she could, then she jabbed her thumbs in its eyes. It shrieked in rage while she shrieked in terror and pain.

Blake had stopped screaming. He was gone. He was being *consumed*. The five that killed him were so busy with his body that they forgot all about her.

She ran into the forest, stumbling in shock and pain and alarm. She ran for maybe an hour before collapsing next to a log, then fell asleep and woke as a monster. A vicious thing, a hungry hungry predator that stalked humans and killed them and ate them.

She was *not* going to talk about it. The others would kill her for sure. Probably not Kyle, but Lane and Roland certainly would. Parker, too, and perhaps even Hughes. Hughes had already shot at her once.

But she wasn't infected. At least not anymore. She was immune. Her body fought off the virus and she recovered.

Right?

That's what happened, right?

She wasn't going to *turn* again.

Was she?

She didn't think so. She wasn't stupid. She knew how viruses and immunity worked. Every virus meets effective resistance in some people, even among populations that have no immunity. Some people got Ebola and lived. Some people used to get smallpox and live. Some survived the bubonic plague. Even Native Americans, who had no effective resistance to European diseases, survived in small numbers. No virus killed everyone. Otherwise the human race would no longer exist— though the health of her species wasn't looking too good anymore.

But no, she was no longer infected. She was immune. She probably wouldn't get sick again even if she recontracted the virus.

Probably.

But that's not necessarily how the others would see it. They might look at her and see *carrier*. Typhoid Annie. With blood and sweat and spit boiling with the virus even if it no longer affected her. Maybe they'd be afraid she'd relapse.

And maybe she would.

What if the disease is less like the flu and more like AIDS or malaria or herpes? Malaria victims relapsed. People with herpes had relapses. Maybe she ought to stay away from everyone else for the rest of her life.

She had no idea, so she wouldn't tell anybody. She didn't dare.

She also couldn't tell anyone because she couldn't bear the fact that she'd killed people. She actually ate people, or parts of them anyway. Her mind had been completely and utterly bent.

She did worse things to her fellow human beings than everyone else in that grocery store put together, including Lane and Bobby and Roland.

And she knew now why Lane recognized her. She had attacked his crew in a house somewhere in the area. It must have happened within the past couple of days. She killed one of his people and he saw her do it.

The reason Lane couldn't remember where he saw her face was because he was cycling through his memories of all the healthy people he'd seen and met. He came up empty because it never even occurred to him—and why would it?—that when he saw her face, she was one of those things.

Parker sat silently in the cooler and plotted. He couldn't take it anymore. He liked exactly one of his companions—Hughes—and to hell with the rest.

Wouldn't be a bad idea, once he got to a proper location, to dig trenches around a house or a cabin and fill them with Punji sticks. The Viet Cong did that during the Vietnam war. They smeared shit on those sticks to infect everybody who stepped on them. That wouldn't work with these things. Sure, an infection would *eventually* kill them. They weren't vampires. You didn't have to stab them in the heart or shoot them with silver bullets or cut off their heads. But they had to be taken down instantly. He'd need a deep trench, a moat, and some really long sticks.

Okay, everybody," Lane said from his guard post near the door. Annie hated that he stayed put up there. She knew why he did it. He could see almost everyplace in the store when the light was good, but mostly he did it to make sure no one got past him and out. "We can't stay here any longer." He had his hands on his hips. "It's too dangerous. I'm sending two of you out on another run for some bicycles. Maybe Annie and Kyle, but first I want to be sure Annie's up for it."

She didn't like that he was even thinking about her, let alone talking about her. It was only a matter of time before he figured out where he'd seen her before. She wanted to melt away into the walls.

"Annie," he said. "You okay, hon? Let's go talk in the back."

Hon? Who the hell was he kidding calling her *hon*? As if he had any affection for anyone but himself. She didn't even want Kyle calling her *hon*. Not yet, anyway.

"Come on," Lane said and headed back toward the bathrooms. Roland took his place at the front door like the guard he was with his arms folded over his chest and the butt of his pistol prominently protruding from the top of his pants.

She patted her right pocket. She still had Bobby's small knife. She wasn't going anywhere near Lane without it, especially not alone. But she didn't move. She just stood there next to the empty donut rack.

"Come on," Lane said again. "I'm not going to *do* anything. We just need to talk."

He sounded reasonable, like he was concerned for her well-being after a really rough night, but she didn't buy it. She walked toward him with tremendous reluctance, knowing he could force her if he had to and that he would.

He stopped in front of the men's bathroom. "Let's go inside. So we can talk privately."

She froze again. He could see that she was afraid. It was all over his face and hers.

He put his hands up like he was surrendering. Then he untucked his gun from the front of his pants and tucked it into the back of his pants.

As if that made any real difference. "I swear to you, Annie, I just want to talk."

He sounded so sincere, almost hurt that she was afraid of him, as if she'd misjudged him. It was an act, but a damn good one because she actually felt, against her better judgment, like she was being unreasonable. She wanted to pat her right pocket again and feel the knife, but he'd notice if she did. And the knife wouldn't help anyway because she'd have to fish it out and unfold it before she could do anything with it.

"Annie, please," Lane said.

She found it amazing that she was just as afraid of being rude as she was of being alone with him in the bathroom. What kind of dysfunctional thinking was that? It was nuts, but people felt that way all the time, and dangerous men knew how to exploit it.

She followed him into the bathroom but did not lock the door. The men's room was the mirror image of the women's room, only with more graffiti on the walls.

His tone changed at once.

"What's up?" he said, but he didn't say it the way friends and acquaintances say it. He said it like an angry boss wondering why an employee can't get their shit straight.

"Excuse me?" she said. "You're the one who wanted to talk."

He leaned against the paper-towel dispenser and folded his arms. "You said your memory came back."

She swallowed like she was gulping a frog. He saw. She was never any good at hiding her nervousness. "It did."

"Well?"

"Well, what?" She felt her face flush hot. "I remember a lot of bad things now like everyone else."

"Something that made you scream. Something that gave you fits in the night."

"What does it *matter*?" She shifted her weight from one foot to the other. "It has nothing to do with you or this store or the boat we need to be getting to."

"It matters," he said, "because you don't want to talk about it. Because I'm trying to decide if I should send you back out there or if you should stay here and cool off or whatever it is you need to do to get better."

"Why do you *care*?" she said. "Send someone else if you don't think I can handle it."

"Listen. I know you're not stupid. And I'm pretty sure you're smart enough to know that I'm not stupid either. I sent you and Kyle out yesterday for a reason. It can't be that hard to figure out why."

Because she and Kyle were competent enough to get the job done and not ruthless enough to disarm Bobby and come back in here shooting.

"Okay," she said. "So send me out again. I'm fine. Really. I wasn't last night, but I'm okay now."

She wanted so badly to pat her right pocket and feel her knife there against the front of her leg, but he would know.

"There's something you're not telling me," he said.

"You don't want to hear my shit story. My entire family is probably dead."

"Probably? So you did not see them die."

"I didn't say that."

"Yes, you did."

"What do you *care*?"

"Because I know you from somewhere."

She thought about the gun tucked into the back of his pants. She couldn't see it, but there was no way she'd forget it was there. And neither would he.

"You and I will not be okay until I know where I've seen you before," he said. "I can't for the life of me figure out why the *fuck* I can't place you, but you know. Don't you? I saw it written all over your face when you woke up this morning. You admitted to everyone that you got your memory back, and now that you remember, you can't even look at me."

She would have killed him the night he saw her face if he hadn't run out the back of that house. She must have looked horrendous then, and horrendously different, but he was going to figure it out eventually.

"I don't know, okay?" she said. He was right. She couldn't look at him. Not in the eye. "I don't remember everything."

"You're *lying.*" He grabbed her shoulders and pushed her against the wall.

She turned her head away from him.

"Don't," she whispered. "Please."

"I wouldn't care, Annie, if you weren't so obviously hell-bent on keeping it from me. Were you with those *people*? The ones who robbed me last week? I don't remember seeing you with them, but I must have. I must have. It's the only thing that makes any sense."

"No," she said. And she started to cry. She tried not to, but she couldn't help it.

And she realized at that moment that she had a decision to make. She'd have to do one of four things. She could continue to lie even though he knew she was lying and wait for him to resort to more extreme measures. She could scream and hope someone would help her, though Roland would probably put a stop to any of that. She could fight him, though the odds that she'd get her knife out and open in time were minuscule. Or she could tell him.

She decided to tell him.

S he did it this way: She said, "I need to show you something. It's not what you're expecting. And it's not what you're going to think when I first show you."

After a momentary pause, he said, "Okay."

"What I'm going to show you will answer your question," she said.

He looked intrigued now and a bit more at ease. Exactly what she wanted.

"But before I show you," she said, "I need you to understand that it's not what it looks like. Okay?"

"Okay."

He trusted her! She could tell. He looked at her in a way he hadn't before. You can tell when people trust you and when they don't. It's obvious. And Lane trusted her, at least at that moment.

She was going to show him something and he was going to lose his goddamn mind. Which was fine. As long as it bought her a couple of seconds.

"But I need you to promise me something," she said.

"Promise you *what*?"

"I need you to promise me that you understand in advance that what I'm about to show you is not what it looks like. So after you see it, you need to let me explain."

"Explain it to me first," he said.

"I can't. Because my explanation won't make a damn bit of sense if you haven't first seen it. So just watch and then listen. Okay?"

"Fine." He was a little more dubious now. That wasn't good. But she had a plan.

She positioned herself so Lane couldn't see her back in the mirror, then took off her shirt. The only clothing above her waist now was her bra.

"Annie," Lane said and turned his head. "That's not why I—"

"Shh. Remember what I said? It's not what you think."

"If you think—"

"That's not what this is."

She took a deep breath and rehearsed her next moves in her mind. She'd need at least three seconds and possibly more if her hands shook too much from the adrenaline. And her adrenaline levels were spiking. She could feel her heart beating faster and a warm rush in her throat.

She rehearsed it. Three seconds. She rehearsed it again. Three seconds. And then she did it.

She turned around.

Lane gasped when he saw the bite mark on her back.

Zero-point-five seconds.

She thrust her hand into her pocket and grasped Bobby's knife.

"Jesus Christ!" Lane said as his mind processed what he was seeing.

One second.

She pulled the knife out of her pocket with her right hand. She had her back to him so he could not see what she was doing.

She heard him back up against the far wall and slam into the paper-towel dispenser.

One-point-five seconds.

She grasped the dull edge of the folded blade with her left hand.

Lane gasped again. There was no doubt he knew exactly what he was looking at. Had he figured out yet where he'd seen her face?

Two seconds. She opened the blade with her left hand and pointed it straight out and away in her right.

Two-point-five seconds.

"You—" Lane said as if underwater or in slow motion.

She turned and faced him.

Three seconds.

His eyes widened slowly. At least it seemed to her like his eyes widened slowly. But they couldn't have widened too slowly because she sank the blade of her knife into his throat at three-point-five seconds.

CHAPTER NINE

Everyone in the store heard Lane shouting, but Parker reached the door first. Parker heard banging and scuffling. They were fighting in there. Good grief, did Annie attack *Lane*?

Kyle rushed to the door and turned the handle. Locked.

"Stay back!" Roland shouted from his post near the front. He had his pistol trained perfectly level at both Parker and Kyle. "Do not approach the door while Lane is inside."

Parker heard something that sounded like choking or gurgling.

"Annie!" Kyle said. "What's going on in there?"

Silence.

Parker stepped away from the bathroom door but did not take his eyes off Roland. The asshole was just waiting for an excuse to pull the trigger. "Kyle," Parker said. "Step back or Roland will shoot you."

Kyle took a couple of steps back. Roland seemed to relax, but only a little.

Then, "I'm fine." From Annie. "*We're* fine."

Nothing from Lane.

The hell?

Parker heard a rustle of clothing from the other side of the door, followed by some kind of thump on the floor. He could barely hear what Annie said next. She practically whispered it. "Where's Roland?"

Kyle and Parker traded glances.

Roland was still guarding the front, but Parker wanted to know where Hughes was. He looked around the store. Didn't see him. He assumed Hughes was also hidden from Roland. Carol, he knew, was hunkering down in the cooler.

Why did Annie want to know where Roland was? And what the hell's up with Lane?

Roland, up at the front, had even less of an idea what was happening.

He didn't dare leave the front wide open.

Annie asked again, in a voice slightly louder this time: "Where's Roland?"

"Usual place?" Kyle said. "By the front door." He was no less baffled than Parker.

The bathroom lock clicked again, and in a single swift motion a blood-soaked Annie stepped out into the hall with a *gun* (!) in her hand and fired a shot straight toward the front where Roland was standing.

She missed and Roland dove for cover behind checkout lane number one.

"The fuck!" he shouted.

Parker also dove out of her way. That was the last goddamn thing he expected.

Kyle hit the deck next to Parker. Carol screamed from inside the cooler. Hughes and Frank came running from the direction of what used to be the vegetable aisle.

Annie stood over Parker now and faced the front door where Roland had just been a few seconds ago. She had blood all over her shirt.

"Come on, you sonofabitch!" she shouted.

Holy shit, was Parker impressed. Annie actually had Lane's gun in her hand. And presumably that was his blood. What happened in there?

"Jesus, Annie, give me that gun," Kyle said.

"No," Parker said. "Give *me* the gun. Annie!"

"What did you do to Lane!" Roland shouted from his hiding place.

Hughes and Frank stepped past Annie and into the bathroom. "Jesus," Frank said when he went inside.

"Lane's dead, bro," Hughes called out in his baritone voice. "Best give it up."

Roland gasped and said, "What did you *do*?"

"He's real dead," Frank said. "Jesus, Annie."

Roland popped his hand up and fired a blind shot from behind the checkout lane. His shot went wild and exploded into the potato-chip rack, tearing holes through at least three bags of BBQ Lay's.

"Roland, bro, put the gun down and come out," Hughes said. "You're the last one left. Not much you can do. We'll go easy. We know you weren't in charge."

Roland fired another blind shot. This one went high into the ceiling.

Annie stayed right where she was. She didn't duck from either of Roland's two gunshots. Parker was impressed, but she was about to get herself killed if she didn't get the fuck down and behind some cover right now.

"Annie!" Kyle said. "Get down!"

"Hand me the gun, kiddo," Parker said, "and get in the cooler. I'll take care of Roland."

Parker was still on the floor. Roland couldn't hit him from there unless he stood up first, and Roland was not about to stand up. Annie looked down and made brief eye contact with Kyle. Parker thought she looked psychotic, all jumpy and twitchy and wild-eyed.

"Hand me the gun, sweetheart," Parker said, "and I'll finish this."

Hughes and Frank carefully peered out of the bathroom toward the front.

Annie sat on the floor, her legs splayed in front her, with a stunned look of amazement on her face. She looked right at Parker and did not seem to recognize him.

He snatched the gun from her hands. She didn't resist. Parker wasn't sure she even noticed.

"Kyle," he said. "Get her in the cooler."

Kyle rose, took Annie's hand, and led her away.

Roland stood up in front, fired three wild shots toward the back, flung open the front door, and ran.

Damn, Parker thought. Now he'd have to go after him.

H ughes couldn't believe what he was looking at. Lane lay contorted on the bathroom floor in a lake of dark blood with a three-inch blade sticking out of his neck. Hughes fished around in Lane's pockets until he found the keys to the Chevy, then bolted into the main part of the store just in time to see Parker run out the front.

He faintly heard Parker yell "fucker" and less faintly heard the *pop-pop-pop* of pistol fire, but he knew Parker would miss. It's not that the man was a bad shot. He wasn't. But even a trained man can only aim a handgun accurately in a firefight from a dozen feet at the most. You try running after a guy and hitting him at a distance of more than 100 feet. You can't. Neither could Parker.

So Hughes jogged outside, unlocked the truck, and took out the scoped M-4 rifle from behind the driver's seat. Parker was 100 feet down the street now, and Roland was even farther ahead because Parker had stopped to reload.

But Roland was running away in a straight line. He must have figured he was in the clear since Parker had emptied his weapon. Hughes could hit him through the scope at 300 yards, though, no problem. He might miss once or twice if Roland ran sideways or in a zigzag, but Roland ran so straight he may as well have stood still.

Hughes steadied the rifle barrel on the top of the Chevy's open driver's-side door, glassed Roland through the scope, aimed just over his head to account for the slight drop in the bullet's arc at that distance, held his breath, and fired between heartbeats.

The rifle shot *cracked* loud enough to shatter the world and came echoing back from every direction.

Roland was still running, and he seemed to be running faster.

Hughes considered starting the truck and chasing Roland down, but the asshole might dart into a building and make things a whole lot more complicated, so he aimed again through the scope, glassed his target, held his breath, steadied his hands, and squeezed the trigger.

The rifle shot *cracked* again, and Roland dropped like someone had flipped off his switch. The sound echoed back even after Roland had fallen.

Parker stood bent over with his hands on his knees, gasping for air. Hughes saw him nod in satisfaction.

"You got him," Kyle said. He and Frank stood just outside the front door and squinted off in the distance. Hughes didn't know how long they'd been there.

"I got him," Hughes said.

But something seemed to be troubling Parker. Hughes could even see that from a distance. Roland wasn't dead yet. He was moaning and crawling away on his stomach. So Parker started walking toward Roland with his pistol in hand, and he took his damn time about it. Parker was going to enjoy this. He seemed to want to savor the buildup. He stopped when he reached Roland's prone form. Roland stopped crawling. Hughes heard a small whimper, followed by a sharp *pop*.

"Well," Frank said.

Nobody else said a word.

Then Hughes saw Parker cock his head to the right and stand up straight. Parker was far away, and Hughes couldn't be sure he was reading the body language correctly, but Parker looked nervous.

"Frank," Hughes said. "Get the shotgun out of the truck and take it into the store."

Then he heard it. The sound was faint at first, like a faraway ball game. Hughes could just barely hear it at the edge of his perception.

Then Parker started running back toward him like hell.

"Uh-oh," Frank said.

"We need to get inside," Kyle said. "Now."

"Help me with these guns," Hughes said as he reached into the truck across the seat and opened the passenger door. There was a whole mess of handguns and a few half-full boxes of ammunition in the cab behind the seat.

Hughes tucked the rifle under his arm and grabbed two of the handguns. Kyle grabbed two more and handed them to Frank, then took the last two for himself.

The noise was a little bit louder now. Hughes clearly heard feet on pavement, but he still couldn't see them. They were coming up one of the side streets.

Parker was getting close and waving his arms toward the store. "Get inside, get inside!" he yelled. "They're coming!"

Hughes shut the Chevy's doors. "Y'all get inside," he said. "I'll pick 'em off with the rifle."

Parker arrived, but he didn't stop or even slow down. Just ran into the store full-tilt and practically knocked Kyle over. Frank and Kyle followed him in.

Hughes stood there and waited. He might be able to pick off ten or so before he'd have to barricade himself inside the store with the others. He might even be able to pick all of them off. He didn't see anything coming yet, but he sure could hear them.

While he stood there and waited, the sound kept getting louder. There were more of them than he realized. His bowels turned to liquid. Only a huge number of people—or things—could make that much noise. He needed to get inside—now—before they rounded the corner and saw him. So he backed up toward the doorway and almost made it inside when a horde burst around a corner six long suburban blocks down. There were dozens of them.

No. Not dozens.

Hundreds.

They screamed in unison when they saw him, their screams like the war cries of an army.

CHAPTER TEN

Kyle ran to Annie while Parker and Hughes slammed the door brace in place. Annie still sat in shock on the floor, drenched in Lane's blood.

"Annie," Kyle said and squatted so he could face her at eye level. She stared at an empty point in space over his shoulder.

"Annie!"

She snapped to alertness.

The roar of footsteps and screaming grew louder. Jesus, how many of those things were *out* there? They must have seen Hughes dart in the through the front door before closing it.

Annie heard them now. She turned her head in the direction of the noise and managed to look even more panicked and crazed than she had just a few moments earlier.

"They're coming," she said. "They found us."

"They found us," Kyle said and nodded. He had a pistol in each hand. He tucked one into his belt and offered his free hand to Annie. "Come on. Get up." She took his hand. He pulled her up. "We all need to man the defenses."

Everybody but Carol.

The screams outside reached a deafening crescendo as bodies slammed into the side of the building, shattering glass and shuddering the foundation.

"Fuck me," Frank said.

Carol shrieked, loud enough to make herself heard over the screams of those things and their pounding and shattering.

Hughes, M-4 rifle in hand, took a knee in front of the door and aimed the barrel straight at its center in case the horde busted through.

Annie looked frozen, either lost in thought or going catatonic. Kyle couldn't be sure.

"Annie," he said. She shifted her gaze toward the front door, but otherwise remained frozen. The shattering changed to pounding now that most of the glass was out of the way, the sound like 10,000 hammers battering the boards they'd nailed up.

"Annie!" Kyle said. She startled and looked at him, her eyes finally focusing. "Can you shoot? Can I give you this gun?" He offered her his spare weapon.

She nodded. "Yeah," she said and took it. "I'm sorry, I'm just—"

"Later," he said.

Kyle watched Parker climb onto the counter in one of the checkout aisles and crane his neck upward to try to see out through the gap at the top of the boards.

"I can't see them from here," he shouted over the din. "So we can't shoot them from here."

They should have cut gun slots in the plywood. Jesus, why hadn't anyone thought of that?

"Isn't there a ladder in back?" Kyle shouted to Hughes.

Indeed there was, and Frank ran toward the back of the store.

The screams from the horde outside were lessening somewhat, but the banging, kicking, and scratching picked up. The plywood sheets couldn't withstand that forever. If those things weren't dealt with, *stat,* they'd burst in. Kyle was now glad that Lane's boys had blocked the back door with a Dumpster.

Frank arrived with the ladder. It was a six-foot stepladder, the fold-out kind with a warning on the third step that you're not supposed to stand any higher. But Kyle had to climb up and stand on the top to see over the lip of the plywood. And what he saw out there was unspeakable.

Hundreds of them swarming outside. Everywhere they banged and kicked the plywood. Some closest to the store were being smashed against the boards by the others behind them. They hadn't done much damage yet except to the glass, but the pressure of so many bodies surging forward would be enough to break through eventually.

Parker wanted to see, too, so Kyle stepped off and Parker climbed up.

"Sweet mother of Jesus," Parker said.

Yeah, Kyle thought.

One of those things must have looked up and seen Parker. It screamed and alerted the others, so the sickening war cries resumed. They didn't even sound human anymore. More like a pack of vicious animals. The roar had to be heard to be believed.

Parker used the barrel of his pistol to knock out the remaining pieces of glass at the top of the windows. Then he awkwardly aimed his gun downward—the angle was too high for him to look down the sights— and fired into the crowd. The mob outside shrieked—in anger, shock, hatred, alarm, or what, Kyle had no idea. Whatever those screams were about, the sound was extraordinary.

The store had only one ladder, but there was a magazine rack along one of the walls. Kyle dragged it screeching to the windows and knocked the magazines off the top row so he could stand up there without slipping. He climbed up and could just barely see over the top of the plywood.

He watched, transfixed, as Parker reloaded and fired into the horde. They screamed in pain when shot in the arms or the shoulder, gasped and went limp when shot in the torso, and switched off in an instant when shot in the head. Most of the wounded ones would bleed out eventually, but in the meantime they kept coming as if the pain didn't make the least bit of difference.

It was a gruesome business. Kyle still hadn't gotten used to killing those things or watching someone else kill them. They looked and acted like creatures out of a horror movie, but they *were* still technically human.

Parker's gun was empty. He patted his pockets, but he had no more magazines.

"You want to *help* me here, Kyle?" he said.

"Shit," Kyle said and snapped to it. "Sorry."

"Give me that gun," Parker said. "And go get some cartridges for this empty."

They traded guns and Kyle hopped down onto the floor. He held Parker's empty. Parker fired more shots and Kyle heard more screams.

"Shoot at the ones nearest the windows!" Kyle said, but he wasn't sure Parker could hear him.

Hughes kept the boxes of ammo next to him at his feet. He was still crouched near the front door ready and willing to blast away if the horde came inside.

"Take half those boxes," Hughes said. He didn't turn to look at Kyle, but sensed Kyle's presence and needs. "Shoot as many as you can from up there, but don't use up all of our cartridges. We'll need 'em if those things get inside."

There were six boxes of ammunition. Four for the handguns, a box of shells for Hughes' shotgun, and another box for the rifle. None of the boxes were full.

"How much do we have here?" Kyle said and opened one of the boxes. Only a few dozen rounds were inside.

"About 200 cartridges," Hughes said, "plus a dozen or so for the shotgun. Take two boxes for yourself and Parker and give the shells to Frank. Do what you can."

Where *was* Frank? Annie had taken Kyle's place on the magazine rack and was firing her weapon, but he didn't see Frank.

Hughes seemed to sense his confusion. "Frank's in back," he said. "Doing what I'm doing. Guarding the other door in case they get in."

Those things were not going to come in the back, not with the Dumpster blocking the way. Unless they thought to move it. Could they do that?

Kyle ran to the back and handed the box of shotgun shells to Frank.

Frank wasn't crouched in a fighting position the way Hughes was. He just nervously stood there with Hughes' Mossberg in his hands. It was quieter back there. Those things hadn't seemed to notice the back door, but of course that could change at any moment.

"Thanks, man," Frank said. "Y'all better hope I won't need 'em."

Kyle ran back to the front of the store. God, the noise was horrendous.

Monsters were battering down their defenses. *Monsters.* Kyle didn't care anymore that technically they were sick people. Those things were without language, without remorse, without reason. They even appeared to move without thought, as if they were drawn to murder and biting and cannibalism the way falling rocks are drawn downward by gravity. They formed a relentless force that functioned as a single organism with multiple parts, like a giant bacteria colony made of human bodies gone savage, an army of malevolent meat driven by a higher—or lower—dark power. Lane and his boys were Buddhists compared with those things.

Kyle handed a box of ammunition to Parker, who reloaded and started firing again.

He climbed onto the magazine rack next to Annie and looked down. There was less movement below than before. Some of those things outside were dead. Others were dying. But the rest—the majority—kept surging forward.

"We don't have enough bullets," Kyle said.

"Shut up and shoot," Parker said.

Kyle ejected the magazine, opened a box of cartridges, palmed several rounds, and loaded his pistol. He took no pleasure from killing, not even from killing those things. He was defending himself and his friends. He was keeping Annie alive. But what if Annie got bitten and turned? Would he shoot her? He'd rather shoot himself than shoot Annie.

But if Parker got bitten …

"Kyle!" Parker said. "Shoot them! Shoot them *now* or we're going to die."

Kyle shot them. He emptied his pistol.

But the live ones kept pushing. The live ones kept kicking. The live ones kept pounding. The live ones kept screaming.

And the plywood sheet in front of the ladder snapped in half down the middle.

A nnie screamed as the wood burst inward. Bloody hands reached through a ripped seam and grasped Parker's ankles. He tried to kick the hands loose and back away at the same time, but he had nowhere to go. He fell backward and pinwheeled off the ladder and onto the floor. Kyle hopped off the magazine rack to help him up.

Annie was alone up there now.

"Bring me a crowbar!" she shouted.

Kyle helped Parker up, then grabbed two crowbars, one for himself and one for her.

She and Kyle swung at the hands reaching through the seam while Parker pulled himself together. Annie swung in wide arcs, shattering wrists and forearms and even severing a couple of fingers. She heard howls of pain every time iron struck meat. The mass of the infected pushing inward from outside was relentless. The ripped seam wasn't large enough for them to get through just yet, but it would be soon enough.

Parker pushed her aside and fired through the gap, trying to aim for the head.

Some of them died.

Most of them screamed.

The live ones behind the dead ones kept pushing. They were pushing the corpses of the dead ones through the gap.

"Hughes!" Parker shouted over the din. "We need you over here!"

Hughes left his post near the front door and brought his rifle.

"Shoot the ones in the back," Parker said. "They're pushing the dead ones through the hole."

"We may have to join Carol in the cooler," Kyle said.

"We're dead if we go in there," Parker said. "We'd never get out. Not with this many out here. We stand here and beat them or die."

Another sheet of plywood cracked down the middle. Annie panicked and stepped back.

But then something strange happened. It was like a switch got flipped in her head. Another hole was about to get punched in their fortress, and it was her job to guard it while the others protected the first one. She felt determination wash over her, but her determination wasn't quiet or steady or calm. It was ferocious.

She would happily beat every single one of those things to death with her crowbar.

Fingers appeared in the ripped seam and pushed outward. She smashed them. No harder than stepping on bugs.

The seam opened wider. An infected woman's face appeared. Her hair must have been blond before it became matted with gore, her nose a little bit pointed, her ears slightly elfin. Her cheeks were covered with months of grime and filth. Her blue eyes were so full of primitive hatred, they could have been red.

Annie drove the sharp end of her crowbar straight that face as if she were driving a stake into the ground. She broke through the skull and killed the diseased woman instantly, and it felt exhilarating.

What was this? She was in the fight of her life, but she still had enough flickering self-awareness that she was appalled by her reaction. She had just killed a woman—granted, a disease-ridden hyper-violent juggernaut woman—and she felt exhilarated?

She destroyed another human being's face with a crowbar, and she felt exhilarated?

She tried to imagine how much a steel bar smashing her lips, teeth, and nose would hurt. She couldn't. It was beyond comprehension.

But *did* she just kill a human? Really? She knew what those things were thinking. Everything that once made them human had been stripped away, leaving only muscle and bone and distorted primitive brain function. They hated her and thought she was food.

More faces and arms appeared. Annie smashed every single one of them, and she felt delirious.

Only then did she notice the stench. They reeked of body odor, rotten meat, and shit. She swung again and caved in another one's skull.

Her killing bar glistened with blood, black fluid, and pieces of bone.

Killing Lane was hard, but this was easy. It was easy and it was *satisfying.*

She hated the infected. Hated them with a passion she hadn't felt since … *hungry hungry predator* … since she was one of them.

Hughes pushed the dead things back through the hole with all his strength while Frank dragged up a spare sheet of plywood from the back of the store. This one was uncut, bigger than those they had already used. It would easily overlap with the adjacent boards so they could hammer it in.

"Nails!" Hughes shouted. "And a hammer!"

Frank retrieved a box of nails and a hammer. Hughes used his massive bulk to hold the new sheet of plywood in place while Parker drove in the nails.

Twelve or so feet to his left, Annie swung her crowbar like a maniac as a second wave of those things tried to push their way in. There were nothing but dead ones at the other, smaller opening, but he knew if the live ones pushed hard enough they could knock that entire sheet of split wood out of the window, and there'd be no way Annie could stop them.

"More wood!" Hughes yelled at Frank. "We have to patch up the other one!"

The new sheet was in place and he felt no resistance now, so Hughes could help Annie. But how much more wood did they have in the back? One sheet? Two? And did they have enough nails?

Hughes picked up his rifle and joined Annie. Mutilated heads and arms protruded through the seam.

"Jesus, girl," Hughes said.

He stuck the barrel of his rifle through the slit between an arm and a bashed-in head and pulled the trigger repeatedly.

Screams from outside. More of those things were going down. Soon there'd be nothing but dead ones outside if they had enough ammunition, but they didn't. The best he could do was thin their numbers for now.

Another sheet of plywood on the north side of the store split down the middle.

"Shit," Frank said.

They weren't going to make it.

"Where's Carol?" Kyle said.

"Hiding in the cooler and useless," Parker said as he ran, hammer in hand, to the north side of the store.

"She might have the right idea, guys," Frank said.

"Get another sheet of wood over here!" Hughes said. He and Annie wouldn't be able to hold the gap very much longer.

"How much ammo do we have left?" Kyle said.

Hughes paused and took stock.

"We've gone through most of it," he said. "We're running out and we haven't even killed half of them."

He exchanged glances with Annie. The look on her face. Jesus. She was ready to eat those things alive if she had to. That girl was a killer. But there were just too damned many of them.

Frank returned from the back with another sheet of plywood.

"Put it down," Hughes said.

"Put it down?" Frank said.

"Put it down," Hughes said. "And go get the gas cans."

They had three large cans left over from torching the car lot down the street. Hughes had saved them for the Chevy's tank. He never expected to use them for more arson. He certainly didn't expect to use them to burn down the store, but what else could they do? Their fortress was falling.

He climbed onto the magazine rack and emptied one of the cans over the lip of the plywood barriers. Annie took another, unscrewed the cap, and started flinging the stuff through the second seam, the one crammed with dead things. Parker took the third can and splashed a little gasoline through the seam on the north side of the store, but the seam was so small, he couldn't get much through it, and he dribbled fuel onto the floor and onto his shoes.

The others weren't getting much gasoline on the horde outside, but

Hughes was. He poured it right over the top and doused dozens of them, but some of it spilled on the inside. Some of it got on the plywood. Some of it got on the floor.

Some of it ran down his arms.

He rushed to the sink to wash it off, but the water pressure had finally given out. The tap was dry.

He reeked of fuel. He'd get torched if he didn't wash himself off, so he ran to the now-warm refrigerator and dumped several bottles of Evian on himself.

Kyle and Frank dragged the magazine rack to the north side of the store near the third seam. No gas at all had gotten outside the store over there. The horde was still active, still banging on and surging against the boards. They'd break through any minute.

Kyle and Hughes climbed onto the magazine rack and poured gasoline over the lip while the things outside screamed in unspeakable fury. They were stupid and murderous and relentlessly single-minded, but Hughes wondered if on some level they knew what was going to happen. They still knew what gas smelled like, didn't they?

Hughes' shirt was so drenched with the stuff, he didn't dare fire a weapon. He'd ignite himself instantly. So he pulled the shirt over his head and tossed it on the floor. Then he thought for a second and picked it back up again.

He could light the shirt on fire and throw it onto the horde. Much more effective than using matches. He stood there, now shirtless and ready for war, and said, "Get Carol. We leave in two minutes."

Parker banged on the cooler door. "Carol!" He banged again, a little harder this time. "We're leaving!"

"I'm not going out there!" Carol said, her voice muffled.

The store reeked of gasoline. The horde outside screamed. Another sheet of plywood ripped and started to split.

"We're setting them on fire and running out to the truck. If you stay here, you'll die."

The door opened. Her tear-streaked face appeared.

"You're setting them on fire?" she said and flinched from the sheer volume of sound in the main part of the store. Shrieks and banging and pounding and wet sounds of thwacking followed another awful crack of splitting wood.

"We're going," Parker said. He grabbed her hand and yanked her out. "Now."

"Parker!" Hughes said and ripped his gasoline-soaked shirt in two. "Take this." He handed Parker half the shirt and a book of matches. "You get the north side. I'll get the west side."

Annie—blood- and gore-soaked all over again—took Carol's hand. "Come with me, honey," she said.

Parker climbed onto the ladder on the north side of the store, gas rag in hand. Frank and Kyle, each with a pack of supplies strapped to their backs, stood ready at the door with guns in their hands.

Wait, Parker thought. What was the plan exactly?

"Hold on," Parker said. "Are we running out the door right after we light them on fire?"

"We let them burn as long as we can," Hughes said. "But we don't have much time."

Parker set his fuel-soaked rag on the ladder's top step. He peeled a match out of the pack and swiped it, but it didn't light. He swiped it again, and this time it sizzled and popped into flame. He touched it to his ripped half of the shirt, and with a whoosh it was ablaze.

He heard an even louder whooshing sound from Hughes' direction, following by shrieks from the horde. They were burning.

Parker picked up the burning shirt and pitched it over the gap.

Flames erupted outside the store. Parker felt the heat on his face.

He also felt heat on his back.

The western side of the store was on fire. The *inside* of the store was on fire. The spilled gas had ignited and would burn right through the plywood. And when the fire spread to the ceiling, their sanctuary would turn into a death trap.

The air filled with smoke.

"Are they burning?" Frank shouted.

"They're burning," Hughes said. "We're going to burn too if we don't get out of here."

"We're going to have to run through them," Parker said.

Carol looked like a cornered prey animal.

The flames licked the ceiling now, and the whole western side of the store was on fire. Those things would be able to bust through at any second.

"We open the door," Hughes said, "and run for the truck. Jump in back. Don't bother with the passenger door. That will just slow us down. I'll drive."

Parker gripped the crowbar like it was a handhold on the edge of a cliff.

"Okay," Hughes said. "Let's do it."

Frank unlocked and opened the door.

They ran. Parker and Hughes took the lead.

At first Parker thought they might be okay. At least half of those things were on fire. Some were already dead, either from fire or gunshots. Most of those left alive were still heaving themselves onto the walls of the store even though the walls of the store were on fire.

Not one of them noticed that the people they wanted to kill had just run out the door and were on their way to the truck.

Not at first, anyway.

Some of the infected on the fringe seemed dazed and disoriented by the flames. They had lost focus and were shifting around aimlessly in random directions. A sickening stench of coppery blood, burnt hair, charred meat, and rot made Parker want to throw up, but he breathed through his mouth and ran for the truck.

But first one and then another spotted him. They screamed.

And they screamed in a certain way, different from those screaming from pain and from rage. This sound, a more urgent one, was a sound

Parker understood perfectly. It said, *I see them.*

Others turned.

"Go!" Hughes said. "Don't stop!"

The Chevy was thirty feet ahead. A half-dozen of those things stood in their way.

Parker opened fire. He did his best to shoot at their center of mass, but he didn't aim down the sights. No time. He just fired and hit maybe two of them, and then he was empty.

Hughes opened fire and took out some more.

But there were still at least two dozen left who hadn't been burned, maimed, or shot. And they were charging from both sides and converged like a vise made of meat, hands, and teeth.

Parker's gun was empty, so he jumped in the back of the truck. Kyle and Annie took up the rear. Each had a crowbar. They swung in wild arcs, breaking hands, arms, and skulls. Frank swung at one with his hammer, but he swung too early and missed.

Hughes was out front ahead of everyone, including the horde. He took cover behind the truck and—*crack*—dropped one and then another with the rifle.

And then Carol screamed. One of those things grabbed her.

Hughes pointed his rifle at it, but he didn't have a clear shot. He might hit Carol.

Frank swung his hammer and hit the thing in its back and probably caved in its spine, but it was too late.

It had already sunk in its teeth.

CHAPTER ELEVEN

Annie spun around when she heard the scream. One of the infected had thrown itself onto Carol and she went down. The infected bit right into her shoulder.

Carol screamed again. For a brief and terrible second, she sounded like one of them.

Which was perhaps fitting because that's exactly what Carol was about to turn into.

The one that bit Carol was a man. He had short brown hair and a long mustache. No beard. That meant he had turned recently, and he had kept up appearances by shaving before he was bitten.

And now he was biting Carol.

Frank broke his back with a hammer. He released Carol from his jaws and rolled onto his broken back, his face turned up at the sky and contorted in agony.

More were coming. Hughes shot one clean through the head with his rifle. Kyle swung his crowbar and broke one of their arms. Annie swung her crowbar and hit one in the ear. It went down instantly.

Frank hit one right in the nose with his hammer.

Hughes shot another one through the chest.

They were almost finished. Only a handful remained.

They'd make it. They'd be okay.

Everyone except Carol.

Annie swung her crowbar at one of the last three remaining—this one also a man—but she swung too early. Her blow connected with nothing. She felt her shoulder go out.

And he was upon her.

He knocked her right over and onto her back. She damn near cracked her own skull open on the pavement. He was right on top of her, his mouth open wide and baring his teeth as if they were fangs.

"Annie!" Kyle shouted.

And then something happened. Something she did not expect, something she did not intend, something she did not even think about. It just happened. As if someone or something else was in control of her body and mind.

She bared her own teeth and lunged for the infected man's throat.

The next two things happened at precisely the same instant. Kyle said, "Jesus Christ!" and Hughes put a round through the infected man's head.

He went limp and collapsed on top of her.

Kyle pulled him off.

Hughes came running, rifle in hand. "Jesus, girl. Did you try to *bite* that thing?"

She had indeed tried to bite him.

Annie watched as Hughes and Kyle set Carol down in the flatbed. Everyone else piled in after, except Frank, who climbed into the passenger seat. He said he did it so Hughes wouldn't have to sit up front by himself, but Annie assumed Frank just didn't want to ride next to Carol. He looked at her like she was leaking virus, which wasn't far from the truth.

Annie didn't worry about that at all. It wouldn't matter if she recontracted the virus. Her body knew how to fight it, so she sat next to Carol and held the poor woman's hand and didn't care if the others thought she was reckless.

Hughes started the engine. "We're just going a couple of blocks down the street for right now," he said as he lightly stepped on the accelerator.

"Finally," Parker said as they started to move, "we're clear." Then he punched Kyle hard in the mouth.

He shouldn't have done it. He knew he shouldn't have done it, and he regretted it instantly, but goddamnit Kyle had to be the dumbest person he'd met since all this shit started.

"Parker!" Annie said.

"The fuck was that for?" Kyle said and wiped his mouth.

Frank turned around in the passenger seat.

"S'going on back there?" Hughes said from the front.

Parker ignored everybody but Kyle. "You know damn well what that was for."

Kyle pulled his hand away from his mouth and licked blood off his lips. "What's to stop me from bashing your head in with this crowbar right now?" Kyle said, his face twisted.

Parker pointed his gun at him. He wasn't going to shoot Kyle, and the weapon was empty anyway, but he wasn't going to just sit there and take a death threat over a punch in the mouth.

"For God's sake, you guys!" Annie said.

Parker lowered his gun. Kyle lowered his eyes.

"You damn near got us all killed back there," Parker said. "You *did* get Carol here killed."

"All right!" Annie said.

Carol groaned.

Parker knew he should have apologized, to Carol as well as to Kyle, and he should have done so at once, but he didn't.

"I got Lane and his boys to stand down when they were ready to throw us all out," Kyle said in his whiny little voice. "And I'm about to take us to an island where we'll be safe and where we can start over."

"You disarmed me," Parker said, "when I stood our ground against Lane. And you refused to kill Roland or Robby or whatever the fuck his name was when you had the chance."

"Okay!" Annie said. "Can you guys do this later? Right now we need to take care of Carol."

Hughes slowed the truck. Parker hadn't paid the slightest bit of attention to where they were or where they were going. They'd stopped in the middle of an intersection. On one corner was a mini-mart, on another an ex–Chinese restaurant with its windows smashed in. Two gas stations took up the other corners.

"We stopping for gas?" Parker said.

"We're stopping for Carol," Hughes said. He turned off the engine and stepped out of the truck.

A hush fell over the world. All Parker could hear was a slight breeze in his ears and a ticking sound from the engine. The air smelled decent and fresh. Nothing dead was anywhere near them.

Hughes put his hands on his hips and stared hard at Parker. "You guys want to go at each other later, that's fine, but right now you save it. Frank, we have any water?"

Frank hopped out of the front and unzipped one of the backpacks. "Just gear in this one. But, hey, we still have the night vision."

Thank heaven for small mercies, Parker thought to himself. He didn't care about Carol. Not really. He knew he should. He just didn't. She'd been a burden all along and would have continued being a burden if she hadn't been bitten. He felt a small twinge of sympathy for what she was going through, but he wouldn't miss her. Not really.

He would have felt differently about it a month ago. Hell, he'd have felt differently about it two weeks ago. He didn't know if the old Parker or the new Parker had it right. The old Parker was more humane, but the new Parker would last longer.

Frank fished a bottle of water out of the backpack and set it down next to Carol.

Annie held Carol's hand and stroked her forehead. The girl was reckless.

"Careful," Parker said.

"Shut up," Annie said. She wouldn't look at him.

She'd have to vigorously wash her hands with soap and hot water, and where would she find any hot water? Parker made a mental note not to touch her until she was clean. Not that he had any intention of touching her. He could only imagine her reaction, especially if he touched her right now.

"So what do we do?" Kyle said and wiped his mouth again. He wasn't bleeding much. Parker hadn't hit him that hard.

"Let's just sit here a while," Annie said. She stroked Carol's face with one hand and held Carol's hand with the other.

"I'm sorry," Parker said to Carol. "About what I said a minute ago." It was true that Kyle had gotten her killed, but he shouldn't have said it out loud. She wasn't dead yet.

Kyle glared at him. He wasn't getting his apology. Not now, anyway. Probably not later, either.

"It's okay," Carol said. She sounded weaker already. Maybe she was just tired or resigned or numb with shock over what happened.

"How you holding up?" Parker said.

God, what a stupid fucking question that was.

Annie glared at him.

"I'm sorry—"

"Just shut up," Annie said. "Go walk around the truck or something."

He sort of liked Annie. She was a tough kid, and she wasn't stupid. He'd need to behave a bit better now that she was around. He didn't care if Kyle hated his guts, but he didn't want any more rebukes from Annie.

How long would they have to sit there in the middle of the intersection, though? Were they just going to wait for Carol to die—or to *turn*?

No one seemed to have any idea how long they'd be there or what exactly they were supposed to be doing. Carol obviously wasn't coming with them on the boat. And how were they supposed to get to a boat, anyway? They couldn't drive to Olympia with the roads so packed with cars. Parker wasn't even convinced that they should go to Olympia. Thousands of those things would be hunting in a city that size. There had to be a smaller marina on Puget Sound somewhere.

"Is there anything I can do?" Kyle said.

Parker should have been the one to say that. Annie would have been impressed.

"You can open that bottle of water," Annie said.

Kyle twisted the cap off the bottle of water and handed it to her.

Carol moaned and reached toward her shoulder where she'd been bitten. Her shirt was soaked with blood, but the bleeding seemed to be slowing. It wasn't pooling underneath her.

"Don't touch it," Annie said. "You'll just make it worse."

She'd also risk spreading the infection to everyone else if she got blood all over her hands, but Parker didn't say anything. They were all covered in blood splatters anyway.

"Don't wait for me," Carol said. "Just set me down on the sidewalk."

"The hell we will," Hughes said.

"Shh," Annie said. "We aren't going to do that to you."

"You need to get to that island," Carol said and tried to sit up. "It will be dark soon and you should get going. It isn't safe here."

"We're going to wait," Kyle said.

It took everything Parker had to keep quiet. Carol was right. It would be dark in a couple of hours. Then what? Were they supposed to sit out there exposed as the sun went down while she lay there in pain? Someone should put the poor woman out of her misery.

He supposed the humane thing would be to wait for her to pass out. Everyone passes out for an hour or so before turning. She wouldn't feel a thing when they put her down.

Or *was* that the humane thing to do? They were all risking their lives just sitting there in the intersection. And for what? So Carol wouldn't be awake when somebody put a round through her head? She'd die instantly. She wouldn't feel anything. Instead she had to lie there in agony while knowing she was about to turn into one of those things. Who wanted to spend their last hours that way?

Parker sure as hell didn't. Once this was all over, he'd make damn sure to tell everyone to shoot him dead on the spot if one of those things ever bites him. Kyle, at least, would gleefully take him up on that offer.

"It doesn't hurt anymore," Carol said woozily. She was fading. Good. Maybe they could get out of there.

Nobody said anything. The silence of the world was overwhelming. Parker thought he might hear a pinecone falling as far away as Idaho if somebody didn't say anything soon. He scratched his face. Kyle looked at him sideways as if he'd just belched in church. What was he supposed to do? His beard itched.

Annie kept stroking Carol's forehead. No one else moved or said anything. Frank looked as uncomfortable as Parker felt.

"I didn't want to live in this world anyway," Carol said. "I was just so afraid."

"You don't have to be afraid anymore," Annie said.

"I was silly for being so scared," Carol said. "It hurt for a couple of minutes, but now I'm okay."

No, she wasn't okay. She wasn't even remotely okay.

"You won't let me turn, will you?" she said. "I want to just go to sleep."

"We won't let you turn," Kyle said.

Parker wondered, Who was this *we* Kyle referred to? Somebody had to do the deed, and Parker couldn't see Kyle stepping up for the job.

"Can you not do it now, though?" Carol said. "Can you wait until my little coma?"

"We'll wait, honey," Annie said. "We'll wait."

"I'm sorry to ask you this, Carol," Hughes said. "But … how do you want us to do it?"

"What difference does it make?" Parker said. "She won't feel anything." God, did he actually say that?

"You," Kyle said, "are seriously an asshole."

Kyle could not believe Parker. Just couldn't believe him. The man was shaping up to be a serious problem. Hitting him in the mouth like that? What next? Would he punch Annie? Or Carol?

Maybe Parker would try punching Hughes. Kyle would love to see that.

In the meantime, they had to figure out how get to Olympia, or at least to a marina near the city where they could pick up a boat. Kyle still liked bicycles for the job. They could ride up there in one day, or even in one night if they used the night vision.

Parker was disgusting, but Annie was impressive. She had a wonderful bedside manner with Carol. Kyle thought she should have been in nursing school or even med school, but then he realized he didn't know that she wasn't. He had no idea what she was doing before.

Carol would probably be better off dead if it weren't for Annie, but the way Annie comforted her seemed to make everything okay. Kyle wouldn't mind dying like that, even if—especially if—he'd been bitten by one of those things.

"Thank you," Annie said to Carol.

"For what?" Carol said.

"For giving me comfort when I woke from those horrible nightmares. I'm glad I got to know you, Carol."

"Me, too, honey," Carol said and squeezed Annie's hand. Then she looked straight at Kyle. "Take care of her, Kyle."

Kyle swallowed hard. Carol singled him out to take care of Annie? A warm feeling bloomed in his chest.

But then Parker snorted.

Annie knew something was wrong with her. She was still Annie Starling, but she was no longer the same Annie Starling.

She still suffered some of the effects of the virus. Mother of God, she actually tried to bite one of the infected when it pinned her to the ground. Hughes saw it. *Kyle* saw it. They must have thought she was mad. And she supposed they were right.

The virus was out of her system. Her antibodies beat it back, but she seemed to have new neural pathways in her brain. It happens sometimes. Isn't that what post-traumatic stress disorder is? When something terrible happens to a person, it blazes new neural pathways.

Thoughts and feelings experienced during traumatic events come rushing back when triggered by something associated with the event—a car backfiring can trigger it for someone who was shot. Slipping into a bath can trigger it for someone who nearly drowned.

Neurons that fire together, wire together.

She'd snapped into a state of pure violence when she stabbed Lane in the throat and went after Roland.

It happened again when she beat a bunch of infected to death with her crowbar.

What if she actually did bite the one who had pinned her? Her companions would think she was out of her goddamn mind. They'd start counting down the hours until she went into a coma and had to be shot to death before a monster version of Annie Starling rose and tore them to bits.

Fighting seemed to be her trigger. She might spend the rest of her life having flashbacks and behaving … differently under stress.

She could never tell her companions. Never. They'd shun her.

Or worse.

But she did have an advantage, a secret and enormous advantage.

Unlike the others, she'd be okay if she got bitten again.

Hughes knew everyone expected him to do it. He didn't want to. Hell, nobody wanted to. Surely not even Parker. Parker wasn't a killer. He was just your garden-variety asshole.

Hughes wasn't a killer either, but they'd all look to him to take care of Carol once she slipped into her coma. It's not that he was their leader. The group had no leader. Nobody seemed to be up for it. But Hughes knew his way around guns as well or better than anyone else. He didn't panic. He could think straight in a crisis. The others listened when he barked orders.

No one would listen to Parker if he barked orders. Kyle thought he knew what was best, but he was too immature and naive. Too docile.

Frank was a natural follower. He'd shoot Carol if Hughes told him to, but Hughes wouldn't do that. Frank would be screwed up for life, and Frank was his friend, and Hughes couldn't do that to him.

Annie was far too sweet and kind-hearted.

That left Hughes by default. Doing the deed wouldn't mess him up for life. He was already as messed up as he could be, but he was messed up in just the right way. He couldn't feel anything anymore. He was always a little cold and could become a real hard-ass when necessary, but now he was practically heartless. It was the only way he could keep going.

So when Carol slipped out of consciousness, he drove the truck just past the outskirts of town and asked Frank to help him carry her to the tree line.

Hughes wasn't going to shoot her. They had to conserve ammunition, and they'd already brought enough attention to themselves and given away their location with the noise from the truck. But the biggest reason he didn't shoot her was because enough violence had been done to her body already. He sure as hell wasn't going to bash in her head. He may have become cold and heartless, but he was not a barbarian.

So he gently plugged her nose and covered her mouth. She didn't struggle. He released her a few minutes later and made sure she'd stopped breathing.

Everybody just stood there in silence and shock.

They didn't have a shovel to bury her with, so they pushed dirt and rocks and leaves and sticks onto her.

Everyone helped, even Parker.

Annie sobbed.

They stood around her in a circle when they were finished. Nobody said anything for a long time.

Finally, Annie spoke up. "She was the last innocent person."

Kyle swallowed hard. Frank looked disturbed. Parker didn't seem to know what to do with himself.

Hughes didn't feel anything. Come on, he thought. *Cry.* You saved this woman's life once and now you've just killed her. For fuck's sake, cry like a man.

A nnie later had a terrible thought. It all but seized her with panic. What if Carol had been immune too?

PART TWO

THE ISLAND

CHAPTER TWELVE

They parked the Chevy a half-mile from the bicycle shop and walked the rest of the way, bringing as many supplies as they could carry in their packs. Nothing and no one followed.

The shop's windows had been smashed in and the door left ajar. Somebody had taken some bikes, but dozens remained and they only needed five.

The air inside smelled okay. A little musty, but nothing had died in there recently.

Nobody carried a watch anymore, since day and night were the only times that mattered, but the sun was low in the sky so they knew they wouldn't be traveling. Not at that hour.

The bicycle shop seemed as good a place as any to hunker down and sleep. It wasn't more secure than anywhere else, but it had exits in the front and the back. They might be okay for one night as long as they didn't make noise.

They set five bicycles out front and five out back. If anyone heard anything coming, they could leave in either direction and ride away fast and hard back to the truck a half-mile away.

They slept in shifts and everybody slept dreamlessly. Everybody but Annie.

She found herself in her apartment that wasn't really her apartment sitting on a couch that wasn't really her couch. They were her dream apartment and dream couch. Her sister Jenny sat next to her.

She was infected.

Part of her cheek had been torn off to her jawline. It looked like she'd been bitten on the face. She had blood in her mouth and all over her arms. She even had blood in her hair.

Jenny spoke. Her voice did not match her appearance. She spoke casually as if she were chatting with Annie over breakfast and coffee.

"We're special, you know," Jenny said. "Both of us. Think about it. You know the reason."

Annie woke gasping on the floor and knew at once that she had to get to South Carolina immediately.

W"e need to get to a marina immediately." Kyle's voice. The first thing she heard when she woke up in the morning. She hadn't even opened her eyes yet.

Her back hurt. For a moment she thought she was still at the grocery store, but she opened her eyes and saw bicycle wheels hanging from the ceiling above her. She was in the bike shop now, free of Lane and his henchmen.

Carol was dead.

They were going to ride to Olympia, snag a boat, and sail north to an island, to safety.

But Annie had to get home.

"Before we head up there," Hughes said, "we need to get some more gear."

I need to get to South Carolina, Annie thought. But she didn't say it out loud. She could not tell the others.

They rode their bicycles back to the Chevy they'd parked a half-mile away, loaded them into the back, then drove to the outdoor store in the next town and loaded up three more backpacks with extra supplies. They grabbed fresh clothes, fresh socks, soap, water filters, flint fire starters, hunting knives, hatchets, rope, fishing tackle and poles, sleeping bags, maps and compasses, flashlights, batteries, four more first-aid kits, a couple more solar chargers, and the last two night-vision monocles.

They strapped the packs to their backs, ditched the Chevy, and rode hard toward Olympia.

Nothing and no one saw them, not even when they had to slow

down and weave around cars. Annie didn't understand how that was possible. Where were all the infected? Were they off in the woods? Were they dead? Dying? No, that couldn't be. They'd been attacked the day before by more than she'd ever seen at one time.

Maybe they were coalescing into bigger and bigger hordes.

That would be good and bad. The infected wouldn't be as widely dispersed, which meant she'd run into them less often, but if they were organizing themselves into larger and larger swarms, they'd eventually turn into armies. Pistols, crowbars, and shotguns would be useless. They'd have to be mowed down with machine guns. Or air strikes.

Annie and her companions took what appeared to be the least-traveled roads and weaved their bikes around the old world's detritus: shattered glass, abandoned cars, leaves, tree branches, and human skeletons with their bones picked thoroughly clean.

They didn't enter Olympia. They bypassed it entirely. It was too dangerous.

But her sister Jenny was in there. And Jenny might be immune. She and Annie were full sisters. At least one of their parents was also most likely immune.

Mom and Dad were definitely still back in South Carolina, but Jenny was probably gone. Most people who got bitten didn't turn. They were killed. The only people who turned were those who managed to flee to relative safety after getting bitten. Not many people could do that. One percent at the most.

Annie was lucky. Damn lucky.

And that must be why she and her friends could ride for miles without running into anyone, infected or not. Almost everybody was dead. The world was emptier now than it had been for thousands of years.

The chances that her sister was alive and well were catastrophically bad. Annie could not go into the city and look for her. The others wouldn't go with her, nor would they let her go alone. And how, exactly, would she explain herself? *Oh hey, guys, by the way, I got bitten, I turned, and I ate a few people, but I'm fine now and maybe my sister is too.*

That wasn't going to happen.

But since one or both of her parents were likely immune, and since the eastern United States knew what was coming long before it got there, Mom and Dad might both be okay.

How on earth, though, was she supposed to get to South Carolina?

They found a marina just west of Olympia. All they had to do was ride a couple of miles along Highway 101. She saw it off to the right not two minutes after she first saw the water.

It was a small private marina with just three sailboats, two recreational motorboats, and a weathered wooden dinghy tied to the dock.

A motorboat wasn't an option without ignition keys, so they had to take a sailboat whether they liked it or not. That was fine, though, actually, because as Kyle pointed out, sailboats are like bicycles. They don't need keys and they don't need gas.

Kyle said the largest one would be a bit harder to sail, but not excessively so, and in any case it would be more comfortable and provide better shelter and more room for storage. It occurred to Annie that the larger one would also be safer if the infected swam up to them and tried to climb on. The deck was several feet above the water, which should be enough.

She had no idea what kind of boat it was aside from being a sailboat. She found it surprisingly spacious, even luxurious, with not even an inch of space wasted. It had two bedrooms below the waterline—Kyle called them staterooms—and two foldout beds in the main room. Plenty of space for everyone to spread out.

She wouldn't mind living on a boat like this. It seemed to offer decent protection. And she could sleep in a bed!

It felt like years since she'd slept in a bed.

Parker claimed one of the staterooms for himself. No one argued because nobody wanted to share one with him.

But who was she going to share space with? Kyle was the obvious choice, which made him the wrong choice.

She didn't want to share space with anyone. As the group's only woman, she should have a room to herself. Parker was being a jerk for not seeing that. But only one person could have a room to themselves, since there were five and the boat only slept six.

"I'll sleep on one of the pullouts in the main room," she said.

It was that or share a bed with someone, and that wasn't going to happen.

"I'll share the bed with someone up front," Kyle said.

He could have taken the other foldout in the main room. What did it mean that he didn't? Maybe he didn't want to sleep near her. Maybe he didn't want her to know that he *did* want to sleep near her.

Neither Hughes nor Frank called the other pullout in the main room. The idea seemed to make them uncomfortable. Nobody wanted to say in front of the others that they wanted to sleep near the group's only woman.

How long would the gentlemanliness last?

She sat on the edge of the dock while the others unpacked and Kyle got the boat ready. How many bodies might be floating in it or sunk below the surface? She pushed the thought from her mind, slipped off her shoes and socks, and stuck her feet in. God, the water was cold. The Atlantic Ocean was so much warmer, especially in South Carolina and Florida. The waters of the Pacific felt to her southern skin like ice water. The water was so cold that she didn't worry for even a moment that a submerged infected might grab her ankle from below and pull in her in. No one could survive in that cold for long.

When the boat pushed off into the waters in the late afternoon, she sat on the deck and dangled her bare feet over the side while Hughes helped Kyle with the sails. The boat moved slowly and she figured they'd pick up speed after a while, but they didn't. She had never been on a sailboat before and had no idea they moved so slowly.

But now that she was on one, she didn't want to get off. All she could see, aside from the receding dock, was dark blue water, cloudy skies, and trees. She could almost pretend everything was okay, that the world hadn't fallen apart, that her sister was alive and well and hanging out on the balcony of her apartment in Olympia.

The smell of salt in the air took her right back to her childhood, to the warm sandy beaches where she used to run and play with her dog Andy. The cool wind on her face and her hands, the slush of blue water as the boat made its way forward, the tall spires of evergreen trees, and the Olympic mountain range in all its craggy magnificence—it was all so stunningly beautiful and serene.

"Kyle," she said. "I need to ask you for something."

"Sure," he said.

"It's huge," she said.

"Sure," he said again without hesitating.

"I mean it's really huge," she said.

He paused a moment. "What is it?"

"My sister lives in Olympia."

Kyle tensed up. He seemed to have an idea what she was going to ask him, but he didn't yet know it wasn't quite as bad as he was expecting.

"She did anyway," Annie said. "I mean, I'm not sure if she's ... you know. I realize we can't go in there and look for her, but I do need to ask you something."

He relaxed slightly.

"Can you pull up to the shore next to downtown," she said, "so I can call out her name?"

"Annie—"

"I know," she said. "I know. The odds are one in a thousand that she's still alive and even less that she'll hear me and run to the boat, but I'll hate myself for the rest of my life if I don't at least try."

He opened his mouth to say something else, then closed it again. He did not want to do it, but he understood and was considering it.

"Let me go below and check with the others," he said.

"You're the captain of this boat. You don't need permission from Hughes. You sure as hell don't need it from Parker. You know what Parker will say anyway."

He nodded.

"We have to sail past the city anyway, right?" she said.

"Actually, no," he said. "We have to sail north to get around this peninsula on our right, then we'd have to turn south again to get to Olympia. It's a bit out of our way." He paused and then added, "But only a bit."

"Can you give me like, half an hour?" she said. "And let me fire off one or two shots? We can stop hundreds of feet away from the shore. We can't get attacked."

He thought about that for a couple of moments.

"You realize," he said, "that if anyone is still alive in that city and hears you firing into the air, they're going to come running whether or not they're your sister. What if a hundred survivors show up at the beach and ask for a ride?"

That, she hadn't thought of.

"I suppose that could happen," she said. "You're the captain. You can make a decision. Tell them to get their own boat."

"And what if someone like Lane shows up on the beach and *demands* a ride?"

"She's my *sister*, Kyle. Do you have a sister? Or a brother?"

"I'm an only child."

"But if you did have a sister or brother, would you leave them to die without even trying?"

Of course he wouldn't. Not even Parker, the bastard, was that cold.

"Okay, Annie. For you, we can try. For your sister."

Kyle did not ask the others. He just told them what they were going to do.

Frank said, "Okay."

Hughes said nothing. He didn't look happy about it, but he said nothing. He must have lost somebody. Everyone lost somebody.

Parker groaned, then checked himself and likewise said nothing. So it turned out the man did have an editing function in his brain. He did know how to shut up at least once in a while.

When Kyle took the boat north around the narrow peninsula, Annie saw Olympia's port and low skyline a few miles away to the south. The city was dead, of course, or at least mostly dead, but it looked normal from a distance.

The wind picked up and a sound like a parachute opening in the sails drowned out the little waves lapping the sides of the boat.

Annie had the odd sensation that the boat wasn't moving, that it was stationary, that the waters of Puget Sound were slowly rolling beneath her as the shore slid by. She figured she could swim to the trees and walk into town in less than an hour.

It took almost as long to get there in the boat.

There wasn't much to see up close at first. Just some trees, a few scattered houses, and what looked like a park. The government buildings were still a ways off in the distance. She shuddered when she saw the dome of the capitol building. Such a grand piece of architecture. The most important decisions in Washington State had been made there for more than 100 years. Now it would slowly give way to wind, rain, and ruin. Even the governor was probably dead.

The inlet was narrow, just a half-mile wide at the most, but that still left plenty of clearance between themselves and the mainland. If any of the infected spotted the boat, they'd have to swim a good quarter-mile before even trying to board. They'd either get shot or whacked long before they succeeded.

Hughes stood watch on the deck with his rifle in his hands and squinted at the landscape like he was mad at it. Frank helped Kyle with the sails. Parker remained below.

Soon the port came into clear view. It was absolutely silent and still. She saw no movement of any kind, heard no traffic or heavy machinery operating. She sensed that nothing but fish, birds, insects, and small animals lived in any direction. Just beyond the port was Olympia's downtown. She sensed no life or movement coming from that direction, either. God, was Seattle like this too? It must be.

Only Seattle was bigger.

Much bigger. It must be swarming with the infected.

"Do you see anything?" Frank said to Hughes.

"Nothing," Hughes said, almost like he was disappointed.

"There must be a ton of those things in there somewhere," Frank said.

Annie twisted her face. *Those things.* She hated that term. They were people, human beings. Sick human beings, yes, but human beings all the same. They weren't demons. They weren't aliens. They had an alien-like pathogen in their system, but it could be beaten. Some people recovered. She had recovered. She couldn't be the only one. There's always some percentage of the population that's immune to even the worst kinds of viruses. Jenny could be immune too.

But what, realistically, were the odds that her sister hadn't been killed and that Annie would find her? Practically zero. She knew that. But she had to try, and she'd be forever grateful to Kyle for bringing her here.

The inlet narrowed considerably after they sailed past the port. Downtown was straight ahead. So was the end of Puget Sound. They were just a few hundred feet from the shore and couldn't sail any farther south if they wanted to.

Kyle lowered the sails and stopped offshore from a hotel and marina. "This is as far as we go. We're not dropping anchor because we may need to leave in a hurry."

Annie was shocked to see that the docks straight ahead were crowded with boats. Hadn't *anyone* fled by water? Did the infected take over the city that fast? No way would she find her sister.

Nothing stirred. The city was as silent as the deepest wilderness. Seeing a shattered little town off the interstate was one thing, but seeing a major city—and a state capital at that—in such a condition was something else.

She tasted acid in her mouth. She'd been kidding herself. Not about Jenny. She never actually thought she'd find Jenny. She'd been kidding herself about South Carolina. The East Coast couldn't survive if the West Coast was this desolate. The plague was an unstoppable planetwide biological hurricane.

"Jesus," Frank said.

"Yeah," Kyle said.

"Well," Annie said, "at least my voice is going to carry. I'm going to shout her name now. You ready?"

Hughes nodded. He was ready. And he was ready with his rifle.

"Can those things swim?" Frank said.

"No idea," Hughes said, "but I don't see why not. Question is, will they?"

"Okay," Annie said. "I'm going to call her."

But she was all of a sudden reluctant. The earth was so hauntingly quiet that her voice would carry for miles. Hundreds—no, *thousands*—of infected were going to hear her. The city was quiet, but it couldn't be empty.

She cupped her mouth with her hands, faced the government buildings, and shouted the name of her sister.

"Jenny! Jenny Starling! It's Annie!"

At first she heard nothing but water lapping the sides of the boat followed by a faint and distant echo, but then there was something else. She wasn't sure she actually heard anything. It was like the city's eyelids twitched open.

"Anybody hear anything?" Kyle said.

"I thought I heard something," Frank said, "but I don't know."

"If your sister can hear you calling," Hughes said, "you'll hear her answer."

Annie wasn't sure about that. "What if she's trapped somewhere? Maybe she can't call out."

Kyle put his hand on her shoulder. It didn't make her feel any better, but she appreciated the effort.

"Hughes," Kyle said. "Go ahead and fire a shot. Just one."

Hughes pointed the rifle at the sky. Annie plugged her ears with her fingers. Frank ducked just before Hughes squeezed the trigger.

The crack of the rifle echoed six or seven times off the sides of the buildings.

"That ought to get somebody's attention," Frank said and stood back upright.

It did.

The hotel sat a block back from the marina. Several of its windows were shattered. The front door was blackened by fire. Three human shapes shambled out of it. They didn't run, didn't yell, didn't make noises of any kind.

Annie squinted. Were they regular people? Hughes pointed his rifle in their direction and aimed down the sights.

They didn't look right, didn't walk right. Annie knew that shamble. Knew it well. They were looking for food and hadn't seen anything yet.

"Are they people?" Frank said.

"Don't think so," Hughes said.

"They look ... odd," Kyle said.

"How come they're not running?" Frank said.

"I'm not sure they've seen us," Kyle said.

"They're not people," Hughes said.

Annie bit her lip.

"I've never seen 'em so slow," Frank said.

"That's because they're always chasing your ass," Hughes said. "These haven't seen us."

"Yes, they have," Parker said. He had come up from below. "They see us. They're walking right toward us."

They were, indeed, walking right toward the boat, down the hotel steps and toward the marina. But still they weren't running, nor were they screaming. Annie knew why. They knew they couldn't get to the boat.

They stepped onto the dock.

"Jesus, they're coming right for us," Frank said.

"They can't get to us," Annie said.

"How do you know?" Frank said.

"They aren't running or screaming out to the others."

"You think that's why they scream?" Frank said. "They're alerting the others?"

She nodded.

"How do you know that?" Frank said.

"I just do."

"She's right," Kyle said. "It's obvious, isn't it? I mean, look at them. They're just coming out onto the dock to check us out. Fascinating."

The three figures lurched their way to the end of the dock and stopped. They stared across the water. At Annie.

She shuddered, but Kyle was right. It really was fascinating, as if she was looking at dangerous animals from a distance on a safari.

She was pretty sure two of the three on the dock were men. The third was smaller, perhaps a young woman or teenager. They were filthy and ragged. And twitchy. Annie remember that twitchiness. She didn't know what caused it, but she remembered it. She might even be able to imitate it if she had to.

She couldn't smell them from this distance, but they looked like they smelled bad. And they stood there at odd angles that didn't look comfortable. They didn't shift their weight or sit down. They just sort of stopped when they reached the end of the dock and stood in whatever position their bodies happened to be in when they ran out of boards.

They weren't going to jump in. She wasn't sure why, exactly, but she sensed she wouldn't have jumped in either when she had been infected. They appeared to be unthinking, but they weren't entirely. Their thoughts were deranged, but they did have thoughts. And they remembered certain things from before. She did, anyway, when she was infected. She'd remembered how basic physics worked. She wouldn't have been able to use tools, but she would not have jumped off a building. She would, however, have run into a hail of bullets if someone had shot at her.

Kyle looked at them with a rapt expression on his face. He tilted his head ever so slightly as if he were a curious child. "They sure are strange, aren't they?"

Yes, but Olympia wasn't a zoo. She hadn't come here to gawk. She came to look for Jenny.

"I'm going to call for my sister again," she said.

"Right," Kyle said. He had forgotten. "Hughes, can you spare one more round from your rifle?"

Annie heard something. It was the faintest possible sound, but it was there.

"Shh," Hughes said.

Then she saw first one figure and then several emerging from the downtown area and heading toward the marina.

Feet. She was hearing the sound of feet. Hundreds of feet. Thousands of feet. They had awakened the city.

She yelled again as loud as she could.

"Jenny! Jennifer Starling!"

The sick ones at the end of the dock made grunting and snuffling noises.

"More coming," Frank said. "Eight or nine of them from behind that crab restaurant."

"We can't stay here," Hughes said and tensed up.

Hughes didn't have to tell Annie that she wouldn't find Jenny. She knew. And she wasn't certain that none of the infected wouldn't try to swim to the boat. If hundreds gathered on the marina and so much as one screamed and jumped in the water, they might all pour in after. That's how they worked. Their screams didn't only mean *I see prey*. Their screams also meant *Follow me*.

"Yeah, I think we better get outta here," Frank said.

Annie nodded.

"I'm sorry, Annie," Kyle said.

She was not going to protest. And she was not going to cry. But she was also not going to say, "It's okay."

Kyle raised the sails and turned the boat north. The skyline and shoreline faded into the background. And when the inlet curved to the east, the city vanished forever.

CHAPTER THIRTEEN

Parker felt impressed with Kyle for once. The dumb shit was actually pulling this off. They were on his mythical boat. They might even make it to his mythical island.

Parker never felt entirely comfortable on boats, but they sure beat the mainland these days. That was for damn sure. It wasn't boats that made him nervous so much as the water. Being on the water was fine. *In* the water was not.

Swimming pools didn't bother him, but lakes and rivers sure did. And the ocean—only a pack of those things freaked him out more than falling in the ocean. Human beings don't belong where teeth-baring animals as big as couches live in murky depths where the bodies of the drowned sink to the untouchable bottom.

He'd have a panic attack if he fell overboard, so he stayed below deck, where he didn't have to think much about it. He had his own bedroom down there. And the bathroom worked. The toilet flushed and water came out of the shower. Kyle said that wouldn't last, but they had it for now. The kid deserved props.

Not that Parker would say so. But he'd dial back the insults and the aggression for a while, and he might keep them dialed back for good if this island business worked out.

He felt great below deck. It was warmer down there, for one thing. Even his trusted old army jacket couldn't hold off the bite from the wind off the water.

For the first time in months Parker took long deep breaths and felt himself settle. What if he could spend the rest of his life like this? Wouldn't that be something? He might be able to go back to being the old Parker, the one that wasn't such a big hard-ass. The others might even decide that they like him or could at least tolerate him.

The possibilities were certainly interesting. He wasn't sure how many islands Puget Sound had, but it was a lot. Dozens. Maybe even 100. Some had towns on them with houses, stores, restaurants, bars, and cafés. There were mountains and trees and beaches and vistas. People spent their whole lives in those towns. Parker doubted they were interested in having him as a permanent houseguest, but he knew there were plenty of extra houses. The San Juan Islands were vacation destinations. Rich people in Seattle owned weekend houses up there. Since almost everybody was dead, those houses were probably empty.

Then again, the islands might be incredibly crowded. Surely Kyle wasn't the only one who thought to sail up there. What if instead of an idyllic retreat they found a vast refugee camp?

And if the islands were infected? Well, they couldn't *all* be infected.

Hughes felt relieved when night fell. He did not want to look at Seattle as they sailed past it. The city must be in unspeakably ghastly condition by now. He imagined columns of smoke, toppled skyscrapers, and heaping mounts of dead bodies. Surely his imagination was worse than reality—after all, Olympia wasn't that bad—but he didn't want to know how hard his hometown had fallen.

His wife and son were buried there. Buried deep enough in the yard with a proper shovel where those things couldn't get to them.

He hadn't cried when he buried them. He knew he wouldn't stop if he started, and the city was so dangerous by then that if he couldn't stop, he wouldn't survive.

So he felt relieved when night fell. He could think about something else for a while.

He sat on the deck. The air chilled him, especially when the wind picked up and punched into the sails, but the stars above looked like a Hubble telescope photograph. Hughes had never seen so many before. City lights used to drown most of them out, but there they were in all their billions and glory.

The others remained below deck, except Kyle, who manned the sails.

The wind slacked off a bit after the sun went down, but moonlight lit the way, so Kyle kept the boat moving. He was eager to get to the islands and their new home.

Hughes thought he heard something, but he wasn't sure. "You hear that?"

"Hear what?" Kyle said and cocked his head to the side.

"Shh."

He wasn't sure what he was hearing. It was some kind of low-pitched roar, faint, like ocean waves at a distance, just barely at the edge of his perception. Maybe if the wind stopped blowing and the boat stopped moving, he could figure out what it was.

"I don't hear anything," Kyle said.

"It's far away," Hughes said. "Not close to the boat."

Hughes couldn't see Kyle's face. All he could see was the young man's outline against a darkened backdrop of mountains and a shimmering ceiling of stars.

"Oh," Kyle said. "I think I hear it now. Is that a plane? It can't be."

"It's not mechanical," Hughes said.

And then he knew what it was.

"Oh, sweet Jesus," he said and felt the adrenaline starting.

"What?" Kyle said, alarmed. "What is that?"

"Stay away from the shore. Keep us as close to the center of the channel as you can."

"What is it?" Kyle said, a little too loudly.

"Shh! Don't say anything. Be very quiet."

Kyle crouched next to him. "I'm dropping anchor and folding the sails if you don't tell me what you think you're hearing."

"I could be wrong."

"Tell me."

"God, you'd better hope that I'm wrong. Go get the others."

"Tell me what you think that is."

Hughes swallowed hard. "We're coming up on Tacoma, right? Isn't it just up ahead?"

"Anderson Island is behind us on the left," Kyle said, "so, yes, Tacoma is up ahead on the right."

"Shh. Listen."

The noise was a little bit louder now.

K yle thought the sound was like the roar seashells made when he held them up to his ear, only higher-pitched. Hughes was being paranoid, but fear is contagious, so he went below deck to summon the others.

Parker and Frank were playing cards by flashlight at the dining table. Annie had crashed on the pullout.

"Guys," Kyle said. "I need you all to come up here."

"What's up?" Frank said.

Annie moaned and rolled over.

Parker said nothing.

"Hughes and I are hearing a noise," Kyle said. "We're not sure what it is."

Frank stood up.

Annie sat up.

Parker didn't move.

"Come on," Kyle said. "I need all of you up here. You too, Parker."

The three of them stood and joined him and Hughes on the deck.

"Shh," Hughes said.

Everybody was silent for a couple of moments. The noise wasn't loud, but it was there.

"I don't hear anything," Annie whispered.

"I do," Parker said.

"I do too," Frank said.

How could Annie not hear it?

"Oh," Annie said. "You mean that faraway sound. I thought you meant the boat was making some noises."

"Shh," Hughes said. "Listen and tell me what you think that is."

Everyone shushed and kept quiet for a few minutes. The sound grew faintly louder as the boat sailed north. It sounded a little like a distant stadium roar.

"What is that?" Annie said. She sounded afraid.

"Good God," Parker said. "Tacoma's up ahead, right?"

"It is," Kyle said.

"*How* many people live in Tacoma?" Parker said. "Or used to live in Tacoma?"

"Well," Kyle said. "It's part of Seattle metro, which has, or had, more than 3 million people."

"So there must be thousands and thousands of those things running around," Parker said. "That's what we're hearing. Thousands and thousands of them screaming at once."

K yle desperately wanted them to be wrong, but they weren't, and it was obvious as they got nearer to the city. First they saw the dark shapes of houses on the hills rising above the shoreline, and then, after rounding Point Defiance Park, he could clearly see the dark outlines of cranes at the port and Tacoma's blacked-out skyscrapers.

The noise was intense now. It sounded like the screaming horde outside their grocery store times 100 or even 1,000. And it no longer sounded like a distant stadium roar. It was as if Kyle were standing inside the stadium.

Somebody ought to drop a nuclear bomb on the city.

"What on earth are they *doing*?" Annie said.

"Hunting," Hughes said. "Starving. Fighting each other. Eating each other. Who knows? But I'm sure as hell glad we're not in the middle of that. I'd rather stick my head in a garbage disposal."

Kyle had been a little concerned that his companions might want to stop at one of the nearer islands rather than continue to the San Juans. He didn't want to because the islands of southern Puget Sound were too close to Seattle and Tacoma and far more likely to be infected or, in the best-case scenario, jam-packed with starving and violent survivors like

Lane. The San Juans were farther away from the population centers and much harder to get to. None were connected to the mainland by bridges. They'd be safer there for sure.

That sound from a darkened Tacoma—the sound of thousands of screaming diseased people going berserk—ensured that no one would want to stop anytime soon.

Kyle noticed a glow of light in the sky beneath some low clouds on the northern horizon. Could it be? No.

"Look," he said. "Seattle. It looks like it's lit."

"Well, I'll be goddamned," Frank said. "They got the power back on?"

They couldn't see Seattle yet. Vashon Island stood in the way. They'd have to clear that before they could see the big city. The glow on the clouds above the city, though, was clearly visible above the dark hills in the distance.

But the power wasn't on. The glow was flickering. And the color was off. It wasn't yellow or white. It was orange.

"That's not city light we're looking at," Hughes said.

And that wasn't a cloud over the city. It was a column of smoke the size of a mountain.

Once they cleared the eastern tip of Vashon Island, it was obvious: an apocalyptic firestorm engulfed all of Seattle. Even the forests of Discovery Park were ablaze.

Hughes collapsed onto the deck. Just went straight down on his ass as though his legs turned to jelly. "God," he said.

"That isn't God's work, my friend," Frank said.

Hughes gasped for air. He was breathing fast and hard, but he couldn't get enough oxygen.

West Seattle should have been right in front of the boat, but it was gone, finished, razed by flames to the last blade of grass as if scoured by a tsunami of lava.

That's where his house used to be. Where his wife and his boy were buried. He'd never find the place where the house used to stand. Never find his wife. Never find his child.

Something broke inside him, like a physical tear in his chest cavity.

He thought about pitching himself over the side and into the water, but instead he just pitched himself forward and heaved a shuddering sob. Annie—bless her soul—sat beside him, put her hands on his shoulders, and rested her head against his.

Kyle reacted quite differently. The inferno terrified the animal part of his brain. He could feel the heat as if he'd just opened the oven. But a part of himself that he had no idea existed found the scorching of Seattle exhilarating.

He'd grown weary of cities before the plague started. His work as a computer programmer in Portland had suited him for a while, but hunching in front of a screen for long hours in a cubicle farm wore him down. That was not what humans were designed—either by evolution or God—to spend their lives doing.

Hiking in the wilderness had been his antidote. Cities are by definition artificial, and while they're wonderfully comfortable and even luxurious for those who have money, the landscape of evergreens, ferns, mosses, rocks, streams, soil, wildflowers, volcanoes, and glacial moraines is the *real* world. Look at a satellite photo of earth taken at night. Most of it's dark. The western half of America is only a fraction as lit up as the East because most of it's empty. The flecks of light are just fake little pockets.

Humans evolved to hunt and forage for food. We've done little else for nearly the entire time we've existed. We aren't designed to do anything else except reproduce. Civilization is not our default condition. Kyle felt keenly aware of this whenever he went off into the woods, as though the deep genetic coding in his body and mind were being rebooted. In a way, the infected ones were living a more natural life than Kyle ever did with his stock options and postmodern loft condo in Portland.

Sometimes while hiking on weekends, he idly thought about giving up his cushy urban life to live off the land. It was a fantasy, of course. He'd never actually do it. But he did see the appeal. He had read Jon Krakauer's *Into the Wild* four times.

And now that's exactly how he'd spend the rest of his life whether he liked it or not.

But he looked forward to it. The last thing he wanted was to die in some hideously shattered suburb of Olympia, but now he wouldn't have to. He'd spend the rest of his days in what he always thought was the real world.

Nature would slowly but inexorably overtake every city, suburb, and town ever built until nothing but forest, desert, prairie, and jungle remained. That awful grocery store on that awful street in that awful town off the interstate would soon enough be swamped by grasses and trees and animals and possibly even new bodies of water. If Kyle lived long enough and the infected died off on the mainland, he could watch that process begin and even advance. Seattle was simply being reclaimed a little bit faster.

"How far do you think that fire will spread?" Parker asked no one in particular.

"I don't see why it would stop," Frank said, "until the rains come. What do you think started it?"

"Could be anything," Parker said. "Lightning strike. Gas leak. Boiler explosion. Whatever it was, there's nobody left to put it out."

It had never occurred to Kyle before that fire departments didn't only save people and houses. They saved whole cities from total destruction. Eventually, most cities on earth might burn to the ground. What a revelation. A glorious revelation.

With the old world in ashes, he and the other survivors could give birth to a new one.

E astsound was a tourist town back in the day when there were still tourists. It was not even a town, technically, just an unincorporated community, but it looked like a town, it functioned like a town, and it was effectively the "capital" of Orcas Island, the largest and prettiest of the San Juans.

Romantic waterfront hotels, rental cottages, restaurants, cafés, and craft breweries were all on or within walking distance of the shore. The water is calm as a lake there even during winter storms because the open ocean is forty miles away, the enormous swells and crashing surf blocked by Canada's Vancouver Island.

The San Juans are north of Puget Sound across the Strait of Juan de Fuca, which in some places formed the maritime boundary between the United States and Canada back when national borders had meaning. The only part of America northwest of Eastsound was Alaska. The community was as remote a place in the lower forty-eight as a person could get.

Kyle knew all this because he had been there before, first when one of his friends took him to Orcas on his boat and taught him to sail, and again when he brought an old girlfriend on the ferry for a romantic three-day weekend.

Orcas Island is shaped like a narrow-necked horseshoe, and Eastsound is right there in the neck. If you have your own boat, you can get there from the south by sailing ten miles up the inlet between the eastern and western arms of the island, though most tourists took a ferry, which deposited them ten miles south of town in the village of Orcas.

About 5,000 people lived on the island, roughly half of them in Eastsound and the others scattered in Orcas, Deer Harbor, and the little bits of "countryside" in the island's interior.

The island's residents were about to find themselves with new neighbors.

Perhaps Kyle and the others would be welcome and maybe they wouldn't. If not, there was room to spread out. Most of the island was empty and covered with forest. They could vanish into the trees if they had to. If nothing else, they could live on the boat and anchor it off the island's east coast, where nobody lived and where nobody would bother them.

Kyle loved the journey to Orcas. The route passes through a maze of waterways between forest-covered islands that rise like mountains out of the sea. The area looks and feels primordial when fog hangs in the trees and muffles all sound. Kyle had never seen such beauty anywhere else. The fire and ash of Seattle may as well be on the other side of the world.

They passed some lightly inhabited islands on the way—Center Island and Blakely on the right and Lopez on the left. These weren't private islands, exactly, but they weren't for tourism either. Kyle doubted the few souls who lived there would want any refugees from the mainland. Orcas was the obvious choice. It had more people, more houses, more supplies, more hotels, and more unoccupied second homes. It had a critical mass of year-round residents who knew how to farm, knew how to fix things, and—perhaps most important—knew a thing or two about medicine. Surely at least a few of those 5,000 residents went to medical school.

"We're almost there," he said as they entered the narrow waterway between the island's two forested arms. "This is it. This is Orcas. The town of Eastsound is only ten miles north of here."

"What do we say when we get there?" Frank said.

"We say hello."

Kyle held his breath in anticipation when Eastsound came into view. He recognized the delightful little beachfront hotel where he'd once stayed with a girlfriend. He'd never forget that weekend, but that was thanks more to the charm of the island than the girl, since she broke up with him shortly after they got back to Portland.

Main Street ran four or five blocks along the waterfront. The town was hardly more than a village, but it was larger than it appeared from the water. Another street—which, if he remembered right, was called Beach Street, but he couldn't be sure—ran north to south away from the water. It, too, had restaurants and bars on it and trim prewar wooden houses behind. None of the junky fast-food restaurants and big-box stores that marred that piece of crap town off the interstate existed anywhere on the island. Eastsound—all of Orcas, really—was postcard-perfect.

And it was intact.

"Wow," Frank said.

"Well look at that," Annie said.

"It looks so … normal," Parker said.

Hughes stepped onto the deck from below with his rifle.

Eastsound wasn't on fire. Eastsound wasn't filled with a screaming horde. But as they slowly approached in the boat, Kyle didn't see any people. He wasn't expecting a welcome party, but someone should have seen the boat approach and headed down to the water to see who was coming. They'd been within eyeshot of the town for at least twenty minutes.

"Weird," Kyle said.

"Mmm-*hmm*," Parker said.

That man had an obnoxious tone even when he said nothing. He didn't want to come here, but had he thought for even one second about how nice it will be to check into that hotel and sleep in a bed? Or better yet, in a house?

"What do we do?" Annie said. "Should we check out that hotel?"

"We need to wait," Hughes said. "Kyle, drop anchor. We need to know what the hell's going on in that town."

"Apparently nothing's going on," Kyle said. "I don't see or hear anybody."

"Should we call out?" Annie said. "No one has seen us. It's not like they'd be expecting a boat."

"They wouldn't expect a boat here," Kyle said. "Most people take the ferry and drive in. The dock is ten miles away."

"All right," Hughes said. "We yell to get their attention." Nobody objected. "Hello!" he shouted. His voice didn't just carry. It thundered. "Hello! Anybody in town?"

Nothing stirred. Nobody emerged from one of the houses. No one parted curtains in any of the hotel rooms.

"Fire a shot in the air," Parker said. "That'll get their attention."

"It looks like there's nobody home," Hughes said, "but we have to know for sure."

"Maybe they're off gathering food," Frank said.

"And maybe they're dead," Parker said.

They weren't dead. Kyle was certain of that. The plague hadn't hit Eastsound. Everything looked fine. There were no abandoned cars on the road, no broken windows, no scorch marks, no dead bodies, no reek of death wafting over the water, not a blade of grass out of place.

Frank ducked, Kyle squinted, and Annie plugged her ears when Hughes fired.

The entire island must have absorbed the shock wave from Hughes' gunshot, but not a blade of grass so much as twitched.

"Maybe everyone left," Annie said.

"Apparently," Kyle said. "But why would they leave? This place is perfect."

"Maybe they were rescued," Frank said.

"Rescued from what?" Kyle said. "There's nothing here."

"You don't know that," Parker said.

"Look around," Kyle said.

"You. Don't. Know that."

Kyle may not have known that for sure, but he knew it well enough. *Nothing* bad happened here. He didn't know how and he didn't know why, but Eastsound was empty.

CHAPTER FOURTEEN

A nnie knew at once that she could get used to this place. She hadn't even stepped off the boat yet, but this idyllic little village presented itself like a gift from the gods.

You can't drive to Eastsound, nor can you swim there from the mainland. The infection wasn't there, and with so few survivors left to spread it, how could it ever *get* there?

Even so, she couldn't stay.

The chances that she might find her parents were much better than the odds of finding her sister. How she'd actually get to South Carolina was another matter entirely. When Kyle had said thousands of people lived on the island, she figured at least one or two of them would know how to fly a plane, but everyone seemed to have left. She was less concerned with why there were no people than the fact that there were no people. No people meant no plane ride.

She missed everything about the South, not just her parents. Mild winters; the riot of flowers in springtime; warm, humid summers; and the theatrical thunderstorms that never seemed to develop in the Northwest. She missed Southern food. Southern friendliness. She missed Southern trees that look almost junglelike next to the wintry evergreens of Washington and Oregon.

And she missed the accent. She didn't have a Southern accent, nor did her sister, but plenty of people did, especially older people, and unlike most Americans in the North and the West, she never thought Southern accents made people sound stupid.

Her homesickness felt like a physical ache.

But at least for now she was safe. She could rest. Sleep. Recuperate. Wash. Massage the stress and terror out of her muscles and bones.

She sat on the deck again with her bare feet dangling over the side and looked longingly at the hotel. It was empty. That was clear, so that was where she'd sleep. They shouldn't take over anyone's house. The owners might come back at some point. She didn't think the hotel owners would mind if they checked in without paying. What else were they supposed to do? Money was worthless now anyway.

Her toes were less than a foot above the water and she could see only a foot or so into the water. Anything could be down there, but she refused to pull her feet up. The cool air felt too good on her toes. She wished she could extend them into the water.

Hughes stood next to her with his rifle ready.

"How long should we wait before getting off?" she said.

"A couple more hours at least," he said.

"*Hours?*"

"Hours."

She heard footsteps behind them.

"I don't know, Hughes." It was Kyle. "If there was anything threatening in there, we'd know it by now."

"Maybe nothing threatening in there," he said and gestured toward the town with the stock of his rifle, "but you have no idea what is out there."

Just about every visible inch of the island was covered with trees.

"I'm with Hughes," Parker said. "We stay on the boat."

Annie sighed a little. She understood why the others were nervous, but she wasn't feeling it. Eastsound was the safest place she'd seen by far since the outbreak began.

She wondered what Kyle would say when she told him she wanted to leave.

Thick forest surrounded the town. If you headed in the right direction, you could walk through the trees in a straight line for hours before hitting water. And you could walk *up*. A mountain rose to the east. Kyle remembered driving to the top and seeing Canada's Vancouver Island to the west, skyscraping Vancouver city far to the north; Bellingham,

Washington, to the east; and the magnificent San Juan archipelago far below to the south. It must have taken an hour to drive up there from Eastsound. Walking would take a whole day.

So a horde of those things wouldn't be up there. It took far too much time and effort to walk to the top, and there was nothing but fir cones to eat up there.

Theoretically another part of the island could be infected, perhaps the villages of Orcas or Deer Harbor, but Kyle was certain they'd be just as empty as Eastsound. If the infection had hit those towns, the residents would have fled to Eastsound. And there was no one in Eastsound.

Hughes was just being paranoid. Prudent, but paranoid.

"Let's just give it another hour," Kyle said.

"We give it four more at least," Hughes said.

Kyle flinched. *Four?* Paradise was in view right in front of them, and Hughes wanted to stay on the boat another four hours? They had already been sitting there for at least two.

"I'm not even going in four," Parker said. "I'm sleeping on the boat tonight."

Kyle rolled his eyes. Parker wasn't being prudent or paranoid. He was a drama queen with a beard and a belly who couldn't admit that Kyle had saved his ass. Parker wouldn't even be there if Kyle hadn't practically forced him. He owed Kyle everything. Everyone on that boat owed Kyle everything.

If Parker wanted to sleep there, fine. The rest of them would spend the night in the hotel. And if Eastsound's residents didn't return after a week, they could move into one of the houses. Maybe they'd wait a month just to be decent, but that was it. Those houses would deteriorate if they weren't maintained and lived in. If the owners come back in, say, a year, they'd be glad to discover someone had taken care of the property for them.

He wondered if there was any food left in the town grocery store. That would depend on how long the residents stayed after the plague struck. What if the shelves were empty? What if everyone's cupboards were empty? If they weren't empty already, they would be eventually.

Eastsound was luxurious, but their new lives would still be a challenge. They'd have to fish and farm and trap and hunt. They'd have to chop wood. They'd live like pioneers and homesteaders, though without hostile Indians and with better sofas and beds. By next year, enough of those things would likely starve to death on the mainland that Kyle and the others could pry solar panels off houses in Vancouver and Bellingham and install them in Eastsound. They would not live like royalty, but they'd have enough to be comfortable and enough adversity and hardship to make them appreciate those comforts far more than they did before the outbreak.

It was going to be great. Kyle could never have designed such a perfect life for himself in the old world.

And what about Annie? How much time would have to pass before they moved in together? He knew it would happen eventually, and he was pretty sure she knew it too. She wouldn't live out her days by herself. Not at her age. She wasn't going to shack up with Frank. The very idea was ludicrous. Parker? Not a chance. And Hughes? Hughes was a bodyguard, not a man to bare your soul to and cuddle up with in bed.

No, Annie would eventually move in with Kyle. Even if they did not fall in love—though love was a distinct possibility—they were an obvious pair.

He'd take his time and go slowly, for they had all the time in the world.

Hours passed in languid silence and Hughes began to think Kyle was right. No one was going to stumble out of a house and wave hello if they sat on the boat another hour, nor would one of those things only now finally notice their presence.

The smart plan would be to sail around the island while making a whole lotta racket to see if anything moved in the trees, but more than three hours had passed since he fired his rifle and nothing had happened.

Eastsound looked empty, sounded empty, and just as important, it felt empty. The town and its immediate environs were clear. And that hotel was sure looking comfortable. They could recon the island tomorrow. Nothing would bother them in the meantime.

"Let's move ashore," he said.

"You sure you're okay with that?" Kyle said. Hughes could tell Kyle wasn't actually interested if Hughes was okay with it. He was just being polite.

"I'm still not going," Parker said.

Kyle huffed and said, "Christ, you're impossible."

"Parker," Hughes said. "My man. I'm as cautious as you are."

"No, you're not," Parker said.

"I'm as cautious as you are," Hughes said again. "But now you're just being stubborn. Come on. We'll hole up in that hotel over there and be quiet."

"You want my advice?" Parker said.

"Not really, no," Kyle said.

Annie placed her hand on his arm.

"What's your advice?" Hughes said.

"We stay on this boat for three days," Parker said, "and make as much goddamn noise as we can. Then we get off if everything's clear."

Hughes understood where Parker was coming from. That would, indeed, be the safest possible way to proceed, especially if they sailed around the island once or twice just to be sure. But there is a point where caution becomes excessive, where fear turns into phobia, and Parker had crossed it.

"I've seen you act with incredible bravery," Hughes said to Parker. "Just two days ago you chased an armed man down in the street, killed dozens of those things single-handedly, and set your own house on fire. Stepping onto the beach after all that is nothing."

"I had to do those things," Parker said. "But I don't have to rush off this boat. We have comfortable beds and enough food for days. But I hear what you're saying, so I'll join you tomorrow if you're all still okay."

So, Hughes thought, the island is Parker's coal mine and the rest of us are his canaries. But, hey, whatever. Let him isolate himself if that's what he wants. Better that than dragging him ashore if he's going to be a pain in everyone's ass. Hughes doubted he was the only one who could use a break. Maybe the man would finally settle down after sitting on the boat all alone for a while.

"I'm not the boss of you," Hughes said. "None of us are the boss of you. None of us are the bosses of anyone. So stay here then if that's what you want. We'll be a couple hundred feet away in that hotel over there, and we'll take beachfront rooms. We'll hear if you yell, and vice versa."

Parker's face softened. Hughes stuck out his open palm for a handshake. Parker took it and shook it. "Okay," Parker said. "Good luck. Come back here the minute you see or hear something creepy."

Hughes smiled. Those two might get along fine if the island worked out as advertised.

But he wasn't counting on it. Something was bound to go wrong. There was a damn good reason that town was empty. He didn't know how and he didn't know why, but checking out the island in person was the only way to find out.

They anchored the boat 200 feet out and swam in. The water was so cold that Kyle's lungs briefly seized up, but Hughes insisted it was far better to be cold and wet for a spell than bring the boat onto the beach where it would not be secure.

They left the handguns, but Hughes brought the M4 rifle and held it over his head and swam with one hand to keep it dry. Kyle and Annie brought crowbars. Frank brought his hammer. And that was it. They weren't relocating to the island just yet. This was a recon mission.

Kyle shivered and dripped on the shore and tried to hug himself warm. He had forgotten how rocky the beach was. Soft sand is created by pounding ocean waves, but the water around the San Juans behaved more like a lake, aside from the tides. The silence of the sea made them safer since crashing waves would conceal threatening noises.

"I need to go inside," Annie said through chattering teeth. Her waterlogged clothes sagged off her shivering body. "The hotel will have towels."

Kyle shivered too. Frank shivered. Even Hughes, with all his insulating bulk, shivered a little.

"Agreed," Kyle said. "Our clothes will still be wet, but we can dry off and warm up before we have to put them back on."

"We'll get dry clothes in some of the houses," Hughes said.

"We leave the houses alone," Kyle said. "They belong to someone. We should at least wait until we're certain they aren't coming back. There should be a clothing store on the next street."

They crossed Main Street and followed a handpainted wooden sign in front of the hotel that said "Office." The office was dark, and Kyle had to cup his hands over the glass to see inside, but it did not look abandoned. It just looked like it was closed for the day.

He pushed and pulled the door handle. It was locked, so he knocked. He knew no one would answer, but it felt like the right thing to do.

"Hello!" he said. "Anyone in there?"

"Just break the glass," Hughes said.

Kyle hadn't felt averse to breaking and entering for more than a month. The very concept of breaking and entering meant nothing anymore on the mainland, but Eastsound was different. It still looked respectable.

He felt like a criminal, but he whacked the glass with his crowbar. The shattering was extraordinary. It gave him one jolt of adrenaline and another of fear. Surely that sound could be heard from a mile away.

"You guys okay?" Parker called from the boat. He was hundreds of feet away, but with no wind, no rain, no surf, and no traffic, his voice carried like he was standing right there.

"Just bustin' into the office," Frank said. He didn't yell it, he just said it, and of course Parker could hear him. For a second Kyle was surprised that Parker showed concern for their well-being, but only for a second.

Parker was concerned about his own ass. Anything that threatened them threatened him even if it threatened him less.

Kyle reached through the broken glass, unlocked the door, and stepped into the office. It was just as cold inside as out. The heat had been off for a long time. He could see well enough in the gloom to step behind the counter and grab four room keys.

"Just grab one," Hughes said. "We should stick to one room," Hughes said.

"I need to take off my clothes," Annie said, still shivering.

Kyle handed her a key, kept one for himself, and returned two to the desk. "You take 17. We'll be next door in 18."

"We should get ourselves a raft," Frank said, "so we don't have to freeze our asses off like this every time we go to and from the boat."

"The hell are we going to find a raft?" Hughes said.

"I'll make one out of shoestrings and twigs," Annie said, "if I don't have to do this again."

"There's a dock down the shore a ways," Kyle said. "We can tie the boat there when we know for sure the island is safe."

"It's not safe," Hughes said.

Annie stopped shivering for a moment. "What do you mean?"

"This place looks perfect, right?" Hughes said.

Like heaven, Kyle thought. A city on a hill at the end of the world.

"But it's empty," Hughes said. "Why would a place this nice be empty? People here ran away from something."

"From what?" Kyle said. "There's nothing here."

"I don't know," Hughes said. "But Annie girl, you're coming into room 18 with us. You can dry off and warm up in the bathroom. Nobody should be alone on this island."

A nnie locked herself in the bathroom, hung her wet clothes in the shower, wrapped herself in a towel, and sat on the floor. The room had no window so she couldn't see anything, but she didn't care. She felt warm and safe and comfortable. The floor was cold, but the towel kept the chill out of her shoulders and core. It also covered the bite mark on the back of her shoulder. She'd need to make *damn* sure nobody saw that. The three men on the other side of the door might only keep her safe as long as they didn't know her little dark secret.

But safe from what? She had a hard time believing the islanders ran away from disaster. What disaster? There had to be a benign explanation. Of if they did run from something, whatever it was had moved on.

"The light's weird here, isn't it?" Frank said on the other side of the door. She couldn't see him—she couldn't see anything—but she could hear him just fine.

"The color is a bit strange," Kyle said, "but it doesn't mean anything. It's just something to do with the clouds."

The light in the sky had looked a bit odd, now that she thought about it. It took on an odd fluorescence similar to the light in a meat locker or Walmart. But Kyle was right. It didn't mean anything. Frank was just a little on edge. They were all a little on edge, especially Parker.

She dreaded the thought of getting dressed again. She'd freeze the minute she put her wet clothes back on.

She stood up, wrapped the towel around her body—taking care to ensure that her bite mark was covered—and opened the door. Kyle, Hughes, and Frank were drying off in the next room. None had any clothes on.

"Sorry!" she said and went back into the bathroom, leaving the door ajar so they could talk.

"Kyle," she said, "I understand what you're saying about not breaking into anyone's house, but we need some dry clothes and we don't have time to look for a store. We're going to get hypothermia walking around in wet clothes. And what if we got attacked right now?"

"We're not going to be attacked," Kyle said.

Hughes and Frank said nothing.

"Look at us," she said, "freezing our bare asses off. This is ridiculous."

"She's right," Frank said. "I'm still freezing my ass off even now that it's dry."

"I agree," Hughes said. "Like it or not, we need to bust into somebody's house."

Hughes did wonder if he was being a little bit paranoid. He'd tried to talk Parker down earlier, and now he played that same talk back to himself.

What's fear, anyway? It's not the same thing as terror. He felt terror when those things rushed at him. It's the body's response to a visible threat.

Years ago he figured it out. The fact that you're afraid of something is proof that it's not actually happening. If a man points a gun at you, the only reason you're afraid of getting shot is because he hasn't shot at you. If he was shooting at you, you'd be afraid of getting hit. And if you did get hit, you'd be afraid of bleeding out. And if you had bled out, you'd already be dead.

Fear is about what *might* happen next, which means it might not.

So Hughes thought it through logically. None of those things were in town. Nor were they out in the trees adjacent to town. A different part of the island might be infected, but if those things were close enough to threaten him and the others, they would have heard his rifle shot earlier even if they were too far away to see the boat or hear talking and splashing.

Nor were the townsfolk lying in wait to ambush anybody. That would make no kind of sense.

So why couldn't he relax? Something in the air? In the sky? He couldn't help but imagine someone—or something—watching them from behind drawn curtains. It was his mind and body's evolutionary response to being hunted before we invented the technology that made us apex predators. But he didn't see or hear so much as a squirrel.

He put on his sopping-wet clothes, felt his body temperature drop a little again, and took the others out onto the street.

The light in the sky still looked strange and weirdly fluorescent. He'd seen light like this in the past, usually before one of the Northwest's rare summer thunderstorms. The weather was finally going to change then, and most likely dramatically.

The street was silent. He could actually hear the boat rising and falling on tiny waves way out in the water.

Something else was wrong with the town, but he hadn't yet figured out what. It was right there at the edge of his mind, but he hadn't quite grasped it. That was the reason he couldn't relax.

"This way," Kyle said and pointed to a street off to the left, "will take us to the center of town."

So they went that way. And as soon as they rounded the corner, Hughes figured out what was bugging him.

The street continued in a straight line as far as he could see. And there were no cars on it. None. Not even parked cars.

Annie noticed it too. "Whoa. Where are the cars?"

"See," Kyle said. "I told you. Everyone left. They left in their cars."

"The hell'd they go?" Hughes said. "This is an island."

"There are two smaller towns down the road," Kyle said. "They could have gone to one of those."

"The whole town?" Annie said. "Why would people from the big town evacuate to a small town?"

"Right. But the ferry terminal is ten miles south of here, so they didn't just leave town. They left the island."

"Why on earth would they do that?" Annie said.

"I don't *know*," Kyle snapped.

Kyle and Annie obviously liked each other. Everybody could see that, but now Hughes felt the tension between them. Not his problem. He just wanted some dry clothes and some time to work out this puzzle.

"Sorry," Kyle said.

Annie said nothing.

"I'm freezing and agitated," Kyle said. "I've been dreaming about this place for months, and now that we're finally here, you guys are all freaking out. It's actually perfect that nobody's here. The residents might have run us off otherwise. They might've even shot at us."

"I'd feel better if I knew why they left," Annie said. "But you're right. This is the best place we could be."

Hmm, Hughes thought. We'll see about that.

L et's try that house," Kyle said and pointed to a trim wooden Crafts-man behind a café. The lawn was overgrown, but otherwise the home looked lovingly cared for. The porch spanned the whole front of the house and even wrapped partway around the south side. Two comfortable-looking rocking chairs sat near the front door with a dainty wooden table between them. The porch was practically an outdoor living room. You could see the water from there. Kyle imagined moving in with Annie.

"No breaking in," he said. "Let's first try the doors and the windows. If it's all locked up tight, we'll go to the next one." He didn't want busted windows in the house he hoped to be sharing with Annie.

"Just break a window if it's locked," Annie said. "I'm freezing and need some dry clothes right now."

"The house won't be usable," Kyle said.

"There are plenty of others!" she said and shivered.

Kyle sank a little inside, but he didn't argue. He walked up the wooden steps and heard, and felt, the sickening squish of his sopping-wet socks. After finding dry clothes, he'd need to find a plastic bag to put them in so they wouldn't also get wet when he swam back to the boat. They had all kinds of supplies on the boat, but no plastic bags.

He tried the handle, but it was locked, so he knocked. "Hello!" he said. "Anyone home?"

"Step back," Hughes said. "I'll kick it in."

"Just a minute. Let me try the windows."

Kyle headed back to the sidewalk. He walked around the north side of the house and into the back, where a bedroom window slid open. "Got it!"

The window was only five feet off the ground, so he climbed inside easily enough.

He saw at once that the house belonged to old people. A country-style bedspread and a pair of reading glasses next to an antique lamp on the bedside table gave it away.

The house smelled of must and rotting garbage. At least that's what he hoped it was. He doubted anything had died in there. The smell was faint. It didn't smell like a dead rat or dog or cat or—God forbid—a person. It just smelled a little like the owners had neglected to take out the trash one last time before they left town.

He made his way to the faded living room and opened the front door.

"It's all good," he said. "Smells a little so we should open the windows, but otherwise everything seems to be fine."

Hughes stepped inside and scanned the front room. "You two wait outside. I'm gonna check the place out."

"It's fine," Kyle said.

He'd know if someone was in there. The presence of even silent and hiding humans was strangely detectable. At least he'd always imagined that was the case. Empty houses have a feel, and this one felt empty, like his condo always felt when he returned home from a three-day weekend in the mountains. He heard no sound, sensed no living vibrations, nothing.

Hughes checked the bedrooms as Kyle stepped into the dining room and saw two neat place settings at the table. In the kitchen, the sink and counters were spotless. The people who owned this place were either neat freaks or they cleaned up on their way out so they wouldn't come home to a mess.

"Clear!" Hughes said from the hallway.

"It does smell slightly in here," Annie said. She and Frank were still in the living room.

"It's getting dark, guys," Frank said. "Maybe we should stay here instead of at the hotel. There's more room and more stuff we can use. We can open the windows to air the place out for a bit. It's not like it's gonna get any colder in here if we open 'em."

"And there's a kitchen," Kyle said.

"And more than one exit," Hughes said as he returned from the bedrooms.

Kyle stepped into the kitchen. There was, indeed, a back door in the mudroom behind the kitchen just as Hughes knew there would be. Two exits were great in an emergency, but that also meant the house had two entrances. It would be easier to escape but harder to defend. If it came to that. But Kyle knew it wouldn't.

He opened one of the cabinets and saw a neat stack of plates and bowls. Inside another cabinet were drinking glasses and coffee mugs.

Frank opened the drawer under the microwave. "Flashlight," he said and pressed a button on its neck. A yellow beam placed a blotchy circle of light on the refrigerator.

"Can I see that for a sec?" Kyle said.

Frank handed it over.

The thing didn't weigh much and the light wasn't powerful. It looked like the kind of flashlight that sometimes went dark and had to be shaken. But it worked.

Kyle opened a third kitchen cabinet. And when he pointed the flashlight inside, he knew at once why everyone on the island had left.

CHAPTER FIFTEEN

Twilight settled over the water and chilled the air. Soon Parker would have to go below deck.

The light had been strange that evening. A slight bluish hue washed over everything and bathed the island and inlet with a surreality that he'd found unnerving. It wasn't a portent or anything, but it didn't make him feel any better.

He did, however, feel a bit better when nothing happened after the others went ashore. The town really was empty. The people were gone. Those *things* were gone if they were ever even there. He had overreacted when he refused to go with them, and now he felt more alone than he ever had in his life.

The light continued to wane. Twilight faded to dusk. He could see the dark outlines of houses and trees, but the details had faded to black. The boat bounced and rocked as tiny waves kissed the sides. All was silent. His fear settled in the gloaming and went down with the light. If night wasn't falling, he'd be tempted to swim ashore.

But only tempted. He didn't dare tell the others, but he refused to swim in the ocean. The only reason he didn't refuse to swim in this inlet was because it wasn't really the ocean. It was filled with seawater, sure, but it looked like a lake. He'd do his best to pretend it *was* a lake and try to act fearless when it came time to jump in.

He was not going to do it in the dark, though. Not a chance. Swimming in the dark when he couldn't see land might be even more terrifying than swimming in the open ocean. But if nothing dramatic happened that night, he'd join his friends in the morning and pray they did not see the fear on his face.

His friends. He actually thought of them as his friends now. Before they were simply companions. And they were annoying companions. Necessary, but annoying, especially Kyle. But Kyle had done good with this island. There was no getting around it now. Sailing up to Orcas was brilliant.

It could have gone another way. The island could have been infected, crowded, or hostile, but instead it was empty. The universe had finally taken mercy and provided a respite for him and his friends.

One of his friends was a woman. Their little group was made up of five, but only one was female. She might as well be the last woman on earth. Has Annie stopped to think about the implications of that?

Parker knew he had no chance with her. Kyle was her age and seemed more her style, especially now that he'd scored so big with this island. They wouldn't share Annie. She'd never go for it. Nor would they fight for her. They certainly were not going to rape her. At least Parker wouldn't. That was for damn sure. Hughes would take his head off. Hell, Parker would take somebody's head off for raping a woman.

There had to be other survivors. More people could show up any second. More probably would show up eventually. It just made sense. There had to be thousands of boats in the Puget Sound area, and there were dozens of islands. He imagined a micro-civilization of hardscrabble survivalists arising in the Pacific Northwest's archipelago and slowly, gingerly, moving back to the mainland once those things had died off.

They had to die off eventually. For God's sake, they'd been reduced to mindless psychotics. They had no civilization. They couldn't build things or grow things. They could only destroy things until they themselves were destroyed or killed off by starvation, bullets, hammers, and weather.

He felt lonely on the boat, but he'd still feel lonely even if he was onshore with the others. He'd isolated himself with his atrocious behavior. That had to change. The others might even forget he'd been a jerk if he could be nice for a while. After a couple of weeks they could chalk it up to stress under pressure. That was understandable and forgivable. Wasn't it?

Kyle knew why everyone left the island. "Look." He stepped back from the cabinet while keeping the flashlight pointed inside. The others peered in. "It's practically empty."

Inside was a half-bag of rice, three cans of vegetable soup, half a packet of instant oatmeal, and that was it.

"So?" Frank said.

"So think about it. When was the last time you saw a food cupboard this empty?"

"I've never seen one this empty."

"Neither have I," Hughes said in a knowing tone. He had also figured it out.

"How much do you want to bet," Kyle said, "that the shelves in this town's only grocery store are also practically empty?"

"They left because they ran out of food," Annie said.

"Exactly," Kyle said.

"That means they had somewhere to go," Annie said.

"Or they thought they did," Hughes said.

"Where do you suppose they went?" Annie said.

"Friday Harbor," Kyle said. "They must have gone to Friday Harbor." He didn't know that for sure, but it made sense.

"What's Friday Harbor?" Hughes said.

"Biggest city on the San Juan Islands," Kyle said. "It's the seat of San Juan County. And it's on a different island. You guys remember when the government tried to set up shelters and food-distribution centers?"

"Sure," Hughes said.

"No, but okay," Frank said.

"It didn't last long," Kyle said. "Only a couple of days, really, until the state's trucking and distribution system collapsed along with everything else. At least one shelter and food-distribution center was supposed to be set up in each county. That means Friday Harbor for this area. The government couldn't set one up for each tiny island, so everyone who lived here just went over there. They took the ferry. And they drove. That's why there are no cars here."

"Let's go there!" Annie said.

"To the ferry terminal?" Kyle said.

"To Friday Harbor," she said.

No, Kyle thought. That was not going to happen. Why on earth would she want to go there? "Best-case scenario is it's full of thousands of refugees. We won't have a house or even hotel rooms to sleep in."

"We'd be sleeping outside," Hughes said.

"We'd be sleeping outside," Kyle said.

"But there will be food," Frank said. "At the distribution center."

"Frank," Kyle said. "The distribution system collapsed. So did the ferry service. So did everything else. The people in Friday Harbor ran out of food a long time ago."

"But there will be others," Annie said.

"Others?" Kyle said.

"Other people," she said.

"Of course," Kyle said. "That's the problem."

But Annie said it like she wanted to find other people.

That would not do. No, it would not do at all.

Night fell early this time of year, so they contented themselves with cold vegetable soup for dinner and retired early. They needed rest and could explore the town in the morning when they could see.

Hughes took the couch, his rifle across his chest with his finger next to the trigger guard. His body was exhausted, but he couldn't sleep. All he could do was stare upward toward the dark ceiling with his ears tuned to hypersensitivity like a rabbit's.

He sensed the others were awake, too, even though no one was moving or talking. At last they had some peace, some privacy, some comfort, and the time and space to think their own thoughts.

Hughes wondered what the others were thinking and how they were feeling. They seemed to think they were safe. They were not.

A nnie slept alone in what might have once been a child's room but now looked like the spare room. Kyle and Frank shared the master bedroom and Hughes took the couch. He wanted to be near the front door in case anyone—or any*thing*—tried to come inside.

She felt better than she had in days, partly because she was safe now in a beautiful place, but also because her twisted—*hungry hungry predator*—thoughts had quieted down.

Annie didn't know if her mind had settled because she was recovering or because she was temporarily free of the terror and violence that brought those feelings and thoughts to the fore. She hoped she'd never find out but doubted she'd be so lucky.

Maybe she'd be so lucky if she spent the rest of her days in Eastsound, but she didn't want to, not even after sighing at its lovely serenity. If God came down from the heavens and told her she could never go home, that her parents were dead, that there was nothing left for her in South Carolina, then, yes, she'd happily live out her life here in Eastsound, but that wasn't going to happen. She couldn't know those things, really know them, without going home.

If Kyle was right, if the population of Eastsound had moved to Friday Harbor, then that's where she'd go first. There had to be planes there if it was the capital of the islands. And somebody would know how to fly one.

She wanted Kyle to join her. Hell, she wanted all the others to join her, but she'd never convince them, especially not Kyle. His entire existence had revolved around Orcas Island from the moment she met him. Now that they were here, she couldn't possibly pry him away. Not even if she gave him everything.

Could she give him everything? Part of her wanted to. She caught herself twisting the ring on her finger while thinking about him sometimes. What was that about, anyway? It was just a plain silver ring she'd found in a mall.

But she also needed some distance, not just from Kyle, but from everyone else. She couldn't let anyone see her back with her shirt off.

Obviously she had been bitten, and she had been bitten recently. The wound hadn't entirely healed yet. Maybe when it scars over, she could make up a story about how her sister bit her when they were children.

Her sister. Jenny was almost certainly gone. But her parents might not be. She wondered where they were. They could still be at the house. Or perhaps they fled to an island like she had. They could be on Hilton Head off the coast near Savannah or the Florida Keys or maybe one of the Outer Banks Islands up in North Carolina.

She sank into a sleep that felt like the deep sleep of the dead.

Then found herself barefoot and freezing on the dark streets of Eastsound. The clouds had cleared. A quarter moon illuminated the houses, the trees, and the water. Stars glistened like diamonds shattered with hammers.

She felt a terrible cloying hunger within her and the coppery taste of blood in her mouth.

Oh God. She'd turned again. The virus was back. It never went away. It was only beaten into remission like cancer.

She stepped toward the house. There were people inside. Food inside. Food to sate her terrible hunger. Food to sate her terrible hunger and rage.

Up the stairs toward the door. Was she dreaming or was this real? She had no control over her body, as if a primal alien intelligence manipulated her muscles.

Kyle was inside that house. She wouldn't—would she?

She struggled to gain control, to turn her body around and go back down the steps, but it was futile. She crossed the porch and slapped the door as hard as she could with her palms. She screamed—a terrible scream of hunger and fury—and battered the door again with both palms. She'd wrench the lock if she could not break it down.

Her hair hung down in front of her face, but she did not push it away. It was fine where it was. She liked it where it was.

The door opened. Kyle stood there before her.

"Annie?" he said.

She lunged and bit into his face. He screamed and she screamed and she woke in bed gasping, in animal panic and terror, and it took everything she had not to open her throat up for real and send everyone rushing into her room and asking what on earth was wrong with terrible Annie.

She breathed. Her heart slowed.

No, she hadn't turned. She was just dreaming again. And this dream wasn't a memory.

But she turned onto her side and cried softly into her pillow, knowing that she would never again be the same.

Kyle hated sleeping in the same bed as Frank. He'd take the floor if the house weren't so cold. Instead, he lay as close to the edge of the bed as he could.

He assumed Frank was doing the same. They did not want to touch each other, not out of some latent sense of homophobia—Kyle had gotten over that silliness right after high school—but because he wished he was sleeping with Annie. Frank's very existence in the bed next to him was a rude and obnoxious reminder that he was not. If Kyle had his own bed, he could just forget it and get some sleep, but Frank kept fidgeting and pulling the blankets.

Neither of them could sleep, so Kyle figured they might as well talk. "So you can't sleep either."

"Not a wink," Frank said. "The bed is okay, but I can't turn my brain off."

"What are you thinking about?"

"That everything is going to change again."

"It's all going to change for the better."

"But how will we live? What will we eat?"

"We can fish. Grow food. Trap squirrels. Hunt deer. Raise cows."

"Cows? Where on earth are we going to get cows?"

"There are some farms between here and the other towns. If the cows haven't starved, and they probably haven't, we can bring them closer to town."

"How are we going to do that?" Frank said. "Who knows anything about cows?"

"I don't know, Frank. We'll figure it out. Humans have been raising cows for thousands of years. How hard could it be? Primitive people figured it out."

"I suppose," Frank said. After a long pause he added, "You really think we'll be okay?"

"We are the luckiest people on earth," Kyle said. He turned onto his side and quietly thought about Annie.

P arker woke to the sound of splashing water—a fish jumping in the inlet, perhaps, or one of his companions throwing a rock to get his attention.

He rose from bed feeling more refreshed and alive than he had for months. Today, he thought, is the first day of the new Parker.

Wisps of fog curled in the trees. The sea was flat as a pond. He heard water licking the sides of the boat and a chipmunk or squirrel running along a tree branch on shore. The idyllic village of Eastsound looked like a place where hobbits might live, a peaceful and beautiful retreat free of the death and destruction and mayhem wrecking the continent.

He felt several pounds lighter when he imagined his future self rising from a snug bed in one of the town's little houses, tossing a log onto a crackling fire, and cooking up deer steaks for breakfast for himself and a faceless woman he hadn't met yet.

The water was so calm he wasn't even afraid to jump in. It would be cold—he knew that—but he could be ashore in thirty seconds or so, and then he'd be fine, albeit wet.

He stepped into the boat's cramped bathroom and found a disposable razor and a can of shaving gel on the sink. Cool Ocean scent. Kyle's. Frank and Hughes used Barbasol foam. Parker squirted some into his hand and sniffed. Contrary to the label, it smelled nothing at all like the ocean. The ocean smelled of salt spray, seaweed, and fish. This stuff just smelled like shaving gel.

His face looked like hell in the mirror. His beard was so long now it added ten years to his age and knocked at least another ten off his IQ. And it wasn't just the beard that added ten years. His eyes were baggier than ever. Brand-new lines slashed his forehead. His companions also must have aged years in the last couple of months, though he could hardly imagine Kyle looking much less mature than he already did.

Inside the mini cabinet he found a pair of barber scissors and used them to trim away most of his beard. He did a messy job of it but didn't care because he was going to take the rest of it off with a razor, but he looked like a deranged person with only random parts of his beard hacked away. He chuckled to himself when he imagined what his companions would think and say if he showed up on the island looking like that. They'd want to lock his ass up.

The tap water was cold, but he used it and the gel to get rid of the rest of his beard. The razor burned his skin and left tiny red bumps on his neck, but an old familiar face looked back at him in the mirror when he finished. The original Parker. The pre-apocalypse Parker. The Parker before he turned into a big raging asshole. The Parker none of his companions had ever seen. A new face to go with the new attitude. The instant they see him, he thought, they'll know something has changed.

He climbed the steps onto the deck and heard a door open and close in the distance. Sound really carried nowadays. He still wasn't used to it. Then he saw Annie heading down the street toward the shore with a bounce in her step. She seemed to have slept well and to feel as content as he did. She had a purple bath towel draped over her shoulders and carried what looked like a set of dry clothes.

"Good morning!" she said and waved as though they were old friends. Were they friends? Was it still not too late for him to redeem himself even in her eyes?

He waved back.

"I brought you a towel!" she said, "and some clean clothes. I think these should fit, but if not we can get you some more."

"You're very kind. Thank you." And he meant it. How lovely it was to have friends.

The day was cloudy, but she shielded her eyes with her hand as she looked over the water at him. "Did you shave?"

"I did," he said and smiled.

"You look different even from here! The water's pretty cold, but you'll warm up quick when you dry off. And you'll feel better after a bath even if it's in seawater."

She was right, but not quite in the way that she thought. He'd feel better after his bath because he'd be out of the sea. He sat on the edge of the deck with his feet dangling over the side and thought, *Just look at the shore. Don't look down at the water. Look at the shore and it will be over in seconds.*

But he couldn't help looking down at the water. It was murky, full of algae or plankton or whatever it was that made the Northwest's waters so dark. He was grateful for that. He knew the water was too deep for his feet to touch bottom, and he didn't want to know just how deep. He was no safer in seven feet of water than in seven miles of water, of course. All that mattered is that he couldn't stand on the bottom without drowning. If the water was eighty feet deep and clear, however, he'd be able to *see* that it's eighty feet deep. And he'd freak.

"Come on!" Annie said. "I won't lie, it really is cold, but you'll sort of get used to it after a couple of seconds."

Such a sweet kid, that Annie. She thought he was hesitating because of the cold.

He could strip down to his underwear and save his clothes from getting wet, but Annie might be offended if she saw him practically naked. And he did not want her seeing his paunch or his milky white legs that hadn't seen sunlight for more than ten consecutive seconds since he was eight. He firmly believed no one should go around in public half-naked unless the sight of their half-naked selves made the world better. Parker had never measured up to that standard, and he especially didn't measure up now.

So he removed his army jacket—no sense getting that wet—stripped off his socks, and jumped in.

The water literally took his breath away. His entire diaphragm froze. When he could finally breathe again, he did it by gasping.

No longer did he fear that he'd drown. He'd freeze to death first. He actually felt the heat leave his body and cold pour into his bones as though it were liquid.

The Alaskan current makes the Pacific Ocean so frigid in the Northwest that a person can lose strength and sink in just minutes. The Puget Sound waters are a little bit warmer since the current sweeps past them, but they're still unspeakable. A life jacket will save you from drowning, but hypothermia will still kill you quickly.

Parker swam like he'd die. The only reason he didn't panic was because Annie was standing there with his towel. He could not lose his shit in front of the girl.

When he neared the shore and the water got shallow, he stood up and ran the rest of the way. Water poured off him in sheets.

"Hey there," Annie said. The corners of her eyes crinkled when she smiled at him. She had never looked at him that way before. It was as if she was seeing him for the first time. She handed him the towel and said, "You look ten years younger."

"I feel ten years colder." He wrapped the towel around his shivering shoulders and felt better at once.

"Come on. Let me show you the house. We have hot coffee." They had hot coffee? "There's a wood stove in the living room. Kyle put a few logs on and boiled some water in a pot. The coffee is instant, but it tastes better than Starbucks under the circumstances."

Parker did not care for Starbucks. Pumpkin-spice lattes? *Please.* A regular latte was nice once in a while, but he wanted coffee-flavored coffee, not *pumpkin.*

"I'm sure it's better than Starbucks," he said and left it at that.

He placed his bare feet gingerly on the road and watched for tiny pieces of gravel. The ground actually felt a little bit warm. It had to be cold—clouds hid the sun and the air couldn't be more than fifty degrees—but his feet were even colder from sea.

That icy water, he realized, added yet another layer of protection to the island. Even if those things did try to swim, they sure as hell wouldn't be able to swim to the San Juans from the mainland. Nor would they be able to swim from one island to another. The cold would pull them down as quickly as it would him.

The house wasn't far. Just a block off the main street. It looked like the perfect storybook cottage. Annie carried a set of dry clothes for him and led him up the stairs and through the front door.

He stepped across the threshold and dripped onto a scratched floor made of fir. Kyle sat on a faded brown couch, Frank in a billowy recliner. Both sipped from steaming mugs.

"Whoa," Frank said.

Kyle looked startled when he saw Parker sans beard but didn't say anything.

"Dude, you shaved," Frank said.

"I did."

"Nice of you to join us, my man," Hughes said from the kitchen.

The kitchen. They had a kitchen! Oh, this was grand. Parker could get used to this.

He excused himself to one of the bedrooms so he could dry off and change. The clothes Annie found for him—a pair of blue jeans and a gray pullover sweatshirt that said "Iowa" on it—were a little too big, but that was fine. Better that than a little too small.

He emerged from the bedroom rubbing the towel through his hair.

"What's for breakfast?" he said.

Nobody spoke.

"Oh," Parker said. "There's no food here."

"We'll check the other houses," Hughes said. "This one's empty. Frank, you'll go with Kyle. Annie and Parker will stick with me."

It was at that moment that he realized a new dynamic had shaped up. There was no longer any sort of leadership struggle between himself and Kyle. Parker had receded into the background while Hughes stepped up in his place. Parker just flat lost the argument about where to go and what to do. He had to admit that. He'd assert himself later, and he'd do it a little more delicately than he did before, but now it was time for him to stay back. No one would listen to a damn thing he had to say now, especially right after he'd exiled himself on the boat.

"Food was always going to be the big challenge here," Kyle said, "if not right away, then eventually."

Annie sat next to him on the couch. She held her coffee mug with both hands and blew onto it. Faint wisps of steam rose and dissipated.

"Worst-case scenario," Kyle said, "is we go fishing. When was the last time any of you went fishing? It'll be great."

Annie looked off into space at nothing in particular. Parker couldn't understand why, but he thought she looked sad.

O kay," Kyle said after everyone finished their coffee. "Time to scrounge up some food." He looked forward to it and could hardly wait to see more of the island now that the whole thing seemed to be theirs. "We also need water since the taps aren't working. We should bring the boat in. There's some filters in the backpacks."

"Not yet," Hughes said.

"What do you mean, not yet?" Kyle said. "We need the filters. Along with everything else. The night vision sure would be nice."

"We save the night vision for when we're attacked," Hughes said.

"When we're *attacked*?" Kyle said.

Hughes just looked at him. Looked at him like he was the stupidest person on earth.

Kyle let out his breath. Okay, yes, they would likely get in a fight again at some point. They'd eventually need to raid the mainland for supplies like solar panels. Perhaps a hostile group like Lane and his crew would show up in a boat of their own. And, sure, it was *possible* that some of those things were on the island somewhere, but what were the odds? Everybody had left.

"Hughes," Parker said. "Remember yesterday when you told me to chill? That I was being paranoid?"

Hughes said nothing.

"Has something *changed* since then?" Parker said. "Did you all see or hear something when I was out there by myself?"

Parker, Kyle thought, was finally making some sense. What was up with Hughes, anyway?

"Didn't see or hear anything," Hughes said. "Doesn't mean the island is clear. We've only seen this one little piece of it. We need to search the whole thing."

Kyle resisted the urge to roll his eyes. "It's bigger than you think."

"I know how big it is," Hughes said. "We sailed all the way up it yesterday and I've looked at your maps."

"We can't search the whole forest," Annie said. "It goes on forever."

"Didn't say we had to search the forest," Hughes said. "But Kyle himself said there are two other towns. We have no idea what happened in either of them."

"Man has a point," Frank said.

Kyle pursed his lips. "All right. Let's check out the grocery store and see if there's something for breakfast. We'll round up a few more supplies, either from there or from some other houses, then check out the other two towns. Y'all want to walk or take the boat?"

"Boat," Hughes said.

"I'm not getting back in that water," Parker said.

"Then your ass can stay put," Hughes said, "We don't need you."

Damn, Kyle thought. That was cold. Kyle had more of a reason to be angry at Parker than Hughes did. Parker had punched him two days ago, after all, and his jaw still throbbed. But Parker had behaved better since then. Reducing the amount of stress in his life was doing him good.

"I'd like to find some more clothes and blankets," Annie said.

"And we need some water," Frank said. "I don't know about you guys, but I'm super freaking dehydrated. My piss looks like tea."

"There might be some water left in the store," Hughes said. "Or in bottles in people's refrigerators. We also need to check for gun racks and ammo. We used up most of the ammo back at that grocery store. Let's hold off on splitting up."

Kyle nodded and opened the front door.

"Forgetting something?" Hughes said.

Was he?

"What?" Kyle said.

"Your crowbar," Hughes said.

Kyle felt his face flush. He retrieved his crowbar from the kitchen counter.

They headed out as a group. The house next door, a Victorian with delicately painted wedding-cake trim, didn't look at all like the kind of place where they would find guns and ammo, but Hughes didn't complain when Kyle stepped onto the porch.

He knocked. He felt silly doing it, but he'd feel worse barging in. His civilized habits were coming back in full force now that he was in a place that hadn't been trashed. That was a good thing, but at the same time it disturbed him. How many places like this were left in the world? How long before the entire human race forgot how to behave? Dead bodies, broken glass, burnt walls, trash on the streets, and scarce resources brought out everyone's inner barbarian. Most of the planet must look that way now.

After waiting a few moments for the greeting and welcome he knew wouldn't come, he tried the handle and the door opened. Whoever lived there hadn't locked up—what was the point?—but they did take out the trash. Kyle didn't notice even the faintest of odors. Nor did he sense life or movement or presence inside. The house was empty just like the other one. Surely like all the others.

But this house was nicer than the first. Whoever lived there had enough money to collect heavy wooden furniture from the Victorian era. The curtains were heavy and expensive, as was the marble-top coffee table. The fancy sofa looked a little uptight and uncomfortable—Kyle was a leather-couch guy himself—but the beauty and grace of the whole ensemble was something he never thought he'd see again in his life. The legs on the dining-room table were as thick as Hughes' arms, and the slab of the tabletop itself could stop bullets.

Hughes stayed on the porch with his rifle and kept watch on the street.

Frank and Annie stepped into the kitchen. Kyle heard the cabinets and refrigerator open.

"Score," Frank said. "We've got soup, rice, and pasta in here. A jar of peanut butter and a can of tuna."

"Big bottle of mineral water in the fridge," Annie said, "and some expired orange juice."

Kyle may not have broken into the house, but he had entered the house, and standing there in the living room like a burglar with a crowbar in his hand while Frank raided the cabinets made him feel like the intruder he was. The law had gone silent, but it was still there in his mind.

He forced those thoughts down, though, and focused instead on the positive. He would love sharing this house with Annie. The place next door was nice enough, but this Victorian was like a miniature grand ballroom in a five-star hotel. Whoever lived there had been good solid people. He could tell. That tradition would continue when he and Annie moved in.

He could hardly wait to chop wood for fires, fish for their dinner, and plant a garden in back. No more wasted time. Everything he did from here on out would be of monumental importance. Never again would he be distracted by email, vacuous filler programs on television, phone calls, errands, or making and stressing out about money. None of that crap even existed anymore. Life was now about basics: food, shelter, relaxation, and love. He'd learn about farming and fixing things and generating off-the-grid power. He'd get his hands dirty and keep his nose clean.

Life was better than ever, and it was about to get better still.

But then Hughes came inside and said, "Everybody down on the floor."

CHAPTER SIXTEEN

The herd came from the west, from the direction of the ferry terminal and the other two towns. Hughes had known all along that this might happen. He'd seen no evidence, let alone proof, that everyone had evacuated the island. They had only evacuated Eastsound. And now they were back, shuffling along the road in a daze.

They didn't see Hughes as he shut himself and the others inside.

Frank flattened himself against the front wall as Annie, Parker, and Kyle hit the deck next to Hughes. Then Kyle craned his head up toward the window. "What did you see?"

The dumb shit was going to get everyone killed.

"Keep your damn head down," Hughes whispered and yanked the back of Kyle's shirt.

Kyle got back down on the floor but propped himself up on his elbows.

The heavy curtains in the front window were parted, but a thin mesh curtain was drawn. It was hard to see through it into the house. Hughes had checked that from the front. He wasn't able to see any detail at all through the mesh and the glare from the porch, but movement near the window might create visible shadows.

"The hell's going on?" Kyle said.

"How many are out there?" Parker said.

"I saw maybe ten," Hughes said, "before coming inside. Could be 1,000. Could be just ten. They're walking, not running. They didn't see me."

"How do you know they aren't townsfolk?" Kyle said.

Hughes wanted to punch him. "They *are* the townsfolk."

"Let me see," Kyle said and craned his head up again. "I don't hear any—"

Hughes yanked Kyle back down again and gave him his I'm-going-to-stomp-your-ass-rightfuckingnow look. "You move in front of that curtain, and it'll be the siege at the grocery store all over again. But this time they'll bust right on in."

"You're fucking dead, Kyle," Parker said.

"*Shh*," Hughes whispered. "Shut your ass up. They're right outside."

Hughes could hear them shuffling up the street now. They didn't walk the same as regular people. They ran more or less the same as regular people, but they staggered when they walked as if they were drunk. The herd outside seemed to have no particular destination in mind. They just stumbled into town as if they had nowhere better to go.

They probably wouldn't try to get into the house without a reason, so as long as everyone stayed down and kept quiet, everything should be fine. As long as none of them shambled onto the porch and peered in the window. The glare and the mesh wouldn't work so well from that close.

The bathroom down the hall had only one small window, and since bathrooms are private, the window was high enough off the ground outside that no one—and no *thing*—could see in without standing on a stepladder or something.

"You all get into the bathroom," Hughes whispered, "and lock the door. Don't walk. Crawl. And do it quietly. Crawl slowly. Sound really carries."

"You staying here?" Frank said.

Hughes nodded.

"But—" Kyle said.

"Just go," Hughes said. "Now. And be *quiet*."

They went. He stayed. And he peeked ever so carefully through the mesh over the windowsill.

As many as three dozen filthy, tattered, and diseased human forms dragged their feet at quarter-speed up the street. Their eyes seemed not to focus on anything in particular, as if they were looking through, over, or past things rather than at things. War veterans called it the thousand-yard stare.

They didn't look like that at all when something caught their attention. Then they looked *focused.*

Five-thousand people lived on the island, but they couldn't all have turned. Most were probably dead, their bodies consumed, their bones scattered somewhere back near the ferry terminal—the plague's likely insertion point on the island.

Eastsound's population must have driven there to wait for a boat to take them to Friday Harbor as Kyle had said. But something went wrong. Maybe they waited for a boat that never came, or the boat showed up with a bunch of the infected on board.

And they must have heard Hughes' gunshot the first morning and headed back in the direction of town. But if that was the case, why did it take them so long to show up? Maybe they heard the sound but didn't know exactly where it came from, so they just started ambling about in that general direction. He should have thought of that. Damn, he should have thought of that.

The herd turned left off Main Street and headed right toward the house. Hughes fought the urge to duck. They wouldn't be able to make out the details of his face through the mesh, but they might see sudden movement. If they attacked the house, they'd be inside in seconds. And there would be nowhere to run but out the back door.

Hughes and the others might make it out. They could run for the water. The shore was only 200 or so feet away. How long did it take to run 200 feet? Thirty seconds? The horde would come after them, but they'd get away if they had a fifteen-second head start.

But the herd was between the house and the water. And they just kept coming, more and more of them now. Another two dozen came into view from the west. The nearest ones were less than 100 feet away and coming straight toward him.

Annie heard two things: her own heartbeat in her ears and the heavy breathing of four panicked people. One tiny window at head level let only a small amount of heavy gray light in, but she didn't dare stand anywhere near it. Neither did Kyle, Parker, or Frank.

Kyle sat on the edge of the claw-foot tub with his face in his hands. Frank sat splayed out, stunned, on the floor. Parker stood near the sink and flexed his fingers like he wanted to strangle the infected to death in the street. She leaned with her ear against the door leading into the hallway, straining to hear even the tiniest sound.

"I can't believe it," Kyle said. She felt a fresh rush of panic. *Be quiet already.*

"If you don't shut up right now," Parker whispered in a voice that sounded like hissing, "I'm going to beat you to death."

Annie placed her hand on Parker's shoulder.

"What do we do?" Frank whispered.

Nobody said anything for a few moments. Finally, Parker said quietly, "Let them pass. They obviously don't know we're here."

"And then what?" Frank said.

Nobody replied.

Annie heard faint footsteps outside on the street, but they weren't normal footsteps. They sounded like limping and scraping. She looked at the window. It was too small for a person to fit through, so the infected couldn't get in. They'd have to come in through the door. But that also meant she couldn't get out through that window. She and the others were trapped with only one exit.

The bathroom was a good place to be at the moment because they were invisible, but it would be the worst place to be if the house came under attack.

The window faced the side of the next house, not the street, and she thought about peeking out ever so carefully. She might be able to see some of the street and get an idea what was going on out there. But if she could see the street, the street could see her.

She took a few steps toward it, not intending to stand right in front of it, but to get close enough that she might be able to hear what's going on out there. Parker grabbed her arm and shook his head.

"I just want to listen," she whispered. "They won't see me."

The living-room floor was made of creaky old hardwood. The bathroom floor was tiled in white marble, so her steps made no sound.

She reached the window, ducked underneath it, cocked her head sideways so her right ear pointed upward, and heard a cough. Not a normal cough as if from a person with a seasonal cold, but a sickening wet rasp as if one of the infected was coughing up its own throat.

"Jesus," Parker whispered.

Frank shushed him.

Everyone started when they heard a light tap on the door. Hughes.

"Come in," Annie whispered and unlocked the door.

"Can't," Hughes whispered from somewhere near the floor. "They might see the door open. It's visible from the street at just the right angle."

Hughes must have crawled. He was awfully quiet about it because Annie didn't hear him even though the hallway floor creaked. Hughes was good. It must have taken him a good couple of minutes.

"At least three or four dozen of them out there," Hughes said. "Everybody just stay put and stay quiet and we'll head back to the boat once they've moved on."

Annie sat next to Kyle on the lip of the tub. Parker and Frank sat on the floor, Parker as far away from Kyle as he could get. The two wouldn't look at each other.

Minutes passed. Annie exchanged concerned looks with everyone, but after a few more minutes she felt better. Feelings of terror gave way to fear, which gave way to dread. Then even the dread faded into boredom and torpor. The infected were still out there, but they had no idea anyone was inside the house.

Her body and mind could only sustain the feeling of fear for so long. Eventually, the human brain's pharmacy ran out of adrenaline.

The infected were still out there. They were not moving on. She could hear them. It was as if on some basic level they knew they'd find more food in town than out on the road or in the forest. Or maybe, on another dim level, they recognized Eastsound as home and felt like they had nowhere to go.

The others had no idea what the infected were thinking, but Annie knew the answer was, not a lot. They don't reason anything through. They just hunt down food and react to stimuli. When she was infected, she didn't know her own name. She might have recognized her apartment, but she wasn't even sure of that much.

She tried to imagine what she would have done in their place when the virus still had control of her body and mind, but with each day that passed she had a harder time remembering what it was like to be sick. At best, her memories of those events were like the memories of a dream that would dissipate like wisps of steam if she didn't consciously try to hold onto them.

Another hour passed. Nobody moved. Nobody said anything. Nobody was relaxed—that was for sure—but they all had an easier time keeping calm. They were safe for now as long as they didn't make any noise or try to go anywhere.

"What if," Kyle finally said, "we try to imitate their movements and behavior? Pretend like we're part of the pack?"

"That," Parker said, "is the stupidest idea you've come up with yet. And that's saying something."

"We don't look anything like them," Hughes said.

"Only because they're filthy," Kyle said. "But they aren't filthy when they first turn. The freshly turned ones don't get attacked."

"Man has a point," Frank said.

"Think about it," Kyle said. "Let's say we took one of those things, somehow managed to give it a bath and put some fresh clothes on it, then took a picture of it while it was just standing there inert, when it wasn't biting somebody's face. If we showed that photograph to someone who didn't know any better, would they be able to tell that they were looking at one of the infected?"

Hughes shook his head. "No. I don't think so. But that doesn't matter. Those things aren't just standing around posing for pictures. They're moving. And they move strangely. I don't think you can imitate them. They recognize us just as easily as we recognize them."

"They move as a herd," Annie said. "We'd have to move with them. Go where they go. But right now they seem to be stalled. They're just randomly milling around."

"They'll have to move on at some point," Kyle said.

"Then all we have to do," Annie said, "is go the opposite direction. We wait until they move on, then run to the boat."

"And what if they stay out there all week?" Frank said.

"They won't," Kyle said.

"You don't know that," Frank said. "You have no idea what goes on in their … heads. They used to live in this town. Doesn't seem like they're going back to their own beds for the night, but they seem to remember this is where they belong."

"But why are they here *now* all of a sudden?" Kyle said. "They weren't here this afternoon. They weren't here yesterday. They probably haven't been here all week or even all month."

"They heard my gunshot yesterday," Hughes said on the other side of the door. "Just took them a while to get here. They didn't know where the sound came from exactly. They only knew the direction."

Annie felt herself sink. Hughes was probably right. It made sense.

"They looked tired," Hughes said. "Like they're dehydrated and hungry."

Annie opened her mouth, then clamped it shut. For the briefest moment she forgot she wasn't supposed to tell them she had been sick once herself. She wanted to say they knew to drink water when they found it, and that they also knew not to drink seawater. She remembered that much at least.

"The island has freshwater on it somewhere, right?" she whispered.

"There are five freshwater lakes on Orcas," Kyle said. "That's where we'll get our own water."

Parker looked incredulous. "In case you haven't noticed," he said, "the island is *infected*."

"We'll get some more ammunition and sweep it and clear it," Kyle said.

"You are amazing," Parker said. "Absolutely fucking amazing."

"Those things are going to die, aren't they?" Annie said. "When winter comes. I mean, what, they're just going to sleep on the street out in the open? They're going to do that in January?"

"Doesn't really matter," Frank said. "They could bust into some houses, but it's no warmer in here than it is out there without a fire going."

No one said anything else for a long, long time. The day slowly drained away. Nobody moved inside the house. Annie heard only an occasional grunting or scraping outside. Some of the infected were still out there. Eventually she noticed the light getting dimmer.

"Sun's going down," she whispered.

"Yeah," Parker said. "We *noticed*." She frowned at him, but he didn't see her. He was looking at the window. She could tell he wanted to peek outside as much as she did.

Late evening faded to twilight. Annie heard a faint hissing outside the window and felt a squirt of adrenaline.

"What's that?"

"Rain," Kyle said.

Yes, the sound was just rain. Annie exhaled. She was still on edge. It was just barely raining outside. It sounded like little kisses on the leaves and the grass.

"Well that's just great," Parker said.

"Actually, it's perfect," Kyle said.

"You guys hear rain?" Hughes said from the other side of the door.

"Faintly," Annie said. "It's a light drizzle. It could stop any second."

"If it picks up," Kyle said, "those things might move on."

"They might come in *here*," Parker said.

"You should all hope it rains like a sonofabitch," Hughes said. "Because that way they won't hear us when we make a run for it."

Parker knew he'd been right to sleep on the boat the first night. Goddamnit, if he'd stayed there just a couple more hours, he'd be fine right now.

The rain picked up. It was steady now, and loud. It drummed on the roof. The house was freezing inside. The autumn rains had finally arrived, and the Northwest had a short autumn. Winter, the rainiest time of the year in this part of the country, comes early and would be upon them in no time.

Parker consoled himself with the wonderful fact that most or all of the infected would die of exposure if not starvation. Homeless people used to live on the streets of Seattle and Portland during the winter. They were losers, for sure, but at least they had the sense to get out of the rain and sleep under a bridge wrapped in blankets. The infected, near as he could tell, were still out in the elements. They wouldn't get hypothermic and die in the next couple of hours, but at least they hadn't come in the house. Yet.

He could barely see a damn thing at this point. Even though the sun had gone down, there was still probably more light outside than in the bathroom. A few stray rays still bounced around in the atmosphere, but the darkness in the house was about to become absolute.

Hughes tapped on the door. "Coming in." He couldn't whisper anymore and expect to be heard over the downpour, so he spoke at regular volume.

Parker didn't even see the door open. It was too dark. Which meant those things wouldn't have seen it even if they were out there on the porch.

Maybe that's exactly what they were doing. Gathering on the porch and pressing their faces and hands against the front glass. The windows were not boarded up. They could come right in if that's what they wanted. How long until they got sick of the cold and the rain and some dimwitted switch flipped in their heads that made them remember, *Oh yeah, houses. Houses are dry!*

If a band of those things opened the front door and shambled on in,

Parker wasn't sure he'd hear them over the sound of the rain. They'd just *be* in the house.

As far as he knew, that had already happened.

Somebody should have brought back the night vision.

"You see anything?" Parker said to Hughes.

"They're still out there," Hughes said. "Wandering aimlessly. They don't seem to mind getting rained on. Probably won't be many left in the world this time next year. Not in this part of the world, anyway."

"But this time *this* year," Parker said, "we're trapped on Kyle's little island of horrors."

"Now's our best chance to get out of here," Hughes said.

Heat bloomed in Parker's chest. "And go where?"

"The boat," Hughes said. "Where else?"

I'm not doing that, Parker thought. I am not. Doing that.

Not in the dark.

"They won't see us," Hughes said. "It's raining so hard they won't hear us, either, so we need to go before it stops."

Now?

No.

Parker couldn't do it. No way. Assuming he even made it down to the water before getting bitten, he couldn't possibly jump in the sea and swim to the boat in the dark. He wouldn't see it. He wouldn't even see silhouettes. Not at night in a rainstorm. He might as well go out there blindfolded.

If he didn't get bitten, he'd freeze or he'd drown.

That water was so cold, he'd sink to the bottom in minutes if he got lost. And it was raining so hard, he wasn't sure he'd even be able to tell which way was up.

"Can't," he said.

"Yes, you can," Annie said.

"No, really, I can't."

"Then stay here," Kyle said. "The rest of us are going. And we need to go now."

Jesus, they really were going to do it. Why in the hell didn't they just wait in the house until morning? The house was only a couple hundred feet from the water. If they timed it right, they could probably make it. Hughes had his rifle and could shoot at least some of them. The others had crowbars and hammers.

"Let's go in the morning," Parker said, "when we can see where we're going."

"The whole point," Hughes said, "is to go when we can't see because they can't see either. And with this rain coming down, they won't hear us."

"We should fan out when we hit the water," Annie said. "First one to find the boat hollers out."

"You people are crazy," Parker said.

"Those things," Hughes said, "could bust into this house any second."

"The bathroom door has a lock," Parker said. "They can't get in. And they won't even try if they don't know we're here."

"What makes you sure they won't figure out that we're here?" Hughes said. "Or that they won't come inside and just camp out there in the living room?"

"We go out there, we die," Parker said.

"We stay in here, we die," Hughes said.

"This is your fault, Kyle," Parker said.

"*My* fault," Kyle said.

"We should have checked the whole island before we got off that boat," Parker said.

"Agreed," Hughes said. "But it's not Kyle's fault. It's my fault. I should have insisted."

"It's Kyle's fault," Parker said.

"You can all blame me later," Kyle said, "after we're safe."

Parker noticed they'd raised their voices, not in anger but because the rain was coming down even harder. It sounded like a Pineapple Express coming ashore. The Pacific Northwest gets storms like that all the time in the autumn and winter. The weather forecasters called these storms atmospheric rivers, and that's exactly what the storm sounded like—a river pouring onto the roof of the house. It was going to rain like that for hours. The sea must be boiling. The perfect place to drown in the dark.

"So here's what we do," Hughes said.

"Fuck," Parker said.

"Stay here and die then," Kyle said. "The hell do we care?"

"So here's what we do," Hughes said again. "We go out the front, and we go out quietly. We walk. We don't run, we walk. And keep low. There might be just enough light in the sky that we'll form silhouettes if we don't stay low. Should only take us a minute or two to get to the water. It's a straight shot, okay? That street goes directly down to the shore, so we won't get lost if we stay on the pavement. If you're spotted or grabbed, run. Don't scream, don't yell out to the others, just run. But do yell if you're the first one to the boat. I don't think our voices will carry as far as the beach from out there in this rain, but if so, who cares? We've got lights and guns on the boat."

"I don't have a weapon," Parker said.

"You should have brought one," Hughes said. "But you don't need one."

"The hell I don't," Parker said. "You all have weapons."

"I'm not going to shoot in the dark," Hughes said. "We're not swinging crowbars in the dark, either. We'd take our own heads off."

"Actually," Annie said. "Maybe we should. One of us should go out swinging ahead of the others to clear a path on the road."

"You hit one of those things in the shoulder," Hughes said, "and it's going to scream. Then we're well and truly fucked. And you might still hit one of us in the head. Too easy to get turned around and confused out there."

"Please wait until morning," Parker said. His voice sounded pathetic even to himself. The others knew how scared he was now, but he didn't care.

"This will be over in five minutes," Hughes said. "Two minutes to get to the water and three minutes to swim. The boat has a propane heater. We'll warm up and we'll be okay. Five minutes."

Parker put his hand on his face and rubbed his eyes with his fingertips.

"Fine," he said. "Okay."

He didn't say "okay" because he thought Hughes' plan was sound. He said "okay" because he'd rather die with the others than all by himself.

This could go one of two ways. He'd either be torn up by teeth on the road or he'd panic and drown in the water. Toss a coin. One or the other.

And if he gets only partly ripped up by teeth, he'll die twice. The first time from biting, the second from drowning.

D arkness filled the house so absolutely that Parker couldn't tell if his eyes were open or closed except by feel. He groped his way out of the bathroom and into the hallway, poking Annie in the neck and elbowing Frank in the ear.

"Sorry," he said.

Somebody banged into a wall.

Parker could navigate his own house well enough in the dark, "seeing" it in his memory. That, he figured, was how blind people got around, only they'd learned to "see" a much wider swath of the world than their own bedroom and hallway. But Parker did not know this house. Nor did he know the streets outside. He'd have to feel his way hundreds of feet to the water on a street full of predators. And if by God he made it that far, he'd have to "feel" his way to the boat.

Drowning or teeth? Which one was worse? Getting chewed up would hurt more, but sinking into a dark sea where his body would never be found, his lungs filling with burning saltwater, frightened him more than anything else in the world.

Maybe he should just run. Run like he's on fire, throw himself into the water, and swim toward the boat so fast and so hard that nothing could possibly catch him. He might get lucky and bang into it. Then he could pull himself up the aluminum ladder. It could work. He had a very small chance of making it.

But only if he ran. Because otherwise he'd panic and freeze.

"Don't run," Hughes said when they got to the living room. "We'll only make it if we go slowly."

Every cell in Parker's body screamed bullshit. This was flight time. But on some level he knew Hughes was thinking more clearly. He probably did have a better chance of survival if he emptied his mind and did exactly what Hughes told him. Just surrender. Surrender to the plan and don't think about it. Just do it.

He took a deep breath.

The rain sounded louder, clearer, and closer when Hughes opened the door. Parker could just make out a swath of dull gray light overhead. That was the sky. There were no stars, only clouds, and there was no ambient light from a city in any direction to light up the underside of the clouds.

Parker could not see the street. He could not see any houses. He could not see the porch he knew was in front of him. He could not see the steps he'd have to descend. He could not see the rain thundering down onto everything.

Nor could he see those *things* he knew still wandered around out there. He'd never make it all the way to the water without bumping into at least one of them. And then what?

He'd shit himself to death, that's what.

"Take it slow," Hughes said quietly. "And remember. No yelling until you get to the boat."

When he crossed the porch, Parker saw the water. It looked like a faint gray splotch below the slightly lighter gray sky. He could make out no details, let alone the boat. He saw only the faintest possible shade of gray and exploding purple and black shapes on his retinas, the same dark kaleidoscope he saw while falling asleep.

When his feet found the first step leading down to the sidewalk, a torrent of rainwater lashed his face, chest, and arms, soaking and freezing him instantly as if he stood in a cold shower. Water even got in his nose.

And the noise was incredible, like a 100,000 hands slapping the ground. It came from every direction and made him dizzy. He struggled against the urge to sit on the steps.

Instead he reached out in front of him and found Hughes' back. He grabbed onto the man's shoulders, but Hughes turned and told him to let go.

"We're more likely to bump into those things if we don't split up," Hughes said. Was that really true? "Just stay on the road and take it slow."

Somebody shushed them. Parker thought it was Annie, but he couldn't be sure. He wasn't even certain he heard somebody shushing them, the rain was so loud. Maybe that's all he heard.

Those things were out there. They could be three feet in front of him. One foot in front of him. Three inches in front of him. How would he know? It was like stepping out into a minefield. A living, breathing, moving minefield with fangs that would take him apart as thoroughly as a Claymore.

He almost fell forward when he reached the sidewalk and expected more stairs. Someone—or some *thing*—bumped into him from behind. "Just me," Annie said and gently pushed him.

He was going to lose his mind before he got to the water. The infected were everywhere, swarming around in the dark. Maybe they could see better. Maybe they could hear better. Maybe they could smell better. They could certainly fight better against an unarmed man. All they had to do was bite Parker just once and he'd be finished.

Actually, if they bit him just once, he would join them. Good God. Talk about an advantage. If only *that* dynamic could be reversed. If healthy people could "tag" the infected and cure them, the human race could increase its numbers. And its advantage.

He'd rather drown or be eaten than get bitten and turn. That much he knew. But the water was still so far away. Hundreds of feet away. There could be twenty of those things between him and the shore.

Parker swallowed hard and froze. He couldn't move in any direction. Annie bumped into him again, but this time he stepped out of her way and then stopped again. He blinked his eyes, squinted as hard as he could, but saw nothing. He heard only rain.

In a detached way, he realized he was freezing, but he didn't care. It wasn't important. His body shook and it shuddered, but he couldn't walk. His heart pounded in overdrive. His breathing grew faster and shallower. He couldn't get enough oxygen. He'd faint if he didn't get more, but he couldn't. The air was drenched in water. He already felt like he was in the sea. *Was* he in the sea? Did he make it to the shore already? Was it time to swim?

No, he was still on the street. Wasn't he?

God, what was happening?

He no longer knew which direction he was supposed to be going. He could hardly even stay upright. His head felt like it was caught in a whirlpool and his stomach fluttered they way it did when he leaned too far back in a chair. He bent his knees and reached for the ground.

Squatted. Placed his hands on the pavement. There was a good half-inch of water pouring over the street. His fingertips found gravel and grit.

Then someone bumped into him. He didn't know who it was. Annie again most likely. But he smelled the stench of body odor and heard a deep guttural exhale, a half-grunt, half-sigh that sounded like it came from an animal.

Oh God. It was one of those things.

One of those things had just walked right into him.

He scrambled on all fours and ended up slipping and rolling onto his back. Water poured into his eyes and his nose. He jammed his eyes shut and blew out his breath.

No idea where that thing was. It seemed to have vanished. The feeling of panic ebbed slightly. He could think again.

He was on the street. And he had to *move*. He needed to stand. Walk to the water. Swim to the boat.

Shit. The others could be there by now. How long had he been standing there? They wouldn't leave him, would they? And where was that *thing* that had just walked into him?

He stood up. And bumped into another one. It grunted. Its breath smelled like a carcass. It grabbed Parker's arms with cold hands.

He screamed.

It wasn't a horror-movie scream. It didn't even last a full second. It was more of a startled gasp, really, or maybe a yelp. Completely involuntary on his part. But it was just enough that the thing that gripped him knew it found prey.

It tightened its grip and pushed into him. He felt it, but he couldn't see it.

Jesus, where were its teeth?

What he did next was instinctive. He didn't think anything through, didn't plan, didn't calculate. He just reacted. His arms were pinned to his side, so he kneed the thing in its groin and head-butted it in the face.

Only then did Parker realize the thing was shorter than him or he might have head-butted it right in the teeth.

It cried out in anger and pain and Parker shoved the thing down to the ground.

There was nothing he could do about what happened next.

It screamed.

If there was any doubt before about what their screams meant, there was not anymore. The sound had a perfectly clear and unambiguous purpose. It said, *Found prey.*

Parker stood. So much rain poured off his body that he felt heavy. He still couldn't see, had no idea which direction he was facing, but he knew where that thing was. It was on the ground three feet in front of him. It screamed again and he kicked it in the face. He felt and heard a sickening crunch as its face broke. It flopped to the ground, silent.

He turned around, found the faint gray smudge of the sea in the distance, and ran. If he crashed into anything or anyone, he'd shove it aside or run right on over it.

He could not see the ground. Could not see his feet.

So he did not see the curb.

He didn't go flying, exactly. His right foot just spun underneath him. He went up and then down.

He may as well have been hit by a bus. His abdomen slapped the ground like he'd just done a belly flop. Air exploded from his lungs. His stinging palms felt sandpapered. He tried to breathe and could not. He gasped for air, but his diaphragm and lungs refused to cooperate.

He heard footsteps in front of him and the faint sound of a human voice beneath the drum of the rain saying, "This way." It sounded like Hughes, guiding the others.

Parker still couldn't breathe. He got up onto his knees, but he still couldn't breathe.

Everything stopped. He stopped hearing the rain, stopped feeling the wet and the cold, and completely forgot that those things were out there in the dark.

Because he couldn't breathe.

Nothing else mattered until he could breathe. He keeled forward, desperate to draw breath, but he couldn't.

He was going to suffocate.

But just as suddenly as he had stopped breathing, his lungs exploded with air. Parker took one gasping breath after another. He was not going to die on that sidewalk. Not if he got up and ran.

He stood again and felt like someone had stabbed an ice pick into his knee. His palms felt shredded to ribbons. He couldn't run. Couldn't walk without limping. He was just about done.

But he limped, dazed, certain he wouldn't make it, but drowning now seemed better than being killed by one or more of those things. At least he wouldn't turn into one of them.

The water was not far ahead of him. He heard splashing. His companions were wading in and pushing off toward the boat. He could see the water a little bit better as he got closer.

He heard Annie cry out, "I see the boat!"

Footsteps behind him. Footsteps moving fast. Running. Lots of them.

Screams behind him.

Those things knew where they were. Those things knew his companions were getting into the water.

Parker ran. He didn't know how, but he did it. A switch flipped and the pain vanished from his knee, his hands, and his belly. He'd either make it to the water or die like a gazelle on the African Savannah in seconds.

He hit the water at full speed and it tripped him. Pinwheeled him forward and face-first into the sea. His injured knee slammed into a rock below the surface and the pain exploded again. He saw white flashes behind his eyes and felt his stomach leap up his throat, but he pushed himself into the dark water and swam ahead blindly.

Splashing behind him. Lots of splashing behind him. Those things had followed him in.

Why were they swimming? They didn't jump in off the docks in Olympia, but *now* they were getting into the water?

He swam. Not properly the way he learned as a kid in the pool at the YMCA, just a frantic and panicked blind paddling scramble away from the shore. He was hyperventilating. He couldn't help it. The adrenaline in his system reached its biological maximum. His heart pounded away like a hummingbird's. He had to breathe fast and hard and deep and then even faster, but the water was almost ocean-like in its choppiness, and he got some in his mouth and his nose every time a wave swept into his face.

So much water washed over his head that he could no longer tell if he was above water or not. But he had to breathe, and he had to breathe fast, and he if he didn't find the boat *now* he would drown.

He had no idea where it was. No idea any longer which way was the shore, so he slowed down and tried to stand on the bottom so he could fill his lungs and get his bearings, but his feet found no purchase. The sea had no bottom. He had swum too far, he was sinking, and he was going to drown. Those things were somewhere behind him, but he was going to drown.

But then his feet touched the bottom. He was submerged over his head, but his feet found the bottom, and he pushed upward as hard as he could, ignoring the explosive pain in his knee, and launched himself back toward the surface.

His face broke through and he gasped. *Go. Just go. The boat has to be up ahead somewhere.*

Annie's voice cried out ahead of him.

"I found the boat!"

He could barely hear her over the rain and the waves.

Something gasped and gurgled and splashed much closer behind him.

Go. Toward Annie's voice and don't stop until your hands grasp that ladder.

He swam. And this time he did it correctly, the way he was taught. No furious dog paddling, but the proper crawl stroke with the proper method of breathing.

"Here!" Annie cried. "Here!"

She just might save his life.

The surface of the sea exploded with light from the boat. Someone had flipped on the power switch and turned the darkness to daylight.

"Parker!" Annie screamed from the deck. He saw her face. Pure terror and shock and alarm at what she was seeing behind him. "Parker, *hurry!*" she shouted, hysterical now.

Somehow he swam faster. He didn't think it was possible. He felt like a torpedo on the water's surface, his feet behind him kicking in the water like a propeller. And he felt a strange sort of high and detachment. A deep and serious calm settled inside him. He moved fast, but time seemed to slow. He heard everything and noticed the tiniest details. Hundreds of individual raindrops striking the surface of the illuminated sea created hundreds of individual splashes and ripples. He heard every drop of water kicked up by his feet. He was going to make it. His body was damaged, but it was performing magnificently under the threat of imminent death.

The boat was less than twenty feet ahead of him now. He saw it clearly. The others were all on deck now, not just Annie. Kyle and Frank wielded crowbars. Hughes pointed his rifle directly at Parker.

And fired.

Parker saw the barrel flash and heard the *crack* of the shot at the same instant he felt a bullet pass so near his head that it might have taken off some of his hair. From not four feet behind him, he heard a smack and a gurgle.

"You're clear!" Hughes shouted. "Get up here! Now!"

Parker reached for the ladder and felt a rip in his shoulder as he overextended. Frank stood there waiting. He reached out his hand. Parker grasped it with his good arm. Frank pulled him up and onto the deck. Parker rolled over and lay on his back, gasping.

He coughed water out of his mouth and his nose and heard another loud *crack* of Hughes' rifle. He was safe. He didn't die. None of them died. Everyone was okay.

But his relief shattered at once when he realized they had nowhere to go.

CHAPTER SEVENTEEN

The storm blew over and brought back the night sky, including a quarter moon. All was not lost. Kyle could see just fine now, and he knew what to do. There was never any chance they could build a new world without setbacks, but everything would be fine. The others would see.

Adjacent to Orcas was another smaller island. He forgot its name, but no matter. Hardly anyone lived there. Just a handful of houses. There certainly wasn't a town, nor was there ferry service. The few people who lived on the island had to come and go on their own.

So that was the place. Kyle would take his companions there to shelter for a few days until everyone regained their strength and their nerve.

He guided the boat into the passage between Orcas Island and the other one. No one—and no *thing*—was going to bother them there.

"We can sleep here," he said and dropped anchor. "We're a mile from land. Only the open ocean is safer."

No one objected, not even Parker.

God, the islands were beautiful in the moonlight, like emerald mountains in a liquid pearl sea.

"We can head over to that small island in the morning," he said.

"Not a fucking chance, Kyle," Parker said.

Parker was angry. Kyle understood. He understood perfectly. And frankly, he couldn't blame Parker. He almost died in the water off Eastsound. If Hughes hadn't shot that thing that was swimming up from behind him, he probably would have died. Kyle would never forget the terror on Parker's face at that moment.

"You can stay on the boat again if you want," Kyle said. "We'll all understand. But you should know that hardly anyone lives on that island. The entire population I think is less than two dozen. It has to be safer than Orcas."

"You don't know that," Hughes said.

"He fucking well doesn't," Parker said.

"Guys," Frank said.

"Okay," Annie said. "Everybody stay calm."

"I'm perfectly calm," Parker said. "Why wouldn't I be perfectly calm? Kyle's island of horrors didn't *actually* kill me."

"We'll sail around the island in the morning and check it out," Hughes said. "See what we see."

"Of course," Kyle said. "But there's probably nobody on it. The residents would have starved by now if they didn't go somewhere else."

"You hear that?" Parker said. "Kyle found us a safe place, but we'll starve to death if we stay there."

"All right," Kyle said, "you know what—"

"We have a week's worth of food on this boat," Hughes said. "We won't starve tomorrow."

"What do we do when it runs out?" Frank said.

Kyle had a plan, but it was better to wait and fill the others in later. Nobody wanted to hear it right now, especially not Parker. But ultimately it didn't make a damn bit of difference what Parker wanted. Kyle's plan was solid. The others would see that.

But he did feel disappointed and chastened. Orcas Island hadn't worked out, not yet. The place was a mess. A dangerous mess. But his new plan would work out just fine.

It had to.

If Eastsound was infected, what were the odds that the other islands were clear?

The odds were not good. No, they were not good at all. Friday Harbor was out. So how on earth could Annie find someone to fly her to South Carolina?

She couldn't.

She'd have to drive there. Or walk. That wasn't going to happen, not by herself. Frodo in *The Lord of the Rings* had better odds of taking the ring of power to Mordor. And he had a much better reason—

Wait.

Boom. She got it. There might be a way.

If only ...

But she could get herself killed, or even all of them killed. So many ways it could go wrong. It would be the biggest risk of her life, but if it worked, it could change everything.

First she'd have to tell them.

God, she'd have to tell them.

They went ashore in the morning. Hughes approved the idea after Kyle sailed around the island's perimeter. It was but a fraction of the size of Orcas, just two miles long and one mile wide. Nothing stirred on the shore or in the trees. The mere handful of houses visible from the water looked abandoned.

This time they used a small private dock instead of swimming ashore. They had to. Each had only one set of dry clothes. The air temperature outside barely reached fifty degrees Fahrenheit. Six inches of rain must have fallen the previous night. Building a fire from soggy wood wasn't possible. If they swam in the sea again and couldn't dry off, hypothermia would kill them just as surely as a pack of those things.

The dock seemed to belong to the owners of an enormous house a few hundred feet up a grassy hill. A trim gravel path wound its way up to the expansive porch. One other boat—a motorboat, not a sailboat—was lashed to the dock. Somebody might still be on the island. They'd have to be careful.

Hughes stepped off first. He brought the rifle and had Frank take the shotgun. The dock sounded hollow under his boots. Kyle followed, then Frank, then Annie, then Parker.

Hughes saw no signs of trouble at or near the house, but it was hard to tell for sure from this distance. "Do we have binoculars in any of those

"I don't think so," Frank said.

"Should have got some binoculars."

They started up the path. Gravel crunched under their boots. Nobody said anything. Parker limped and grimaced and grunted once in a while, but even he didn't say anything.

The path wound its way a safe distance from a short stretch of cliff about sixty feet above the water before turning again and heading straight to the house.

Whoever built that house had serious money. It looked like a cross between a gigantic log cabin and a small mountain lodge. The roof was pitched to let snow slide off even though snow rarely fell at sea level in the Northwest. The walls were painted the color of wood, the window trim green like the forest. The front porch, held up by fat log pillars, was as big as a small apartment. It would be a nice place to rest up if it checked out.

When they were less than 100 feet away, Hughes raised his right hand and said, "Hold up." Everyone stopped.

"Hello!" he shouted. "Anyone home?" He somehow expected his voice to echo, like it had in Olympia, but it didn't. All he heard was the creaking of timber.

"We're friendly!" he said. "We're not here to take anything!"

No movement. No sound.

"Looks like nobody's home," Kyle said.

Hughes frowned. Somebody had tied a boat to that dock. Kyle was being complacent again, and complacency kills. It would not have even occurred to Kyle to call out ahead. He'd have just strolled up the path and knocked on the door—or, worse, just walked right on in.

But all seemed to be well until they reached the overgrown lawn in front of the house. Two corpses lay on the grass. Hughes saw a third around the right side.

"Everybody get back." He raised his rifle and pointed it in the direction of the dead men. "Use some trees for cover."

The forest began just a dozen or so feet from the gravel path. Hughes took a knee as the others scrambled into the woods.

The corpses weren't skeletons. Whoever had been killed here hadn't been eaten. Looters, perhaps, shot by whoever owned the property.

"Hello!" he said again. "We're not here to steal! If there's anybody home and you don't want us here, just say the word and we'll go!"

Nothing. No movement. No sound.

"Frank," he said. "Cover me. I'm going to check out the porch."

He switched weapons with Frank. He'd need the shotgun for close-quarters fighting while Frank needed the rifle to cover him from a distance.

They were short on ammunition, but they had enough for a firefight if it came to that. They couldn't fend off a horde, but they could handle a pissed-off gunman or two.

He passed the corpses in the grass. They hadn't shaved in weeks. Their clothing was filthy. One had a pistol in his right hand. A shotgun lay on the grass near the other. Hughes figured the dead man on the side of the house was the owner. Most likely the man was defending his property against two intruders. The three of them must have shot each other to death at the same time.

Hughes retrieved the shotgun from the grass—a 12-gauge Baikal MP220—then held his breath and extracted the pistol from the second corpse's grip. A Jennings J22, an absolute piece of crap. It jammed constantly, which might explain why two men couldn't take one down without everyone getting killed. He placed the Jennings in his jacket pocket and vowed not to even try firing it except as a last resort.

Nobody was home—nobody left alive, anyway—but all the same Hughes banged on the door with the flat of his fist. "Coming in! And we're armed! We don't want any trouble, so if there's anyone in there, now's the time to speak up."

No answer, not even the creak of a floorboard.

When he opened the door, it took everything he had not to throw up.

Parker gagged when he stepped into the house. He could taste the stench of rot. This wasn't the first time he'd breathed putrid air in the last couple of months, but he'd never get used to it.

The dead man in the chair must be the homeowner. He was covered with fat flies. Parker had no idea who the three men outside were, but it seemed awfully unlikely that a stranger would make his way to this house on a remote island just to blow his own head off.

It was obvious that he'd blown his own head off, because his oozing fingers still gripped the shotgun. Another weapon, then, for the taking, but no one was in any kind of hurry to extract it.

The house was unusable. It didn't make the slightest bit of difference where in the world Parker went. Death preceded and followed.

But there was a guesthouse alongside the main house that had looked like a separate wing of the same house from the shore below.

He, Hughes, and Frank made sure both were clear, then everyone sat on the porch in front of the guesthouse.

"We'll be all right here for a while," Kyle said.

"Well isn't that a relief," Parker said. "Don't worry about all the dead people, folks. *Kyle* here thinks we'll be fine."

"We're only going to rest here. Until we're ready for the next phase of the plan."

Parker exchanged glances with Frank. Hughes raised his eyebrows. Annie looked a little perplexed.

Parker had his green light. "Listen up, Kyle. Your ass is done making plans for the rest of us. Done. That's twice now you damn near got us all killed. Both times because, despite what you look like, you're twelve fucking years old."

"All right!" Annie said.

Parker ignored her.

"From here on out, you're not allowed to piss without permission from both me *and* Hughes," he said.

"That's enough," Hughes said and stood up.

Annie glowered at Parker. Kyle wouldn't look at him.

"Fine," Parker said. "What's your plan, bright boy?"

Kyle sat on the top step of the porch and rested his elbows on his knees. "You are going to hate the idea. Of that I have no doubt."

"Oh, I don't doubt it either. But let's hear it. Let's have everyone hear it so we can agree to take your pissing privileges from you."

Kyle sighed. Annie looked away and into the trees.

"We have the guns and ammo from the dead guys in the grass," Kyle said. "Most likely every house on this island has more. These people lived in the middle of nowhere. The cops aren't minutes away—they're hours away, if not days. They were in charge of their own security. They had to be."

"That worked out well," Parker said. At least the corpses outside didn't smell too bad from a distance.

"So here's what we do," Kyle said. "We hit every house on the island and stock up as much as we can. Then we get back on the boat and go sweep and clear Orcas."

Nobody said anything.

"We can sweep and clear from the water," Kyle said. "We don't even have to get off the boat until we've killed most of them."

Nobody said anything.

"That's it?" Parker said. "That's your plan?"

"That's the plan."

"Your plan is that we go to war."

"You have a better idea?"

Parker did, in fact, have a better idea.

"Not a *terrible* plan," Hughes said.

"The hell it isn't," Parker said. "You know what we do? We take this boat and sail up to Alaska. Every single one of those fuckers is going to freeze to death *stat* in Alaska. Most of them are probably meatsicles already."

"You want to live off the land in Alaska?" Annie said. "Where it's too cold to farm?"

"We can hunt," Parker said.

"Hunt what?" Kyle said. "Bears?"

"Would you rather hunt up there or be hunted down here?" Parker said.

"Guys, I think I'm with Parker on this," Frank said.

"Well, I'm not," Annie said. "I'm from the South. I can't survive on an ice cap."

"Sweetheart, Alaska isn't an ice cap," Parker said.

"I'm not your *sweetheart*."

Kyle stood up. What, did he want to fight? He'd get his ass kicked for sure.

"Everybody just chill," Parker said. "How about we sleep on it and discuss it again in the morning?" He would not change his mind— that was for damn sure—but maybe by morning everyone would be a little less touchy and see that peace in Alaska was better than war in Washington.

"Fine," Kyle said.

"There are islands up in Alaska, you know."

Kyle sighed.

"We could go up for the winter and then come back down," Parker said. "See if those things have died off."

Kyle nodded, but Parker could tell he wasn't listening. Nor was he interested.

But Kyle needed to get interested. The dumb shit moved through life as though he had duct tape over his ears, but what he needed was duct tape over his mouth. Kyle had managed to convince *Parker* that Orcas Island was safe. He was as persuasive as he was naive and delusional, and his ludicrous ideas were sure to get everyone killed. The group needed joint leadership by Parker and Hughes with Kyle beaten down and shamed into obedience. That's exactly what was going to happen, and it was going to happen first thing in the morning.

They carried half their supplies up the hill and into the guesthouse. The rest had to remain on the boat. It would take two trips to bring everything up, and if they had to make a run for it in the dark, there'd be no time for two loads of gear. It was a good plan, but they mistakenly left behind the backpack with all the night vision in it.

When darkness fell they used a half-dozen candles for light inside the guesthouse. Parker parted the curtains, looked outside, and saw nothing at all. The moon was down now, the darkness absolute. "We should go get the night vision," he said. "In case something happens tonight. Flashlights are fine for getting around when everything's normal, but not if someone—or some *thing*—busts their way in here at four o'clock in the morning."

"Agreed," Hughes said.

"Me too," Kyle said.

"I'll go," Parker said.

"I'll go with you," Kyle said.

"The hell for? I don't need you to hold my hand."

"I need to burn off more calories," Kyle said. "I'm not tired yet and I'll go crazy here in this cabin."

"Fine," Parker said. "Grab a flashlight."

He didn't want Kyle along, but whatever.

Outside, the flashlights barely lit anything. Parker could see the ground in front of his feet okay, but everything else was as dark as before. He'd have to be damn sure to stay on the gravel path where it wound near the edge of the cliff. The stars sure looked great, though. And he could see the sea below and the black shapes of more islands off in the distance.

The air was cold. Parker used to enjoy the cool air of the Pacific Northwest, but that was back when climate control still existed. The main house had a fireplace, but the guesthouse didn't. And all the wood was wet anyway.

His and Kyle's feet on the gravel path made a hell of a racket. No one, and no thing, would be able to sneak up on the house in the dark. Not on the path, anyway.

"Cold out here," Kyle said.

Parker said nothing.

He had never used night vision before and wondered how well it would work with so little ambient light in the atmosphere. There was some light from the stars at least. His eyes were adjusting. He could almost, but not quite, make out individual pieces of gravel on the path.

The cliff was up ahead somewhere. As long as he stayed on the path, he'd be fine, but he felt spooked not knowing quite where the edge was.

And what was back in those trees? He wasn't entirely convinced the island was clear. Hence the night vision. This island, whatever its name was, was more likely clear than Orcas, for sure, but he'd thought *that* island was safe even though it was not. It made no difference how he or anyone else felt. The island was either safe or it wasn't.

Anyway, those things weren't the only possible threat. Three dead bodies up on the lawn and a half-decomposed corpse in the main house made that abundantly clear. Humans could be predators too. How many human survivors were behaving like Lane and his boys? Most of them, probably.

And what about mountain lions? And bears? Did big animals live on this island? Parker had no idea.

He and Kyle remained silent all the way down to the boat. Parker had assumed Kyle wanted to talk, perhaps even apologize, but he wasn't talking.

They reached the boat and went below to retrieve the backpack with the night vision in it.

"I want to try it out," Kyle said.

Parker felt tempted to argue on general principle, but he wanted to try it out too.

The night-vision devices were monocles. They only worked in one eye. Parker took one out of the box and attached it to his head over his left. He flipped the switch and gasped in astonishment. He could see everything below deck, even things his flashlight wasn't pointing at.

The flashlight itself was so bright, he had to squint and point it at the floor. He already knew these devices rendered everything in green for whatever reason, but he had no idea he'd be able to see so *much* rendered in green. He could read a newspaper if he had one.

"Wow," Kyle said when he turned his on.

"These are extraordinary," Parker said. "Turn your flashlight off."

They both turned off their flashlights and Parker could *still* see everything. He wasn't sure he'd still be able to read, but he could find his way around in the dark without any problems.

When he stepped up onto the deck, the full awesomeness of the night vision revealed itself. The sea and the islands were bathed in otherworldly green light, as if an alien sun had just appeared in the sky.

"Holy shit," Kyle said. "All this just from just starlight?"

"And the stray beams of moonlight still bouncing around," Parker said.

He couldn't make out the distant islands in detail, but he could see the boat, the sea, the dock, their own island, and the roofline of the house up the hill perfectly.

"Imagine," Kyle said, "if we'd had these on Orcas. We could have walked through that horde in the dark and been *fine*. We'll have a huge advantage when we go back there to clear them."

Parker wanted to punch Kyle in the ear. Instead he went below again to retrieve the backpack with the other night-vision devices and returned to the deck.

"It's too bad these only work in one eye," Kyle said.

Parker exhaled. "They only work in one eye so that your *other* eye can adjust to the darkness. You wouldn't want to be blind if the damn thing ran out of batteries."

That wasn't the only reason, of course. You'd need to know what everyone else can and can't see in case you're trying to hide in the shadows. Wasn't that obvious?

They trudged up the hill. Parker could see everything now. He could make out individual pieces of gravel without any problem. He could see individual blades of grass. He could see every single needle and leaf on the trees at the edge of the forest. And the number of stars overhead was simply extraordinary. At least ten times the usual number.

The trail became steeper as it wound its way toward the top of the cliff on the left.

"We're going to be okay," Kyle said as they walked.

"All we're doing here," Parker said, "is delaying the inevitable."

"Man, can't you stop being yourself for even five minutes? If we're safe now, we can be safe in the future."

"Doesn't matter if we're safe here because we'll die if we stay. You said so yourself. We'll starve to death. We can't grow any food. There's no farmland on this island."

"There are no farms in Alaska, either, but that's where you said you wanted to go."

"Farms or not, people live off the land up in Alaska."

"People live off the land here."

"No, they don't. The people who lived here loaded up on supplies from Seattle. This island is not a self-contained system."

Kyle stopped and turned around. He looked like a glowing cyborg with that night-vision thing on his eye. "We're not going to stay on this island. We're going back to Orcas."

"The hell we are."

"We'll sweep it and clear it and start new lives there. We'll plant crops and build irrigation ditches and raid the mainland for solar power. We'll cut trees for firewood and sleep in beds and raise chickens and barbecue deer steaks and eat apples and cheese for dessert."

"Good God, listen to yourself. Apples and cheese? Are you fucking kidding me?"

"Apples grow here, you know. And cows live on that island. It can't be that hard to figure out how to make cheese. We can hit a library on the mainland and bring back books that teach us how to do all that stuff."

They weren't far from the cliff edge. He'd missed it coming down when all he had was a flashlight, but he could see it now with the night vision. There it was, yawning over the beach below and the bright green sea beyond.

Parker started walking again. Toward the cliff. Kyle followed.

"What I want to know, Kyle," Parker said, "is why you think you get to make these decisions for everyone. Nobody appointed you captain. Every decision you've made since I met you has been a disaster."

"We'll vote," Kyle said. "And you'll lose. You can go to Alaska by yourself if you want. No one will stop you because no one will miss you."

Parker stopped in his tracks. Kyle stopped too.

"Excuse me?" Parker said. He flushed with heat and anger. And shame. Anger because Kyle had said it, and shame because he knew Kyle was right.

"You're welcome to stay, but no one will mind if you go. You treat everybody like shit. It should be obvious even to you that everyone hates you."

"Annie doesn't hate me."

"Of course she does, Parker."

And with that Kyle turned back around and started walking again.

Parker didn't plan what happened next. He had no idea he was going to do it until he was already halfway through doing it. And once he was halfway through doing it, it was too late to stop.

He reached behind Kyle and ripped the night-vision monocle off his head.

"Hey!" Kyle said.

Then he grabbed Kyle by the shoulders, planted a boot in the small of his back, and shoved him straight forward with all the might in his leg toward the edge of the cliff.

Kyle sprawled face-first into the grass, but he didn't go over. He flipped onto his back and looked toward Parker, but he couldn't see without his night vision. It was lying on the path. Parker could see the panic on Kyle's face as his blind eyes darted around. Kyle instinctively crab-walked backward a step before remembering that the cliff was somewhere behind him. It was, in fact, less than twelve inches behind him.

Parker couldn't believe what he'd just done. Some part of his brain misfired. Or the lizard part of his brain, the id part of his brain, the part of himself that had evolved on the African Savannah to deal with predators, prey, and survival, had just come uncorked. It spasmed. It erupted. But just for a second.

Like the one and only time he hit his wife Holly.

Jesus, he had actually tried to kill Kyle. Tried and failed.

"Shit, Kyle, I'm sorry." He reached out his hand to help the poor bastard up, but Kyle couldn't see.

"Heeeeeelp!" Kyle screamed. It was a horrible scream. A terrified scream. Even the horde across the water on Orcas Island must have heard him.

"Parker's trying to kill me!"

"No, Kyle—"

"Help!" Kyle screamed again, his face flushed with raw animal panic. He didn't even hear Parker's apology. He thought Parker was about to kick him over the edge.

"Wait," Parker said and took a step back.

"Help me!"

"Kyle, it's okay. I didn't mean it."

The front door of the guesthouse banged open. Parker saw flashlight beams like green searchlights sweeping across the grass.

"Kyle!" Hughes said. "We're coming!"

"Parker is trying to kill me!"

"Wait," Parker said, panic rising in his chest. "Jesus, Kyle."

"Kyle!" Annie screamed.

"Down here!" Kyle said. "Help me!"

There was nothing Parker could do. Nothing but wait for the others and apologize and surrender.

He heard three pairs of boots running on gravel, followed by the *ca-crunch* of Hughes' pump-action Mossberg.

Kyle lay on his back, the rim of oblivion somewhere behind him and a crazed Parker somewhere in the dark out in front of him.

The bastard actually tried to throw him over the edge.

Kyle couldn't see anything without the night vision, but he'd kick and punch and scratch and lunge and even bite the sonofabitch if only he could figure out where he was.

Flashlight beams swept down the hill. Annie called out his name.

"Down here!" he shouted. "Help me!"

Hughes, Annie, and Frank arrived within seconds. Parker was keeping his distance. He couldn't try throwing Kyle over the cliff again. Not if he didn't want witnesses.

Annie was breathless. "Kyle!"

"What's going on?" Frank said.

Kyle couldn't see the look on Hughes' face, but he could tell by the man's posture and general bearing that he was gearing up to break Parker in half.

"He ripped off my night vision and tried to throw me over the cliff."

Annie gasped and looked at Parker, who was moaning and covering his face with his hands.

"That true?" Hughes said and pointed his shotgun toward Parker.

"Get him away from me," Kyle said. "Take him somewhere and shoot him."

Annie gasped again.

"Now hang on a second," Frank said.

"Parker!" Hughes said and pressed the barrel of the shotgun at the side of Parker's head.

Parker looked up and panicked. "I can explain."

"I'll take that as a yes," Hughes said and grabbed the asshole by his shirt collar.

"No, wait!" Parker said.

Annie stepped toward Kyle. He squinted at the brightness of her flashlight, though it only seemed bright in one eye, the eye that remained adjusted to the dark while he wore the night vision. She recoiled when she saw how close he was to the edge.

"Did you or did you not try to throw Kyle over that cliff?" Hughes said.

"I—"

"It's a yes-or-no question."

Annie sat next to Kyle, though farther away from the cliff's edge, and put her hand on his knee.

"We were walking up the path," Kyle said, his breathing and heart rate beginning to slow. "And we got in an argument. He ripped my night vision off and tried to kick me over. Damn near succeeded too."

Parker stood on the path and winced at the flashlights in his face. He still had the night-vision monocle over his left eye. He looked like a creepy robot-person in a bad science-fiction movie.

"All this time," Kyle said, "we were worried about getting attacked by looters or the homeowner or another pack of those things. But the biggest danger of all was right here beside us. He's worse than Lane. Lane never *actually* tried to kill any of us."

Annie stood and helped Kyle up. He didn't need help—he wasn't hurt—but he took her hand anyway. He'd wanted to take her hand since he met her.

"We need to get rid of him," Kyle said.

"Please," Parker said. "Kyle, I'm sorry."

Kyle wouldn't look at him. It would only make doing what had to be done that much more difficult. He felt an enormous swell of an emotion he wasn't familiar with. This was something new, something he realized now that he should have felt a long time ago.

Iron had entered his veins. Iron and ice. It felt exhilarating and right. No more fucking around. "Take him to the edge of the cliff and shoot him."

"Agreed," Hughes said and grabbed Parker again by his shirt.

"Wait," Annie said. "There's something I need to tell you."

PART THREE

ONE OF THOSE THINGS

CHAPTER EIGHTEEN

Hughes killed the boat engine when he and Frank made it halfway up Orcas Island's main inlet. They'd need to row by hand the rest of the way so those things wouldn't hear.

"This is the dumbest thing I've ever done in my life," Frank said.

"It could work," Hughes said. "We won't know until we try. And we have to try because this could change everything."

They'd taken Parker upstairs in the main house and left him in a sealed room. The gag-inducing stench from the corpse downstairs had seeped into the walls. Kyle and Frank boarded up the windows from the outside and Hughes screwed some kind of lock onto the door from the hallway, most likely a sliding bolt from one of the bathrooms.

Not that any of that was remotely necessary. They'd tied him to a chair, his ankles bound together with rope, his wrists cinched tight with a second rope, his waist strapped to the back of the chair with a third, and his arms yoked to his ankles with yet a fourth. Parker could hardly breathe, couldn't look up, and if they didn't let him go or at least loosen him soon, his back would give out.

What were they going to *do* with him?

The others seemed to be at an impasse. Kyle and Hughes were prepared to shoot him and throw him over the cliff before Annie took them aside out of earshot. Parker had no idea what she said, but it startled them and bought Parker some kind of reprieve.

"Guys!" he shouted. "Please! Can you loosen these ropes? Just a little?" He doubted anybody could hear him. They didn't want to. That's why they left him tied him up in the other house.

He still couldn't believe what he'd done. And he wasn't just horrified that he failed and got caught. He'd be no less despondent had he succeeded. The only person he'd ever killed was Roland, and he did that to save himself and the others.

How many people sentenced to life in prison for murder were little different from him? Psychologically normal until one day they slipped and changed everything forever in a matter of seconds. Maybe everyone had it in them to kill under the right (or wrong) circumstances. Just look at those *things*. Even a Buddhist monk would turn into a cannibalistic predator if that virus got into his system.

On the other hand, maybe Parker wasn't psychologically normal. Perhaps he'd had a murderous personality all along that just hadn't been triggered yet.

He deserved to be punished. They had the right to put him in jail, so to speak, at least for a while. But they didn't have to restrain him like Hannibal Lecter.

They must be planning to let him go at some point, though. Why tie him up and stick him in a room if they were still going to shoot him?

But Parker didn't know what he didn't know. The only reason they hadn't killed him was because Annie took the others aside. She hadn't taken them aside to object. She took them aside and said something so shocking it brought Kyle right down on his ass.

What did she *say*?

"Guys!" he shouted. "Please! Somebody talk to me!"

Nobody answered. Nobody came.

A nnie sat on the brown leather couch in the guesthouse. She could see her breath and felt the cold seeping into her backside and legs right through her clothes. Hughes and Frank hadn't returned yet from Eastsound. Kyle sat in a recliner on the opposite side of the room. He seemed a little afraid of her now. She couldn't blame him.

"How long do you think they'll be gone?" Annie said.

"Depends on if the town is still overrun," Kyle said. "If those things have cleared out, they should be back this evening."

"They aren't *things*," Annie said. "They're people. With a virus. And viruses can be cured. How can you still not understand that?"

Kyle would never look at her the same way again now that he knew. *Maybe* he'd look at the infected ones differently. Eventually. He should.

But for now he looked pensive, still processing what she'd told him. Hughes and Frank were shocked too, but Kyle seemed more disturbed than the others. He had a thing for her. That was obvious. But now he wouldn't stand or sit anywhere near her, as if she could transmit the virus by breathing on him.

"You don't know that it's curable," he said. "Maybe it is. Maybe it's even preventable. Or maybe you are just really damn lucky."

Eastsound looked clear from the water. Hughes saw nothing moving in any direction. The town appeared as empty as it had been a few days earlier. Those things must have moved on.

He and Frank rowed ashore as silently as possible. This time they were better armed and better equipped. They had enough ammunition to take down a medium-size herd. They also had night vision in case they got pinned down again.

Hughes considered waiting for nightfall before hitting the beach. He and Frank would have the advantage this time since they could see in the dark. But the town really did seem to be clear, so they pulled the rowboat onto the rocky shore and set out.

They started with the pharmacy, where Hughes easily found what he needed, then hit the sporting-goods store. Hughes wasn't entirely sure what he was looking for in there, but he'd know what he needed as soon as he saw it.

"How about this?" Frank said and held up a fishing net. It was big enough to hold a few gallons of fish. The net was attached to a hoop two or so feet in diameter at the end of a six-foot-long pole. Perfect.

"Grab two of those," Hughes said. "And we need some more rope and a roll of duct tape. Can't forget the duct tape. Might not make it back

262   Michael J. Totten

without duct tape."

He saw something else that caught his eye. Bear spray. He had never heard of bear spray before, but it sounded promising, and when he read the label he knew it was exactly what they needed.

The stuff was the same kind of pepper spray used against human assailants. Hughes once bought his wife a small can the size of his finger for her key chain when she was still able and willing to leave the house. The bear spray, though, came in a can the size of a beer bottle. It's industrial-grade mace, more or less, and according to the label, the entire can empties in ten seconds if you hold down the button. This shit will drop anything with a respiratory system for at least a half-hour.

"Sweetheart," he said, "where have you been all my life?"

"What did you find?" Frank said.

"Big-ass can of mace." Hughes held it up. "For bears."

"Not just for bears," Frank said and grinned. "So we have everything we need now?"

"We have everything we need."

They returned to the boat and shoved off. After paddling out 100 feet or so, Hughes raised his Mossberg in the air and fired a single explosive shot, one that would be heard for miles in every direction.

Then they waited.

It no longer made any difference if Kyle and Hughes still planned to shoot Parker. His back would kill him first. The way they'd tied him up forced him to lean all the way forward, and he'd been stuck in that position for at least twenty-four hours.

"Help!" he moaned. "You guys have to loosen me up! You're torturing me!"

It really was torture. He wasn't exaggerating. The human body can't be contorted like that for such a long time. If they ever planned on letting him go, they damn well better get him comfortable, fast, or he'd turn homicidal again.

He never should have tried to kill Kyle, but he was beginning to wish he'd succeeded. Living with guilt and suspicion was far preferable to living with guilt, imprisonment, torture, and the threat of execution or exile.

He heard a boat engine approaching in the distance. Apparently they'd left and were now coming back. Was that why they hadn't answered? Maybe they'd let him go now. Or at least let him know what in the hell they were planning.

Kyle heard Hughes and Frank on the gravel pathway outside. He opened the door and stepped onto the porch. Hughes carried his shotgun in his right hand and a brown paper bag in his left. Frank followed.

"Did you get it?" Kyle said.

"We got it," Frank said. "It was a bitch and a half and we damn near got killed, but we got it."

Annie joined Kyle on the porch. She crossed her arms and hugged herself to keep warm. "Where is it?"

"Still down at the dock," Hughes said.

They left it down at the dock? Unguarded? "It that a good idea?"

"It's not *going* anywhere," Frank said.

"I don't want to bring it up until we're ready," Hughes said. "Too dangerous."

Kyle heard faint yells from Parker upstairs next door. "My back is killing me! Loosen my ropes! Please!"

Everybody ignored him.

"How did you get it?" Kyle said.

"With *great* caution and care," Hughes said.

"You get the other stuff?" Kyle said.

"Right here in the bag." Hughes held up the brown paper bag.

"Well, come on in then," Annie said. "We should get started."

They went back inside. Kyle closed the front door behind them.

Annie sat on the couch and rolled her sleeve up over her elbow. Hughes took several syringes out of the bag. Kyle winced. This was not going to be pleasant.

"There are all kinds of goodies in that pharmacy," Hughes said. "I picked up some narcotic pain meds and some antibiotics. We'll need both for sure at some point."

"Maybe we should give some of those pain meds to Parker," Annie said.

"Hell no," Kyle said.

"Why not?" Annie said.

"Because fuck him, that's why."

"He's in pain. You heard him. And it's only going to get worse."

"You should take some of those pills. This is going to hurt."

"I can take it. I've been through a lot worse."

"No. I mean, this is *really* going to hurt. None of us has a clue what we're doing."

"I trust you."

"You want me to do it?"

"Like I said, I trust you."

"Well, you shouldn't. I have no idea what I'm doing."

"It's okay."

"I'm not a doctor and this isn't a hospital. Take two of those pills. Hughes, give her some pills, will you?"

Hughes unscrewed the cap on a little orange bottle and gave Annie two pills. She swallowed one without water.

"We should wait a half-hour or so," Kyle said. "Let that pill start to kick in."

He picked up one of the syringes.

"How much of my blood do you think we'll need?" Annie said.

"Enough to fill this whole thing," Kyle said and tapped the needle tip with his finger.

Parker drifted in a delirious state made of one part sleep and another part pain. The agony in his lower back remained constant even while he slept. It was part of his body now as if it had always been there and always would be. He even began to make some sort of peace with it. He'd stop resisting if only the pain would stop getting worse.

The door opened downstairs and he snapped to alertness. He reflexively tried to sit up, but of course he could not, not with his wrists yoked to his ankles as if he were chained to the floor.

"Jesus Christ," he heard Kyle say. "I will never get used to that smell."

Parker no longer even noticed the smell of the corpse downstairs on the couch. That was the least of his concerns now. Only two things mattered to him anymore. He couldn't move, and his lower back felt like someone had reached in with a pair of pliers and yanked things out.

He heard several sets of feet on the wooden steps. The whole crew was on its way up there. To let him go? Shoot him? Read him the riot act?

The door opened. Kyle appeared with a syringe in his hand with Annie beside him and Hughes and Frank behind. Hughes had the Mossberg, but he pointed it at the floor.

"We have a job for you," Kyle said.

"I'm sorry for what I did," Parker said.

Kyle's face remained flat. "You mean you're sorry you didn't succeed."

"No," Parker said, suddenly desperate all over again to have his ties loosened and to feel even the slightest bit of relief in his back. "I snapped. I wasn't thinking. It could have happened to any of us with all this shit that's going on."

"But it didn't. You're the only murderer here. But it doesn't matter anymore because we have a job for you."

Parker looked again at the syringe in Kyle's hand. It was filled with dark liquid.

"We debated whether or not to tell you what's going on," Kyle said. "I didn't want to say anything because I don't think you deserve it, but the others convinced me."

"Can you please loosen these ropes? Then we can talk. My back is killing me. I can't stay hunched over like this anymore."

"Unfortunately for you," Kyle said, "your job requires you to remain precisely in that position."

Parker groaned. He had a bad feeling about where this was heading.

"What's in the syringe?" He wasn't sure he really wanted to know.

"Blood," Kyle said.

A wave of panic hit him and his entire body seized up. Were the sadistic bastards going to *infect* him?

He pulled against the ropes with everything he had left. "Get me out of here! Let me go and I'll never bother any of you ever again!"

"Relax," Kyle said. "This is Annie's blood."

Parker settled down, but he could still feel his heart pounding in his chest and the blood rushing in his ears. He was hyperventilating, and it was hard for him to breathe in this position.

"Annie is immune to the virus," Kyle said.

She was immune? Really? "How do you know?"

"Because I got bit," Annie said. "Look." She turned around and lifted her shirt up. Parker saw an obvious human bite mark below her shoulder.

"Jesus," Parker said. "You got bit and it didn't affect you? Are you sure you were bitten by one of those things?"

"Oh, it affected me," she said. "I became one of them."

Parker didn't move, but he felt like he fell onto the floor.

"I spent days as one of them before my system defeated the virus. It's hard to be sure. My memory of that time is vague."

"Jesus, Annie," Parker said. "Did you—kill people?"

"I did," she said and swallowed. "I attacked and killed some of Lane's crew shortly before he took over the grocery store. He saw the whole thing. That's why he recognized me. But he couldn't place me because it never occurred to him that I was infected when he saw my face. He didn't think anyone could turn back."

"My God," Parker said. So that's why she looked like such hell when Hughes first brought her home. That's why she was covered in so much blood. She'd bathed in the blood of her victims. "Annie, I'm sorry."

He shuddered as he tried to imagine her running around as one of those things and hunting people, biting people, *eating* people. Then he paused. "What does this have to do with me? And why is your blood in that syringe?"

"We're passing Annie's immunity onto you," Kyle said. "At least we're going to try."

Parker was truly confused now. He thought they were going to punish him. But this wasn't punishment. This was a gift. They weren't going to kill him then. There's no way they'd draw blood from Annie's arm and inoculate him only to kill him or exile him later. He breathed easier.

"So you're going to stick that in my arm?" Parker said.

"I'm going to stick this in your arm," Kyle said. "It's best you don't move when I do it. I'm not a doctor. It hurt something fierce when I stuck this in Annie. I'll try to make it relatively painless even though you don't deserve it, but it is going to hurt."

"We're pretty sure," Annie said, "that the antibodies in my system are in my blood and that they can be added to yours. So you'll be immune just like I am. In theory."

"Have all of you gotten the injection?" Parker said.

Kyle's face remained flat. Annie looked like she was going to say something, but she hesitated. Hughes shook his head.

Then Annie spoke up. "You're the first."

He was the first? That made no sense. He was the bad guy. So why was he first?

"Why?"

"Because we don't know if it works yet," Kyle said.

Nobody said anything else. Nobody even looked at him. They just stood there and waited for him to figure it out for himself.

"You motherfuckers," he said. "You wouldn't dare."

"It's the only way to be sure," Kyle said and plunged the syringe into Parker's arm.

CHAPTER NINETEEN

Parker wept silently. He no longer cared about the pain in his back, nor about the pain in his arm where Kyle had jammed in the needle. He was one of the last human beings on the face of the earth, yet he had no more value to anyone else than a lab rat.

How long, he wondered, before they brought the next needle in? The one that would infect him. And what would they do with him once the results from their little Nazi experiment came in? If he turned and stayed turned, they'd shoot him. That was clear. But what if he turned back into Parker, like Annie had turned back into Annie? Were they still going to shoot him?

Probably. Since shooting him was the plan in the first place.

Maybe after he turns, he'll have enough strength to rip through the ropes and break out of the bedroom. The virus didn't give those things extra strength, but it did seem to make them less sensitive or concerned about pain, like psychotics hopped up on angel dust. Maybe he could bust his way free and eat Kyle.

He actually laughed at the thought, a horrible grim laugh even though there was nothing funny about it. He didn't want to eat Kyle. He didn't want to eat anybody. Yet he laughed at the thought. Perhaps this was the beginning of acceptance.

Acceptance. Yes. He'd have to accept this. It's not like they gave him a choice. They were going to stick him with an infected needle, and he'd either turn back like Annie did or he wouldn't. And then they were going to kill him.

He wondered what it would be like after he turns. Would he be aware of what's happening? Would he remember the person he was before, when he still knew his name and where he had come from? Annie said her memories of that time were vague, which suggested she was still sentient on some level. She wasn't sleepwalking. Otherwise she wouldn't remember it.

He hoped he would at least remember his name. Please let him at least remember his name.

The front door downstairs opened and he tensed up. This was it. They were on their way up. He only wished they could wait a little bit longer and give him more time to make peace with the terrible transformation awaiting him.

Then he wondered: Where on earth did they get the fluid for the second injection?

A horrendous racket downstairs. Lots of banging and scraping.

He heard Hughes say, "Grab his hands, Frank!" and Frank said, "I'm trying!"

Grab whose hands? Kyle's?

Then he heard Kyle's voice. "Steady. Get it onto the stairs."

Get what onto the stairs?

Something heavy banged into the wall.

And then something growled.

No.

It couldn't be.

They wouldn't.

He heard a new voice he didn't recognize. It struggled and strained as if it were gagged. Parker's entire body flushed with red heat.

The commotion reached the top of the stairs, and soon they were outside the bedroom.

"Okay," Kyle said. "Hughes and I have a hold of it. Frank, open the door."

Parker heard grunting and snarling. He wanted it to be some sort of animal, but no. He knew what it was.

One of those things.

Madness and mayhem out in the hallway. Annie stepped back as Kyle, Frank, and Hughes wrestled with the thing they had captured in Eastsound. This one really did look like a thing. Annie felt no kinship or bond with it whatsoever. Not even pity.

It was a male. Maybe thirty years old. It was covered in gore and it stank of a charnel house. Its eyes were like intelligent animal eyes, seeing and focusing but lacking compassion and decency. Its face was red and swollen and puffy. Hughes had stunned it with pepper spray designed to repel grizzly bears, which made it furious and explosive.

Hughes and Frank had placed some kind of fishing net over its upper arms and tied its wrists together behind its back. They covered its mouth with duct tape. It could still kick and head-butt and throw its weight around. It thrashed about so violently, she feared it might get its arms free, rip the tape off its mouth, and start biting.

Annie held the Glock. Her job was to guard that thing while the others tried to control it.

This was not at all what she had in mind. When she said they should inoculate Parker and then infect him, she meant they should inject Parker with the virus, not let one of those things actually bite him. But Kyle insisted—no, he *demanded*—that they do it this way. His sadistic determination frightened her almost as much as this thing did.

Hughes grabbed its bound wrists with one hand and the hair on the back of its head with the other. Kyle and Hughes each managed to hold one of its shoulders. They had it positioned in front of the door like they were going to use it as a battering ram.

It managed to scream even with its mouth taped shut. It sounded human and not at the same time. Parker hollered on the other side of the door, but the thing in the hall made so much noise with its muffled yelling and thrashing that Parker's screams were hardly even noticeable in the background.

"Annie," Hughes said. He gripped the thing's head and held its writhing arms still as best as he could. "I need you to open the door, step out of the way, and then aim that Glock at this creature's head. We're going to get it down on the floor in front of Parker and then rip the tape off. Let it bite Parker one time and one time only. Then shoot it. Do not hit any of us and do not hit Parker. You got it?"

She nodded, trembling.

Parker screamed from the other side of the door. Surely he knew by now what was happening.

She reached for the doorknob and the thing lunged at her. It rammed the top of its head into her shoulder and groaned into the tape. She flinched and stepped back.

"Sorry, Annie," Kyle said.

"Jesus, this thing," Frank said.

Hughes gripped its hair and pulled back its head. "Okay. You're clear."

She reached for the doorknob again, twisted it, flung open the door, and stepped back.

Parker, tied to the chair, strained and thrashed as violently and hysterically as that thing. "You motherfuckers! You're going to burn for this!"

"Get it down on the floor," Hughes said and kicked the back of the thing's knees with his boots. It went down just a few feet from Parker.

Parker's face was red from the straining. Spittle flew from his mouth. "You're the most wicked people alive. I never did anything half as bad as what you're doing right now. Kyle, after I turn, I'm going to rip through these cords and chew off your face."

Annie tried to aim at the thing's head, but she couldn't keep her hands steady and the gun bobbed all over the place.

"Frank," Hughes said. "Lift Parker's pants leg. Expose his ankle."

God, Annie thought. Lifting his pants leg so that creature has something to bite. She wanted to look away but couldn't. She'd need to shoot that thing if it got loose.

Hughes turned its head sideways, slammed it into the floor, and leaned all his body weight into its back. "Rip off the tape, Frank. Do it *carefully.*"

Parker wept. He seemed too tired and resigned to yell anymore.

Frank tried to yank the tape off the thing's mouth, but he flinched and pulled back, afraid of losing his fingers—and worse. Unlike Parker, he had not been inoculated. None of the others had yet been inoculated. No one even knew if the inoculation would work.

"Try again, Frank," Hughes said. "This thing's head isn't moving."

Frank reached toward its face with a shaking hand, grabbed a corner of the tape, pulled, and jumped back. He scrambled six feet backward to get clear of its teeth.

The tape was still over its mouth.

"Damnit, Frank," Hughes said and ripped the tape off himself in a flourish. He did it so quickly, the squirming thing had no time to react. But now its head was free and its teeth were bared, the virus cocked and loaded, the worst biological weapon the world had ever seen.

Parker jerked as if he was being electrocuted in his chair.

Annie should have known what would happen next, but somehow she didn't. She knew the bite was coming. She anticipated Parker's screams. She knew she'd have to blow the thing's brains out before it bit somebody else.

But she didn't foresee what happened first.

It belted out a scream unlike anything she had ever heard in her life, even from the others she had encountered. Those things didn't take kindly to being detained and controlled by their food. If malevolent violence had a sound, this was it.

She felt shocked and appalled all over again that she had once been the same kind of thing that made such a noise.

It lunged like a big cat and bit Parker's ankle.

Annie turned away as Parker screamed in horror and agony. She knew that sound because she had made it herself when she had been bitten. It came back to her in a rush, the knowledge that she was finished, that the dark waters were rising, that she would transform into a thing so mindless she'd be a brain-dead woman walking, yet walking all the same and biting and spreading the disease that burned down the world.

But then she recovered. She came back from the other side as if she had been resurrected.

The same thing might happen to Parker.

Please, she thought. Let him recover. Let him live. She needed him to rise whole from that chair.

She snapped back to alertness when Hughes took the pistol from her trembling fingers and blew the thing's brains onto the floor.

"Kyle," Hughes said. "Frank. Get rid of that body. Throw it on the lawn outside next to the others. And try not to get too much blood on your hands."

A nnie was angry. Kyle could see that. She wouldn't talk to him. Would not even look at him.

He sat on the front steps of the guesthouse while she slammed kitchen cabinets and banged things on the counter. He wanted to go in there, but he wouldn't be able to say the right thing, not after the violence upstairs in the main house, and especially not since they all knew more violence was coming whether or not Parker recovered.

They hadn't yet discussed who would shoot him when this was all over, but Kyle would make sure he got the honor. He would insist. It was his right.

P arker was beyond pain now. The part of his brain that received and interpreted it had switched off. The rest of his conscious mind would shut down soon enough. Only a distorted version of the lizard brain would remain.

It was all over for him even if he recovered, but a tiny flickering part of him hoped he'd recover anyway. For Annie's sake and for the few healthy humans left in the world. If her immunity could be passed on to enough people, she might prevent this scourge from becoming an extinction event, but he'd never know. He'd be dead either way. So he also hoped, for entirely selfish reasons, that when he slipped out of consciousness, it would be lights out forever.

Please, he thought. Just let me go. Let me go to sleep and never wake up.

Hughes wasn't easily disturbed, but what happened in that room was the worst thing he'd seen since the death of his family. And this time he was to blame.

What was wrong with him?

He should have insisted they do it differently, that Parker be injected rather than bitten.

It was possible that the virus could only be transferred through saliva and biting. Kyle was right about that much. They didn't actually know that the blood carried the virus. None of them had witnessed a person getting infected from contact only with blood. But they'd figure it out. If Parker didn't turn after being injected, *then* they could have brought that awful thing into the room.

That would have been the civilized way to handle it.

Kyle could be awfully persuasive. He was persuasive when he was naive, and he was persuasive when he was vindictive.

That made him a dangerous man, one of the most dangerous Hughes had ever known. He didn't *seem* dangerous in the slightest, not like Lane or even like Parker, and that's what made him worse than either. Not even Hughes kept his guard up consistently enough, and Hughes was more allergic to dangerous people and ideas than just about anyone.

What really shook him was how Kyle had seemed like the most decent of the whole bunch after Carol. Yet look at what he did. Look at what he made all of them do.

Annie slipped out of the guesthouse and into the main house. The rotting corpse in the living room smelled worse every time she walked in there. She was hoping she'd get used to the sight and the smell, but no.

She crept up the stairs so Parker wouldn't hear, and he was

whimpering and moaning when she reached the door leading into his room.

Yes, it was his room now. His very own room of torment and horror. No one else in her group would ever use it for any other reason.

Parker hadn't turned yet. The sounds he made were too soft and too—human. He wasn't screaming or violently thrashing about.

But oh God, was he going to scream after he turned. No one had gagged him or taped up his mouth. Perhaps they should have, but this way his bellowing would allow them to monitor him from a distance. Annie would need to find something to plug her ears.

She pressed her hands against the door as if she could feel the energy inside. She couldn't, but all the same she tried to transmit some peaceful energy of her own across the grim threshold. It was useless, of course, but she didn't know what else to do with herself.

She wanted to say something, anything, but it would only make Parker feel worse. From the sounds he was making, she figured he was in some kind of delirium. Perhaps that was best. Delirium is its own form of anesthetic.

"I'm sorry," she whispered, knowing he couldn't hear her but needing to say it.

She hoped with all her heart that he would recover and make all this worthwhile. It would be a major breakthrough, especially for a small band of survivors without any medical training. She might be able to save lives in the future, but for now she just hoped Parker pulled through so that something decent could result from the horrible thing they had done to him.

The horrible thing that was her idea, sort of. His body would be shot through with holes and broken at the base of the cliff right now if she hadn't told the others about her immunity and suggested they test it on Parker, but she had no idea it would be such a nasty business.

Another thought occurred to her, something no one had mentioned yet and probably had not even thought of, partly because it was a bit early for that, but mostly because the idea would terrify everyone else.

If her immunity could be transferred, they couldn't stay in the Pacific Northwest. They'd need to find an operational medical facility, one that could study her and mass-produce a vaccine. Certainly no such facility existed anywhere near Puget Sound. They might have to travel hundreds or even thousands of miles. She'd need to tell the others. And she'd need to tell them sooner rather than later.

If Parker recovered.

And there was one other thing. If Parker came back, he'd be the only person in the world who understood what she'd gone through. She needed him to recover.

She needed him to survive.

The whole world needed him to recover and then to survive.

Kyle hated that Annie was mad at him. He was beginning to think she'd always be mad at him, or at least think of him differently than before. They could not have a future together if they couldn't get past this.

Parker had been right about one thing. Ruthlessness has to be met with ruthlessness. Kyle had been too soft. The cozy and comfortable morality of high-tech Seattle and Portland had no place in a world where life was brutish and short. Kyle understood now. Annie needed to understand it, as well. They needed to talk.

Annie thought she had sneaked over to the main house to visit Parker, but Kyle had seen her leave. He wouldn't say anything. It would just create one more thing for them to fight about. Instead he waited on the couch for her return while Frank and Hughes chopped wood for a fire in back.

She came back a half-hour later. And she looked startled when she opened the door and saw Kyle sitting there waiting.

"I know why you're upset," he said.

"You do, huh?" she said.

"It was pretty gruesome what happened up there."

She shook her head. "You don't get it at all."

"What don't I get?"

"Every day since this virus appeared has been gruesome. I never even imagined the things I've seen the last two months. But what happened up there was worse because it was pointless. We didn't have to do it that way."

"It was the only way to be sure."

"Bullshit."

"We could have injected him with infected blood," Kyle said, "but we still don't know if it would work. It's not like we have anyone else around here to experiment on."

"You hate him. And you want revenge."

"I don't hate him."

"Of course you do. Not that I blame you. I'd hate him too if I were you."

"You're saying you don't hate him?"

"It's hard to hate someone after tying him to a chair and force-feeding him to an infected. You heard what he said."

"I heard what he said."

You're the most wicked people alive.

"It doesn't bother you."

"Why should it? He's wrong. This was your idea, Annie. And it was a brilliant idea. This is science. Progress. We're not the Center for Disease Control here, but there's a chance we'll all be immune by the time this is over."

Hughes and Frank came in from outside. Kyle needed to dial the argument down. He didn't want to fight with Annie at all, and especially not in front of the others.

But Annie retreated to her room and slammed the door hard enough to rattle the windows.

Annie collapsed on the bed. She lay on her back without bothering to put her head on the pillow. All she wanted was a long, deep sleep and the peace of oblivion.

It was not going to happen.

"Shit!" she said and bolted up.

"You okay in there?" Hughes said from the living room.

She crossed the room and opened the door.

Kyle was still on the couch, and now Frank was sitting next to him. Hughes was on his feet and looked ready for anything.

"We are so stupid," Annie said.

Hughes seemed to relax slightly. No, she hadn't seen one of those things out her window, and no, she wasn't about to stab Kyle.

"We can't do this," she said. "We need a doctor."

"What now?" Kyle said. "We're already doing it."

"No," Annie said. "I mean we *really* need a doctor."

"You sick?" Hughes said.

"I'm fine," Annie said. "But Parker might not be."

Frank raised his eyebrows. Kyle rolled his eyes.

God, they hadn't thought this through at all.

"Have any of you ever donated blood?" Annie said.

Frank shook his head.

"No," Kyle said.

"Can't say I have," Hughes said.

"I give blood every year," Annie said. "Jesus, I can't believe I didn't think of this until now."

"What?" Kyle said.

Hughes looked crestfallen. He closed his eyes. He had figured it out. "Your blood type."

"Yeah," Annie said. "My blood type."

"What about it?" Kyle said.

"I can only donate blood to people who share my blood type."

"Oh," Kyle said. "Shit!" He was still mad from their fight, and now she was just pouring it on.

"Do you and Parker have the same blood type?" Frank said.

"I have no idea," Annie said. "We didn't ask him. He might not even know his blood type."

"Do you know yours?" Hughes said.

"Well," Annie said, "if I had type O, Parker's wouldn't matter. O is the universal donor. But I have type A. Which means I can only donate to people with type A or AB."

"How many people have type A or AB?" Hughes said.

"Less than half," Annie said. "About forty percent of the population if I remember correctly."

"I have type B," Frank said. "I was in the Army. We all got tested. In case something happened."

"And if Parker's is different?" Hughes said.

"He'll have an allergic reaction," Annie said.

"What does that mean?" Hughes said. "Will it kill him?"

"I don't know!" Annie said. "But either way it's pretty unlikely that he'll be immune to the virus if his blood rejects mine."

Kyle put his face in his hands and groaned.

"So if you're A and I'm B," Frank said to Annie, "we know I can't get an injection. But we still have a forty-percent chance it will work out with Parker."

"No," Annie said, "we have a forty-percent chance that his body won't reject the transfusion. We still have no idea if the antibodies in my blood will kill the virus in his."

"So what do we do?" Frank said. "Should we ask him his blood type?"

"*Now?*" Kyle said. "It doesn't make a rat's-ass bit of difference what his blood type is now. It's already in his system, and so is the virus. This'll either work or it won't."

"No sense going up there and looking like a bunch of amateurs in front of him," Hughes said.

"But we are amateurs," Annie said. "And you know what else?"

"What?" Kyle said.

"Even if this works, we're still screwed," Annie said.

"Why?" Frank said.

"I assume," Annie said, "that since none of you have donated blood, you don't know your blood type. Am I right?" Kyle squeezed his eyes shut. "Which means you can't have a transfusion. I can't pass my immunity on to you even if it does work with Parker. We've already failed."

But they had already moved forward. And Parker turned in the night. They all heard it happen. The walls weren't soundproofed and no one had gagged him.

He roared is if he wanted to swallow the world.

Annie cried into her pillow and refused to come out of her room even to eat.

CHAPTER TWENTY

Frozen. Trapped. Pinned. Tied. Tied to a chair. Tied to a chair by his prey. By his food.

A hungry hungry predator shouldn't be tied. Cannot be tied. Cannot be tied by his prey, by his food, or he can't get to his prey, to his food.

Pain in his back. Pain in his arms. Pain in his legs. Pain because he was tied.

Every muscle flexing, relentlessly flexing.

The ropes were strong, but he was stronger. He'd show them. He'd show his prey, his prey and his food, that he was much stronger.

Push.

Pull.

Yank.

Strain.

His back afire and his eyes ready to burst, but the ropes would break because he was hungry strong.

His prey would pay. With blood, organs, sinew, tissue, and bones.

He would devour them all, rip them apart with his hands, with his teeth, all his prey in the world, his cattle run wild, he would devour them all and still not be sated, this terrible hunger, so hungry.

His tongue on his teeth so sharp and biting and strong. Stronger than rope.

He smelled his prey down the stairs and outside. He screamed at his prey down the stairs and outside. His prey, his food, his prey heard him. They did. He'd find his prey, explode at his prey and rip their throats, screaming and gnashing, from the necks and, biting and thrashing, their torsos from limbs.

Every muscle flexing, relentlessly flexing, burning with acid, his mind exploding with rage and anguish gone nova, and the rage and the pain and the pain and the rage and his throat raw and burning from screaming.

Violently shaking in wrath and pain, the chair was going to topple, his throat would burst in his own neck from screaming, then a whispering voice, a tiny flickering thought in the back of his mind: Oh my God.

A side from the raging of the thing that used to be Parker, a day passed in tense silence. No one knew what to do with themselves or what to say.

Hughes spent most of his time on the front steps staring out at the sea and listening to the bellowing from upstairs next door. He had to keep at least an ear on Parker in case the man somehow broke free. There was no way to be sure Parker wouldn't rip through his ropes and break down the door in the state he was in.

Annie stayed in her bedroom. Kyle sulked on the couch and in the kitchen, his presence and energy baleful enough to keep the others away. Frank wandered around the property, never venturing far in case something happened. Meanwhile, Parker's voice thundered hard enough to blow down the walls.

Hughes couldn't sleep. The guilt got to him. He, Kyle, and Frank would not be able to get a vaccine from Annie's blood even if Parker did happen to recover. Maybe they shared her blood type and maybe they didn't. There was no way to tell. It's not like the Red Cross had an office nearby where they could get tested. Pharmacies had instant pregnancy-test kits, but they did not carry blood kits. They'd need a doctor for that, and a lab. Hughes doubted a functioning medical facility existed anywhere within 1,000 miles of the Puget Sound region. Maybe on the East Coast something was still up and running. Maybe.

So Hughes just lay there in the darkness and stared at the ceiling, hating himself and what they'd done to Parker. Their nasty experiment would have been justified if it produced a vaccine, but they had not thought it through.

The thing that used to be Parker finally quieted down, but Hughes still couldn't sleep. He couldn't take the suspense or the weight of what would happen next. What if Parker did recover? There was a forty-percent chance that he shared Annie's blood type, after all. And maybe the inoculation would work. Then what? Hughes no longer had it in him to shoot Parker. Not if Parker recovered. Hughes could have shot him that night on the cliff, sure, no problem, but he couldn't execute a man who was tied to a chair after putting him through such unspeakable hell.

Something else bothered him too. Annie had amnesia for a while after she came back. Parker might too. He might not have any idea what had happened. He might not remember that he tried to kill Kyle. He might not remember coming up to the island. He might not remember Kyle at all or that the plague even existed. He'd be innocent in his mind. Innocent and confused. Then what? Shoot him anyway?

No.

Hughes could never execute a man for a crime he didn't remember committing. Wasn't right. He wouldn't do it.

Nor would he allow it.

Would Kyle be willing? *Really*? What would Annie think of him then?

Hughes thought he heard sounds coming from the next house. Moaning. Parker. The moaning sounded—human. Was Parker awake? Had he recovered?

Hughes bolted off his bed and grabbed a flashlight. He heard doors opening in the hallway. The others were also awake and must have been thinking the same thing.

They converged in the hall. Annie looked as if she had not slept for days. Kyle looked nervous. Frank was just beat.

"I'll bring the shotgun," Hughes said. "Nobody else bring any weapons."

"I'm bringing one of the Glocks," Kyle said.

"The hell you are," Hughes said.

"Kyle, no," Annie said.

"Goddamnit, you guys," Kyle said. "I'm not going to shoot him right now, but we don't know what kind of state he's in. He might still be dangerous. He could have torn through his ropes."

"That's why I'm brining the shotgun," Hughes said. "And you will stand down. Leave the Glock."

"Fine!" Kyle said.

Hughes led the others through the dark and into the main house. Was it just his imagination or was the corpse in the living room getting riper by the hour?

They crept up the stairs.

Annie opened the door.

When he shone his flashlight on Parker, Hughes could see that the man was still tied. Tied up, hunched over, exhausted, and in terrible pain. A dried pool of brain matter and blood covered the floor where the thing that bit Parker was shot, but it looked like Parker had vomited the gore up himself in the night.

"Hey man," Frank said and knelt next to Parker, taking care to avoid the dried blood. He put his hand on Parker's shoulder.

"Careful, Frank!" Hughes said.

"It's okay," Frank said. "He's passed out."

"You don't know if he's—"

Parker snapped his teeth around Frank's thumb and index finger and clenched like he wanted to chew them clean off.

Frank screamed.

"Jesus Christ!" Kyle said.

Annie gasped and backed into the far wall.

The thing that used to be Parker growled and gnashed his teeth together around Frank's thumb while Frank screamed and pummeled Parker's head with his free hand.

Hughes pointed the shotgun at Parker, but he couldn't shoot or he'd hit Frank.

"Get him off me!" Frank shouted.

"Jesus, Parker, shoot him!" Kyle said.

"Oh, God, get him off me!" Frank said.

Hughes jammed the butt of his shotgun into the side of Parker's head, splitting one of his ears open. Frank pulled his hand free and Annie rushed up and helped him get away.

"Fuck me," Hughes said. The thing that used to be Parker looked at him with inhuman malevolence and growled like a wolf ready to pounce and rip out his throat. "I ought to blow your head off right now."

The thing that used to be Parker screamed. Crimson blood covered his teeth and his chin, the muscles between his eyes curled into a knot of aggression.

"Do it!" Kyle said.

"God!" Frank yelled.

Not yet, Hughes thought. How long did Annie say she lasted as one of those things? Shit. She didn't know. The experience warped her sense of time beyond recognition.

A trail of drizzled blood led from Parker's chair to the corner of the room where Frank sat moaning in pain with his chewed-up hand in his lap and Annie's arm around his shoulder.

Goddamn it. Hughes was going to have to put down another one of his friends. It never got any easier. Maybe that was okay. Maybe it shouldn't get any easier.

"Everybody out," Hughes said. "Kyle, help Frank."

"No one can help me," Frank said.

Nobody said anything.

Kyle took Frank's left hand, his good hand, and pulled him up. "Come on, man. Let's get you out of here."

The thing that used to be Parker screamed again. It sounded nothing like Parker and hardly even looked like him anymore.

"I knew this was a bad idea," Frank said. He didn't sound angry. He sounded defeated, resigned, as if he'd known for months he'd get bitten eventually.

Kyle and Annie each took one of Frank's arms and led him out into the hallway. Hughes looked one last time at the thing that used to be Parker, shook his head, closed the door, and slammed home the lock.

"He is *so* dead," Kyle said, referring to Parker.

Probably, Hughes figured. It didn't look like Parker was coming back. In the meantime, Frank absolutely was going to die. They could try injecting him with Annie's blood and hope for the best, but he was the only one whose blood type for sure didn't match. And he'd never find out if the experiment with Parker would succeed or fail. Frank would never know whether or not he died for nothing. Perhaps it was better this way, since he probably would die for nothing.

He would be but the first. Hughes, Annie, and Kyle couldn't last much longer, either. Just a few days earlier, eight people were holed up in the grocery store back on the mainland. Now they were just three. Kyle's island was a bust. A nice idea, but a bust. Passing Annie's immunity on to everyone else was likewise a bust. They were stuck on a remote island without any food while winter was coming. Where were they supposed to go now? How were they supposed to live?

Kyle led the way down the stairs. Annie eased Frank down one step at a time. Hughes took up the rear with his shotgun as if Parker might bust through the door at any second.

"Just shoot me," Frank said. "Get it over with." He didn't sound anguished or even in pain anymore. He was just done.

"We're not going to shoot you," Hughes said.

They were back in the living room now. Hughes could practically feel the rotten stench of death on his skin like a sickening film. Kyle hurried forward and opened the front door.

"Fucker practically bit my thumb off," Frank said. "It *hurts*. I don't want to wait. What's the point of living twelve more hours in this kind of pain?"

Hughes wouldn't shoot Frank even if he were unconscious. He'd ease him out of this world the same way he eased his wife out of this world, and then Carol. By closing Frank's mouth and plugging his nose after he went into his coma. It made no difference if Frank would feel pain or not. Enough violence had been inflicted on his body already.

"Hand me the shotgun and I'll do it myself," Frank said.

That was not going to happen. Hughes wouldn't allow it. "Frank—"

"I have the right to die how I want."

"Frank, honey, let's sit you down," Annie said.

"I don't want to sit down!" Frank said. He sounded angry now. "Just give me the damn gun, Hughes."

Hughes thought about it. The man did have a point. He should be able to die how he wants. Blowing his head off with a shotgun might make sense if he were on this island alone, but he wasn't alone. Frank was with friends. Nobody wanted to look at his body with his head blown off his shoulders.

"None of you have to watch," Frank said. "I'll go into the woods."

But they'd hear the shot, Hughes thought, and somebody would have to go into the trees and retrieve the shotgun from Frank's hands.

Hughes could always let Frank have the Jennings J22 he'd pulled from the corpse in the grass. It was a bad gun. Hughes had no intention of ever firing it. He could let Frank take that one to his grave. And yet he still hesitated. Something deep inside him rebelled at the thought of Frank shooting himself. There was a right way to do things, and that was not it.

"Come on, man," Frank said. "Show a dying man a little fucking mercy, why don't you."

Hughes looked his friend in the eye and exhaled. Frank was a brave man. Most people would suck up the pain if it meant they could live another half-day and avoid a violent death, but not Frank. Hughes admired that. He wasn't sure he'd be able to do that himself.

"Bye everybody," Frank said. "Take care of each other." And he took off running down the hill toward the water.

"Frank!" Annie said.

Toward the cliff.

"Let him go," Hughes said.

"He's going for the cliff, isn't he?" Kyle said.

"Probably," Hughes said.

"The cliff Parker tried to throw me over," Kyle said. "We should throw his ass over it, too, on top of Frank."

Frank ran with everything he had, as if he feared the others were chasing him. He didn't look back or even slow down, but he screamed when he went over the edge.

A nnie couldn't take it. She wanted to get off the island—to where?—and headed off into the trees.

"Where are you going?" Kyle said. She did not turn back to look at him.

"I need to get out of here," she said. Her tone was final, uncompromising.

A faint trail covered in fir needles led into the forest. The path had probably been used, and was possibly even created, by whoever owned those two houses, but it was nothing like the trails in the national parks or even the national forests. This was more like an animal path. Wet leaves brushed against Annie's pants as she walked, and she winced in pain when a thick branch from a low-lying bush jammed into her knee.

Carol was dead.

Frank was dead.

Kyle had been damn near pitched over the cliff.

Parker had turned into a monster. No, she and Kyle and Hughes *turned* Parker into a monster on purpose.

She tried and failed to force down the heat welling up in her chest.

How much longer could their little group last?

Not long. Not like this. There were only three people left now. Herself, Kyle, and Hughes.

She didn't know how she felt about Kyle anymore, but at this point it hardly made any difference. If they lost just one more person, the group would not be a group. It would be a pair.

No way could two people survive in this world by themselves.

If Parker recovers, they'd need to keep him alive.

The forest was cold but beautiful, and it put her slightly at ease. She could hardly believe beauty still existed in this world. It seemed wrong somehow, impossible, but there it was.

The sky overhead was dishrag gray, so no sunlight slanted down through the trees, but that seemed fitting and right. Gray skies suited these dark evergreen woods. The deep greens softened the color of steel from the sky and were even enhanced by it. Moss covered the branches and trunks and looked almost translucent in the thin light of late autumn. The ground felt spongy and soft under her boots. If there was one advantage to being stranded in the Pacific Northwest at the end of the world, it was the copious amounts of freshwater.

Annie followed the path and wondered how long they'd have to wait before deciding that Parker would never recover. She wasn't even sure how long she took to recover.

Think back, Annie. How many days were you infected? How much time passed?

She remembered chasing people through a forest. She remembered attacking Lane's earlier crew and killing one of his men on the front porch of a house. Were Roland and Bobby with him then? She didn't know. She didn't see them. Or, if she did, she couldn't remember. It's not like she could tell one human being from another when she was infected. To her diseased mind, all human beings were just food.

She did not remember sleeping when she still had the virus. Her sense of time from that period was fuzzy, off, as if she had been drugged or asleep. Yet she had *some* sense of time passing.

Three days. She couldn't be sure, but that's what her gut—or her subconscious—told her.

Three days. She lived for three days as one of those things, then woke on the forest floor with temporary amnesia.

Now she was in another forest, and her sense of time was slipping again. How long had she been out walking? How far did she walk from the compound and her companions?

Annie didn't know. She could be on the other side of the island now for all she knew. Maybe too far away for the others to hear if she called out for help.

Maybe far enough away that the infected could be lurking in the trees without having any idea that healthy humans—food—were holed up a ways down the trail.

Cold fear took hold of her. She turned around and headed back, careful to make as little noise as possible, turning her body to the side as she passed between bushes to minimize rustling sounds.

She saw the houses through the trees ten minutes later. Her heart rate slowed. Ten minutes. She had only been gone for twenty then. Kyle and Hughes were still out front, standing right where they were when Frank took off down the hill toward the cliff.

"You okay?" Kyle said.

"Three days," Annie said.

"What's three days?" Hughes said.

"I was sick for three days," Annie said, "before I came back."

"You sure?" Kyle said.

"No," Annie said. "But I think so."

"So Parker needs two more days," Hughes said.

"One day," Kyle said. "He turned two days ago."

"Parker needs two more days," Hughes said again. "In case Annie isn't remembering right. In case it takes longer for him to come back. Hell, we should give him a week just to be sure."

"We're not giving him a week," Kyle said.

Hughes was right, but Annie was not going to stand there and argue with Kyle. Not less than an hour after Frank jumped to his death.

She went into the house. It wasn't much warmer inside, but at least there was no wind. She shut herself in her room again, partly to get away from the others and partly because privacy and solitude were luxuries she hadn't had in a while, and she didn't know if she'd ever have them again.

How could she have been so stupid? She knew about the problems with blood type, but she was so blinded by the sheer awesomeness of making a vaccine. She could give it to her friends right away and later to others.

They needed professional help. They needed doctors. Even if Parker never recovered, they still needed doctors. If a blood vaccine doesn't work, maybe something else would. But where on earth could they possibly find any doctors?

Twenty-seven hours later, Parker woke up. All the muscles in his body, including muscles he did not know he had, felt like they had been mashed against his bones in a vise. Even his eyes hurt when he tried to move them or blink. He felt a knot in his back as hard as a bowling ball, and it wouldn't stop spasming. All he could do was endure it through clenched teeth.

He was tied to a chair with blood and gore on the floor in front of him. He was thirsty, so thirsty, and he tasted blood in his mouth.

Why ...

Oh. God.

How long had he been tied up?

"Help!" he cried. "Help me!"

His entire body ached like it had never ached before. The pain felt like it had crawled inside him and subsumed his identity. He could hardly think about anything else. Nothing made sense.

He gasped.

Ignore the pain. Think. How did you get here? Who tied you up? Did your friends tie you up?

Who *are* your friends?

Hughes. Frank. Annie.

Kyle.

Shit. He had tried to kill Kyle. The others tied him up and—

Oh, God. One of those things. They had turned him into one of those things.

Did he bite *Frank*? Or did he dream that?

"Frank!"

He did, didn't he? He actually bit Frank. He remembered it clearly now. The others had come into this room and he bit Frank. Was Frank okay?

No, Frank would not be okay. Unless they gave him the vaccine first. But why would they give him the vaccine? They didn't know if it worked.

Then it hit him. The vaccine worked! Parker was immune just like Annie. They could all inject themselves with her blood and they'd come back if they ever got bitten.

"Guys! I'm back!"

The pain receded somewhat. It didn't hurt any less, but he felt a rush of exhilaration that made him not care.

But then he realized, of course, that his friends were going to come upstairs and shoot him. They couldn't let him live now. Not after he tried to kill Kyle and actually killed Frank.

He was the old Parker again, but the old Parker hit his wife. The old Parker damn near shoved Kyle over the cliff. The old Parker didn't want to kill Frank, but it was the old Parker's fault that Frank died.

He felt beyond exhausted emotionally, as if he had cried for a month without even stopping to sleep. But he cried anyway.

Kyle heard Parker yelling—in English. The sonofabitch was actually back.

Their little experiment worked. Annie's immunity could be transferred, at least to somebody with the right blood type.

Amazing.

Too bad Kyle didn't know his own blood type. It was too risky to chance it. Odds were sixty percent that his body would have an allergic reaction if he injected himself. He didn't know what that meant. Would it kill him? Maybe, maybe not. But sixty-percent odds of something terrible happening were unacceptable.

In the meantime, Parker. The sonofabitch was actually back.

Kyle knocked on Annie's door. "Parker's awake!"

Hughes emerged from his own room. "I heard."

Annie flung open her door. "He's awake?" she said, a little too gleefully, Kyle thought. Things were about to get ugly again.

"You didn't hear him?" Kyle said.

"I was asleep," she said. She looked like she had been crying.

"Let's go," Kyle said.

"We need to get one thing straight first," Hughes said.

Here it comes, Kyle thought.

"We haven't decided what we're going to do with him yet," Hughes said. "So don't fuck with him. Hear?"

"As long as you don't let him go," Kyle said.

"We'll discuss that later," Hughes said. "After we find out what kind of state he's actually in. He might not remember what happened. He might not even recognize us."

Right, Kyle thought. Annie didn't remember when she recovered either. What if Parker didn't remember?

Well, so what, Kyle thought. The man was dangerous either way. That's been established. He can't be allowed to go free even if he doesn't know his own name.

"I'll bring the Mossberg," Hughes said. "Just in case."

Outstanding, Kyle thought. Maybe that creep job will try something and we can end this once and for all.

They passed the corpses in the grass outside and entered the main house. Kyle could hear Parker groaning in his room from the stairs.

Hughes pointed his shotgun at the door and gestured for Annie to unlock and open it.

She did.

Parker was still tied to the chair, his wrists still bound to his ankles. The side of his head was swollen. Blood drained from his split ear and onto his shirt. Despite himself, Kyle felt a flush of sympathy for the man. He looked like hell and must feel even worse. He deserved it, but still.

"Help," Parker said.

So Kyle hadn't been hearing things. Parker actually returned from the walking dead. Or in his case, the tied-to-a-chair dead.

"Look at me," Kyle said.

Parker groaned, but managed to raise his head. "Kyle."

"Yeah," Kyle said.

"You remember what happened?" Hughes said.

"I don't know," Parker said. "What happened to Frank?"

"He remembers," Kyle said.

"Did I—"

"Yeah," Kyle said. "You did."

"Did you what?" Hughes said. "What do you remember?"

"Did I *bite* Frank?"

"You killed him," Kyle said.

Parker moaned.

"The disease killed Frank," Annie said.

"Like hell it did," Kyle said.

"I attacked Lane's people," Annie said, "when I was sick. Was that me or the disease?"

Kyle said nothing. She was right, but so what? Parker was a murderous bastard whether he had the virus or not. Otherwise he wouldn't be tied to that chair. Frank would be fine.

"What happened to Frank?" Parker said. "What exactly happened?"

"Threw himself off the cliff," Hughes said.

"Oh God," Parker said. "Just shoot me."

"Oh, we will," Kyle said.

"Later," Hughes said.

"Yeah," Kyle said. "We'll shoot you later. *Count* on it."

Parker groaned again. "I'm in terrible pain. Can you at least untie me for now?"

"In your dreams," Kyle said.

They gathered in the living room of the guesthouse but didn't speak for a while. Everyone needed to process what had happened. There was a lot to think about.

Annie had more to think about than anyone else.

Were they going to shoot Parker now? Banish him? Let him rejoin the group?

Against her better judgment, she sympathized with him. She knew how it felt to transform and how it felt to come back. Just as important, Parker must sympathize with her more now than he did. They'd been through the same hell. Parker was the only one in the world bonded to her like this.

His hell was worse, actually. He bit and killed one of his friends.

It wasn't entirely for nothing. She did pass her immunity onto him. He got lucky. They got lucky. Apparently Parker did have the same blood type. The odds were forty percent. But she couldn't pass her immunity onto the others. Just trying might kill them.

But the disease was preventable! If only they had a hospital, a lab, and some doctors.

And what about Kyle? Did Annie have a future with him after everything that had happened the past couple of days?

She finally spoke up.

"We need help."

Nobody argued.

"We're down to three now if we don't include Parker," she said.

"We're not including Parker," Kyle said. "So yeah, we're down to just three."

"Frank is dead," Annie said.

"Because of Parker," Kyle said.

"Because of us," Hughes said.

"None of this would have happened if he was a civilized person," Kyle said.

"Nor would this have happened if we'd done things differently," Annie said. "It's amazing that he's alive at all. *My* blood could have killed him. The virus sure as hell should have."

"Oh don't worry," Kyle said. "The virus didn't finish him off, but we will."

"Mmm," Hughes said. Annie had no idea what that meant.

"You kill him," Annie said, "and our experiment will be a complete waste."

"It's a complete waste anyway, Annie," Kyle said. "Someone should explain to you the notion of sunk costs. You passed your immunity to him. Great. But you can't pass it to us whether or not we keep him alive."

"We need doctors," Annie said.

"What does that have to do with anything?"

"What we really need is the Center for Disease Control."

"Where is the CDC anyway?" Hughes said.

"It's in Atlanta," Annie said.

"You sure?" Hughes said.

"I grew up near Atlanta," Annie said. "Sort of near Atlanta. I'm from South Carolina. I know that part of the country as well as Kyle knows this part."

"What do you want to do?" Kyle said. "Send them an email?"

Annie looked hard at Kyle.

"You've got to be fucking kidding," he said.

Hughes' face was unreadable.

"The West Coast was hit first," Annie said. "Washington before Oregon, and Oregon before California. We're at ground zero here. This is the worst place in the world for a vaccine to pop up."

She watched Kyle's face carefully. He was crestfallen. And angry. He knew that if she convinced Hughes, there would be no little new-world utopia for him in Eastsound.

"You may be right," Hughes said, "but I'm going to say something anyway because it needs to be said."

"Go ahead," Annie said.

"We don't know you're the only one," Hughes said. "For all we know, ten percent of the population has built-in immunity. I might have it myself and not even know it. Parker might have already had it. We don't know if we've accomplished a damn thing here except getting Frank killed."

"That's possible," Annie said. "But for all we know, I'm a freak of nature and medical science." She let that sink in for a moment before continuing. "Although my sister might be immune too, and possibly one or both of our parents."

"Where are your parents?" Hughes said.

"South Carolina. Assuming they're still alive. They might not be. My sister probably isn't."

She accepted now that she would never see Jenny again. She hadn't finished grieving yet for her sister, but she would finish in time. When she could.

"The East Coast was hit later," Annie said. "They might have suffered less damage. They might still have functioning medical facilities if they fortified them well enough in advance."

Kyle closed his eyes. He did not want to hear this, but he could not close his ears.

"CDC is in Atlanta," Hughes said. "In the South. In the *East*."

"Do I need to say it?" Annie said.

Hughes looked at her intently and shook his head.

"You're saying we should go to *Atlanta*?" Kyle said.

"I didn't say it," Annie said. "You did. And yes, I think we should go there."

"That's insane."

"They can develop a vaccine," Annie said. "They can test your blood type and inoculate you on the spot if you're a match."

"You have no idea if the CDC still even exists," Kyle said. "It probably doesn't!"

"It might," Hughes said. "It's 4,000 miles away from ground zero. But the roads are impassable. We can't take a boat. And none of us knows how to fly."

Kyle put his face in his hands. He looked exhausted, a defenseless emotional wreck at the mercy of forces beyond him. His dream to start over on Orcas Island was sound. It was a beautiful idea, but it was a fantasy.

"So we walk," Annie said.

Hughes knew they wouldn't have to walk the whole way. They could wait for winter to set in and for most of those things to die off. Ride snowmobiles over the Cascade Mountains, drive a truck on the open roads of the American deserts, and take a boat down the Mississippi River to the Gulf of Mexico. That would get them most of the way, but Atlanta was more than 100 miles inland in Georgia. Winters in the American South were too mild to kill all those things. The trip would be dangerous, more dangerous than anything any of them had ever attempted before, but it could be done.

One unsolved piece, however, remained: Parker.

Kyle paced back and forth in and out of the kitchen. The kid seriously needed a Xanax.

"We can't kill him," Annie said.

"He tried to kill me, Annie," Kyle said. "He tried to kill *me*. For no reason at all."

"You damn near got him killed on that other island," Hughes said. "You damn near got all of us killed."

"That wasn't me," Kyle said. "It was those things. And nobody died on that island."

"You're still alive," Hughes said.

"I didn't try to kill anybody. He did. Doesn't intent mean anything to you people?"

"We punished him pretty severely, bro," Hughes said. "Let me ask you something. Is what he did to you worse than what we did to him?"

Kyle paused before speaking again. "We had to do it that way." He sounded a little unsure of himself.

"We most certainly didn't," Hughes said. "Not that way."

"Frank got killed because we did it that way," Annie said.

"You're still mad that we set Parker up to be bit?" Kyle said. "Frank still would have died if we'd done it your way and injected him. Frank died because Parker bit him, not because Parker was bit. This is on all of us, including you. Especially you, Annie, because the whole thing was your idea in the first place."

Annie bit her lip. Kyle was right about that much. Hughes agreed with Annie that they couldn't kill Parker. Not now. Not after what they'd done to him. Not when they were down another man.

"I need him," Annie said.

"What do you mean, you *need* him?" Kyle said.

"He's the only person who understands what I've been through. Hopefully he's the only one who ever will. God forbid you ever have to go through it."

"It's not all about you," Kyle said. "It's certainly not about your damn feelings. This is about safety for all of us."

"There's safety in numbers," Hughes said. "Three of us aren't enough. Hell, four aren't enough."

It was time for Hughes to step up and take charge, not just when everyone's lives were in danger, but to take charge in general. He wasn't up to it before—and truthfully he still wasn't—but he no longer had any choice. He'd been content to let Kyle and Parker argue about where to go and what to do, but those two were incompetent. Parker was unstable and dangerous and Kyle was naive and a dreamer. Kyle took it hard when things didn't work out, much harder than Hughes had expected, and he was no less capable of the wrong kind of violence than Parker.

So Hughes would take charge of them both, whether they liked it or not. They wouldn't fight him. Nobody fought Hughes for long.

"Parker won't be a problem," he said. "We broke him."

"He'll kill us in our sleep if we let him go," Kyle said.

"And then what? Try to survive by himself? No one can survive by himself anymore. Anyone who tries to be self-sufficient in this world *will* be killed in their sleep. Look, it's like this. He just went through the most wrenching experience of his life. We all went through the most wrenching experiences of our lives when the plague struck, but it happened again to Annie and Parker."

Annie shuddered. Hughes thought she might start crying, but she didn't. The girl was tough.

"With Annie it was bad luck," Hughes said. "But *we* did it to Parker. He's going to have the mother of all attitude adjustments. He and I are going to have a little talk. And when I'm through with him, he will be in compliance."

"You're going to talk to him?" Kyle said. "That's your big plan? You're out of your goddamn mind if you think he'll stop being a lunatic because you *talked* to him."

"Kyle," Hughes said.

"What?"

"I'm going to ask you a question. You don't need to answer me now. You don't ever have to answer me. But I want you think long and hard and carefully before you say anything else. I'm going to ask Parker the same question."

He paused for effect, then continued.

"I'm going up there to talk to Parker right now. I'm taking the biggest kitchen knife I can find with me. I'll use it to cut his ropes and I'll use it to get his attention." Hughes smiled. No one says no to a big scary black man with a butcher knife. "And I'm going to ask him the same question I'm about to ask you."

Kyle paused before speaking again. "What's the question?" He sounded slightly more cooperative now. At least he was curious.

Hughes had the man's full attention. He paused another moment and made Kyle wait for it.

"What kind of man do you want to be?"

CHAPTER TWENTY-ONE

Kyle retrieved the rest of the supplies from the boat. He went alone. Everyone said they understood, but they didn't, and he needed some time to himself.

Hughes had said only Annie and Parker faced the most wrenching experiences of their lives since the plague struck, but that wasn't true. It had also happened to Kyle. And it had happened to Kyle repeatedly.

No one had ever tried to kill him before. Those *things* didn't count. They were no longer people. An actual human being had tried to murder him in cold blood. The others had no idea how that felt, nor did any of them have the decency even to ask. And now Kyle was supposed to be friends with this person? To travel across the damn country with this person?

That was but one of the numerous wrenchings of Kyle Alan Trager.

The second was Annie. He loved her. He could admit that to himself now. It was his blessing and curse, but it was mostly a curse. She'd never love him back. He saw it all over her face. In her posture. Her distance. Her coldness.

And she had turned into one of those things. She'd killed people. Bitten people. Turned people. Even eaten people. For all he knew she had bitten and turned and killed and eaten some of his friends.

She had turned into one of those things, but he loved her anyway. She would always be by his side and forever untouchable.

That was the second of the numerous wrenchings of Kyle Alan Trager.

The worst, though, was the island.

He'd worked everything out. A community of survivors on Orcas, safe and secure in the most luxurious setting for thousands of miles in any direction. They could start over, not only with their own lives but with the story of the human species. They'd live simply, but they would not have to live primitively. All of humanity's knowledge was stored in books. They could rebuild slowly and sustainably, free of all the detritus and junk of the twenty-first century. Best of all, free of the plague.

But it wasn't to be.

His dream had shattered, and he suffered alone. The others did not even care. They weren't interested in the first place. All they had done was come along for the ride. They never saw the potential, the beauty, nor did any one of them thank him for taking them there when it looked like everything would work out.

And now they wanted to give up on all of it and walk into the jaws of a pitiless continent.

A nnie moved the rest of her belongings into her room in the guesthouse and shut the door. Wind whistled outside her window as evergreen boughs rose and fell on the other side of the glass. She could see her own breath and thought about putting on a hat and some gloves.

Instead she crawled shivering into bed fully clothed and pulled the cold covers up to her chin.

She shuddered when she thought about Frank.

And Parker. Oh God, poor Parker. He really got run through the wringer. She knew what it was like. She was the only one who knew what it was like.

For all she knew, they were the only two people on earth who knew what it felt like to have everything that makes us human stripped away and replaced with nothing but ashes.

At least now she was freed from her terrible secret.

Parker was not Jesus. He hadn't died for her sins. He suffered for his own. He suffered something awful, but he suffered *for* her, in a sense, and relieved her of a terrible burden.

It might turn out that Parker suffered for everyone, even Kyle. If a vaccine could be one day made from her blood, Kyle could get an injection and become immune too. He'd survive if he gets bitten. So would Hughes.

But for now, what on earth was she supposed to do about Kyle? How was she supposed to feel about him? Had he turned into somebody else? Or was he never the man she thought he was in the first place? She had no idea. The man was a stranger. Kyle himself might not know who he was anymore. Earlier she had felt almost certain that she had a future with him, but the road ahead was unmapped and unlit. For now she did not want to touch him, did not want to look at him, did not even enjoy thinking about him.

She closed her eyes, shivered under the covers, and thought about the house she grew up in and how warm her bedroom was in South Carolina, how summer nights were often so hot, she had to sleep on the bed instead of in it.

December hadn't arrived yet. Charleston was still almost balmy this time of year. Charleston was always balmy compared with the greater Seattle area no matter what time of year. How much colder would the snowy mountains of Idaho be? The high deserts of Wyoming? The windy frozen plains of Nebraska?

She'd shatter in that kind of cold. Of that she was certain. But that was the point. Only healthy humans could survive in those places without technology during the winter. The landscape would be littered with the frozen remains of the infected and those they had desiccated. Until they reached the American South, anyway. Winter was not going to kill all the infected ones there. But if she could make it to Atlanta, she'd make it to Charleston. She'd have to risk everything, and she probably wouldn't make it, but she found herself smiling and crying because she had finally found a way home.

The others would likely never see home again. Hughes could never visit his family's graves even if he could manage to find them amid Seattle's rubble and ashes. Parker would never see his old street, wherever that was. Kyle would never see Portland again or build his little dream town on that island.

Maybe he could find one in the Atlantic. Maybe.

Parker was going to change. He had just passed through an unspeakable transformation, but he wasn't done yet. Not even close. He had no idea what was coming, that the virus would rewire his mind.

Neurons that fire together, wire together.

She shuddered.

Would he forgive her? Blame her? Blame himself? Blame Kyle? Blame Hughes? Blame all of them? Even Frank? Would he kill them all and then himself in a moment of blackness?

Or would Parker see in time that he was Annie's blood brother now, that he, like her, just might help save what's left of humanity, that without him, Atlanta would not be possible. It wouldn't even be thinkable.

She scoffed. Saving humanity. It sounded ludicrous even when she didn't say it out loud. Who was she to save humanity? Who was Parker? Who were any of them? They were just people. Ordinary people who were lucky to still be alive. Annie was immune by sheer chance. Parker was only immune because he tried to kill Kyle. Annie was not worthy. Parker was even less worthy.

But they would go to Atlanta or they would die trying.

Parker could hardly move after Hughes cut his ropes. And he could hardly believe it when Hughes told him he wasn't going to be shot, stabbed, or hurled over the cliff. Parker deserved any and even all those fates, but by the grace of God, fate, and Annie Starling, he was given another life.

He should have died in that room. He had survived the worst pathogen ever to strike his species. It obliterated everything but the body. As far as Parker knew, he and Annie were the only ones who had ever come back.

He owed her his life. They all did. Not just because of her blood, but because of her decency. She had saved him not only from the disease, but from the cliff.

Hughes told him the plan. He'd agree to any plan at this point—not that Hughes had asked his opinion.

They were going to Georgia. By land. To find doctors.

It made sense, but Jesus. The odds of survival didn't look good. His odds of surviving if he did not go, however, were worse. The biggest reason he'd go with them, however, aside from the fact that Hughes didn't give him a choice, was because he wouldn't leave Annie.

They had a faint flickering *chance* of making it, that the Center for Disease Control was still there, that doctors could take blood from Annie Starling and make a vaccine. And didn't Annie say she was from next door in South Carolina? The girl was practically going home.

"You sorry?" Hughes said.

"More than you'll ever know," Parker said.

"You need to demonstrate that to the others."

"I know."

"They're waiting for you outside."

"I have no idea what to say. What could I possibly say?"

"Don't worry. I've got it all scripted out."

Parker blinked at him.

"Think of it," Hughes said, "as a reinitiation."

Parker tried to stand, but his back gave out. So did his legs. He was broken. "I need some help."

Hughes set down the butcher knife, bent over, and all but pulled Parker up on his feet. Damn, that man was strong. He was the last person Parker ever wanted to cross.

He leaned on Hughes as they made their way down the stairs and through the wretched living room.

Annie and Kyle were waiting for him outside, as Hughes had said. For a moment Parker expected to see Frank. For the briefest of instants he had forgotten, and he felt lacerated when he remembered. He could still faintly taste Frank's blood in his mouth. It would take Parker a long time indeed to ever feel healthy and clean. He wasn't sure he ever would.

Annie looked nervous. Kyle just stood there, molten with hatred. Parker could not meet his eyes.

The front lawn was an expanding graveyard. The original two corpses still lay there, plus a third corpse, the body of the thing that had bitten him.

Hughes told Parker to stand next to the corpses, close enough that he could smell them. The others kept their distance.

"Hi," Parker said.

Annie said hi and looked embarrassed, though Parker had no idea why. Kyle said nothing.

"I don't know what to say," Parker said lamely. What could a person say after all that?

"My man," Hughes said. "I told you I've got this all scripted."

"You could start with *Kyle, I'm sorry*," Kyle said.

"Okay," Parker said. "I'm sorry. Honest to God, Kyle, I'm sorry. I'm even more sorry about Frank."

"We all are," Annie said. "It's our fault, not yours."

"Annie," Kyle said.

"Later," Hughes said. "Right now, you," he said to Parker, "are going to take a vow. I've already prepared it. You get no say in what's in it."

Parker swallowed. "Okay."

Hughes didn't say *you will accept this or die* because he didn't have to. Parker was in no position to argue. The others had the right to dictate terms. Besides, he was standing next to three corpses. Hughes no doubt chose that location on purpose. It made an impression. It would have made even more of an impression if Frank's body were there too. They were going to bury him, right? They couldn't just leave him at the bottom of the cliff where Parker deserved to be.

"Raise your right hand," Hughes said.

Parker raised his right hand.

"I'd make you put your hand on a Bible," Hughes said, "but we don't have one. Repeat after me."

Parker straightened up. This was serious.

"*I, Jonathan Anthony Parker*," Hughes said.

"I, Jonathan Anthony Parker," Parker said.

"Do hereby swear to serve and protect Annie Starling for the rest of my life," Hughes said.

"Do hereby swear to serve and protect Annie Starling for the rest of my life," Parker said.

"She is the most precious person alive."

"She is the most precious person alive."

Annie choked up.

"I will guard her with my life."

"I will guard her with my life."

"I will keep her from harm and follow her to the ends of the earth."

"I will keep her from harm and follow her to the ends of the earth."

"If I ever again commit violence against anyone in this group, I shall be, and deserve to be, summarily executed."

Parker swallowed hard. He knew that was justified, but it was difficult for him to say. He said it anyway. "If I ever again commit violence against anyone in this group ... I shall be, and deserve to be, summarily executed."

Kyle stared at him, and stared at him hard. Kyle wanted to execute him that instant and add another corpse to the lawn. That was clear.

"You have no other role," Hughes said, "none whatsoever, from now until the end of the world."

"I have no other role," Parker said, "none whatsoever, from now until the end of the world."

"You didn't have to repeat that part," Hughes said.

Parker understood that, but he wanted to say it anyway.

Hughes shook his hand.

Kyle just stared.

Annie looked uncomfortable. Parker wanted to hug her, but he doubted she'd be all right with that. He was pretty sure Kyle would deck him. Or stab him.

Annie stayed behind as Hughes and Kyle headed toward the house. On his way up the stairs, Hughes turned back, silently beckoning Parker to come with him.

But Parker wanted to walk in with Annie, and she wasn't moving. Was she waiting for him, or did she intend to stay outside by herself? He couldn't blame her if she wanted some space—especially from him—but there was no one else in the world he'd rather be near. She might be the only person on earth who could forgive him in her bones for what he did to Frank.

"Well," Parker said to Annie. "I guess I'll go in then." He didn't know what else to do or to say. It would be a long time before any of them ever trusted him, and it would take almost as long before he trusted himself.

His back felt like someone had beaten him half to death with a hammer. The side of his head felt exactly as it should after someone smashed in the side of it with the butt of a shotgun. He walked slowly and a little lopsidedly. Annie walked beside him as he struggled.

"I won't let you down," he said and winced from the pain.

"You'd better not," she said.

"I understand if you don't believe me."

"We'll see."

They walked in silence for a couple of moments. Parker did his best to keep the pain to himself, but there was only so much he could hide it.

"How was it up there?" she said. "Do you ... remember much?"

He blew out his breath. "I remember. It was bad." He wished he could forget, at least for a short while like she had, but he knew he never would.

She nodded and looked at a place in the distance, at something Parker couldn't see, as if she remembered something she could never talk about or knew something she hadn't yet told him.

He stopped at the bottom of the stairs and grabbed the handrail. This wouldn't be easy. He thought he might lose his balance, but Annie placed her hand on the small of his back so he wouldn't fall.

END OF BOOK ONE

ALSO BY MICHAEL J. TOTTEN

The Road to Fatima Gate
In the Wake of the Surge
Where the West Ends
Taken: A Novel

Made in the USA
San Bernardino, CA
19 March 2014